JAGGER

JAGGER

KRISTOPHER RUFTY

SINISTER GRIN PRESS

Sinister Grin Press Austin, TX
www.sinistergrinpress.com
February 2015

Cover Art by Frank Walls
Text Design by Brian Cartwright

This one's for Steve Beaver

CHAPTER ONE

Standing over the remains of his mangled pit bull, Clayton hocked up a wad of phlegm and spat on it. He wanted to kick the worthless dog, but knew it was a waste of energy. Bruiser was dead. Couldn't do much more damage to him than that.

Besides, there wasn't a great deal of the dog left that he *could* kick. Bruiser fought a decent battle. He just wasn't good enough a fighter to survive it.

And what made it even worse, Clayton actually liked the mutt.

"Fucking runt," he muttered.

He knew Bruiser couldn't hear him and didn't care. Still felt good saying it.

Running a sweaty hand through his shoulder-length hair, he groaned.

What the hell am I going to do?

Not only had he convinced himself Bruiser would win this fight, he'd convinced Brock Shuller so much that the wealthy prick had placed a large bet on the dog. Brock was someone who hadn't earned his income through legal resources. And if Clayton couldn't whip up a plan to recover Brock's losses, he'd be in just as bad of shape as Bruiser.

Just like Ralph.

He shivered thinking about what had happened to that poor bastard. Brock had lost five grand on Ralph's German Shepard. And all they found of Ralph a few days later was his head. The skull had been sawed open like a bowl and packed full of dog shit. People said clumpy brown trails had oozed from his nostrils and mouth.

Ain't nobody gonna stuff me full of dog shit.

JAGGER

He looked at the remains of Bruiser again. He felt squirmy inside. Not only had the dog put Clayton's life in danger, he had to clean this mess up. Luckily, Freddy was here to help. Not too bright of a guy, but Freddy admired Clayton. And more often than not, Clayton used that to his advantage.

"Freddy! Where you at, man?"

"Back here!" His voice was not at all manly, more like an elderly woman. Whenever he spoke, the pitch fluctuated like an audio cassette about to be eaten by the tape deck.

"Get out here, man! I need help cleaning up this shit!"

There was a bang on the other side of the wooden stall's wall. Something crashed, a metallic rattling resounded from wherever Freddy was. "But it's *your* shit to clean up!"

Groaning, Clayton turned around, finding a small hole in the wall directly behind him. Had Freddy been watching him all this time? He suddenly felt very bizarre and awkward.

The short, plump man waddled around the corner. His gait reminded Clayton of penguins he'd seen on the Discovery Channel. The flab on his body jiggled as he shuffled forward. He glanced past him and saw the bloody chunks of fur that remained of Bruiser.

And grimaced.

"My God," Freddy said, his voice traveling upward. "Looks even worse now."

"Well, you don't think he's going to make himself pretty, do you?"

"Guess not," mumbled Freddy. "All that time I spent making him tough, wasted. *Bah!*" Nose wrinkled, Freddy swiped his hand at the pit bull. "Pathetic."

Clayton put his hands on his hips. He stared at the dog. Strips of its fur and flesh were gone, showing a corner of the rack of ribs underneath. The throat had endured the majority of the damage. A wide chunk had been torn out, leaving a tube exposed that dangled like an old sparkplug wire coated in gooey crimson.

"Brock bet a lot of money on you," Freddy reminded him.

"He bet it on the dog."

"Yeah, but you know what he does if he loses."

Clayton made a face, knowing exactly what he did. An image of Ralph flashed in his mind. He shook it away.

"And that was just five grand," continued Freddy.

"What was the total lost on Bruiser?"

"Between Brock *and* his business associates—twelve."

Clayton's legs suddenly felt as if they were filled with warm liquid. He dropped to his knees, splashing in a sticky puddle of dog blood. "I'm fucking dead…"

"You told him it was a sure thing…"

Clayton remembered his pitch to Brock. How poised and convincing he'd sounded. And *cocky*. Arrogant. Bruiser had won three fights in a row, and he'd become convinced his dog was unstoppable.

Brock might have bet knowing he'd lose, just to prove a point to me for being so full of my own shit.

Ralph's head was full of shit…

Clayton absently rubbed his hand over his scalp. He looked around the old barn as if an answer to all his problems was hidden somewhere around him.

Freddy had used his parents' dilapidated barn for all the dog fights. And it was a good spot, too. Tucked far away from civilization. The police had never once been by to investigate, though they must have known of its existence. Clayton had always assumed that was because a guy like Brock had bribed most of them.

Now he was twelve thousand short and it was Clayton's fault.

Bullshit. It was Bruiser's fault. He was the one killed by a damn half-breed.

"You got all quiet," said Freddy.

He wanted to stand up, grab Freddy by the shoulders, and shake him until he understood why he'd lost the mood for conversation. Instead, he just sighed.

"Scared of what Brock's gonna do to ya?" Freddy asked.

"Duh, shit, fuckwad."

"Don't have to get all bitchy about it."

"Why don't I? I'm probably gonna die, don't you understand that?"

"Maybe not."

"Really? You got twelve thousand just lying around that we can pay him back with?"

"No, but he owes me a favor. Maybe I can get him to give you a little time to come up with some money."

Hearing that didn't make Clayton feel any better. That wasn't a solution, nor was it a plan. All Freddy could do, if he was even telling the truth, was delay the inevitable.

Drag it out.

Somehow, the idea of prolonging matters made him feel even worse.

But it was also more than he could come up with on his own.

"What kind of favor does he owe you?" asked Clayton.

Freddy's thin lip curled, showing a speck of brown teeth. "Don't worry about that."

Clayton, on his knees, looked up at Freddy. "You really think it'll work?"

"I can convince him," said Freddy. "He'll hold off for a little bit, but he won't forget."

"Good. I just need some time to think. Try and come up with something."

Maybe I could ask Teresa?

Doubtful. She'd kicked him out. He should have known if he was going to bring other women into the bed he shared with his girlfriend, he needed to make sure there were no stains left behind.

Besides, she didn't have that kind of money.

"I do this favor for you," said Freddy, his breaths turning wheezy.

"You have to do a favor for me."

Clayton noticed the goofy grin on Freddy's chubby face, a tight line between two pudgy cheeks. Freddy swallowed hard, as if a rock was in his throat. It was loud, the thick wetness dropping into his stomach.

"What the fuck you talking about, Freddy?"

"If you want me to buy you some time, you've gotta do something for me."

Clayton felt himself shrink inside. "You're not getting weird on me, are you?"

"No, not weird. I just think it's deserved. I've been kissing your ass for so long, I think it's time you showed me some appreciation. You're already in the position for it, on your knees."

"You want me to *kiss* your ass?"

Clayton shook his head. "Not kiss my ass. Kiss me somewhere else. Actually…just put the whole thing in your mouth, leave out the kissing and just do some sucking."

An icy flutter clung to Clayton's spine. He saw where this was going and wanted to tear Freddy's throat out. But the overwhelming possibility that he may be able to help with Brock kept him on his knees, on the dirt floor.

He's lying. Brock doesn't owe him shit.

Brock did seem to go easy on Freddy, though. Sometimes Brock took Freddy along to the many strip clubs he owned. Clayton remembered the rumors about Charlie. He'd given Freddy a hard time, punched him in the stomach or something. People said Freddy told Brock about it and he was the reason Charlie was found dead in Dinky's Pond.

Clayton held up his hand. "Freddy…"

"Lick those lips." He laughed a nasally, weasel-like laugh.

"You're not serious."

The laughter stopped. His smile dropped. "I am serious."

There wasn't the slightest glimmer of humor anywhere on Freddy's face. He wasn't joking. His eyes lowered to Freddy's crotch, where it jutted in the front like a small tent in the fabric.

Clayton's mouth felt awfully dry. "You really think I'm going to… *blow* you?"

"You're goddamn right I do. I'm telling you, I know Brock, and I can probably get him to go easy on you."

"What if I do it and he don't go easy on me?"

Freddy shrugged. "I ain't gonna talk to him unless you do it."

"I've always been nice to you, man, even when all those fucks would give you shit. You really gonna make do this?"

"You ain't always been nice to me. You just put up with me. *Shee-it*. I think you're cool, and it's fine with me if you think I'm a shit. But I ain't helping you unless you help *me*."

Freddy rubbed a thumb over his zipper. Then he flicked the tiny tab. He put both hands on his hips, thrusting his expanding bulge in Clayton's face.

I'm really gonna do this. I'm gonna suck a cock. Fuck! FUCK!

Clayton's mouth was parched, his lips dry and brittle. So, he did just what Freddy had suggested—he licked them. It helped very little. The inside of his mouth felt like it had been coated in a layer of putty. His tongue felt heavy and dry.

"Come on," said Freddy. "We ain't got all day."

"All right, Freddy, just shut the hell up. Don't talk. You're making it worse."

Grinning, Freddy gave his hips a little shake. Loose change and keys jingled from his pocket.

Raising his hands to Freddy's zipper, Clayton's fingers twitched as they clamped down on the tab. Freddy chuckled above him. Not wanting to look at his ugly face again, he kept his eyes pointed forward.

And slowly pulled the zipper down.

An uncircumcised, contorted penis fell out of Freddy's pants, slapping Clayton across the nose. He jumped back with a gasp.

Freddy's penis looked like a pepperoni stick that was still in the shrink-wrap. Warts lined the underbelly down to the hairy scrotum. It was slightly damp and gleamed under the dim lights inside the barn. He could smell the stale odor of sweat and shit.

Goddamn, does Freddy ever wash himself?

Freddy took his cock in his hand and tapped Clayton on the lips with it. Knowing he was signaling for him to open wide, he did just that. Slowly, Freddy eased it into his mouth, as if afraid he may do something stupid, like bite. As much as Clayton wanted to, he didn't dare.

He'd never sucked a dick before, but he'd watched enough porno and had enjoyed the act enough times himself to know the routine. He wondered if he'd ever be able to enjoy having this done to himself again.

He thought about it, concluding that nothing could rob him of the pleasure a blow job gave him.

"Wait," said Freddy.

Relief flowed through Clayton. It was a joke. All this time, Freddy had been messing with him.

Leaning back on his legs, Clayton released a long breath. He started to smile.

When he saw Freddy tug his cell phone out of his pocket and angle it above his crotch, his smiled fell away.

"Gonna record this," said Freddy.

"Come on, man..."

"Something for me to remember it by."

Clayton's eyes started to burn. For the first time since he was a kid, he thought he might cry.

"I'm ready," said Freddy, holding the phone out so he could see the screen.

Clayton wanted to protest, but knew it was pointless. He was in a situation that didn't have any paths that could lead him out. He would have to suffer this humiliation if it meant buying him some time.

"You better not show the video to anybody," said Clayton.

"Think I'm stupid? I don't want anybody knowing you sucked my cock."

Clayton didn't respond. He formed his lips around the cap of Freddy's manhood.

Moaning, Freddy reached behind Clayton's head and took a handful of his lengthy hair.

Then Clayton got started.

CHAPTER TWO

Something wet dragging across her bare feet tickled Amy awake. She jerked her legs up, swatting at the thin sheet swaddling her body. She felt it flutter back down over her toes.

Heavy footfalls started at the foot of the bed and made their way around the side. She heard the jingling of metal tags growing louder. "Let me sleep," she said.

The sheet skimmed across her skin as it was shoved away. A large head pushed into the gap between her shoulder and neck. She felt a wet nose sniffing the side of her neck.

Flinching, Amy tilted her head and squirmed away from the edge of the mattress. "Stop!"

Opening her eyes, she was met with a wide blur of slurping red as it licked a sticky path from her chin to her hairline. She could see the wide nose and jutted maw coming at her face for another lick. Amy dodged the lashing tongue, throwing her arm up and bumping a collar. The tags jangled even louder. As she stirred about, she heard an excited whine of somebody being thrilled she was awake.

The bed bounced when he leaped onto it, toppling her onto her side. Laughing, Amy rolled onto her back. The sheet had been thrown aside, uncovering her bare chest to the cool air of the room. In nothing but her panties, her skin was tickled by a heavy coat of dog fur as thick legs stood on each side of her.

"Jagger! I'm awake! I'm *awake!*"

He pounced the bed, shaking her. His wide mouth hung open, panting. Dots of drool spattered her breasts. Shivering, she tried to pull the sheet over her, but it was pinned down by his big paws.

Amy folded her arms under her breasts and smirked. "Getting a nice look?"

Jagger huffed.

"If you want me to take you out, you have to let me get up."

Knowing this was their every morning routine, Amy still liked to kid around with her dog. Since he was roughly twenty pounds shy of two hundred, it was all she could do. Wrestling was no longer an option. He'd accidentally hurt her more than once and she'd had to put an end to their horseplay. Sometimes he got excited and forgot she was nowhere near as strong as he was, but a squirt from a water bottle reminded him.

But she still allowed him to cuddle.

He was very good at that.

As if to remind her of his abilities, he slowly lowered himself. She opened her arms so his fuzzy chest could settle down on hers. Hugging him, she folded her arms around his wide neck and her legs around his hips. It was almost like a hugging a large hairy man.

He lowered his head, resting his maw on her pillow, beside her head.

"Oh, Jagger." She scratched behind his ear. "You're all the man I'll ever need."

He huffed through his nose as if agreeing.

"You know I love you, right?"

Another sigh, as if he was bored and tired of her constantly reminding him.

She scratched his large, dangling ear. She felt him tense up, lean his head into the scratching. "Like that?"

Jagger moaned his appreciation.

"No wonder they itch. Your hair is curling into your ear!" She laughed. "I must have a fetish for hairy men. What does that say about me?"

Amy laughed.

Being a Mastiff mix, Jagger's hulky body concealed hers underneath a pile of thick, brown and black fur. She imagined he looked as if he'd sprouted a woman's arms and legs and a head of long lemon-colored hair. Though he could easily crush her, he felt light and soft on top of her.

His breed was known to be gentle by nature. And Jagger knew when to be delicate, really. Usually he was content with snuggling or being Amy's footrest whenever she sat on the couch. He rarely did much other than sleep these days unless he was outside or at the park.

Just don't get him wound up, things get broken.

Glasses, picture frames, a chair. She'd lost many things during Jagger's animated sprints through the house. Her bank account could attest to all the money spent on replacements and repairs.

Once he'd accidentally run into the bathroom door while trying to follow her inside. She was sitting on the toilet when his head had burst through the cheap wood. With his head lodged there, he seemed to smile as he'd watched her empty her bladder. This ordeal prompted her to replace the doors inside the house with something more durable. So far they'd held up. Only a few bonked noggins over the following months, but he eventually grasped he wasn't going to get through.

"Hey. Are you going to let me up?"

Jagger sighed into the pillow. She moved her scratching fingernails to his side. His hind leg kicked, hitting the mattress like several whacks from a hammer. She felt the bed shake under her back.

But he didn't move.

"Want to go out?"

He tensed. Held his breath.

"Huh? Want to go outside?"

His head lifted, but he didn't look at her. It was as if he was pretending he was focusing on the wall.

"Come on, handsome. Let's go outside."

That was the command he wanted to hear. Jagger leaped off the bed. The floor groaned under his landing. Spinning around in a splurge of circles, he barked. It was a profound noise that vibrated the walls. Her framed college diploma hanging on her bedroom wall trembled.

"Hush," she said, sitting up. "Want to wake up Aunt Teresa?"

Jagger tilted his head at the mention of her friend's name. A flap of his jowl hung away from his mouth, showing curved teeth.

Teresa had crashed on the couch again last night, making it three nights in a row. Hopefully it would be the last for a little while. Teresa had been Amy's best friend since eighth grade and Amy loved her like a sister. But she was growing tired of the skulking pessimist Teresa become.

That damn Clayton Fortner.

How did Teresa ever wind up with such a total loser who mooched off her every chance he got? He hadn't held a job longer than a month. Never seemed to have any money and always owed somebody some.

Amy hadn't liked him right away. And when she'd confessed this to Teresa it had almost ended their twenty year friendship.

Two weeks ago Teresa found some stains on her bed sheets that were still a little damp. Clayton didn't even try to deny he'd been fooling around on her.

So she'd kicked Clayton out, but he kept coming around. Begging her for money, asking if he could crash there for the night. And Teresa would give him the money, would allow him to stay, which usually led to them having sex and to Teresa's head becoming even more messed up.

Finally, Teresa had had enough and came to Amy for help. She supposed Teresa being here was her way of attempting a Clayton Fortner detox. He'd really screwed her head up, and still was, so some time away might help get the gears working smoothly again.

Now she felt lousy for wishing Teresa would leave. She could stay as long as she wanted.

Amy swung her legs off the bed. She put her hands down on the sheet, and felt wet spots from Jagger's slobber.

Talk about stains on the sheets.

At least she knew who was responsible for these.

Grimacing, she lifted her hand. Bubbly spittle coated her

fingertips. She wiped the drool on the sheet and stood up.

On her way to her dresser, she rubbed Jagger under the chin as she walked by. His head reached above her hips and she felt the cold swipe of his nose on her skin.

Amy opened the top drawer. In the corner of her eye, she saw this motion imitated in the vertical mirror on the closet door. She looked to the side and studied her reflection. Her tawny skin looked smooth in the dim morning light coming through the window and her wild mess of yellow hair seemed to shimmer. One leg, slightly pushed forward, showed the curve of her thigh and the narrow lines of muscle. It looked nice, almost as if she was posing for a picture. Angling her rump out, she jutted out a hip and watched the dimple appear in the side of a buttock where the seat of her panties didn't reach.

Smiling, she turned so she could see her front. And frowned at Jagger's drying drool sprinkled across her breasts.

"If only all the men drooled over me like you do."

Jagger bumped her legs from behind, making her stagger forward. She looked at him from over her shoulder and pretended to scowl. "Watch it, pal."

He ran his tongue across his lips, mouth hanging open. Slobber drizzling from his jaws made little puddles of foam on the carpet.

Great.

She looked around her room for the container of antibacterial wipes, but didn't see it. She must have left it in the kitchen, so Jagger's slobbery mess on her skin and the floor would have to wait.

Turning back to the opened drawer, she took out a bra. She shut the drawer, then opened the one underneath. She grabbed the shirt on top and bumped it shut with a hip. Then she bent over, opened the third drawer and removed a pair of running shorts.

She walked back to the bed with Jagger right on her heels, nudging the backs of her thighs with his nose. It felt like cold kisses on her skin.

"All *right*," she said. "I'm hurrying. Jeez." She dropped the clothes on the bed. She turned around and stuck her arms through the straps of her bra. "Talk about impatient." Reaching behind her back, she snapped the bra in place. "But I suppose if *I* had to pee really bad like you do, I'd be antsy too."

She realized she did have to pee, so she quickly dressed, then slipped her feet into her sandals. She returned to her dresser, taking the hairbrush from the top. The handle was wrapped in hair ties and felt ribbed in her hand. On her way to the bedroom door, she ran the brush through her hair, cringing whenever the bristles snagged a tangled not.

Finished brushing, Amy took one of the hair ties she'd wrapped around the handle and tossed the brush onto her bed. Jagger seemed tempted to fetch it, but evidently changed his mind. She pulled her hair back. As she twisted the tie around her hair, Jagger tried to squeeze between her and the wall.

"You can't go out that way," she told him. "Come here."

She patted the thigh of her right leg. Jagger, catching the hint, stepped back and came around to the appropriate side.

"Get back," she whispered, opening the door.

Jagger rushed into the hall, his wide girth knocking the door out of her hand and her against the frame.

"Shit," she said. "Jagger!" She kept her voice down to a harsh whisper as she hurried after him. She could feel the vibrations of his heavy plodding in the floor.

His collar stopped jangling when he reached the living room.

Amy stood halfway up the hall, shaking her head.

Then she turned back and made a detour into the bathroom.

When she was finished, she entered the living room and found Jagger sitting on his hindquarters beside the back door, a beefy paw tapping the leash that hung from a hook beside the frame. His flappy ears hung behind his head like a nun's veil.

The air in the room was heavy with the stale odor of cigarettes. Amy looked over at the couch. Teresa was sleeping on her stomach in a thin tank top and a pair of panties that barely covered the lower arcs of her buttocks. The blanket was bunched around her calves as if it had eaten her up to that point. Her arm hung off the side and bent at the elbow when it touched the floor. An ash tray filled with a chimney of crinkled butts was within her reach.

She looked away from Teresa and headed to the door. Putting her finger to her lip, she quietly shushed Jagger. "You're being too loud. You're going to wake up Teresa."

"Too late," said Teresa in a groggy voice. She lifted her head. "I've been awake for a few minutes."

"Sorry," said Amy.

"What time is it?"

Amy glanced at the wall clock. "Almost eight."

"Shit." Teresa groaned. "How do you get up like this every morning?"

Amy patted Jagger's head, waggling his ears. His fur was soft and smooth under her hand. "My nearly two-hundred pounds of alarm clock here."

Teresa crawled to her knees and sat back on her legs. Her dark hair hung around her face in tangled waves. The dark shapes of her breasts could be seen through the white tank top. It jutted in little points in the front. "Taking him for his walk?"

Nodding, Amy took the leash off the hook. "Want to join us?"

Teresa groaned.

Laughing, Amy bent over, pulled the clasp toward her and clicked the leash on. The rabies tag clinked against the metal fastener.

"How can you *handle* him?" asked Teresa. "I picture you skiing on your heels down the road."

Amy laughed. "It gets like that sometimes, if he sees a rabbit or something. Or if the Rileys' chickens are out."

"Chickens. Gross." She grimaced. "Ugly little things."

"Anyway, we're going to head out and make our lap around the neighborhood. Sure you don't want to come with?"

"I'll pass. Too early to be in the sunlight. That's the vampire in me."

Teresa worked nights at Honkers Truck Stop, but since she'd called out her past few shifts, Amy wondered if she still had a job. Might be best for Teresa, if she didn't. Honkers, a shithole that catered to the lowest dregs of society, was a place locals stayed away from. Unless they were like Teresa and cursed to work there. The clientele was made up of travelers, who Amy assumed were probably all serial killers passing through.

Seemed if you had a great body and willing to exploit it, you could work there.

Glancing at Teresa, on her knees on the couch, lightly rubbing the top of her thigh, Amy had to admit Teresa more than had the required credentials.

Jagger moaned from beside her. Amy looked down and saw his big head tilted up at her. Though his limp jowls draped the edges of his mouth, she could still see his pout.

"All right, Jagger, let's get going."

Amy unlocked the deadbolt, then the knob. She pulled the door toward her.

"What do you want for breakfast?" asked Teresa.

"What are you in the mood for?"

"Waffles."

"That sounds great."

"I'll get started on them."

"Waffle iron's under the counter," said Amy, putting her back against the door.

"I'll find it."

"See you."

"Bye."

Amy opened the screen door, giving Jagger's leash a gentle tug to inform him to stay put. He obliged, allowing Amy to exit first. She read in a dog training book that it was essential to teach large-breed dogs that the owner should go outdoors first. That way, the owner was less likely to get a dislocated shoulder when the dog jerked forward.

Holding the screen door open with her rump, she stood on the deck. She clucked her tongue. Jagger, knowing the cue, walked forward. His nails clacked across the wooden boards as he walked onto the deck.

From the coolness inside, it felt hot and damp in the early morning heat. Birds chirped from all directions and the watermelon smell of fresh-cut grass hung in the air. Amy could tell it was going to be another record-breaking summer day. There was a balmy mugginess behind the cool and no breeze seemed to come.

Amy pulled the door shut. She stepped away from the screen door. It closed slowly, clicking when it shut. She checked the doormat and didn't spot the envelope she was looking for.

Damn.

Janice Wilson, a woman who owned a singlewide in her park, was supposed to have her lot rent on the deck by 9:00am.

She's still got time. It's not even eight yet.

Amy doubted she'd see the money anytime soon, but hoped it would be here when she got back. Amy had decided if it wasn't turned in this morning, she was going to have another talk with Janice. Possibly threaten to make her take her trailer somewhere else. Always late on the rent, Janice was normally remained two months behind. But now the past due was advancing to three. The only reason Amy remained indulgent about the payment neglect was because of Nathan, Janice's little boy.

Jagger walked beside her to the steps, keeping a good amount of slack on the leash. She knew he wanted to run into the yard and cock his leg as soon as possible, but he remained calm. Again, he let her take the lead when it came time to go down the steps. He was always much calmer with the leash on, but indoors he seemed to forget everything he'd been taught by Amy and the instructor from his obedience classes.

JAGGER

The grass was wet with dew and rubbed wet trails across her sandals as she approached the fence gate. She'd probably have to mow before the weekend. Her backyard was enclosed in a chain-link fence with a gate on each side and one in the rear. She'd had it extended when Jagger was a puppy, knowing he would need an enclosed area to play in. Plus, it added a bit more security from her tenants. Being the owner of Eagle's Nest Mobile Home Park, she needed any she could get.

When her father still lived in the house, he never kept any kind of fencing up. And he hadn't needed to, back then. Over the years, he'd let the park go to hell, and now a fence almost felt like an obligation. Hopefully one day she'd have amended the park from the shunned reputation it had obtained over the last decade or so.

Wishful thinking, she knew.

Raising the latch, she swung the gate inward and went out first. Jagger followed closely behind. She switched the leash to her other hand, pulled the gate shut, and started walking. As they neared Jagger's favorite peeing tree, she felt him moving toward it. The slack in the leash went taut.

"Stop," she said.

Jagger tugged once more, then eased up.

They stopped at the tree. Jagger lowered his nose to the humps of root jutting from the ground like a serpent's back. His snuffles made little clouds in the dirt as he kept his nose down, walking to one end of the tree before turning around and coming back. Convinced nothing had tried to claim his spot, he shifted his weight to two legs and cocked his hind leg into the air. A stream of dark yellow gushed out, hitting the tree as if it were being sprayed from a hose. It seeped down the bark, creating a foamy puddle in a crevice between two roots.

Jagger's eyes were partly closed, his head tilted slightly as if relishing the relief. It seemed Jagger would never stop.

"Aw, buddy. Had to go, huh?"

The power of Jagger's stream lessened, turning to a sputter. Then it ceased to a drip. He snorted once and lowered his leg. Then he shook all over, a fluttering current that rustled his fur as it traveled down his spine and into his tail.

He was ready to move on.

CHAPTER THREE

Clayton felt things scuttling through the gorge between his buttocks and sat up with a sharp cry. He tried moving his right arm but it was numb and useless. So he used his left hand to dig his fingers in, scratching and clawing as he whimpered. His fingers squished little crawly things, smearing moist trails along his skin. Felt like ants when they crunched under his fingertips.

Rolling away, he felt something like scratchy quills brushing his skin. When he was sure he was far enough away from the ants, he angled his hips and looked behind him. Other than thin dark streaks of squished ants, he saw nothing on his skin. He let out a relieved sigh and dropped onto his back. The movements made his muscles throb, pulsating with sharp jabs of pain. He felt as if he'd been beaten with a hammer.

As he tried to catch his breath, he looked around. Tall grass surrounded him.

A field?

Weeds tilted in a gentle breeze that felt good on his sweaty skin. He looked up and quickly regretted it. The stinging glare of the sun caused his head to pound. Turning away from the brightness, he shielded his eyes with a hand. That helped some, but the pain was still there.

Birds chirped nearby in a chorale of quick melodies. He could hear the faint buzzing sounds of June Bugs or bees. Hopefully it was June Bugs. But knowing his luck, he was probably laying on top of a hornet's nest. After the clash with ants, he wouldn't be surprised.

He quickly spun away. Other than weeds his body had crushed, there was nothing there to see. He felt the bristly patches of tall grass tickle him between his buttocks.

I'm naked.

JAGGER

Clayton shrunk inside. He shot up. Pulling his legs to his chest, he hugged his knees. He looked down at himself. Completely nude. Even his socks were gone.

He looked around.

What the hell happened?

He tried to recall how he'd gotten here, but his memory was met by a dark curtain. All he could conjure up was what Freddy made him do last night.

No…not last night.

It was the night before. Last night was something different.

Holding up his hand, his arm felt as if it were pumping a river of tingling grits. His fingers felt stiff and numb. He couldn't bend them yet, couldn't make a fist.

My knuckles!

They were scabbed with blood. The two in the middle looked worse.

An image of a foot stomping his hand flashed in his mind.

I was on the ground. People were kicking me.

At least he'd put up some kind of fight. He let his hand drop onto his raised knee.

Clayton straightened his legs and winced at the pain it caused in his back. Looking down at his front, he saw a collection of bruises spread around his chest and stomach. The one in the middle was shaped like a shoe.

So he was right about being kicked.

Twisting around, he checked his ribs and saw more bruises there. He tapped the blemished skin, cringing. It really hurt there. He wondered if any were broken.

He didn't think so. Other than some dull pressure, it didn't hurt when he breathed.

Brock said he'll extend the deadline!

Clayton flinched at the voice. He looked around. Nobody was out here but him.

The voice had been in his head.

"What the hell?" he muttered.

He saw guys leaning over him. *Brock requests a tiny deposit on your debt!* Somebody slapped him. The others laughed.

"He's crying!" said a fat one in a flannel shirt.

The rest had gotten a big kick out of that.

"Make him cry some more," said someone he couldn't see. Sounded like Freddy.

"You're recording this?"

"Just a memento."

"It better not go on the internet."

As if he was looking through the point of view of some tragic character in a strange movie, he watched as feet and fists assaulted. His vision flashed whenever they struck him.

Clayton felt the blows and hits as if they were happening right now. Each bruise on his body seemed to jolt him with phantom pain.

He remembered it clearly now. Last night, he'd gone into Charlie's Mart to pick up some cigarettes and put ten bucks' worth of gas in his truck. He was on his way out to pump it when they grabbed him.

And brought me here?

That he couldn't be sure of. More than likely, they took him to the barn and delivered Brock's message through an ultimate ass-kicking.

Freddy must have spoken to Brock.

Yeah. I thank my lucky stars for that.

He felt awful. His whole body ached and throbbed. They'd stripped him, dumped him here. Left him to make it back on his own. His cell phone was in his truck, so he couldn't call anyone.

My truck!

Clayton had no clue where his truck might be now. They probably left it somewhere with the tires slashed.

At least they didn't kill me.

JAGGER

Not yet. But they'd definitely made it clear he *would be* dead if Brock didn't recover the money he'd lost on Bruiser.

"I'm dead fucking meat..."

And he was naked in a place he didn't know. Some kind of field. At least the weeds were high enough to hide him.

Can't stay here all day.

He thought he could, if he really wanted to. Looking ahead several feet, he saw a large tree, full with dark green leaves. The hefty branches reached out, throwing wide ponds of shade on the ground. The weeds stood firm around it like an unmoving carpet of tall grass. Looked like the perfect spot to get out of the sun.

He wasn't sure what time it was, but he could tell it was still early. The day still had a kind of softness to it, though the sun was out. And the air felt thin on his skin, not heavy with heat. Soon he wouldn't be able to stand it.

The shade will help with that.

Was he really going to stay here all day?

Figure that out later. Right now he needed to piss, then get under the shade.

Clayton gave one last look around. Other than a border of barbwire fencing, he saw nothing. Not even a barn, silo, or shed. Just wide open space.

And the tree.

Clayton stood up, his ligaments popping and stretching. It might have felt good if he wasn't so sore. Hobbling like an old man with arthritic hips, he made his way toward the tree. Though he saw nobody out here, he didn't want to point his member into the wind and start peeing.

After a few minutes, he reached the tree. He stepped around to the other side of it.

And jerked rigid when he saw the tractor parked with its hood up.

"Shit!"

A big man in overalls and a straw hat was working on the engine.

His head turned. He looked right at Clayton. Smiling at first, his lips dropped into a frown.

Scampering as if his feet were on hot coals, Clayton hurried around to the other side of the tree. He leaned back against it, his skin scratched by the jagged bark.

Somehow he hadn't noticed the man or the giant piece of farming machinery in his first glance. He supposed the tree had blocked his view of it.

"Who's that?"

Clayton tensed when he heard the deep voice.

"Boy, I done saw you. Might as well tell me what in Sam's hell you're doing out here."

Clayton could hardly breathe through the tight place in his lungs. "I'm...naked..." he stammered.

"Done seen that. Whatcha doing on my property?"

"I..."

Clayton didn't really know what to tell him.

Sorry. Some goons roughed me up because I lost their boss a lot of money on a piece of shit dog.

No. He couldn't say that.

"You what?" asked the farmer.

"Some people jumped me last night. I woke up here."

"Naked."

"Yuh-yeah...naked."

"That's a damn shame, boy."

Yeah. A shame.

He heard the farmer's sigh. Weeds rustled as the man walked toward him.

Clayton's stomach felt tight and sick. He had no idea what the farmer would do to him. He'd seen too many crazy movies featuring hillbillies that liked to force men to squeal like pigs.

In this moment, Clayton regretted his life. If he was offered a restart, he would gladly take it. He wouldn't have started hanging out with Glenn Tutterow in high school. He wouldn't have started smoking weed. And he wouldn't have dropped out of school. Then he would have never come into contact with Freddy and the rest of Brickston's dogfight elite. At one time, he'd had aspirations of working in comic books. He hadn't drawn anything in fifteen years, but he used to be really good at it.

Should've gotten as far away from this shit town years ago.

The footsteps stopped. Clayton could see the dark streaks of the farmer's shadow on the weeds. He stood just a couple yards behind him, on the other side of the tree.

"Well...I ain't gonna make you come out from behind the tree just yet. I know you're a little...indisposed at the moment."

"You can say that again."

"Give me a few minutes to get my tractor running again. Damn thing likes to stall on me. Probably the carburetor. Needs replacing. Once I get it running, I'll give you a ride back to my house. Let you borrow some clothes."

"Th-thanks."

The farmer sighed again. "Name's Mitch."

"Clayton."

"Can't say it's a pleasure to meet you, boy."

"Can't say I blame you."

Mitch snorted. "You can use my phone, if you need to. I doubt you got one on your...person. Got anybody you can call to come pick you up?"

Clayton considered calling Freddy, but decided that would be a poor choice. He was almost convinced Freddy had been among the group last night, documenting the whole assault. What was it with him wanting a library of Clayton's misery?

No matter what happened in the end, he would make sure he at least got to beat the hell out of Freddy.

"Yeah," said Clayton. "I know someone."

Teresa.

"Good. Hate for you to walk back into town. Can't give you a ride myself since I've got work to do."

"You're doing plenty," said Clayton. "Thanks, again."

"Sure."

The weeds made scratching sounds against Mitch's pants as he walked back to the tractor. Clayton waited until he heard the knocking sounds of Mitch working on the tractor before he finally peed. As he drained his bladder on the ground, he wondered what Teresa was going to say when he called her. He had no doubts she would come pick him up. He just didn't want to listen to her nagging him about his life choices.

She's got a lot of room talk. She works at Honkers for christsake.

At least it was work, she would say. Which was more than what Clayton had. And he hated to admit it, but she was right. Clayton was great at getting jobs. Not being able to keep them was one of his many flaws.

It took Mitch twenty minutes to get the tractor into working order. The engine puttered to life, popping as it seemed to choke on the gas. A tangy scent of burning fuel filled the air. He heard the clutch groan and the tractor started moving. Mitch drove around to Clayton's side of the tree. He covered his genitals with one hand.

Mitch was older than Clayton had expected, judging his voice. He looked like someone's grandfather. Heavy and broad, his body was fit with muscle gained from years of hard work. His face was what gave away his age. It was tired and a bit haggard, with a fresh beard brushing grey stubble on his cheeks.

"Hop on," Mitch shouted, above the ruckus of the engine. He patted a flat surface behind the seat.

Clayton nodded. He walked to the rear of the tractor and climbed up. The metal was cold under his buttocks when he sat down.

Mitch started driving. Clayton stared out into the rolling fields, enjoying the scenery, but hating his life.

CHAPTER FOUR

Amy walked along the verge of the gravel road, letting Jagger stroll in the tall grass. Every few feet he stopped to smell the ground or some discarded litter. He never lingered longer than a few seconds unless it was to lift his leg and sprinkle his mark.

Thankfully, the Rileys' chickens were out of sight, so Jagger wasn't tempted to run over there. He paused when he heard their squawks and screeches, ears perking. But he didn't seem very interested.

Ellie Riley had been getting the newspaper from her driveway when they'd walked up. Amy had to chat with her for a few minutes while Jagger sniffed around.

Ellie was a nice lady, though she could be, at times, afflicted with complaints. As always, she griped about the weather. Didn't seem to matter what the temperature was it was never what Ellie wanted it to be. She told Amy she saw on the forecasts that this week would be the hottest Brickston had seen in years. But a nasty thunderstorm would probably hit in a couple days, bringing even more humidity with it.

Amy wasn't looking forward to that. Usually bad storms knocked down limbs and she had to call a landscaping crew to clean up.

Costs a damn fortune.

An expense she didn't want, but it was one that she could handle if needed. Her father had not only left her the trailer—*mobile home*—park, he'd left her his savings account, property, and two insurance policies. Being the only child, she'd gotten it all. Mom had died when Amy was a teenager, so she had nobody to split the money with. But if she could give all of her inheritance to have her mom back, she'd gladly do it.

Amy hadn't been close to her father. Pete Snider hadn't been an approachable guy in his life, even with his family. So, like most people,

JAGGER

Amy and Mom had kept their distance. He'd been somebody who was there in the evenings to eat dinner with and watch him fall asleep in the recliner. He'd come to Amy's graduation, had paid for her education, and had put down the deposit on her old condo in Cool Springs. Other than holidays and birthdays, her communication with Mr. Snider had been scarce.

And she regretted it. She would have loved accusations of being a daddy's girl. But her reality was far from it. He had never been mean to her or had abused her, but he hadn't been especially loving or emotional. Hardly supportive, he'd never offered any kind of advice or displeasure in any of her affairs.

She couldn't recall ever seeing him smile.

But he gave me his empire.

Standing at the bend in the gravel road that horseshoed through Eagle's Nest, Amy sighed. She'd left the secluded mobile homes behind. Rundown singlewides were on either side of the narrow track up ahead in weedy cubicles of overgrown yard. Some were dotted with bullet holes in the tin siding. Others had chunks missing that showed patches of the insulation inside. Nearly all of them had some kind of junk car parked in the yard. Most had several garbagy cars. A couple times a month police showed up at random lots to interrupt domestic disputes or drunken fights, the majority happening at Carlos Lozano's lot. Even now, standing where the road curved, she could see Carlos outside in long black shorts and gaudy white T-shirt. He stood in front of his bright orange Impala, its hood up. A small crowd of Mexican guys stood around while Carlos tinkered around the engine. Amy had heard rumors that Carlos and his buddies were all members of some kind of gang.

People had even been murdered in Eagle's Nest. And a lot of the neighbors assumed that somehow Carlos was responsible, though Amy didn't think so. He'd never been anything but nice when she'd collected the lot rent, though his eyes seemed to lock on her breasts.

In the three years Amy had owned Eagle's Nest, she'd almost sold it a few times. The only buyers she'd managed to find only wanted it for the land. They'd planned to bulldoze the landscape and clear it out, which meant everyone who lived here had to hitch up their trailers and move. The majority of them didn't have the financial resources to go anywhere else. They could hardly afford to live as it stood now and were trapped here. If Amy got rid of the park, they'd have nowhere to go.

And sometimes Amy felt trapped too. As much as she wanted to leave, she knew she never could, which was why she'd moved back into Dad's house, leaving her condo and her old life as a dental assistant behind.

She hated her father had let this community become a slum. She remembered how nice it used to be here, when the people were actually decent.

They're not all bad now.

The majority of them were. And it was her father who'd allowed them to park their trailers here. He'd allowed drug addicts to move in, to operate their illegal businesses right out of their backyards. It was his fault Eagle's Nest was such an economically disadvantaged place to live. Plus, he'd stopped keeping it up like he was supposed to, but Amy planned to restore it to how she remembered it being when she was a kid. When there were big gorgeous trees full of pink and yellow flowers, yard decorations, and an annual event on Fourth of July when they used to set up tables and everyone in the trailer park would provide some kind of food. She remembered it being so much fun.

Some day. I'll make sure we do that again.

She turned back, started for home, guiding Jagger along. He panted as he walked, his nails scraping the dirt into little tanned clouds around his paws. The road was so dehydrated it looked like powder gravy mix and crunched like sand under Amy's feet.

"Ready to head back home?" she asked Jagger.

He walked along, not acknowledging she'd spoken. His ears perked for a moment as he stared ahead, then drooped back down. Foamy lines ran along his curled lips. If anyone were to stumble upon Jagger when he looked like this, they would assume he was rabid. She made sure he always had his tags on, so people would know he wasn't.

The road straightened out ahead of her. She passed the Rileys' lot without slowing down. Surely the chickens would be out by now and Jagger would want to gobble them up.

Janice Wilson's trailer was on a slight rise to her right. She had the biggest yard of all the renters, though she hardly kept it up. Amy paused, giving Jagger's leash a gentle tug so he would know to stop. He listened, sinking down on his rear. He was tired already. She worried about his weight, but Dr. Alasba told her his heavy size was normal and if she kept up the daily walks, all would be fine. The lifespan of dogs like Jagger could reach ten years. He was four now, but acted like a senior already.

Her throat tightened as she tried to picture what her life might be without him.

Don't start thinking about that. He has six good years left.

She looked at Jagger's snout, the sagging jowls that gave him a joker's grin. Was that gray hair she saw feathering down the compacted maw? Turning away from Jagger, she peered up the short hill to Janice's trailer. The weed-choked lawn needed mowing. Patches of wild onion spread through like troves of green tails. Children's toys were scattered around the yard in brightly colored debris like the remnants of a toddler apocalypse. She saw a clubhouse near the front door with a yellow ceiling and blue walls.

A little boy walked out, waving a plastic baseball like a sword. She could hear him providing the swooshing sound effects with his mouth.

Jagger's ears perked again. His panting stopped. A low whine emanated from his throat as his maw closed. Watching Nathan play made Jagger want to join him. Jagger wasn't a dog that openly trusted people, but he loved the little boy a lot.

Outside alone. Again.

Nathan usually played outside without any kind of supervision.

38

Social Services had been dispatched here more than once and each time left without taking the kid, for whatever reason.

Amy would never forget the evening she was driving back from the gym and had nearly hit him with her car. He'd been in the middle of the road, crying in nothing but a shirt and soggy, loaded diaper. He'd had on no shoes or socks, which left his feet bare and his toes scuffed. When Amy had taken him to the trailer, she'd found Janice had fallen asleep—*passed out*—on the couch and Nathan had wandered outside and couldn't find his way back home. Amy had returned to her car, the smacks of Nathan's punishments combined with his screams coming from inside the trailer.

Now, seeing the kid play in such a scraggly yard, without his mother keeping an eye on him, made Amy sad. Her heart broke for him. Such a cute little guy with a traditional little boy hairstyle of flat bangs that touched his eyebrows and poked out around his ears.

At least he's dressed this time.

She thought about walking up to the trailer and checking on Janice. Make sure she hadn't passed out drunk again. Now would also be a good time to get the lot rent.

Amy sighed.

She couldn't do it. For whatever reason, she would feel like a merciless bitch for knocking on Janice's door.

"Come on," she said to Jagger. "Let's go home before Nathan sees us and wants to play."

They walked the rest of the way back to the house without stopping. The good feelings had left her and now she felt tired and miserable. Even Jagger seemed depressed.

Birds hopped along the grass beyond the road, pecking at the ground, and Jagger ignored them. In the woods that enclosed Eagle's Nest, Amy could hear things scuttling about, but Jagger didn't even glance in the direction of the sounds.

Maybe the heat was getting to him. Being a typical North

JAGGER

Carolina summer day, it felt much warmer now than when she'd left. The dew on Amy's grass was dried when they reached the yard. She wasn't sure how long they'd been gone, but she guessed no longer than forty minutes.

As she walked around the side of the house, she glanced at her Jeep parked under the carport.

The space beside it was empty.

Where's Teresa?

Amy hadn't seen her on the road, so she must have driven out the other way, the direction Amy had avoided this morning.

I might've seen her if I'd kept going.

She stared at the empty spot for a moment, then walked to the fence. She opened the gate, squatted next to Jagger, and unhooked the leash. He trotted into the yard, his collar jangling like a pocketful of change. He took the steps in one big sprint and reached the door well before Amy got to the deck.

She tried the knob. It was unlocked.

Thank God. I would've been locked out.

Amy didn't keep a spare key outside, so she would have been stuck on the deck until Teresa got back.

Where the hell is she?

Amy opened the door and didn't attempt to stop Jagger when he dashed inside. The cool air from the air conditioning felt great on her hot skin. It dried the sweat, gluing her tank top to her back. Reaching behind her, she plucked it from her skin and fanned herself as she walked into the kitchen.

Jagger headed to his food and water. The auto-feed jugs stood next to each other underneath the counter where she kept the trash can. It was a metal unit with a locking lid since Jagger used to knock over the old plastic container so he could raid it for scraps.

The waffle iron was on the counter, opened and unplugged. Two cooked waffles sat on a plate next to it. They were large golden discs. The squared pattern was slightly darker, making it resemble an edible checker board.

The waffles are done. So she didn't go to the store because I was out of something.

Where *did* she go?

Amy found her answer written on a note that had been stuck to the fridge by a magnet.

Had to leave—Teresa.

"Well that explains nothing," said Amy.

Jagger, slurping from his water auto-filler, stopped lapping long enough to raise his head. His maw was drenched. Runnels sluiced down his jowls, making soft ticking sounds when they dripped onto the floor. He ran his tongue across his snout, then lowered his face back to the water.

Amy touched the waffle. It felt cool and a little greasy, like a damp sponge. She grabbed the top one, put it on another plate, and opened the microwave. The rotating plate inside was dirty with overcooked spatters. She set the waffle inside and shut the door, then tapped some numbers on the pad.

As it warmed, she fetched the syrup from the small closet-like pantry. Then she took the orange juice from the fridge, grabbing the butter dish along the way. She put them on the small round table. The microwave beeped as she was getting a clean glass from the cupboard.

Sitting at the table, she used a knife to cut off a square of butter. She smeared it across the reheated waffle. After she had it gleaming, she doused the waffle in syrup, watching the squared indentions fill with thick brown. She even made a sticky puddle around it.

Yummy.

Jagger walked slowly to her, turned a circle, then laid at her feet. He put his head down on his outstretched forepaws and was sleeping before she'd taken her second bite.

CHAPTER FIVE

Janice had watched Amy from a window in her living room. Leaning against the wall, she'd tilted her head to see through the glass. The young woman had stood in the road, partially blocked by the trees, with her giant dog. She had been watching Nathan play. And, Janice assumed, had been thinking how horrible of a life Nathan must have.

He's got it made!

Though Amy Snider had never done anything to warrant it, Janice couldn't stand her. There was really no reason for the dislike. It was just there, like a feeling someone has and can't explain why. They really should get along, considering they were close to the same age. Amy might be a couple years younger, though not by much. Both were probably considered attractive by men all over. Janice would bet in other circumstances they might even enjoy going out and doing what girlfriends did.

But Amy was still basically Janice's landlord. And Janice had never respected anyone with any kind of authority above her. Though Janice owned the trailer, Amy owned the land it sat on and the septic tank and well in the ground. Everything else belonged to Janice.

Now, sitting on the couch and smoking a cigarette, Janice felt antsy. It was seeing Amy outside that had done it. She'd come to get the lot rent, Janice was sure of it. For whatever reason, she'd changed her mind.

Must know I don't have it.

Janice had assured Amy she would bring it over this morning. There was a delay in her unemployment check, so what money she actually had needed to go to utilities. A food stamp card took care of groceries. At least they'd put the money in the account on time. Nothing like being owed money that just wasn't coming in like it was supposed to.

JAGGER

Amy must be thinking the same thing.

Nathan's laughter drifted through the opened window. With the A/C unit outside on the fritz, all she had to cool the trailer with was the breeze from outside that never seemed to be enough and some ceiling fans. If her check ever got here, she would go pick up some of those cheap window fans. Wouldn't help much, but having them was better than nothing.

Janice stood up, leaned over, and flicked the ashes off her cigarette into the empty beer can on the coffee table, a leftover from last night. She hadn't gotten so bad she'd started drinking in the mornings, but she feared she would be before long.

Crossing the room, she stopped at the same window she'd spied Amy through. She looked down. The bushes were overgrown and springy branches reached up to the window screen.

Nathan was out front, trying to twirl his plastic baseball bat like a staff.

She really did care about him. Whether it was love or not, she couldn't say. Yes, she was his mother. She'd carried him the full nine months and birthed him. She'd breast fed him as a baby and cried when he said his first word.

Dada!

Some accused her of not caring about Nathan, and she supposed she'd never given them any reason to think otherwise. There were times when she assumed they might be right. She wanted to love him like a mother should.

She just couldn't.

When Janice had found out she was pregnant, she'd wanted an abortion. She'd gone as far as setting up the appointment. Eric had talked her out of it. He had that kind of influence over Janice. He'd been the one who'd seduced her into the affair that led to her being thrown out of the home she'd once shared with Trent, her husband of seven years.

I spread my legs. Can't put all the blame on him.

But she could put *most* of it on him. And she did, constantly. Usually the nights she cried on the couch until the beer finally made her pass out.

Like last night.

Eric had ruined her life and Nathan was the constant reminder of how much she hated it. Eric had convinced her to move into the trailer with him. Not a great life, but it hadn't been unbearable for a little while.

Not until Nathan was just eight weeks away from being born and Eric killed himself. Washed down a dozen sleeping pills with some vodka. The eternal sleep cocktail, she liked to call it. Many nights she'd been tempted to make one for herself.

Each time she was tempted, she felt something nudge her inside—a cold feeling, unlike the sorrow she usually felt. At times she wondered if it was remorse.

On nights like that—like last night—she'd find herself stumbling down the hallway on the slanted floor that had never been leveled correctly. The alcohol made it even more treacherous, causing her to stumble into the walls, using her elbows to keep from falling. By some miracle she'd wind up in Nathan's room. He'd gotten too big for a crib, so he slept on a child-sized mattress on the floor. It was the best she could do for now. One day she would get him a frame of some kind.

Last night she'd stood over him, watching him sleep, and had felt as if she might be able to actually love him.

After making it back to the couch, she'd prayed for the first time since she was a teenager. And she'd asked God not to let those feelings burn off with her hangover in the morning.

So far, they hadn't.

She'd even cooked breakfast this morning, not forcing Nathan to eat oatmeal again. He'd been so happy eating eggs. He'd sung songs to her. Even with her terrible headache, she'd allowed it.

It had been the best morning they'd had in years.

Please God, let us have more. Help me to love my son.

JAGGER

Outside, Nathan tried to twirl the bat onto his shoulder as if he was a soldier with a rifle. The fat end bonked him on the forehead. Janice heard the smack from where she was standing, and winced as if she'd been the one hit.

Dropping the bat, Nathan looked confused and a little stunned by what had happened. A red blemish blossomed on his forehead, spreading like spilled fluid. It wasn't blood, just a rapidly forming welt. He started to cry, but not like most kids who'd unleash a pitiful wail. He knew better. Usually when he cried like that, Janice was quick to make him shut up. Though it was clear that he wanted to cry and express the pain he was in, he didn't.

And this made Janice cry.

"Mama?"

Janice's sobs stopped at once. Nathan had heard her. If he realized she was close by, he might want her to console him. That was something else she didn't know how to do.

Biting her lip, she huffed through her nose. She screwed her eyes shut, taking deep breaths.

But didn't answer him.

A couple minutes later Nathan was playing again as if nothing had happened.

CHAPTER SIX

Deputy Mark Varner wanted some doughnuts, but when he saw the line of cruisers in Glory Doughnuts' parking lot, he drove past. He'd give his colleagues time to get out of there, go back later.

Damn, guys. We already have a bad enough reputation for being lazy.

Shaking his head, Mark braked at the stoplight. He was driving through downtown Brickston, or what he liked to call Fast Food Central. Being a small town, they still had a vast array of popular chains, all within walking distance of each other.

Gazing into the rearview mirror, he could see the large pink doughnut on the sign. He sighed. His stomach grumbled to tell him how angry it was for being teased.

Patting his stomach, Mark said, "Be patient. We'll come back in a half-hour."

The light blinked green. Mark pulled his cruiser through the intersection. Other than him, nobody waited in either direction. Traffic was nearly nonexistent around this time. It was late in the morning, but the people in Brickston usually didn't start filling the roads until closer to lunchtime. He enjoyed these calm moments. It was rare that he had to rush off on some kind of call before noon. And what he had to worry about afterward wasn't much.

A big change from the night shift.

Working nights had nearly made him quit being a cop. During his downtime, which was rare, he found himself reading over pamphlets from the community college. A lot of people believed nobody was ever too old for a new career. Mark tended to disagree. He was in his mid-thirties and had been a cop for thirteen years. In his eyes, his options were becoming more limited by the week.

JAGGER

Mark turned left at the next intersection, heading toward the crummy district. Low income housing and government-funded living were all that was back here. Back when he worked nights, he could have parked his car out here and just waited for the calls. Sometimes he missed it, though he was usually quick to come to his senses.

He supposed those rare nostalgic feelings stemmed from how much time he'd spent here. He had memories, though none of them were quite pleasant. Not all of the people back here were criminals. Some were just prisoners of their convictions, victims of bad decisions. And he felt sorry for them.

Others had settled in this area, comfortable with how badly they'd screwed up their lives. Those were the kind of uneducated idiots Mark couldn't stand. The worthless losers who thought they were smarter than everybody, though they'd gained nothing doing things their own way.

He quickly drove through Clancy, not bothering to take any of the side roads and going in deeper. He didn't want to or need to. It was dead out here this morning, other than one guy wandering around talking to himself.

He reached a stop sign, clicked the blinker, and let the car crawl through. He gave one last look at Clancy before turning left and leaving it behind.

So much for being sentimental.

He was glad to be driving away, feeling slightly better about his current position after seeing where he used to be assigned. But he still didn't know if he wanted to be a cop the rest of his life. It had already cost him marrying Miranda. He was shot in the leg by a guy hopped up on meth a month before he was supposed to become a husband. Miranda had already started moving into his tiny house and was there when they'd called to tell her he was being rushed to County Memorial Hospital.

They'd postponed the wedding. Miranda was patient and supportive during his recovery. A week after the leg brace had come off for good, she'd told him she was leaving. She was going to move back in with her parents in South Carolina and start over.

"You should do the same with your life," she'd said, tears making her eyes twinkle under the light in his kitchen.

"I don't know how," he'd told her.

And it was true. Still, he'd taken her comment to heart and began thinking about other possibilities his life could bring him.

And that bag of surprises was a small one, more like a pouch.

"Not much else you're good at, Marky-Mark," he mumbled.

The radio sizzled and whistled high and sharp, tearing him away from his piteous recollections. Mark winced at the shrill loudness filling the car.

Carla's voice came on, distorted and somehow sexier than in person. "Unit five, what's your twenty?"

He snatched the mouthpiece from the cradle, raised it to his mouth, and thumbed the button on the side. "Dispatch, this is Unit five. I'm heading west on Honey Well, going back into town. Over."

There was a pause. She most likely knew he'd been in Clancy and was wondering why since she hadn't sent him there. The crackling static was starting to make him antsy.

"Your superior is requesting your assistance at the local gathering of your peers, Deputy."

Mark groaned. Somebody must have spotted him driving past Glory Doughnuts and were now summoning him back.

"Carla? Did they really call you and make you dispatch me over there?"

"That's an affirmative, Mark. Said the coffee is just right this morning and the doughnuts are fresh."

Mark didn't want to be seen with nearly all the other on-duty officers at the doughnut shop, but they really wanted him there. If he didn't show up, it would make him look like a jerk.

"All right," he said. "Heading over there now."

"One more thing," she said.

JAGGER

"Sure."

"Make sure somebody brings me some coffee and a half-dozen?"

Smiling, Mark nodded, though he knew Carla had no way of knowing he'd done so. "You got it."

"Would it by chance be you, bringing me the sweet treat?"

Mark felt the back of his neck growing hot. He'd known Carla had made her way around other officers in the past, yet somehow it seemed different whenever she flirted with him. As if there was something that yearned for more than a few nights in her bedroom. And that was exactly what kept him away. He didn't want anything serious until he'd figured out what to do about himself.

"We shall see on that one," he said.

"That's good enough for me," she said. "Signing out."

"Over."

The radio went silent. He returned the mouthpiece to the cradle and drove the rest of the way to Glory Doughnuts in silence. His mind had gone blank and he made sure it remained that way.

Pulling into the parking lot, he found an empty space between two other cruisers. He shut off the car. Sitting behind the wheel, he willed himself into the content policeman character. The others seemed to buy it, so he must be putting on a good show each time.

There's a career. Actor.

Smirking at the thought, Mark climbed out of the car. He felt the heat of the day breath on him as he shut the door. It made his uniform feel even thicker and heavier against his skin, a bit clingy and sticky.

Adjusting his belt, he started for the shop, already enjoying the sweet aromas drifting from inside.

CHAPTER SEVEN

Clayton climbed into Teresa's car and slammed the door. She didn't drive off right away. Even though he wasn't looking at her, he knew she was looking at him. He could imagine what she was thinking as she noted his black eye, scuffed nose and split lip. She couldn't see the bruises under Mitch's clothes, but she probably knew they were there.

"My God, Clayton..."

"You should see the other guy."

"That's not funny."

Clayton sighed. He tugged at the flannel shirt that was two sizes larger than what he usually wore. Teresa still wasn't driving away from Mitch's two-story farmhouse. He looked out the passenger window and could see Mitch watching them from a bay window. He looked concerned through the frown that furrowed his brow.

"Let's get out of here, huh?"

Teresa swallowed. It made a wet plopping sound. She was about to start crying.

He saw her nod, then turn around in her seat. The car shifted gears and they started moving backward. She got the car turned around and was driving up the gravel driveway with cornfields on either side when the tears did come.

Clayton turned his head slightly. He could see Teresa. She sat forward a bit, both hands on the steering wheel, tears streaming down her face. It looked as if she was grinning from how her lips were pulled back. But he knew she wasn't. She was fighting with all she had to hold back her true reactions to his condition.

"I'm sorry," he muttered.

Teresa shook her head, still crying. "When's it going to stop?"

JAGGER

"What do you mean?"

"This." She waved her hand. "All of this. You."

He knew what she'd meant, but had decided to keep playing dumb. It was the same trick he used to pull on his parents when he was a teenager.

"I can't keep bailing you out of trouble," she said, sniffling.

"Who asked you to, anyway?"

She turned to him, eyes wet and runny with tears. "You did."

"Oh...right."

"And of course, I came running like a good little doggie every time you whistle." Though her voice was still shaky, she seemed to have stopped crying for the moment.

An image of Bruiser's mangled remains popped in his head. The ripped open throat, the stringy bits spilled onto the floor, turning the dirt clumpy.

Clayton focused on Teresa's legs to take his mind off Bruiser. It helped. The sun didn't reach below her stomach. Tanned and smooth, her legs still gleamed in the soft shadows as if she'd rubbed them in lotion. Her skirt hung back on her thigh down to the curve before her rump. He could see the seam of her dark panties.

He looked at the rest of her. She wore a sundress that hung low on her chest, showing the bulging slopes of her breasts. She must have had a strapless bra on underneath because he couldn't see any hint of her nipples in the front, and all that was on her shoulders were the noodle-thin strings of her dress.

She looked great, like always. She wore no make-up, but she had the kind of face that didn't require it. He would bet she had some kind of Indian in her blood from the black hair and how dark her skin always seemed to be. It was the smoothest he'd ever felt. Slick and velvety, his hand would glide across.

He felt stirring in his pants.

"Stop staring at my tits, Clayton."

"I wasn't," he said, facing the front. At some point they'd gotten on the main road and were heading back to Brickston. "I was looking at your legs."

She rolled her eyes. "Whatever."

She's really pissed.

And he couldn't blame her for it. But right now, he really needed her not to be.

"Thank you for picking me up," he said.

"My fucking pleasure."

"What do you want from me?"

"To stop this bullshit."

If only he could. "I'm trying."

"Are you?" She turned to him. "Are you, really?"

"I'm trying to try." He sighed. "Got any cigarettes?"

"You don't?"

"I don't even have my wallet."

Teresa thrust her chin forward. "Glove compartment."

Clayton's knees brushed the dashboard from how close the seat had been moved forward. Reaching between his legs, Clayton pulled the lever and the lid dropped open. The cigarettes rolled out. He caught them before they fell between his legs, then flung the compartment lid up. It clicked shut.

"Grab me one too," she said.

Clayton opened the flip-top box. A lighter was inside with the few remaining cigarettes.

Hopefully she has another pack somewhere. These won't last us long.

He pulled out the lighter with two cigarettes. He pinched both cigarettes between his lips, using the lighter to light both cigarettes at once.

He passed one to Teresa.

"Thanks," she said.

"Sure."

JAGGER

She rolled her window down a crack. Wind gushed in, pulling the smoke out and flinging Clayton's hair across his face. He cracked his window as well. The heavy gust slackened, and the draft seemed to settle the force throwing his hair around. He tried running his hand through it, but his fingers got tangled in the knots. He felt clumps of dried blood matting it together. Letting his hand drop in his lap, he sighed.

He needed a shower.

"Going to tell me what happened?" she asked.

"Does it matter?"

"To me it does."

Knowing she cared so much should make him feel good. Instead, it annoyed the hell out of him. He wished she *didn't* care. It would make his being mean to her so much easier. "Some guys kicked my ass."

"What'd you do?" She puffed on the cigarette, blowing the smoke out the side of her mouth. The wind snatched it through the window.

"Why do you automatically assume it's my fault?"

"Isn't it?"

Clayton flung his hand up, letting it slap his leg. "Well...yes and no."

Teresa didn't say anything. He realized she was waiting on him to elaborate. And he was angry at himself when he realized he was going to.

He told her about Bruiser and Freddy's claim that he could get Brock to take it easy on him for a while. Naturally he'd left out how he had to get Freddy to do this.

"So they beat you up anyway?"

"Yep."

"And this is good?"

"It's not great, but it's better than them killing me."

Teresa looked pained. "Think they really will?"

"If I don't get Brock twelve thousand dollars, yes."

"You should go to the police."

"Oh, sure. And tell them what? 'Hi. I've been helping some people run a dog fighting thing and my dog was killed. Lost some people a lot of money. Can you help me?'" Clayton shook his head. "They'd bust my ass."

"I'm sure they'd give you some kind of deal."

"I'd go to jail no matter what. If I wasn't killed before then, somebody would knock me off in there."

"But they'd lock up this Brock guy, right? They wouldn't put you in the same place as him."

"Please. I wouldn't make it that far. Brock has cops on his payroll. He's a *dick*."

"Well...how do you plan on getting him the money, if you're not going to do the smart thing?"

Teresa's comment stung. He felt himself starting to sweat, despite the cool air blowing from the vents. He scratched his head hard enough to make his scalp burn. "I've been thinking about that."

"Oh?"

On the naked tractor ride back to Mitch's house, it had been all he could do. The only option he felt he had was simple, and it probably wouldn't work.

"I've got to get another dog and win some fights."

Teresa groaned.

"It's either that or kill them all," he quickly added.

"Do you even hear yourself when you talk?"

"Unfortunately."

Teresa tossed her cigarette out the window. It was a bad idea considering they were in a rural area that hadn't had rain in two weeks. Might start a fire and burn the whole town down.

Maybe I could burn the barn down. It'll get them off my back even longer until I can figure some things out.

Teresa sighed as if she'd heard his idiotic thoughts. He looked over at her. She had her elbow on top of the door panel, leaning her head against her hand. Her fingers were burrowed into her thick, raven-black hair and held it away from her face.

JAGGER

Damn, she's so pretty.

He couldn't help thinking that every time he saw her. Sometimes the sight of her stole his breath. Other times it made his chest tighten with pain. Then other times he wanted to grab her by the shoulders and shake her really hard. He'd never been a guy who could hit a woman, but he was fond of shaking them if he had to.

"Where am I taking you?" she asked, sounding irritated and ready to be done with this car ride.

"I don't really know. I guess we'll try Charlie's Mart first. Hopefully my truck's still there."

Teresa didn't acknowledge he'd answered her.

Clayton leaned back. He smoked the rest of his cigarette and held it until the cherry burned out. Then he tossed out his window.

As he was rolling the glass up, he saw Charlie's Mart up ahead on the right. It was a small brick building with four gas pumps out front. The parking lot was oddly shaped and awkward. No matter how many cars were parked there, getting in and out was a hassle.

His truck was parked at the edge, the front facing the road.

"I'll be damned, they actually left it."

"Luck you," she said.

Clayton frowned.

Teresa slowed the car down to pull into the parking lot. She drove over to his truck and parked next to it. Leaning up, Clayton looked past Teresa so he could see his truck. From where he sat, it looked okay. The windows hadn't been busted. The tires on this side were still inflated.

Maybe they left it alone. How could they expect me to get them their money if I had to pay to get my truck fixed?

"Thanks for the ride," he said, opening the door. "I won't bother you again."

He started to climb out.

"Clayton!"

He paused. "Yeah."

"Wait."

Clayton dropped back down in the seat. He felt like he was about to be scolded by a teacher for shooting spitballs. "What?"

"Look at me."

He didn't want to, but he turned his head. Their eyes locked. He felt that tingling pinch in his chest. His heart started to pound, making it hard to swallow.

Her dark eyes were full of hurt that *he'd* caused. But behind those sad orbs was love for him that hadn't been broken.

He was about to apologize again when she suddenly leaned over. She gripped his shirt and pulled him close. Her lips pushed against his. It hurt where his lip was split, but he didn't stop her.

They kissed, fervently and quick, unable to get enough of each other. His hand reached between her legs. It was stopped only for a moment by her closed thighs, but she parted them so his fingers could delve. They slipped behind her panties and went in.

She gasped in his mouth. He moved his hand back and forth inside her wet heat, thrusting with his fingers. She clamped her thighs around his arm so he couldn't he pull it away.

"I love you so much," she whispered.

He felt the breath of her words on his lips. He smiled.

They started kissing again.

CHAPTER EIGHT

Jim Riley stuck the empty coffee can into the bag of chicken feed and scooped some out. He scattered it around the yard, throwing little grits all over. It looked like bug poison on the grass.

The chickens ran toward the feed, wings spread and chests fluttering. They clucked and screeched with eagerness as they pecked at the ground. The little ones were getting big. Soon they'd be laying eggs of their own. Might be a good idea to start keeping them separated. He didn't want to have an out of control fowl population on his hands.

Amy would have a fit. She didn't like the chickens he had now, though he gave her fresh eggs every month as a courtesy. She didn't mind taking them, no sir. And she also didn't mind reprimanding him whenever they wandered out of his yard.

He didn't have a fence, or the money to put one up. Usually the coop at the edge of his backyard was all he needed. They were decent birds and kept close to home most of the time. Every so often they made their way into the neighbors' yards or up the road toward Amy Snider's place.

He actually liked when they snuck over there. That meant he would have to bring them back, so he'd have to pay a visit to the Snider place.

Last month, he'd caught her sunbathing in her backyard. On her back, she had been on a blanket folded out on the ground under her. He hadn't been able to see her eyes behind the sunglasses, but how her chest had moved, he could tell she'd fallen asleep. She'd had on a purple bikini that was just a triangle over each nipple and a small patch covering her groin.

He was sixty-one, but his penis wanted to grow rigid like a teenager's whenever he thought back to how her body had seemed to shine under the sunlight. It had looked coated in oil, bright and tanned and slippery.

He imagined his hands sliding all over her skin as he massaged her. Her large breasts filled his hands when he grabbed them behind the triangle-shaped shields of her bikini top. He just knew they would feel soft and springy, yet a little firm.

He'd watched her for several minutes from behind the trees at the verge of her property while his chickens had searched the ground around his feet for food. Wanting a closer look, he hadn't dared to try.

The big dog had been sleeping beside her.

Amy never went outside without the big beast. He'd heard neighbors say he weighed somewhere around two hundred pounds.

Jim didn't doubt it. Seeing him sleeping beside Amy, he'd looked like a bear lying next to Goldilocks—a sexy Goldilocks sparkling under the late May heat.

He wondered if she was lying out in the sun right now.

Probably not. She was just walking that big monster a little bit ago.

Wearing those short shorts that barely covered her full ass. Her legs had looked muscular and curvy, leading up to her buttocks that flared out before reaching her flat lower back.

Looks like she has jelly beans packed in her shorts.

And he bet they tasted as sweet as candy.

Jim licked his lips.

"Jimmy-tot! Get your hand out of your pants!"

Jim jerked at the humiliating shout from his wife. His heart lurched. He looked down and saw his hand had slipped into his robe and down his pajama pants. "I was scratching it!" he shouted back.

"Sure you were!"

Groaning, he pulled his hand out of his pants and turned around. Ellie stood on the top step at the back door. The wooden frame had warped and leaned slightly to the side, so she had to hold onto to the aluminum railing to keep from falling.

Seeing her now in her pink robe, with her once-pretty hair pulled tightly behind her head, made it hard to believe she used to look something like Amy back when they had been just a pair of frolicking youngsters. Way back when they couldn't keep their hands off each other.

He supposed Ellie's body was still all right. She had an ample bosom, but it was becoming too heavy for the skin that connected them to her chest. So her breasts drooped more than he liked. Her legs were in great shape, tight and lined with muscle from working hard all her life. They were just so pale he could see the blue smears of her veins through the skin. Wide hips combined with a tight waist gave her a nice hourglass figure, though he could go without her slightly pudgy belly.

Her face could be better. The wrinkles and stress lines made her look ten years older than sixty. And she smoked like a damn chimney and had a cough that never went away. Sometimes they fooled around, and when she got too worked up, she'd launch into a coughing spell that caused her to pee herself.

At least she doesn't look as bad as me.

Jim had no hair left worth combing, other than the frizzy patch that wrapped around the back of his head. The skin under his chin hung like a beard of flesh and he had gray hairs sprouting from his ears, around his nipples, and even more grays infesting his pubic area. His legs were scrawny with knobby knees that popped with nearly every step he made.

"I'm thinking you like those damn chickens too much, Jimmy-tot!"

She'd called him that as long as he'd known her. Whenever she referred to him by his proper name, he sometimes didn't realize he was supposed to acknowledge her.

"Can't help I itch," he said. "Sometimes when I itch, I have to scratch, you know."

"That's the kind of scratching you should do in private, where nobody can see."

He wanted to remind her that their backyard was *private*. Thanks to the trees that surrounded them and the woods behind them, it looked as if they lived in complete seclusion. He didn't say that, of course. Being snarky would only cause her to get louder. He might not be able to *see* his neighbors, but they could hear Ellie's loud mouth whenever she got aggravated.

"Aw, leave me alone," he said, turning his back to her. He bent over, ignoring the pain in his lower back, and scooped out another helping of chicken feed. He flung his arm out. The grain pebbles sprinkled across the yard in an arc.

He heard the steps groaning as she came down them.

"Breakfast is almost done," she said. "The grits aren't quite boiling yet.

"Fine."

They'd only been up for four hours, so naturally she'd waited that long to cook it for him.

"And yes, I put a lot of butter in them."

"Good. I don't like them to be dry."

"I know. They taste like salty bricks." She stepped next to him, crossed her arms, and watched the chickens strut about. Her arms pushed against her robe, making a gap at her chest. He saw a glimpse of a white slope and the purple jut of a nipple. "I got more coffee going, too."

Jim looked away from his wife. "Thanks."

She bumped him gently with her hip. "Going to be another hot one today, isn't it?"

"Seems like it."

"I saw Amy walking around earlier. You'd think she would know better than to dress like that in this neighborhood."

"Hmmm? Didn't see her."

He felt Ellie's unbelieving eyes on him. "Oh? I thought that was why you was in the bathroom so damn long earlier. Watching her walk around."

"Nope."

"Uh-huh."

He hated when Ellie accused him of being a peeper. It wasn't because she was wrong, but how she seemed to always know exactly what he was up to whenever he was doing it. And Jim didn't *want* to ogle Amy Snider. He just couldn't help himself. After all, he had a daughter around Amy's age, and grandkids. He shouldn't be lusting after a woman other than his wife anyhow.

"That dog of hers would keep anybody from messing with her," he said, hoping to get the focus away from his bathroom visit.

"Oh, please. That dog's a giant softy. He won't do nothing to nobody. He's all show, but really that's all you need."

"I suppose."

"I worry about her a lot," said Ellie.

And Jim supposed she truly did. Through her gossiping was a woman who didn't know how to accurately express her concern. Jim could see it, but others would be fooled by it.

He walked over to one of the nests. He saw a couple of eggs inside.

"Got some this morning?"

"We do. Looks like four."

"I'll check the others."

"I got it. I'm sure the grits are about done by now."

"Probably right."

She turned away from him and headed to the rickety steps that led to the back door. He watched her walk like someone who didn't suffer from achy hips. She never seemed to be in any kind of pain. The pink tail of her robe fluttered a little and he got a glimpse of the bottom of a buttock. It was pale and curved, dimpling where it curled to her thigh.

He looked back at the nest. He had four here, hopefully there were some more in the others. The chickens had their little constructed egg baskets all over his backyard. If he could gather up a dozen, he'd take them down to Amy Snider.

JAGGER

Maybe she'd be lounging out in the sun.

"Grits are done!"

Jim jumped at Ellie's shout. Looking over his shoulder, he saw the window above the sink had been lifted. He could see the pale smudge of her face leaning down.

"All right!"

Damn. She was bound to give him a heart attack today for sure.

He headed for the back door, ready to eat.

CHAPTER NINE

Clayton slipped out of Teresa's bed, leaving her sleeping. She hugged the sheet to her chest and had a long dark leg sticking out and draped across the mattress. She wore an anklet made out of string that she might have created herself. He hadn't noticed it before, but liked how it was all she had on her smooth skin.

He looked around for his clothes. They were thrown all over the room. When they'd come back to Teresa's apartment, she'd eagerly torn the borrowed wardrobe off his body.

Clayton found his socks near her dresser underneath Teresa's panties, and picked them up. Standing, he caught a glimpse of his bruises in the vanity mirror. They were sore and made his skin feel tight behind each purple blotch. Some were ruddy around the dark edges where Teresa had kissed him.

"Too make them better," she'd said, rolling her tongue over the dark blots.

Where's the flannel shirt?

It took a moment to locate it, but he finally found it under the bed. With the clothes collected, he snuck out of the room and walked down the very short hall to the bathroom. He went inside, closing the door behind him.

He stood in front of the mirror. His hair was still knotted with blood, and now stuck out on the sides and in the back from Teresa's gripping hands.

She'd invited him over to take a shower. And he planned on doing so. Because of their detour into her bedroom, he really needed one now.

He cut the water on, twisting the dial all the way to the H. He pulled the tab on the faucet. Water sprayed down, pelting the tub. He knew it was going to make the bruises and scrapes hurt, but he didn't care.

Clayton turned away from the tub. He stepped up to the toilet. Bending slightly, he lifted the lid. Angling his penis down with a fingertip, he felt the dried crust of Teresa's release coating him. He began to urinate. It was thick and gloppy as it sputtered out. The tip was a little sore and burned some from so much rubbing.

Finished, he returned to the tub and stepped inside. He pulled the pastel-checkered curtain behind him.

The inside of the shower was stocked full of shampoos, conditioners, lotions, and skin treatments. It looked as if she ran a beauty supply store from her bathtub. He didn't know where to begin. His shower was simple. A bottle of shampoo with the conditioner already added and some soap. Nothing to it.

This...this was a nightmare.

There were different types of shampoos, each with a matching conditioner. Not knowing what to choose, he randomly selected a yellow bottle.

Cleans your hair without the fuss!

"What the hell does that mean?"

He didn't know. If it would get the blood out of his hair, it would be fine.

He lowered his head into the spray, his hair falling around his face as it became soaked. The water hammered his scalp, feeling good while also aggravating the soreness there.

He was gentle but washed in a rush. He was out of the shower and on the bath mat drying off with a towel he found hanging from a bar within five minutes.

He put Mitch's clothes back on. He noticed how soft his skin felt now under the heavy garments.

Using Teresa's overly large hairbrush, he ran it through his lengthy hair. It moved through without difficulty. As he brushed, he studied his hair in the mirror and noted how much more it shined under the bulbs above the glass.

Looks good. And healthy.

And he wasn't fussing, just as the bottle claimed he wouldn't.

When he was done, he hung the towel over the curtain rod so it would dry. Then he stepped to the door, quietly pulling it open.

He stuck his head out. Steam drifted out, feeling like a warm moist breeze on his face. He turned one way and didn't see Teresa anywhere. He looked in the other direction and jumped.

Teresa stood there, naked, holding a can of Coke out to him. "Thirsty?"

"Damn it, Teresa!" He leaned against the frame, holding a hand to his heart. "Scared me to death!"

Teresa pretended to pout. "I'm *saw-wee.*"

Heart pounding, Clayton breathed heavily. He took the Coke, glimpsing her great body. He really was thirsty, and was glad she'd offered. "Thanks," he muttered.

She leaned forward, sniffed. "Somebody smells like a *hot* woman."

Clayton closed his eyes, sighed. He heard Teresa laugh and opened his eyes to see the white of her teeth through her big smile. It brought one out of him as well.

He popped the tab and raised the can to his mouth, guzzling a couple heavy swigs. The soda burned his throat as it went down, but was cold and tasted wonderful.

He lowered the can, belched softly, and sighed.

"Hit the spot?" she asked.

"Big time."

"Too bad you're already done. I was going to join you."

"Yeah, well...I was about to leave."

The good humor on her face fell away. "Leave? Where were you going?"

While he was lying in bed with Teresa snuggled up to him, he'd been on the verge of falling asleep when he'd suddenly seen his skull packed with dog shit, just as Ralph's had supposedly been. It had shocked him away from being cozy. He'd begun to think more about his options.

And he'd concluded once again that he had none.

There were no rich relatives he could borrow the money from, and he wasn't about to start robbing liquor stores in hopes of raising enough funds. Really, all he could do was get another dog so Brock could win back his losses, maybe even a little extra.

And the dog had to be good.

"I going to Clancy," he said.

Teresa made a face. "You've got to be out of your mind."

"Nope. Just hanging from the end of my rope."

"Why are you going there?"

"To see a guy about a dog."

Compared to Clancy, Brickston was like Paris. Low income housing made up the majority of the small town. Without proper funding, the roads weren't kept up and had tar-sealed cracks spreading across like black varicose veins. Holes peppered the blacktop like acne and Teresa nearly ran off the road to avoid hitting them.

Clayton hadn't wanted her to come, and now that she was here, she wished she hadn't.

She hit the auto-lock button on the door. There was no deep thump, so they were already engaged.

"They're locked," said Clayton, confirming.

"Just being sure."

"That's your third time checking," he said.

"And it probably won't be the last."

Teresa gave a glance out her window. Shoddy, abandoned-looking houses sat close together with only a narrow path of yard separating them. The backyards looked as if they were conjoined into one long track. Some were intersected by rusted fencing, but most were not.

Teresa felt her lungs tighten as she looked around, making it hard to breath.

They came to a stop sign. She slowed the car down. Before it had come to a complete stop, a man in a tan tank top and cargo pants full of holes reeled to her window.

"Oh, shit," Teresa said through a gasp.

Clayton leaned over. "Oh, don't worry. That's just Rosco. He's harmless."

He didn't look it. His bugged eyes were wide and frantic. He had sand-colored hair that stuck up in spikes around parts that were flat and matted as if he'd added gel to just those pointed areas.

"Hey!" he shouted through the window. "Hey!"

Teresa drove off. She looked in the rearview mirror and saw him standing in the road with his arms held out. He was shouting something she couldn't understand.

"Are we almost there?" she asked.

"Yeah." Clayton pointed to Teresa's left. "It's right up there. See the white house?"

Teresa saw it. The house sat atop a small hill. A small driveway angled up, nearly reaching the house, and was crowded with old cars.

She parked behind an old Fairlane that was raised on cinder blocks. Its hood was up, but nobody seemed to be outside working on it. The white body had faded to the color of stone. Dark spots peppered the rear end and the fender was marked with tarnished streaks the color of caramel.

Teresa left the engine running. "Are you sure we should be here?"

Clayton seemed nervous, but his voice was calm when he said, "It's fine."

"There has to be another way of going about this."

"I can't think of any."

"Why this guy?"

"Stan's the only person I can really turn to at this point. Everyone else is in Brock's pocket."

"And Stan's not?"

"Nope. People think he's too crazy to be trusted."

Teresa felt a tingling pop in her stomach. "Great. And you think you can trust him?"

"What choice do I have? We knew each other in high school, so I can probably trust him more than most."

Teresa tried to come up with an idea that would solve all his problems. Her mind was blank. She couldn't improvise anything for him. If only she had more time to think, she might be able to figure something out.

"Since you insisted on coming along," said Clayton, "I should warn you about Stan."

"Warn me?"

"He's very strange."

"Define 'strange'."

"The drugs have really fucked his head up. Made him crazy. He's *extremely* paranoid, so just go with whatever he says. If you disagree with him, he might think you're an enemy."

"An *enemy?* Are you serious?"

Clayton nodded. "He's completely bat-shit, but he's very smart. He went to medical school or something and actually *graduated*. He could have been a doctor, but..."

"But now he's bat-shit crazy?"

"Exactly."

"Just wonderful." Teresa sighed.

"You can wait out here, if you want."

"Are you kidding me? I'm a sitting duck out here. I'd rather be with you."

Clayton smiled. "Really?"

His reaction was genuine. She'd only experienced his true

personality on a few occasions. This was one of them. Her comment had really made him feel good.

"Yes, really. Why else would I be here with you?"

Continuing to smile, Clayton nodded.

I'm such an idiot.

She could have been eating waffles with Amy and yet here she was. In Clancy, with a guy she wasn't sure was still her boyfriend. She wasn't sure she *wanted* him to be, either. But she knew she cared an awfully lot about him. And that made her feel even more stupid.

Stan isn't the only one who's bat-shit crazy.

Chapter Ten

A scrawny young guy with a bald head and a long goatee that hung down his throat answered the door. His eyes looked tired and lazy, rimmed with red. The purple bags underneath were puffy and swollen. Teresa would guess he wasn't much older than thirty, but his haggard face made it hard to tell for sure.

He greeted them with a, "Huh?"

Clayton, leaning against the glass storm door, cleared his throat. "Hey, Hap. Is—uh—Stan here?"

How does Clayton know these people?

Hap was opening his mouth to reply when he suddenly flew back. Another man appeared in his spot, taller, with oily bangs that hung in his purple-shaded eyes.

His arm shot out, hand gripped Clayton's shirt, and yanked him inside.

Teresa, gasping, reached for Clayton's back, but he was already gone. The storm door slowly closed.

"My, God!"

Teresa didn't know whether to dash inside to save Clayton or call the police. She was reaching into her purse for her cell phone when the storm door opened again.

A woman stood there, smiling. It was a lovely smile that stretched wide on her mouth to reveal her teeth. She still had them all, though they were stained. Her cheeks were pushed up to her eyes, making them squint around the glistening blue colors.

"Well, hi there," she said.

Teresa stood frozen, one hand inside her purse. The woman continued to smile. Her hair was the color of fire and hung to her shoulders in straight lengths.

"Um..."

The woman's eyebrows rose. "Want to come in?"

"Um..."

She waved a hand. "Don't mind, Stan. That's just how he greets people."

What the hell kind of place is this?

"Is Clayton...?"

"He's sitting on the couch," assured the woman. "Come on in. Or you can wait outside. No skin off my tits." She stepped away from the door, letting it slowly swing shut.

Before the latch *snicked*, Teresa stuck her fingers into the gap and caught it.

Was she really going in there?

Yes.

Removing her hand from her purse, she adjusted the strap, then the front of her dress, and went inside.

The room smelled like a combination of cigarette and weed-smoke mixed with something that made Teresa think of tacos. She saw a sectional couch before her. Clayton was sitting on the end closest to her, with the tall guy right next to him. His arm was thrown around Clayton's shoulders, pushing his neck down and making his head lower.

Clayton turned to her. "Hi. Teresa, this is Stan."

Stan slowly leaned his head forward, appearing on the other side of Clayton's face. "Greetings," he said.

"Huh-hi."

"Please, sit down." He gestured toward the opposite end of the couch.

Teresa looked around. The room was a mess. The coffee table was covered in clutter that had spilled onto the floor. Old fast-food bags, some burger cartons, a couple pizza boxes, and what looked like several empty rolls of aluminum foil.

A loveseat that matched the couch was to her right. Hap laid on it, his arm extended above his head and hanging over the arm of the couch. He looked asleep.

The woman who'd invited her in sat where the sections of the long couch connected. She wore denim cut-offs that looked more like briefs. She crossed a leg over her knee. Her pale shin was marked with scabs and scratches. Seeing Teresa was looking, she patted the empty cushion beside her. "Take a load off."

"O-okay. Sure…why not?"

Teresa walked on legs that felt filled with warm jelly. She expected them to give out at any moment. Thankfully, they didn't. She reached the couch, turned around, and dropped down beside the woman. She made sure there was space between them.

Teresa looked at Clayton. His eyes rose, mouth twisting upward as if to apologize.

Teresa shook her head, hoping he understood she would not easily forget this.

"Teresa, is it?" asked the woman from beside her. She put her hand on Teresa's knee and gave it a soft squeeze.

Teresa's reflex went off, making her leg jerk. The woman kept her hand there. "Um…yes."

"Hi, Teresa. I'm Daisy. That sleeping sack of uselessness over there is Hap. And you've already met Stan."

Teresa's eyes landed on Stan. He wore blue athletic pants that looked too big for him and a bright yellow T-shirt that was dark with stains. His hair was parted down the middle and hung in his eyes in greasy strands. Stubble painted his cheeks dark. It looked as if he hadn't bathed—or slept—in weeks.

He probably hasn't.

Daisy smelled nice, though. Being so close to her, she was thankful she didn't smell stale and dank. Her scent was like a mixture of flowers and soap, how the woods smelled after it rained.

JAGGER

"Want to watch TV?" asked Daisy.

"Huh?"

"TV." She pointed past Teresa.

Turning, she allowed Daisy's finger to guide her to the flat screen TV on a stand across the room. It was nicer than the one she had at home. Looked at least fifty-five inches, maybe even bigger.

How'd they afford that?

Drug money.

No doubt they operated some kind of drug business from here. Judging Daisy's wardrobe of cut-off and nearly translucent white shirt, Teresa figured she was probably a prostitute of some kind.

"No TV," said Stan. "I'm talking to Clayton. Don't need the distraction."

Since she'd come in here, Teresa hadn't heard Stan say even one word to Clayton. He just sat leaned close to him, his arm around Clayton's shoulders. They looked like buddies about to pose for a picture.

She'd never seen Clayton so uncomfortable. And it broke her heart knowing what he was going through just to try and make things right where he'd screwed up.

She realized she would have to help him through it.

He doesn't have anybody else to turn to.

Teresa decided she would be that person.

"St-Stan?" said Clayton.

"Yyyyeah?"

"I have a bit of a strange question to ask you."

"There are no strange questions, Clayton. Only strange intentions."

Clayton's brow creased. "Um...okay."

"Ask your question, man. Quick."

"Can I buy a dog off you?"

Stan jerked his arm away and shoved Clayton. He threw his arm up as if he was about to block a punch from Stan.

"What'd you ask me?" said Stan, voice rising. His eyes seemed to grow unnaturally wider than humanly possible.

"Stan?" said Daisy. "Be civil. Clayton's a friend."

Stan's head whipped toward Daisy. Though Teresa didn't see how it was possible, his glassy eyes stretched even wider. The shimmering orbs flicked as if he were a puppet, by fingers crammed inside his skull to operate them.

"Friend?"

Daisy nodded, still smiling. "Yes. Friend."

"Friend good?"

"Yes, honey."

"Okay..." Stan nodded as if reassuring himself. "Good. Clayton friend of Stan?"

"That's right," said Daisy.

Hap still slept, oblivious to the insanity Teresa and Clayton were witnessing.

What the hell's going on here?

Stan scooted away from Clayton, turning so he could hang a leg on the couch. Knee bent, he pulled his foot against the other leg. When he spoke, his voice was very calm and friendly. "A dog you say?"

Clayton smiled. Teresa could tell it was forced.

"Yes," said Clayton.

"Pardon my confusion. I am familiar and quite comfortable with people coming here and requesting all sorts of things from me. And I am always happy to oblige. Sometimes they ask for my product, and other times they ask for Daisy."

Daisy looked at Teresa, wiggling her eyebrows and beaming as if Stan had complimented her.

"Other times they ask for Hap," he extended his hand toward the sleeping loser on the couch. "But I have to say, nobody has ever come to me wanting one of my dogs. What kind of sick fetish do you have, my man?"

"No," said Clayton. "Not...gross..."

JAGGER

"You have dogs?" Teresa heard herself ask.

"Oh, honey, yes," said Daisy. "A whole lot behind the house full of them."

"I train them," said Stan. "They are my guardians to the portals."

"What's the...?"

Daisy put her hand on Teresa's thigh and gripped. "Don't ask," she whispered. "You'll get him started and he'll never stop talking about the portals."

"I heard that," said Stan. "And she's right. The portal discussion is for another visit, I'm sure. Just know they are everywhere. And at any moment, one could open up and gobble your ass!" He snapped his finger, the harebrained tone switching back to something more rational. "But right now time is of the essence. Am I correct?"

How Stan enunciated his words reminded Teresa of bad impressions she'd heard of William Shatner.

"Yes?" said Clayton, forming it into a question instead of an answer.

"Word on the street is you are in some water of the hottest temperature."

"How'd you know?" asked Clayton.

"The street told me. My ear is always on it."

Teresa was starting to get a headache, listening to Stan talk.

"How much do you owe our mutual antagonist Brock?"

"Twelve grand."

Stan whistled, making Hap stir. His arms and legs stroked the air like a puppy having a bad dream.

Stan ran a hand through his greasy hair. His fingers gleamed slightly when he lowered his hand. "That's quite a debt, old friend."

"I know. I'm out of ideas on how to pay him back. Didn't really have any ideas to begin with."

"What are you planning to do with one of my dogs?"

"Hopefully win back Brock's money."

"I see." Stan tapped his chin with a finger. "I assume you mean the fights, correct?"

"Correct." Clayton frowned. "I mean—right."

"I have one that's pretty tough, but is he tough *enough*, I wonder?"

Clayton looked hopeful. "I'll take anything at this point."

"Keep in mind, my dogs aren't giant killing machines like you're used to, but they are great protectors. I trained them myself."

"To guard you from the portals," said Teresa.

Stan smiled. "A smart one you've got here, Clayton."

"Thanks," said Clayton.

"But she is correct. They are protectors, not merciless killers."

"If they can hold their own in a fight, is all that matters to me," Clayton said.

"Maybe. Maybe not." Stan continued to tap his chin, his eyes flitting back and forth, as if trying to keep up with the rapid-fire of thoughts behind them.

"Is everything all right?" Teresa asked.

"I don't know," said Daisy. "He's thinking about something."

"Yes, I am," said Stan.

Clayton leaned forward, resting his elbows on his knees. He pressed his fingertips together. He reminded Teresa of somebody waiting on bad news.

He is. No matter what Stan can do for him, it won't be good.

Stan snapped his finger, jerked rigid, and shouted, "Hap!"

Hap jumped up, feet pounding the floor. "What?"

"Fetch me Bruticus!"

"Yeah, okay."

Hap shambled out of the room, his shoulders hunched and arms dangling limply in front of him. His hands smacked against his green shorts.

A wicked grin made the skin on Stan's face crinkle like tissue paper. One eyebrow lifted higher than the other. "If this works, I might

JAGGER

just have the solution you're looking for."

Teresa's skin started to crawl. Goose bumps pebbled up her arms. Rubbing them, they felt like tiny points under her fingers.

"Let's go down cellar and wait for Hap. I'll get things ready."

Stan rolled back and flipped over the top of the couch. He dropped. There was a bang that shook the debris on the coffee table when he landed on the floor.

Clayton stood up. "What are we going to do?"

Stan's head appeared above the couch, wild eyes narrowed at Clayton. "A science experiment, Ygor! I hope you brought some goggles!"

He unleashed a deep throaty guffaw that made Teresa's chest hurt just hearing it.

CHAPTER ELEVEN

The dog unleashed a shrill howl that drilled into Clayton's ears, tormented, filled with pain. Flinching, Clayton hiked his shoulders as if preparing to be hit.

The black dog bumped Teresa's leg when it darted past, making her stagger to the side. She screamed, stepped over to Clayton, and hugged his arm. Her face pressed against his bicep.

He felt a warm wetness seeping through his shirt. Her body trembled against his.

She's crying.

He was nearly to tears, himself. Clayton hugged his arms around her back and pulled her tighter to him. She pressed against him, her arms bent up in front of her breasts, wrists crossed.

"Get the dog, Hap!" shouted Stan. He stood behind a table erected from stands and an old door.

Hap had been standing next to him, but now he ran across the basement, leaning over with his arms out. The dog dashed away from him. His claws clicked across the cracked cement floor in the chase. Gaining on the dog, Hap suddenly flung himself forward. His hands opened to catch the dog's tail.

And missed.

He belly-flopped onto the hard floor, blasting out his breath. Wheezing, he rolled onto his side, his face scrunched up and red, groaning through cracked, pursed lips.

Stan slammed his fist down on the makeshift table, making it rattle on top of the spired legs.

Daisy carefully climbed down the mildew-slick stairs, gripping the wooden railing that was just as coated and slippery. She leaned her

JAGGER

head down to peer in. "What the hell is going on down here?"

Stan looked up at her. He jabbed his finger into the air. "Stay out of this, Daisy! Go back upstairs!"

Stepping out from behind the table, Stan tossed the empty syringe behind him. It landed on the table with a soft tap and rolled to the other side. Earlier it had been full of red liquid that had reminded Clayton of fruit punch.

Hap had brought the dog inside from what Stan had called the dog pen, which was actually just a fenced in backyard crowded with dogs of a variety of breeds.

The dog wasn't very big, probably no larger than a Collie, but its body was like that of a German Shepard. Its fur was solid black except for a white patch on its chest.

Putting the dog on the table, Hap had leaned over it to hold it still. Unaware of what was about to happen, the dog had panted away, glad to be receiving all this attention.

It had barely acknowledged Stan pinching a flap of skin above its neck and stretching it up. When he'd stuck the needle that looked big enough for elephant vaccinations into the taut hairy piece, the dog had only slightly whimpered.

Time had seemed to drag as they waited. For what, Clayton hadn't known. Stan had yet to tell him what he was trying to accomplish. All he'd known was Stan wanted them to keep quiet.

And watch.

The dog had closed its mouth. Growled. Then its maw had lunged at Stan, snapping with a sound like two boards being smacked together. Stan had successfully dodged the bite, but knocked into Hap who'd released his hold of the dog.

Then the black canine had dived from the table.

And now won't stop running around and screaming!

It released another agonizing wail and sprinted to the other side of the basement, its head low.

"What's wrong with it?" cried Teresa. "Why does it keep making those sounds?"

Clayton felt Teresa turn in time to see the poor dog crash against the concrete-block wall. It squealed with the dull thud of its head striking the wall's unyielding hardness. Staggering back, the dog look dazed before plopping down on its rear end. Its tail curled out like a dark grin on the concrete. It gazed back at Clayton, panting. Its tongue hung out the side of its mouth, like a dehydrated section of pink rubber between teeth slick with blood.

Then its eyes burst, popping like two balloons filled with milk.

Clayton jerked Teresa back as if they might be struck by eye shrapnel. "Shit!"

Teresa screamed against Clayton's chest.

Daisy screamed behind them on the stairs. Apparently, she hadn't obeyed Stan and gone back into the house. "Holy shit!"

The dog's chest exploded, blowing open in a cloud of red and black fur as what looked like a fatty heart hurled between the jagged tips of bone. It smacked the concrete and splattered with a juicy clap.

Stan stopped running. He stood a few feet away from the dog, hands on his hips, upset as if a car he'd been working on still wouldn't start. Shaking his head, he looked at the ceiling.

The dog dropped onto its side, rolled to its back. Its feet stuck in the air, stiff and rigid.

Huffing, Clayton gaped at the dog. He was so out of breath, he felt as if he'd been chasing around after the dog with Hap and Stan.

"What happened to it?" he heard himself ask. His voice sounded scratchy and dry.

Stan sighed. "Well...obviously he didn't take to the injection."

For the first time since their arrival, Stan seemed almost normal. His eyes had lost their wild gleam, and his lips were no longer peeled back over his teeth. He seemed almost calm.

Too cool for Clayton's liking.

JAGGER

"What was that stuff you injected it with?" Clayton asked.

Stan turned around. "Hap!"

From the floor, Hap groaned.

"Clean this mess up."

"Okay..."

Stan walked to the corner of the basement to an old picnic table. The bench seat had been removed, so Stan could stand directly in front of it. On top was an assembly that might have passed for a mad scientist's laboratory. Clayton saw tubes running this way and that, curling and twisting as they were connected to tin cans that once stored vegetables or soups. A propane tank was in the back corner, with a blue hose running from the nozzle to a beaker with a small writhing flame underneath. An old two liter bottle of soda had been cut in half, with a plastic funnel crammed into the mouth. It dangled above a white mixing bowl.

Stan leaned over the table, putting his hands flat on its moldered surface. Lowering his head, his bangs fell into his eyes, hiding them. "Works on people..."

He'd spoken so softly, Clayton almost hadn't heard him. "The shit you injected him with?"

Stan nodded.

"What is it?" Clayton asked.

Stan turned around, leaning his lower back against the table. He folded his arms over his chest, crossing his ankles. He glanced at the stairs and frowned. "Daisy, if you're going to be down here, help Hap clean up the mess."

Daisy looked nervous as she nibbled on her bottom lip. Looking down, her eyes grew as Hap walked by, dragging the lifeless dog by its back legs. It moved stiffly like small furniture, making a soft scraping sound across the concrete.

"I'll pass," she said and turned around. The heavy clacking sounds of her shoes could be heard as she climbed the stairs. Light expanded in the dim stairway when she opened the door and was swallowed by the darkness when she closed it behind her.

She was away from this awful scenario. Just closed a door to it and was done. Clayton wanted to be with her. Upstairs. Where it somehow seemed less maddening than down here.

He regretted coming to see Stan.

"Adrenasyl."

"Adrena-what?"

"Syl. It's what I call it." Scratching his head, Stan made a face as if concentrating. "Never given it to a dog, though." He shrugged. "A concoction I whipped up. A synthetic version of hormones and increased muscle mass."

"A steroid?"

"More than that. Much more."

"And you sell that to people?"

Stan's eyes rounded, reverting to their psychotic glare. "Oh, yes. Men looking for that extra edge, the perfect body that looks chiseled out of stone by a homosexual artist. I give them fighters that can't feel pain, buff fuckers that can take hit after hit, their teeth flying, bones breaking, and yet they keep fighting."

"And you make it? That red stuff...?"

"Adrenasyl."

"Right. You *make* it?"

Stan bumped a shoulder in a half-shrug. "I take the common items, take what I want from each, add Stan's Secret Sauce, and presto, we have Adrenasyl."

"What's in it?"

"A good magician never shares his secrets."

Rattling from the side made Clayton jump. Looking over the top of Teresa's head, which was still pushed against his chest, he saw Hap had reached a lift door. He was pulling a length of chain out from the clasps. It was the same door he'd entered the basement through with the dog.

Before...

JAGGER

He remembered how happy the dog had been, prancing around, its wagging tail slapping Hap's legs.

So stupid. It had no idea.

"Of course," said Stan, "common side effects are severe mood swings including depression, outbursts of anger, increased blood pressure and cholesterol, nose bleeds, and poisoning of the brain which triggers insanity and madness. Paranoia."

Clayton wondered if Stan had been sampling some of his own secret sauce.

"It reacts to each person differently," Stan added.

"And you gave it to the dog?"

"You saw me do it."

Clayton pulled away from Teresa's intense hold. Her hands gripped his shirt, and he had to pry them off. Her eyes were soaked in tears that made them pink and puffy. Wetness had covered her cheeks and formed a damp moustache above her upper lip.

He leaned in, gave her a gentle kiss, and stepped away. On his way to Stan, he licked the salty moisture of her tears off his lips.

"What were the plus sides?" asked Clayton. "Why did you even attempt it on that poor dog?"

The lift door suddenly rose with a rusted groan. Clayton's heart gave a punching lurch that stole his breath.

All heads turned to Hap.

He smiled bashfully, shrugged. "Sorry."

Then he grabbed the dog's forepaws and started pulling as if he was moving a heavy trash can. The grass rustled when its back swished across.

Stan fumed at Hap for a moment, leering at him with a face full of rage. It seemed to drop away as Stan turned back to face Clayton.

"To answer your question, I sell it to local farmers also. They use it in their livestock. Never had any problems."

You've got to be kidding.

Clayton thought of the several independently owned restaurants in town that advertised as getting their meet from local farmers.

I've probably eaten burgers tainted by Stan's Secret Sauce.

His stomach felt queasy and jittery.

"My mess up," said Stan, "I used too large of a dosage on a smaller animal. But it *has* to be given in large doses for it to work at all."

"And how do you plan on fixing that problem?"

"I need a big dog. A *big* dog. Something that can handle that much."

Clayton sighed. Where was he going to get a dog big enough for Stan's magic potion to work?

You're not really going to pursue this any further, are you?

He figured he was. It was either a hundred dogs dying in order to get this plan to work, or Clayton dying. And Clayton might be considered a tad biased in the situation, but he would rather he be the one who got to live.

A part of him still wished he'd never come here. But the idea was in his head now, and he knew he would try anything to make it work.

"Do you have any big dogs?" asked Clayton.

Stan's arms dropped to his side. "What are you, some kind of sadist? You expect me to keep pulling my own goddamn loyal companions to save your ass? No way. The rest is on you. This one was on the house, but the next is going to cost you."

"Cost me?"

"You get the dog. I'll provide the rest. We'll work out an arrangement for payment later."

Clayton didn't like how that sounded, but didn't really care. He was the meat of a hell sandwich no matter how he approached his situation.

"How big of a dog do you think we need?"

Stan crossed his arms once again. His lips moved, though no words could be heard. He looked like somebody reciting a silent prayer.

JAGGER

"Over a hundred pounds," he said. "For sure. Heavier would be better."

"Might as well get a fucking horse!"

Stan held out his hands. "I don't make the rules!"

"Yes, you do. When it comes to this you're making *all* the rules."

Sighing, Stan's lips fluttered. "Fine. I'm the almighty keeper of the rules."

"Where do you expect me to find a dog that damn big on such a short notice?"

"Not my problem."

"Seriously, man. Where?"

"Try the animal shelter."

"I'd never pass the background check. Besides, it would take too long."

"The animal shelter doesn't do background checks. And they always have large breeds in the back. Bunch of sad bastards too. Dumped by their owners because they got too big for them handle."

"Isn't there an adoption fee or something?"

"Oh, yes."

Clayton groaned. All the money he had was in his wallet, which was in his truck that sat in the parking lot at Teresa's apartment. And that equaled to around forty dollars. He wouldn't be able to afford it.

"I'll cover it," said Teresa.

Clayton turned around. Teresa stood where he'd left her, hugging herself. Her shoulders were bunched around her head. Though it was hot and stuffy in the basement, she seemed to be shivering.

"What'd you say?" he asked.

"I'll handle the adoption fee."

"Why?"

Clayton hadn't meant to ask, but it had come out anyway. He'd assumed after this spectacle, she would be done with Clayton and would leave him to his issues.

But she's not.

And he had to admit he was glad to have her with him through this. Maybe she was worth keeping. She might even be the *one*.

His smile seemed to warm her some. She stopped shaking as much, and let her arms slip down her front. She tugged at the edge of the skirt in a nervous habit she probably wasn't aware she even had.

"I want to help you," she said. "I want you to be done with all this. And if we have to adopt a big dog so Stan can put that stuff in it, then we *will*."

Clayton felt Stan's hand slap down on his shoulder. "Good woman you've got there."

Still smiling, Clayton agreed.

CHAPTER TWELVE

The animal shelter was fresh out of large dogs. They had plenty of adults on canine death row to choose from, but none seemed to have the qualifications of what Stan needed.

The animal control guy said they had a Rottweiler, but he'd been malnourished by a previous owner and was being nursed back to good health before adoption. He wouldn't be ready for a few weeks.

So the animal control guy tried to sell them on a puppy, and though Teresa played with them all much longer than Clayton liked, he declined the offer.

Heading back to Teresa's tiny Ford Focus, he realized they would have been screwed had there been a large dog to take. Where would they have put it? On the roof?

We would've had to go back and get my truck, then come back here just to get the damn thing to Stan's.

"I'm running out of ideas," said Clayton, crossing the front of Teresa's car.

"Let's get a paper."

"What for?"

"Maybe someone has a dog in the classifieds."

Clayton felt jittery inside. "Yeah. A lot of times they're just *giving* them away." He wished they would have thought of this sooner.

"Yeah," said Teresa, smiling.

Though he doubted she was having much fun doing this, she seemed happy. Maybe it was just the little thrill of working on something together. He'd allowed her into his world, and though it was a sullen place that Clayton wanted to be free of, she was still glad to be close to him.

They left the animal shelter behind. As they drove away, Clayton could hear the faint yelps of the dogs wanting them to come back.

Teresa got the car on the road, heading back to town.

"Want some lunch?" she asked.

Clayton was surprised to find either of them wanted food after their morning. "Sure."

"How about Mickey's?"

"The burger place?" She nodded. "No thanks. For all we know, their beef's pumped full of Stan's toxic fruit punch."

"Ew." She grimaced. "Yeah, I forgot."

They decided on Burger King. The meat there was processed and probably only partially authentic, but it was better than the alternative.

They went through the drive-thru. Clayton ordered two double cheeseburgers, large fries, and a Coke. Teresa got a Whopper Combo and a Coke. When they got their food, Teresa drove to an empty space and parked.

She opened the white paper bag and dug out Clayton's food and handed it to him. When she retrieved hers from inside the rattling bag, they peeled the wrappers away and began to eat.

The food was greasy and good. The buns were slightly damp, but still soft. Clayton finished all of his before Teresa. He was guzzling what was left of the Coke through the straw when she stuffed her trash into the bag.

"All right," she said, smiling. There was a glossy sheen on her upper lip from the food. "Ready to get going?"

Remembering what they were supposed to be doing made the food feel like a rock in his gut. A thick, gassy burp caught him by surprise. He nodded.

"I'm not thrilled, either," she said, cranking the car. The air conditioner coming from the vents was warm, but quickly cooled. "Let's just get it over with."

Clayton nodded again. Now she sounded as if she were the one making the plans.

Better her than me. My plans suck.

Teresa drove them out of the parking lot and onto the main street. A gas station wasn't far away, just ahead on the right. She wasn't going fast enough that she needed to slow down when she turned in. There was plenty of space up front, so she pulled into the first available spot.

She put the car in park and leaned to the side. The seatbelt ran between her breasts, pulling the dress taut around their large mounds. She started digging through a ditch in the compartment that was full of change.

Holding out his hand, Clayton said, "Don't bother. I've got change."

Teresa looked up. "Oh, sorry..."

He hadn't meant to sound so annoyed, but he really was. She'd paid for the food, was going to pay for the dog at the animal shelter, if they'd had one. He could at least cover the cost of a newspaper.

"Be right back," he said. He opened the door, climbed out, and was about to close it when Teresa stopped him.

"Throw this away?" She held out the Burger King bag.

"Yeah, sure."

"Thanks." She smiled.

Taking the bag, he closed the door, blocking his view of her peace-attempting smile. She must have been able to tell his pride had been challenged. Now she would go out of her way to not insult him, though she hadn't done anything wrong to begin with.

Clayton tossed the bag into a plastic drum that was being used as trashcan. He stepped over to the coin-operated rack, and stuck his hand in the pocket.

And felt nothing.

Shit.

He'd forgotten all about not having his own clothes. He was still in Mitch's big and tall wardrobe.

Now he'd have to go back to the car and ask Teresa for some

change.

Sighing, Clayton turned around and walked back to the car. He went around to the driver's side. As he approached, the window came down, the tiny motor whirring. Teresa leaned out.

"What's the matter?" she asked.

"I...uh..." He scratched his head, though it didn't itch. "I don't have any stupid change."

Teresa gave him the look of a mother whose kid just told her he'd wet himself. She turned back inside the car. Clayton could hear the coins jangling as she sorted through them. A moment later, she reappeared, holding out her fingers. Coins were pinched between them.

He took the money, muttered, "Thanks," and headed back to the newspaper racks. He slipped the coins through the slot and pulled the gate down.

There were no papers on the rack inside. All that was left was in the display window. He took that one and let the gate slam shut. He rolled up the newspaper, tucked it under his arm, and walked back to the car.

It felt like he was moving around inside an oven from the heat on his back. It warmed the shirt, making it stick to his sweaty skin.

From the weighty heat outside, getting back inside the car was wonderful. Cool air blew all over him. He shut the door. Leaning back in the seat, he sighed. He didn't feel like moving right away. His belly was full and the air felt too great to bother with anything else.

"Let me see," said Teresa.

He felt the paper being taken from his lap. With his eyes closed, he listened to the crinkly sounds of her unrolling the paper. He figured she was reading the table of contents to find out where the classified section was.

"Got it," she muttered.

More thin rustling sounds of the pages being turned, followed by silence.

Clayton felt his body going light, tingling as the inklings of a nap came to meet him.

"This is bullshit!"

Teresa's shout snapped him awake. Sleep had been slowly covering him with a comforting darkness, but now he was once again blinded by the glaring light pouring in from the windshield.

Clayton turned to Teresa and found her wadding the newspaper into a black and white ball. She threw it behind her, leaned forward, and crossed her arms on the steering wheel under her face.

"Not good news?" he asked.

"There wasn't anything in there that can help us."

Us.

"No big dogs?" he asked.

"No."

Clayton groaned. The heat drained from his body, making him feel cold and achy and exhausted. He dropped back into the seat.

That's it. It's over.

He wanted to cry, but instead he turned to Teresa. "Thanks for trying," he said.

"Some big help I was." Her voice had sounded flat behind her arms.

"You did plenty."

"Oh, sure." She sniffled. "Now what?"

Clayton sighed. "I guess we head back to your place so I can get my truck."

"And then?"

And then it's bye-bye Clayton.

He was tempted to flee Brickston, hit the road. But he had nowhere to go. No friends or family anywhere. Nobody. Other than Teresa, there hadn't been anyone in years that even seemed to care about him.

And even if he did run away, Brock would find him. He couldn't hide from a ruthless guy like that.

And if I ran, Brock would probably do something to Teresa.

JAGGER

Yesterday he probably wouldn't have minded so much, if it meant he was in the clear. Today changed things. She'd proved she actually cared about him and all his pathetic flaws.

"I'll go talk to Brock," he said. "Tell him I can't pay him back."

Teresa's head shot up. "Don't do that."

"It's better I just get it over with. Dragging it out's going to make me go insane."

Teresa closed her eyes. Her lids scrunched up, the corners of her eyes wrinkled with her brow. She looked as if she was in pain. "I can't believe I'm doing this."

Clayton wasn't sure which part of their day she was regretting, but he wouldn't be surprised if it was all of it. "Don't blame yourself..."

"No. Not that." Eyes still closed, she bared her teeth. "I know where we can get a dog."

Clayton sat up fast. "You *do?*"

She nodded. A high-pitched squeak resonated from her throat. "Yes. I thought about asking my parents for the money to pay Brock back, but I know they won't give it to me. Amy won't give it to me, either. I know she won't."

Amy. Clayton remembered meeting her at Teresa's one time. She seemed stuck up, and he was certain she didn't like him very much.

"And this is a dog we can actually get?" he asked. "Not just something we're going to find out isn't going to happen?"

"No. He's there. It's Amy's dog. And he's *big.*"

"How big?"

"As big as me, if not bigger."

Clayton laughed. He drummed his hands on the dash. Amy had a dog, and he felt some kind of sickish thrill knowing it belonged to her.

A thought struck him, making him stop his celebration. If she'd known where to find a dog all this time, why was she just telling him now?

He asked her.

"Because," she said. Finally, she opened her eyes. "I hoped there was another way. But now I see there's not one."

CHAPTER THIRTEEN

Amy felt great. She always did after the gym. Her muscles were a little sore, but they throbbed with energy. She felt as if she could run for miles as she drove her Jeep. A couple times she caught herself going well above the speed limit and had to force her foot to ease up on the gas.

And she liked how the evening's warmth felt on her body after a good work out. It was warm and yet cooling at the same time. It left her feeling motivated and peppy, in a good mood that she tried to keep for the remainder of the day.

Loose hairs dangled in her eyes. She brushed them back, cringing at how knotted and oily her hair felt. First thing she was going to do was take a shower. Wash the funk away from her body. She never used the showers at the gym. Rarely did she even go in the locker room. Too many women, comfortable with their bodies, walked around completely naked, trying to strike up conversations with her. Amy knew she had nothing to be ashamed of when it came to her looks, but she still had some kind of modesty. Those women did not.

She remembered when a woman had tried to talk to her about a spin class while smearing herself with lotion. Amy had sat on the bench, trying to get her jeans on. The woman, standing before her, had coated her skin in lotion that smelled like strawberries. Amy had never felt more uncomfortable in all her life as she'd struggled to pay attention to what the woman was saying while rubbing her breasts and making them shine under the dim lights.

No more for me.

Now she went in with only a water bottle and her iPod. She kept to herself as she worked out, the way she liked it. No conversations, just Amy and the machines. In and out in two hours.

JAGGER

The sign for Eagle's Nest appeared on the left up ahead. One thing she had already taken care of was getting the marker fixed. Before, it had angled into the ground as if sinking into the grass. But now it was level again and she'd paid to have a new sign put on the posts.

It looked nice—colorful and almost cozy.

If only the rest of the park would be so easy to fix.

She slowed the Jeep. Nobody was approaching from the other way, so she swung onto the gravel road.

The horseshoe drive was full of holes and trenches that made the Jeep bounce as she drove. She'd probably have it paved before the end of summer. Her only qualm about doing so was keeping it up afterward. Asphalt cracked so easily, and she'd have to get it patched and coated in fresh tar every so often. She'd be paying for the blacktop for the rest of her life.

The trailers that were in the worst conditions came first. On either side, huddled close together like cars in a parking lot, was beaten singlewides with small patches for yards. The tin siding had rusted into web-shaped blemishes that seemed to be spreading across the exteriors like infections. Others had bullet holes peppering the outside. *Bullet holes!* Tarnish ringed the tiny dots. Amy had often wondered where they'd come from. Was some drunken asshole shooting at his home? A drive-by?

This is redneck country, come on. No drive-bys here. Not yet, anyway.

Still, somebody had caused the holes.

Amy passed two abandoned trailers with weed-choked lawns. Left behind cars occupied the driveways. Their windows and windshields were coated in dust and pollen.

I really should come up with some kind of code of conduct. Have everyone sign it. Make them keep their yards up. And if their trailers need repairs, they have to get them done.

It would be hard, like introducing a new law. Some would be fine with it, but there would be others who'd protest. Plus, so much time had gone by without any kind of rules like that, she'd be trying to teach old dogs new tricks. And some of them might try to bite her for it.

Speaking of dogs...

She wondered how Jagger was doing. Just as she usually would on gym days, she'd left him in the backyard to get his second dose of exercise while she was gone. Being fenced in, she didn't have to worry about him getting into too much trouble. Sometimes she came home to fresh holes he'd dug, but that rarely happened.

He's probably ready to eat.

And so was Amy. She'd been dreaming about chopping up a salad even before she was done working out. She had the supplies in the fridge. She'd even gotten a bag of cubed ham to sprinkle on top.

Her mouth watered. It was hard to believe just adding some ham chunks and spinach to a salad made so much of a difference.

She drove past the Rileys' trailer. Neither was outside. Probably eating supper.

It's past supper time. You're the only who hasn't eaten yet.

Maybe they were relaxing in the living room, watching TV. Not much else for them to do.

Picturing them lounging in front of the television, looking bored, depressed Amy. She didn't look forward to being their age, when every day was based on a routine.

As she steered around the arch of the dirt road, she saw Janice's trailer to her right and felt another kind of depression. Slowing down, she leaned forward and looked out.

Nathan wasn't in sight. *Thank God.* It was about this time of the day when she'd nearly run him over. A light was on in the kitchen, offering a pale shimmer in the waning light of the day.

Frowning, Amy sped up. Hopefully an envelope would be waiting for her, but she doubted it. What was she going to do about Janice? Amy had made it clear that the single mother had to at least pay her *something*. If she still didn't give her any kind of rent, Amy would be forced to act.

How, she didn't know.

JAGGER

Amy didn't think she could be cruel enough to make her leave.

But I can't let her keep her trailer here for free.

Amy felt a jittery sensation in her belly. She didn't want to worry about Janice right now. It would only sour her mood. All she wanted to concern herself with at the moment was whether to chop the salad before or after her shower.

After.

That was an easy decision. If Teresa wasn't home, she might not even get dressed. Just brush her hair and let the air dry her body.

She felt a slight tingling between her legs at the idea. Something about being naked was exciting, even if the only person there to see her was Jagger.

And that's also a little sad.

More than a little, she realized, but she didn't care. It was her life, and she'd gotten used to it. So much so, she kind of looked forward to spending some time alone with her big guy.

Wouldn't matter. Teresa was bound to be back by now. Amy had tried reaching her friend a couple times today, and each time had gotten her voicemail. Amy figured Teresa was probably trying to get some things straightened out at her job. Probably explaining things to her boss, begging him not to fire her.

From how nearly perfect Teresa's body was, Amy doubted he would be quick to let her go. The place was called Honkers, and Teresa had two massive horns that many customers would be thrilled to squeeze. Most likely, Teresa would have to work tonight, and that would give Amy her house back for one night, at least.

Maybe naked salad chopping is in my future after all.

She smirked at herself as she reached her driveway. At the end of the park, it was a narrow track that etched through the woods. If she were to keep going, the dirt road would take her back to the main road.

Sometimes she fantasized about driving past and seeing where she wound up. No destination in mind, no time limit on when to be back—just freedom.

She'd never do it, though. Not only would somebody have to look after Jagger, the dog would miss her too much. And she had a life here, whether she truly wanted it or not.

Branches brushed the sides of her Jeep as she drove up the driveway, making soft squeaky sounds. Maybe she should trim them back. If she waited too much longer, they'd scrape the paint. She had a saw that would probably do the job. Save her some money by doing the work herself and that was always a plus.

She drove out of the trees and the space in front of her expanded and opened up to her front yard. The brick house sat before her. Bushes lined the front. She saw the solar lights that ran along either side of the sidewalk had already turned on. Even in the dusk of light, she could see her grass was getting high. Tomorrow would be a good day to mow, though she wouldn't mind doing it right now. The lawn tractor had headlights and cutting grass at night was actually fun to her.

When she saw the empty car port, her ambitious demeanor took a soft blow. Teresa wasn't here. And though she'd entertained the idea of being alone with Jagger tonight, she felt depressed that Teresa hadn't come back.

Now I'm getting a little worried.

Teresa could have at least let her know she wasn't coming, or at least let her know where she'd been all day. It wasn't like Amy demanded Teresa to share her every move, but she would have thought she'd have said *something* by now.

Hey, I'm staying at my place tonight.

Hey, working tonight. Call you tomorrow.

Hey, you're a shitty friend, fuck you.

Some kind of message would do.

Sighing, Amy parked the Jeep under the port, leaving enough space for Teresa's car in case she did come over. The shelter threw darkness on top of her. Twisting the key, the engine cut off. The sound of crickets and frogs drifted into the silence inside the Jeep.

Amy relished the sounds of summer nights. If she wouldn't sweat herself into dehydration, she would open the windows in the house and sleep with that gentle chorus around her. Spring nights were great for that, though the crickets and frogs weren't nearly as loud as they could be this time of the year.

Opening her door, she raised her foot to catch it so it wouldn't bump the metal stilt of the car port. She had nice scratch on the door from that happening in the same spot more than once.

She grabbed her purse and empty water bottle from the passenger seat, then hopped out. She bumped the door with her rump. She felt the cool smoothness of the fiberglass through her tight gym shorts. The fabric was so thin it felt as if she just had a darker sheen of skin over her.

"Jagger, I'm home!"

Usually by now he was waiting for her at the fence, on his hindquarters, whining softly, his tail thwacking troughs into the ground. Checking his usual spot, she didn't see him there.

And felt a pinch of concern.

Frowning slightly, she headed forward. She stepped out from under the carport and the shadows it created. The light was pale, and when she looked down at her arm, her skin seemed tawny and smooth. The woods that enclosed her property were oily smudges, paling by the moment as the sky turned an even thicker shade of purple. Shadows piled down from their branches, and Amy could see the quick blinks of fireflies scattering like green ashes.

Lovely.

It did nothing to relieve the anxiety trying to build inside her.

So he's not waiting for me. It wouldn't be the first time.

As she neared the fence, she realized how wrong she was. This *was* the first time. She couldn't remember any other time as she fished her keys out of her purse.

Still, Jagger didn't come.

The keys should have done it.

It was like a kettle call to him. When he heard them jangle, he knew something was about to happen, and it brought him galloping to her, his flabby skin rippling on his body in furry waves.

No Jagger this time.

Her frown pressed her face even tighter as she walked along the fence. Gazing into her backyard, she didn't see him anywhere. Her heart drummed painfully in her chest, stealing her breath and drying out her throat.

He's in there. He has to be. Maybe he's on the deck.

Stopping, she turned so she could see the deck. She'd forgotten to leave the outside light on, so it looked as if a dark screen covered the wooden platform. She saw no other shapes that shouldn't already be there.

Nothing that indicated a sleeping dog.

Or a dead one.

Amy gasped.

He's not dead. He's just...

What?

She had no clue. But he'd been healthy and fine when she'd left, and he still should be.

Now she ran, gliding her hand along the top of the fence for support. She reached the corner and turned.

The gate hung open.

Amy stopped running. "Oh, no..."

She'd closed it on her way out. She was certain. Jagger had been standing there, watching her walk to the car. She'd even blown him a kiss.

"See you in a bit, big guy!"

Jagger had barked.

She hadn't forgotten to close the gate.

How's it open now?

Amy dropped her purse. The water bottle hit the ground and rolled to the side. Her keys slipped from her fingers and clanged when

105

they landed.

Her arms felt weak and useless. Her knees started to shake. Where was he? Where'd he go?

She leaned back her head and called for him.

He didn't come.

CHAPTER FOURTEEN

"This is Jagger," said Amy.

Mark Varner took the cell phone from Amy. He turned it around so he could see the picture. "Wow," he said. "He really is big."

"About one-eighty."

Mark whistled softly. The picture featured Amy, sitting on a park bench, legs spread with the big mastiff's back between them. He could see the tawny juts of her knees on either side of the dog like glossy points.

Jagger was a handsome mutt with a thick pelt of black and brown, low-hanging ears and jowls that sagged like dough from his compacted maw. Even though the photo was on a small screen, Jagger's bulk was easy to interpret. His paws looked nearly as big as a toddler's catcher's mitt.

"And he wouldn't hurt anybody," said the older woman in the pink robe.

Ellie, he reminded himself. The robe jutted from her chest because of large breasts. She sipped from the coffee Amy had made.

Nodding, Mark reached forward, just missing Amy's smooth leg and grabbed the mug Amy had given him. He took a sip. Though the coffee had cooled some, it still tasted good.

"Well," he said, giving Amy back her phone. He took a deep breath, trying to construct what to say. "To be honest...I'm not entirely convinced you had an intruder."

"I saw the white van," said Ellie.

"I know," he said. "But there's not any evidence of anybody being here."

"Look harder," said Ellie.

Sighing, Mark said, "The road horeshoes out, maybe they took a wrong turn, and instead of turning around, they just drove through."

JAGGER

"No," said Amy. "Somebody came here and let Jagger out."

"Or took him," offered Ellie.

Amy gasped. With wide eyes, she gazed at Mark as if asking him whether or not it was true.

I wish she'd go the hell home.

Ellie was making it worse. Stirring the pot, getting Amy riled up.

"Let's not jump to any conclusions," he said. With the flick of a wrist, the cover of his notepad swung up. He used his thumb to close it. "I'm going to take another look around before I leave."

As he put the notepad into a front pocket of his shirt, he started to stand. Amy reached out and grabbed his arm.

"You can't leave," she said.

Mark saw what little hope she'd been clinging to drip into total desperation. He knew she thought if he left without figuring something out, it was over for her poor dog.

And he hated to think it might be.

But dogs ran away all the time. Nothing against the owners, but the mutts would catch a scent and follow it. Sometimes to their deaths. Even after someone like Amy probably spent a small fortune to spoil them, feed them, and keep them healthy.

Stupid things.

Mark hated dogs. His sympathy for Amy was genuine, but he felt nothing for the missing dog.

"I'm actually off duty," said Mark. "I can come back tomorrow to follow up after I visit your friend..." The name escaped him. He was patting his chest for his notepad when Amy stood up.

"Teresa."

"Right. Did she respond to your text?"

Amy frowned as if she had no clue what he was talking about. Then a light seemed to come on in her eyes. "Oh, right."

Amy got up, passing Ellie, who sat in the recliner. Ellie patted Amy's hip as she went by, offered a consoling smile, and turned to Mark.

The smile died on her face.

"You think there's no hope, don't you?" Ellie whispered, almost accusing.

Mark held out his hands. "I have no theories at the moment about any intruders. There's not much I can do, personally. But for the dog, it's really a job for animal control. If I can't find any evidence of somebody tampering around here, then I have nothing to go on."

"I'm telling you, I saw a white van. I was trying to round up my chickens with my husband, and I saw it turn into the driveway."

"Right. Amy Snider's driveway."

Ellie nodded.

Frowning, Mark looked toward the kitchen which could be easily seen from the small living room. He saw Amy leaning over her sink. The faucet was running. She cupped her hands under the stream and splashed some water onto her face.

He felt sad watching her. This dog must have been everything to her.

Way to go, Jagger. Make a pretty woman like that cry.

He looked at his watch. It was almost ten. He'd been here for over two hours. He wanted to go home, have a beer, and catch the replay of the Braves game.

I was heading home. I was so close to being done for the day.

But the call had come over the radio and he'd been the closest one. He'd listened as other units responded with excuses and delays. Something had nudged him, had told him to answer the call. So he'd informed dispatch he would look into it on his way home.

Had no idea I'd be here half the damn night.

"Are you going to look for the white van?"

Mark sighed. "Got a license plate number?"

"Well...no..." Ellie's voice sounded almost ashamed that she didn't. "I told you already..."

"By the time you got your chickens rounded up and you could

come check, Amy was already home."

"Right. Screaming for Jagger like some kind of banshee."

Mark felt a burst of sadness in his chest. Amy was probably devastated. Like a wife coming home to find her husband had run off with another woman.

Most likely the dog's somewhere in the woods, being a dog. But I'm not going to spend my whole night searching around.

Amy came back into the living room. She held three bottles of Bud Light between her fingers. Mark's mouth salivated as he gazed at the dark slick glass that left Amy's fingers slightly moist.

In her other hand was her phone.

Mark nodded at the smart device. "Anything?"

Amy shook her head. "No. If she's working, I won't hear from her until she goes on break." She held out a bottle by the neck, offering it. "Drink?"

Mark wanted to. After this long day, it would be great. "I shouldn't..."

"You're off duty, right?" said Ellie.

"Well..."

A corner of Amy's mouth lifted. An eyebrow slightly arched. "Well?"

Mark felt himself smile. "What the hell?" He took the bottle. It felt cold and slippery in his hand. Tiny water beads trickled over his fingers.

Amy was about to offer a beer to Ellie, but she held up her hand. "None for me. I've got to get home. I'm sure Jim's wondering where I'm at."

"Are you sure?" asked Amy. Though her question had sounded legit, Mark had been a cop long enough to know when somebody was putting on a show. And he could tell Amy was ready for her neighbor to leave.

"I'm sure. It's getting late, and I'm sure I'm being missed."

Smiling, Amy said, "You tell Big Jim I said 'hi' and thank him for letting me borrow you for a bit."

Ellie smiled at that. "You bet. Wish I could have helped more."

"You've helped plenty." Amy stepped back so Ellie could stand. "I'd probably still be in the yard yelling if you hadn't come along."

Ellie hugged Amy, gently rubbing her back. "Call me if you need me."

Amy closed her eyes and hugged her back. That gesture was as real as emotional acts could get. It also made Mark wonder how long it had been since Amy had been hugged.

"Thank you," said Amy. Thin drips of tears trembled from her pinched eyelids.

Ellie pulled away from the hug. She pointed at Mark as Amy escorted her to the hallway. She didn't speak, nor did she have to. Mark knew she was ordering him to fix this situation.

Mark gave her a slight nod, just a subtle response. But it must have been the one Ellie wanted. She lowered her arm and turned away. A moment later, she vanished into the darkened hallway with Amy.

The cold glass bottle was making Mark's fingers numb, so he switched it to the other hand. He didn't know if she should sit back down, or wait for Amy to get back and ask him to.

And he didn't know why he was about to drink a beer with her.

And Ellie is leaving. We'll be alone.

A warm tingling sensation moved from his chest into his stomach. This was the first time he'd been alone with a woman in almost eight months.

Relax. You're here for work. This is hardly a date.

But he was off duty. And Amy wanted him to stay.

She's vulnerable right now. She doesn't want to be by herself.

This could lead to other areas Mark was out-of-practice in as well.

And he would be the biggest jerk in the world if he took advantage of anything else other than this beer. Amy was acting like a girl who'd asked a male friend to come over after she'd had a fight with her boyfriend. The possibilities where the moment could take them were pretty vast.

But Mark wasn't the kind of guy who'd prey on an emotional woman. He'd despise himself later for it.

Mark sighed. Sometimes he hated his conscience. If he were anybody else, he'd work Amy's distressed temperament and confusion to his benefit. She'd regret her actions after her mind was clearer and she realized what she'd done, but Mark would have gotten what he'd wanted by then.

I'm an asshole for even thinking that.

He should leave.

"Sorry about that," said Amy, appearing from the corner of the wall.

When she smiled, he knew he wasn't going to leave just yet. Earlier she'd told him she'd just returned home from the gym, and she still wore the clothes she'd exercised in—a form-fitting top that barely reached her navel. It left a tanned bar of bare skin around her waist before the matching shorts that looked spray-painted on. The seat hardly covered her buttocks and left her thighs bare to the curves of her rump.

It'd be rude if I didn't drink the beer.

"No problem." He held the bottle up. "Are you sure you don't mind?"

"I wouldn't have offered it to you, if I minded."

"Right."

Idiot. Don't say too much. Just let her talk. That's what she wants, really. An ear other than her own to hear what she has to say.

"Would you rather sit?" she asked.

"Sure."

Mark sunk back into the couch. The comfy cushions hugged his back and legs. If he could take his shoes off and prop his feet on the coffee table, he could easily fall asleep.

Amy grabbed the other two bottles and stepped around the coffee table. She returned to her spot on the couch. There was a good amount of space between them, but she was still closer than she had been earlier.

Mark could smell a mixture of lotion and sweat radiating off her body. It reminded him of the beach, women tanning, their dusky skin gleaming with sweat and suntan oil.

Amy twisted the cap off her bottle, so Mark did the same. The sounds of their chugs filled the room. The beer splashed the back of Mark's parched throat. It tasted cold and good, tingling and satisfying as it went down.

"That's good," said Amy, breathy and quiet. She softly belched. "Excuse me."

Mark smiled. He liked when a woman didn't pretend she didn't do things like that. But if she suddenly lifted her rump and ripped a rapid-firing fart, he might be a little offended. Mark took another heavy swig. He held the bottle out and saw half of it was already gone.

Slow down.

Amy slapped her empty bottle on the table with a hollow clang and reached for the other. She needed to take it easy as well. He wanted to say something to her, but remained quiet. It wasn't his place to lecture.

"I can't believe this," she said, twisting the cap off the second bottle. She raised it to her lips and drank. Mark watched her throat work as she swallowed.

"I know," he said. "A shock to come home to, I'm sure."

"Are you a dog person?"

Mark took a deep breath. She didn't know he couldn't care less about them. "I don't own one, no."

"But you like them."

"Sure," he lied.

"Well, Jagger's not like other dogs. He just has this...personality to him. It's like he *knows* me. I mean, really knows me."

"I'm sure he does. He sees you every day, knows your habits, your behaviors. Knows when you're upset or happy."

JAGGER

Amy gave him a glance, smiled, and drank some more. The bottle came away from her mouth with a fizzy pop. "Sometimes I think it's sad that my soulmate is a damn dog. Tonight, I'm realizing it's not just sad, it's pathetic."

Soulmate?

Mark wondered just how lonely this woman truly was.

"I'm surprised you haven't asked me yet," she said.

Something like wings fluttered in Mark's chest. What was she referring to? A jumble of questions trampled his mind all at once.

"Uh..." was all he managed to mutter.

"Most people ask me about his name."

For a moment, Mark had no idea who she was talking about. Then he realized it was the dog, and he should have known that.

With a bit of disappointment over her question, he drank more beer. "It is an interesting name," he said after swallowing.

Amy stared ahead, smiling as if she were watching a home movie projected in front of her. "When he was a puppy, he just had such a wonderfully cute face. His lips poked out like this." She stuck hers out to show him, then laughed. "'Sympathy for the Devil' was on the radio and I thought it was crazy how much he resembled him."

"The devil?"

Amy laughed, gently swatting Mark's leg. "No! Mick Jagger."

"Ah."

Mark called up an image of the photo and thought he saw the semblance.

"It's not so similar now," she said. "But when he was a puppy it was uncanny."

Mark raised the bottle to his mouth and was surprised to find it empty. Only a tiny droplet slipped into his mouth. He put it back on the table.

"Want another?" asked Amy. "It's on the house tonight."

"I'd love to..."

"But?"

"But I have to pass. I still need to do another walk-through of your property."

"Sounds so procedural." She lowered her voice. "*Property*."

Mark laughed. When he finished, he saw Amy was staring at him, sort of half-smiling and interested. He cleared his throat.

"You have a really nice smile," she said.

Mark was about to thank her when she smacked the table with the other empty bottle. Far from drunk, the beer had definitely made her more confident and comfortable.

And friendly.

"Well...I..."

She put her hand on his knee. "Thank you."

"For what?"

"For sticking around. You really should have left an hour ago, but you didn't."

Mark shrugged. "Well—I mean..."

"That means a lot to me."

And the beer's making her honest.

"It's my pleasure," he said. "All things considered, it's the best conversation I've had in a good while."

Amy smiled. "We haven't talked about anything, really."

"Compared to my usual nights, it's a vast improvement."

"How about we talk more? Maybe about other stuff? You can hang out for a little bit, if you want."

She looks like she wants me to kiss her.

There was a hopeful glimmer in her eyes. Her lips were slightly parted as if she'd already consented to the idea of having his mouth inserted between their plump curves. But Mark wouldn't allow himself to succumb to the yearning of a desperate woman, no matter how sexy she was.

"I'd like that," he said. "Just not tonight."

That notion of hope dropped away from her pretty face. She lowered her head. "Right. Another time."

"If you're up to it."

She raised her head, lifted an eyebrow. "Challenging me, are you?"

"Just making sure you'll still feel the same in the morning."

Amy laughed. "I see." She tapped the mouths of her empty beer bottles. "When I'm not so *influenced.*"

"Right."

He stood up. He removed the flashlight from his belt. Seeing it, Amy gulped as if the memory of why Mark was really here came back to her. She peered up at him with her large earthy eyes.

"Guess I better get this over with," he said.

"I'll come with you."

"Fine."

Outside, they took their time as Mark swept his flashlight here and there. They stopped to investigate areas he'd missed during his initial search. Sometimes Amy shared a story about Jagger. She told him one about a stray cat coming into the yard. She'd come outside, worried that Jagger was going to kill it, and had to run the feline off after it had chased her giant dog under the deck. She'd needed to use a cooked hamburger to coax him out. And his back had cracked the underpinning, forcing her to replace a whole section of the deck.

Mark laughed at that one. Jagger seemed like a really fun dog, and it was even more obvious to him that Amy practically worshipped her pet.

It's good she has her memories.

Mark couldn't believe he was already thinking as if Amy would never see her dog again. He would bet the dog would be back in the morning, scratching at the door to come inside.

But Amy said the dog has never done this before. And I believe her.

Besides, he couldn't shake the sick feeling inside—like looking for a missing person when there was no hope of finding him.

They arrived at the gate. The one Amy had discovered open after swearing she'd closed it. He believed her on that one as well. Amy seemed to have her head on relatively straight, compared to her neighbors.

He'd been out here many times in the past to arrest someone, and had never once met Amy. He'd met her father a few times. Now there was a son of a bitch if he'd ever met one. He wondered if Amy was close to her old man. He'd never once mentioned he had a daughter.

No wonder she acts like she has some serious affection issues.

"So that's it?" she asked. She opened the gate for him.

"For now."

Amy moaned in defeat. "He's gone, isn't he?"

"Don't say that. Don't give up on me just yet."

"I'm not."

Mark nearly gasped when Amy hugged him. At first, his arms stayed stuck out, rigid, as if touching her might hurt her. He slowly relaxed, putting one arm around her first. Then he added the other and held her. He felt her head twitching against his chest.

She was crying.

He still held the flashlight, angling it away from her. The light cut a short tunnel through the dark and splashed on the ground. Glinting under its smolder was a small brown object, crinkled and mushed, the size of a stumped pinky.

"Amy?"

"Huh?" Her breath was warm as it seeped through his shirt.

"Do you smoke?"

"No."

"Has anyone smoked on your property lately?"

"Teresa smokes, but she does it inside."

He thought he'd detected the odor of cigarette smoke. "But not cigars, right?"

Amy lifted her head and looked up at him. "No. Why are you asking me that?"

"Look."

JAGGER

Amy looked down. He felt her body tense when she saw the crushed cigar illuminated in the flashlight's glare.

CHAPTER FIFTEEN

Teresa's phone vibrating from the nightstand made her jump. She nearly squealed, but managed to keep it in. Clayton had dozed off on top of her, his penis still stuffed deep inside.

But Teresa hadn't been able to sleep.

She couldn't stop thinking about things. She'd become so restless she'd worked Clayton off of her, freeing herself from underneath. She'd felt claustrophobic lying under the stuffy heat and weight of his body. With him off her, she didn't feel compressed and squished, as if she were slowly being suffocated from not just her guilt, but Clayton's lethargic body.

She was just finally starting to doze off when her phone had buzzed.

"Who is it?" asked Clayton, his voice muzzy and thick.

Teresa didn't have to look at the display screen to know it was Amy. She'd called and texted her a few times already tonight. The police had been at her place, and Amy had wanted to know if she'd been over there at all since leaving this morning.

She probably told them I just took off this morning without saying anything.

Not a smart move. Neither was ignoring Amy. If she wanted to draw attention to herself, trying to hide was a great way of doing so.

Reaching out, she felt around the top of the nightstand for her phone. She grabbed it and brought it over. Holding it above her breasts, she thumbed the button on the side. The screen lit up, showing a message for a new text.

It was from Amy.

Teresa suddenly felt even more compressed without Clayton on top of her. She used a finger of her other hand to select the message.

Where R U? Need my bestie right now!

Guilt made her feel exhausted. A single tear escaped her eye, trickling down and going into her ear.

"Amy again?" asked Clayton, more awake now.

"Yeah."

"You'd better write her back. She's probably wondering what the hell you're up to."

"I know."

Teresa stared at the screen. She couldn't force her fingers to type a message.

"Give me the damn thing," said Clayton. He snatched the phone out of her hand.

"What are you doing?"

"Handling it."

Clayton dug his elbows into the mattress. The display screen spilled light onto his shoulders and face. She heard the sliding sounds of his fingers as he wrote Amy back.

A moment later he set the phone down on her bare stomach. The cold plastic made her flinch and hiss through her teeth. Then he lowered his head back to the pillow as if he was going to go back to sleep.

She shook her hips, bumping Clayton beside her. "Well?"

"Huh?"

"What'd you tell her?"

"I pretended to be you."

"I figured that much."

"Told her you were at home, not feeling good and would talk to her tomorrow."

Teresa felt lighter, as if a great weight had been lifted. She was relieved Clayton had handled that for her. She would have kept on neglecting a response and that would only make it look bad.

I'm such a bitch.

She deserved whatever punishment she got. It had been stupid of her to tell Clayton about Jagger. And she couldn't come up with a decent reason as to why she'd done it.

She glanced down at his penis hanging over the top of the rumpled sheet.

No. That is not the only reason.

He screwed her better than anyone ever had. And she got weak whenever she was with him, physically and mentally. She couldn't help herself. She knew it was wrong, but it never seemed to stop her.

Rolling onto her side, she faced away from Clayton. Away from his lean nakedness and large penis. She closed her eyes, trying to demand that sleep come to her.

As she felt herself starting to drift, her mind replayed the day's events.

After telling Clayton about Jagger, they returned to Clancy and had to go through the same awkward introductions as if it was Stan's first time meeting them. After that, his memory seemed to function properly.

"How big's this dog?" Stan asked. He sat on the edge of his couch, eating a slice of pizza from a box on top of four others.

Clayton pressed his fingertips together. "Teresa said somewhere around one-eighty or something."

Stan froze, teeth clamping the pizza, his eyes wide above the pepperoni. His head jerked back, tearing off a gooey chunk. Chewing slowly, he seemed to lull over this information. His throat made a wet clicking sound when he swallowed. He nodded. "It could work."

Stan loaned them some injectable tranquilizers. Three syringes that when he handed them to Clayton, he added he would have to pay him back for these. Clayton didn't ask the total price, just nodded and said he would.

An hour later, they were driving to the countryside of Brickston.

JAGGER

"Want to stop and change your clothes?" she asked Clayton.

He shook his head. "No time. Turn left up there."

Houses had been frequent on both sides of the road for a while. As they'd driven, the houses had been replaced by infinite grassy areas, woods, and farmland. At first she wasn't sure where he'd specified for them to turn. Then she spotted a thin dirt track twisting through a field.

"You're going to pass it," he advised.

Teresa slowed the car down. "That...*path*?"

"Yeah. It's not so bad."

"Maybe not in your truck, but it's going to kill my alignment."

"Just drive slowly."

Though she was careful as she made the turn, the car still rocked when the tires left the blacktop. She took Clayton's advice and drove very slowly, the car shaking and dipping over gullies and holes as she steered them far into the field. Woods appeared on each side of them, blocking out the daylight and throwing a heavy shade onto the path. Flecks of sunlight trembled on the road ahead of them.

Finally, they reached a graveled parking area. Beyond the lot was an old barn. It was larger than any barn Teresa had ever seen before, with two front doors and a loft above it that had been boarded up. Wood fencing ran along the outside of the barn, a metal pasture gate was open as if their visit had been expected.

"Pull up to the fence and park," said Clayton.

"Where *are* we?"

Clayton was quiet until she parked. Then he unbuckled the safety harness, opened the door and said, "Stay in the car."

She opened her mouth to say something, but Clayton was already out of the car. The door banged shut. Teresa's mouth slowly closed. She turned her head, watching him walk toward the barn.

I shouldn't be here.

She could put the car in reverse and drive away from all this. Leave Clayton behind. Go back to Amy's and all would still be okay.

Wait much longer and I won't be able to do that.

Teresa felt pain in her bottom lip and realized she was biting it. She relaxed her jaw, removed her lip. She tasted blood inside her mouth.

Get out of here. Now!

Teresa reached for the gearshift, fingers curled around the knob. She felt her foot push down on the brake pedal. Though cool air drifted over her from the vents, her skin was damp with sweat.

"Just do it," Teresa told herself.

Clayton came out of the barn. Seeing him brought a smile to her face. She couldn't leave him. She was already too far into this and needed to stay by him. Not because she was forced to.

Because I want to. After all of this, he better know how I feel about him.

And she really wished she didn't have feelings for him. She wished she was stronger.

Like Amy.

"Amy," she muttered.

Clayton stood in the opened doorway of the barn, his back to her, hands on his hips. His head was bopping as if he were talking, lengthy hair flapping a bit. Another man came forward, and Teresa realized Clayton was speaking to him. The new guy was short and very fat. He wore a white T-shirt that was faded and the design on the front had lost its color and shape. Even from the car she could see the sweat stains. He was losing his hair on top, thin webby strands fluttered in the breeze.

Clayton turned around. He motioned for her to come where he was.

Teresa nodded, though he couldn't have seen it. She took her foot off the brake and felt the cramp in her calf from how hard she'd been straining to make herself leave. She killed the engine, grabbed her purse, and climbed out of the car.

The heat was like being wrapped in a hot blanket. She felt a breeze moseying over her, but it only seemed to stir the humidity even more.

JAGGER

Walking to Clayton, she kept her arm firm by her side to hold her dress in place. She had on sunglasses, so Clayton's friend couldn't tell she could see him staring at her. By the look on his face, it was as if he'd never seen a girl in a sundress before. He licked his lips and Teresa resisted a shiver.

Clayton reached out, put his arm around her. Though she could feel the heat of his body through his sleeve, making the back of her neck sweat even more, she was glad to have him close.

"This is Freddy," he said.

"Hi," said Freddy, in an unusual shrill voice.

Teresa made herself smile.

"We need to start planning out how we're going to get the dog," Clayton told her.

Teresa's stomach felt as if it was being twisted. She knew why they were here, but hearing him mention Jagger seemed to remind her all over again.

I'm really doing this?

"Okay," she said.

Freddy smiled. His teeth were a light brown, as if painted in coffee. "Is he really as big as you say?"

Teresa nodded. "Probably bigger."

Freddy's dead fish-like eyes seemed to grow. "Wow!" He turned to Clayton. "What a find!"

"That's my baby," said Clayton.

Teresa shouldn't be proud he'd said so, but she couldn't help smiling from it. His arm tightened around her.

"When would be a good time for us to go play fetch?" asked Freddy, giggling like a little girl.

Teresa thought about it a moment. "What time is it?"

Freddy reached into the pocket of his sweatpants. He tugged out a phone. "Pushing three."

Teresa couldn't believe how much of the day had passed. How long would it take them to get ready? What were their plans?

"Amy usually goes to the gym around five."

Freddy whistled. "Doesn't give us much time, does it?"

Clayton stepped away from Teresa. She felt odd without having him close, strangely vulnerable to Freddy's roaming eyes.

"We should start cleaning out the van," he said.

"Van?" asked Teresa.

Clayton was heading into the barn. He glanced at her from over his shoulder. "Freddy's van."

Teresa followed him. Freddy hung behind her, probably watching how her legs worked under the dress. She hated she'd worn something so short and revealing.

If I'd known we were coming here, I would've changed into jeans and a sweatshirt.

She doubted that would have kept Freddy from ogling at her.

Clayton better not leave me alone with him.

"Where is the pooch at?" Freddy asked from behind her.

"Familiar with Eagle's Nest?" she asked.

"Wait," said Freddy.

Clayton stopped ahead of her, turning back. Teresa stepped next to him, then turned around as well. Freddy stood a few steps away, holding out a hand.

"You said her name was Amy?" he asked, his voice rising in pitch.

"Yeah," said Teresa.

"Amy *Snider?*"

Teresa frowned. "You know her?"

"Actually, yeah. I knew her old man *really* well. He's one of the people that funded all this." He pointed his finger up and twirled it.

Teresa looked around. She saw a fenced-in area. There was no light on, so the metal of the fence was a pale glimmer as it made a circle around loose, trodden soil. From where she stood, it looked like a pit.

Where the dogs fight.

And Amy's dad was in on this?

JAGGER

She wasn't surprised, really. She'd known Mr. Snider for a long time and he'd always come across as a very shady person. Even Amy had kept her distance from him whenever possible—which had been most of the time.

"Shit," said Clayton.

"It's kind of fucked up to be messing around with her dog," said Freddy. "Mr. Snider's kind of like our founding father or something."

"You're not going to help me?" asked Clayton.

"She and I used to play around out here when we were kids. Her daddy would bring her to see the dogs. We fed them, gave them treats." Freddy laughed. "She stopped coming around when I tried to poke her between the legs with my finger." He shrugged. "I was ten, didn't know any better at the time. She was just wearing these shorts that were really loose and I could see her undies. They were pink..."

"Dude," said Clayton. "That's messed up."

Teresa was glad Clayton stopped Freddy's perverted recollection.

"Got my ass whooped real hard for that one. My dad was not pleased I'd pissed off Amy's daddy. I don't think Snider ever forgot about it, either. He seemed to always hate me, even after my daddy died."

"Are you helping me or not?" asked Clayton. "Time's running out. We have to get moving if we're going."

Freddy swiped his hand in the air. "Hell with it. Let's go get the pooch."

It took a long time to clean out the van. It was loaded with gorged trash bags, old car parts, and anything else Freddy had decided to toss in there instead of getting rid of. Not only did it smell like a chicken coop inside, there were feathers sprinkled throughout the cargo area's floor. She didn't ask what they were doing there, and nobody offered any explanations. She figured it had something to do with the dogs, or maybe they were also hosting cockfights in the barn.

Again, she wondered why she was here, what she'd gotten herself into. And again she told herself things would be fine once they were finished. When this was behind them, everything would fall back into place.

Teresa didn't believe it and figured she never would.

Close to six in the evening, they were heading to Eagle's Nest. Clayton had the syringes filled with sleeping juice in a plastic shopping bag, as if he'd just come from the store.

Freddy drove, every now and then glancing in the rearview mirror to see Teresa. Where the backseat was positioned, she figured he had a nice view of her legs, possibly up her dress. She decided to let him look. How her legs were pressed together, she doubted he could see everything. He grinned around the cigar clamped between his teeth. Even with the windows in the cab down, the whole van still reeked of the sweetly pungent odor.

Nobody spoke. Teresa couldn't stop shaking. Through the hem of her dress, she could see the tremors of her thighs. No matter how many times she wiped her sweaty palms on her stomach they remained damp.

Her stomach was in pain. She was hungry, yet had no appetite and the dread inside was a nauseating bubble that kept growing. She was betraying her best friend for Clayton. There was no easy way of accepting what she was about to do. She'd tried lying to herself in an attempt of making it somehow seem justified, but there was no getting around the truth. Most likely, Amy would never know. But Teresa was convinced she would somehow be able to tell.

Teresa wondered if she'd ever be able to look her friend in the eye again.

Probably.

Not at first. It would take some time, but eventually she'd be able to block out what she had done. Wouldn't be the first time she'd deceived Amy's trust.

Nick.

Amy's on-and-off-again boyfriend of the last couple years.

How many times had he spent the night in her apartment?

JAGGER

Plenty.

And Amy never knew. At least, Teresa didn't think so. Sometimes Teresa wondered if Amy had some suspicions, but she'd never accused of her anything.

Jagger hated Nick.

He would not go to Amy's house because of the dog, so if Amy wanted to see him, she had to go to him. And Amy had *never* spent the night at his house. Not wanting to leave Jagger alone all night, Amy had adhered to a self-made curfew that had given Nick too much freedom and too many nights of disappointment. Eventually things had progressed to Nick spending his Amy-less nights with Teresa.

And it had been fun. Though she'd wake up in the mornings with guilt sapping her energy, she'd kept doing it until she met Clayton at Honkers. Since then, she'd been devoted just to him.

The van dipping off the road made Teresa gasp and bounce in her seat. Her legs flew wide. Looking up, she saw Freddy watching her through the rearview. How his eyes were scrunched up, she figured he was smiling.

"Just a bump, girl," he said in that feminine voice.

Teresa pushed her dress down, shutting off his nice shot of her panties. Crossing her leg over her knee, she pulled at the edge of the dress and pressed it against the side of her thigh.

Freddy laughed.

"Almost done," said Clayton. He turned around and looked at her. Though he offered a comforting smile, his eyes were grim. "It'll be over soon."

Teresa tried to smile back at him, but the expression felt awkward on her face.

He turned back in the seat, staring forward.

There were no windows in the back, so Teresa couldn't see what was on either side of her. But through the windshield she recognized the reaching branches that seemed to be growing around the power lines. The bouncing and rocking the van made over the trenches in the road was familiar.

They were in Eagle's Nest.

Oh God...

Just get it over with. Hopefully Jagger was outside. It would make it easier. That way they wouldn't have to break in.

The car port was clear. Amy's Jeep was gone. Teresa felt herself relax some seeing that it wasn't there.

When they drove around the side of the car port, past Amy's house to the back, Teresa saw Jagger right away. He was inside the fence, watching them approach. Head tilted slightly, his ears were lifted high. She could see his nose working as he sniffed the air. Not recognizing the van's scent, he ripped into a cacophony of barks.

Raising a hand to her mouth, Teresa watched as Jagger's massive jaws snapped, making sounds like a bear trap. Drool flung from his mouth in thick spatters. For the first time, she noticed how big and sharp his teeth really were. She imagined them crunching around her arm, splintering the bone. Felt them close on her neck.

"Teresa?"

She jerked. "Yeah?"

Clayton, turned in the seat, frowned. "Ready?"

"I don't know..."

"Don't wuss out now," said Freddy.

"Shut up," said Clayton.

Freddy, both hands gripping the wheel, lifted a shoulder in a half shrug.

Teresa leaned forward, watching Jagger chew at the thin links of the fencing as if he wanted to eat his way out of there just to kill them. "I've never seen him worked up like that before," she said.

"He can sense his doom," said Freddy. And smiled. "They all do. You learn to ignore it. Remember you're the dominate species. Don't let them see you're scared. They'll have you then. Always be tough. Speak loud and firm. And if that doesn't work, kick them in the dick. That will teach them *real* fast."

What an evil, fat asshole.

Teresa saw herself slapping him, but didn't dare. Maybe once this was over she'd kick *him* in the crotch. See how he liked it.

A syringe hovered in front of her. For a moment she thought Clayton was about to stick her with it, but she quickly understood he was trying to hand it to her. Thankfully, she'd refrained from flinching away.

Teresa took the needle without speaking. She heard the murky liquid in the plastic tube slosh quietly. He gave Freddy one as well, keeping the third.

"I figure the easiest way to do this is by all of us getting him at the same time."

Wait...he wants me to...

She looked down at the syringe, the pricking tip covered by a plastic cap.

"You'll have to distract him," said Clayton.

Teresa looked up, saw he was talking to her. "Me? Why?"

"He knows you."

Teresa's throat felt as if hands were slowly squeezing it. She nodded.

He knows me. Trusts *me.*

That dog loved her, and Teresa knew it. Not only was she betraying Amy, she was betraying Jagger.

He's just a dog. He doesn't know.

When they exited the van and Jagger saw her, his barking stopped. Seeing how his tail started to wag, she realized how wrong she was. Jagger would know. He would always know.

Tears wetted her eyes, making her vision blurry. She didn't wipe them, though. Not wanting Clayton or Freddy to notice she was starting to cry, she kept her arms down.

The syringe felt odd and wicked in her palsied hand as she

130

removed the cap. Numb inside, she approached the fence.

Jagger whined, wanting her to pet him.

"Hey, buddy," she said in a hoarse voice.

Though it was barely audible even to her, Jagger heard it clearly. His mouth opened, tongue dangled out. His breaths were heavy and fast, excited. Eager.

"Hurry up," said Freddy. She glanced at him and saw he was constantly looking around, checking things out.

She looked back to Jagger and noticed how he ignored the guys, no longer considering them a threat. Since they were with her, he must think they were friends.

Jagger...how wrong you are.

She hoped he would run away from them, maybe even come after one of them. Hopefully Freddy.

Teresa felt the temptation to yell at him to go away. The words burned the back of her throat, trying to force their way out of her mouth.

She remained quiet, kneeling at the fence in front of him. His big paw swiped the fence, claws scraping the metal with a sound like two knives clinging together.

"Damn, he's a big dog," whispered Clayton.

"I think you've got your ticket out of this mess," said Freddy. He pointed his nearly smoked cigar at Jagger. "He's a fucking *beast*."

Teresa tried not to hear them. She raised her hand to the fence. Jagger pressed against it, his weight making the links bow outward. She stroked the poofs of black fur through the oval spaces.

Whining, Jagger pushed even harder, wanting more contact.

He got it when the three needles pierced his fluffy flesh.

Jagger yelped.

Teresa bolted upright, the sheet falling away from her wet skin.

JAGGER

She felt gelid droplets trickle down her sides. Panting, she looked around. The room was filled with darkness. She saw the pale shape of her dresser, the mirror on top glowing like a dim pool in the night. She turned her head and saw the window was open. The curtains swayed inward from the breeze. She felt its cool breath drift over her sweaty skin.

She pulled her legs to her chest, hugging them. Her thighs felt tacky and warm against her breasts, polished in sweat. Her turgid nipples ached as they were pushed back. She rested her chin on top of her knees.

Taking several deep breaths, she made herself calm down.

Just a dream. Just a fucked up dream.

The relief that flowed through felt great. It soothed her aches and chills, relaxed her muscles. Then she heard snoring from beside her. She held her breath. Turning her head slightly, she looked beside her. In the dim smear of moonlight from the window she saw Clayton. Lying on his back, his flaccid penis hung to the side. His chest rose slowly with the soft rattling snore.

It hadn't been a dream. What had woken her in the middle of the night, seized in panic, was a memory.

Lowering her face to the crease between her legs, Teresa sobbed.

CHAPTER SIXTEEN

Amy opened her eyes. The ceiling was bright with daylight. It hurt her eyes to look at it. Closing them, she started to roll over.

And dropped.

Her fall was short. She pounded the floor. Her arm knocked against something hard. Cheek flat on the floor, she groaned into the carpet. Her breasts were smashed against her chest.

Bringing her knee up, it bumped the same hard object as her arm. At first, she thought it was Jagger, but quickly realized it was too firm. There was no soft padding to it. Carefully, she reached out and felt wood.

Now she was confused. What was in her bed?

I'm on the floor.

Okay...then what was in her room?

Opening her eyes, she saw the blurry shape of the coffee table beside her. As even more confusion came over her, she started to notice the weak sensation in her muscles that came on the mornings of a hangover.

I drank last night?

Yes, she remembered. With Mark. The cop.

The cop.

It all came back to her in a painful flash.

Jagger wasn't here. He was gone. She'd come home and he'd been gone.

A draining feeling opened inside her, pulling her heart into her stomach. She felt a terrible cramp in her abdomen.

Jumping to her feet, Amy ran for the hall. She staggered toward the bathroom, falling against the walls and pushing herself up. She pushed the door open, dropped in front of the toilet, and vomited. The stale, beer-tasting froth splashed in the water. Her muscles constricted, legs squeezed and she pushed out another wave. Her body kept heaving, though nothing else came out.

Just beer. That was all she'd had on her stomach last night. No wonder it hit her so hard. No wonder she was sick this morning.

Amy remained squatted a bit longer, and when she decided her body was done punishing her, she sank to the floor. The linoleum was cold on her legs. Hugging the porcelain bowl, she leaned her face against its frigid smoothness. It felt good on her heated skin, almost soothing.

Her forehead felt stiff and moist, as if she'd been frowning all night. The throbbing in her head sent tendrils of pain down her neck. Felt as if a migraine was coming on. She needed to pop some aspirin before it got worse.

Need to eat something.

Her stomach made a fizzy gurgling sound at the thought of food.

Even if it was bread, she needed some kind of food to settle her stomach.

She wasn't sure how long she remained in a pitiful embrace with the toilet, but she finally made herself get up. She walked over to the tub, then sat on its edge.

Amy turned on the faucet, cranking the dial as far to the hot side as she knew she could handle. Then she pulled the switch. The water in the faucet shut off and spray fired from above. Cold droplets dabbed her skin, making her flinch as if she was being bitten by tiny teeth.

Sitting on the edge of the tub, she looked around. She'd left the bathroom door open. Usually she had to close it. Jagger liked to stick his head through the curtain and watch her shower like the canine peeper he was. His face would get drenched and fill the bathroom with the stink of wet dog.

She smiled, remembering how his fur seemed to weigh his face down, making it drag. The expression died when she realized how much she missed it.

Where are you, Jagger?

134

She should go see if he's outside. Maybe he'd come home.

No. Somebody took him.

But why?

Mark thinks he ran away.

He never said as much, but she could tell. He was a nice guy, and had gone out of his way to comfort her, but she knew he was only doing so as courtesy. He didn't believe somebody had come into her yard and dognapped Jagger.

But the cigar...

He did seem a little troubled about that. She wished she would have noticed if it had been there before last night. It could have come from anywhere. Maybe the mailman dropped it there when putting bills in her mailbox.

The mailbox is out front. The cigar was in the back.

Unless he was snooping around.

Like Big Jim Riley.

She remembered that day he'd watched her lying out in the sun. She'd pretended to be asleep, but had known he was there.

Should've gone inside.

Not wanting to embarrass him, she'd allowed him to watch, though she felt sick knowing that he was.

Jim doesn't smoke.

Somebody had left it there. And she could hear a thousand explanations coming from Mark as to why it had been.

He might not even look into the cigar.

He will. He likes me.

And she might like him. Hopefully it wasn't the alcohol last night making her think such things.

The hissing of the shower mixed with the tapping of the water in the tub pulled her thoughts from the cigar. Standing up, she peeled off her top. It clung to her skin and pulled away as if it were melted plastic. Her breasts felt free and no longer compressed. The warm air was wonderful as it drifted across them.

Bending slightly she drew her shorts and panties down her legs. Once they reached her ankles, she gave a little kick and watched them land a couple feet away.

I stink.

A combination of sweat, beer, and vomit.

Gross.

She stepped into the tub, pulling the curtain behind her. The spray was hot and stung when it pelted her achy skin. Soon it felt wonderful, allaying warmth that gushed over her naked body. When she lowered her head into the spray, plastering her hair against her neck, she moaned with pleasure. And she remained in this position for several minutes, until the hot temperature started to dwindle. Lowering the *Cold* dial, the water became hotter. It wouldn't last, so she had to start washing.

She spent the most time on her hair, lathering it until her head felt like a hive of suds. She rinsed and repeated with conditioner. Already, she felt more alert. She spread soap across her skin, coating it in a sudsy white. Then she stepped into the spray, washing it off. Her breasts appeared from under the frothy pelt. They were stippled in goosebumps.

Standing on the bath mat, she gingerly dried herself. She noticed a bruise forming on her arm. Probably from when she'd fallen off the couch.

Amy started to bend over so she could wrap her damp hair in the towel. The soreness in her stomach stopped her. A combination of her spell at the toilet and her previous evening at the gym.

Forget it.

She tossed the towel onto the floor, grabbed her robe from the hook on the back of the door, and threw it on. She tied it taut in the front.

Wiping the steam away from the mirror, she saw her haggard reflection appear on the moist glass. Her wet-tangled hair hung by her puffy face in golden tresses. The puffy crescents under her eyes matched the color of the forming bruise on her arm. She looked as if she'd been punched. Twice.

"Hello, sexy." Her voice sounded scratchy.

And she caught a whiff of her breath. She grabbed her toothbrush and spread a curl of toothpaste on the bristles. She scrubbed until her teeth stopped feeling fuzzy.

Amy left the bathroom. It was much cooler in the hallway as she walked to the living room. Expecting to find Jagger sleeping on the floor, it was bare. Again, she was hit with the shock of his absence.

Her lip quivered. She felt an awful squeezing sensation around her heart. She lifted her eyes to the back door.

Why torture yourself? You know he's not out there.

Though she knew she wouldn't find Jagger waiting to be let inside, she allowed her legs to carry her to the door. She rolled back the deadbolt, pulled the bolt lock out of the brass hoops, and unlocked the knob. Taking a deep breath, she lowered her head. Closed her eyes.

And opened the door.

Something was outside, though it wasn't her dog.

A white envelope.

Look at that.

Frowning, she closed the door, leaving the envelope where it was. She no longer cared to have it. Funny how yesterday it was the only worry she had. Now it hardly mattered.

At least Janice paid me something.

She wondered how much was in the envelope.

Open it and find out.

Later, she decided. She walked to the couch and sank onto it. The cushions felt a tad damp, from her sweating through the night, most likely. She didn't care. She wasn't going to move.

Raising her feet, she propped them on the table, crossing her ankles. The robe slipped open, the edges falling down the sides of her legs, the top spreading around her breasts. She didn't bother shutting it. Nobody but her was here to see.

JAGGER

Not even Jagger.

Tears spilled from her eyes, trickling down her cheeks. She felt their warm drips on her chest, sliding between her breasts. She moved her foot and felt it brush over something smooth and papery. Leaning up, she moved her foot to the side. A small business card was on the table.

What's that?

Sitting forward, she snatched it off the coffee table.

Mark's card.

Flipping it over, she saw another phone number had been jotted down with an ink pen. She looked on the table, saw the ink pen was there as well.

Amy had no memory of him leaving a card, or even adding the extra number to the back. But it was easy to figure out. He'd left this for her.

On purpose?

Of course on purpose. Wasn't like he'd accidentally done it.

She felt like an idiot. To save her the trouble of having to call the station and ask for him, he'd left a direct contact.

But the other phone number? Now that was a mystery.

Whole thing's a mystery. I don't remember him doing it.

Actually, she couldn't remember him leaving at all. Last thing she could recall was them coming back inside after finding the cigar. She'd loaned him a sandwich baggy to put it in. He'd blushed slightly as he confessed to not having any evidence bags with him.

Then what happened?

Trying to recall, she was met by a solid black wall. The most realistic theory was he left right after, then she'd guzzled beers until passing out.

Where are the empty bottles?

She looked around. None were nearby. The table was clear, so was the floor. No bottles.

Amy got up and walked into the kitchen. She stepped around the counter and noticed the sink. Her dirty dishes were stacked in the drainer. The clean dishes that had been in the drainer prior to these were gone.

"What the hell?"

Approaching the trash can, she kept her eyes from glimpsing Jagger's food and water jugs. She opened the lid. A fresh bag was inside.

So I got drunk and took out the trash?

"And did the dishes?"

Didn't seem likely. She turned around, putting her hands on the counter, bracing herself up with her arms. She peered into the living room.

A blanket was bunched up against the arm of the couch, on the side where her feet were. It looked as if she'd kicked it off during the night.

The realization of what happened came to her.

He covered me up. I must have passed out while he was still here. He put me on the couch, got a blanket. He cleaned up after us, took out the trash.

She turned her head so she could see the clean dishes.

He washed them for me?

Amy guessed he had. Probably so she wouldn't have to worry about it. Knew she would be occupied with other things.

She smiled. Though he probably didn't think it was much, it meant a lot to her.

He'd left the card after I passed out.

And he was a gentleman. Didn't do anything he shouldn't have.

Would I have known if he had?

Maybe. But she didn't think he would dare. He was genuinely nice and seemed to really care that she was hurting.

I should call him. Tell him thank you.

Looking at the clock, she saw it was barely nine. She remembered him telling her he worked days. Was he allowed to take personal calls while on duty?

No idea.

Maybe she should wait until lunchtime. Maybe he'd be on break and she could call and thank him. Invite him to supper?

JAGGER

It had been a long time since she'd cooked for anybody other than herself and Teresa. It made her nervous to think about.

Calm down. You haven't asked him yet. He might say no.

Disappointment seemed to take her energy away, mixing with her depression of Jagger being gone. She dragged her feet back to the couch and sat down. She dropped onto her side.

It's like I'm rebounding.

After breaking up with someone special, there was always someone different you poured devotion into. Was Mark going to be hers during her mourning of Jagger?

Mourning...

Amy started to cry.

Please bring Jagger home to me. Safe.

Chapter Seventeen

Mark parked his cruiser in one of the many empty spaces in front of building C of Old Hickory Apartments. It was a small area with four one-level compact buildings. If his memory was correct, there were only four apartments in each. The smaller buildings might not even have that many.

It was more low-income housing, which seemed to make up the majority of the living areas in Brickston. Old Hickory was one of those places that based the rent upon what money you brought in each month.

He grabbed the tiny scrap of paper he'd torn from his legal pad. He'd scribbled down Teresa Hawking's address on it after finding it in the database. She had a few traffic violations she'd been late in paying, but other than that, her record was okay.

Again, Mark wondered why he was here.

Probably wasting my time.

It wouldn't hurt for him to ask her a few questions. Amy had tried getting in touch with her last night, and he had no idea if she succeeded. Either way, Amy said Teresa had stayed over the last few nights and she'd taken off while she was walking Jagger early yesterday morning. So far as he knew, Amy hadn't heard from her since.

Seems odd.

A little. But it's probably nothing.

The Altima registered in her name was parked two spaces down from him. She should be here.

So why couldn't she just contact her friend and let her know she went home?

Mark planned to find out.

He got out of the car, quiet as he closed the door. He didn't know why he took the extra precaution. Wasn't like she could hear him from her apartment. Situating his belt, he started walking.

Mark heard laughter. Kids were playing on the small playground at the far end of the parking lot. They seemed to be having the time of their lives. He felt a small tug of loss watching them run around, swinging, zipping down the sliding boards. It was hard to believe his life had ever been that simple. He had trouble reflecting on his own childhood. The memories weren't there like they used to be.

He wondered how Amy was doing. Was she up yet? Hopefully he hadn't crossed any lines by cleaning up the mess and putting a blanket on her. He'd found it one in the hallway closest, so she'd know he had looked through parts of her house.

Didn't want to just leave her leaning across the arm of the couch.

Amy had been in the middle of telling him about a time when she'd taken Jagger to the park. Some teenagers had been fooling around on a blanket in the woods just off the hiking trail. Amy had spotted them as she'd walked Jagger down a dip in the trail. She'd pretended not to see them, but Jagger had kept tugging at the leash, trying to run into the woods. She'd used both arms to hold him back, but still lost her grip on the leash. He'd darted off into the trees, the leash dragging behind him.

The guy had seen him coming and ran away. Instead of chasing after him, Jagger had sat down beside the young woman. When Amy made it to the blanket she'd seen the woman was hugging Jagger, thanking him through her tears. She'd had on a dress with a ripped hem and a torn pair of panties hooked around her ankle.

Turned out the guy hadn't just wanted a picnic, and though she hadn't been in the mood to give him extras, he'd decided to take them anyway.

And the dog had sensed this and put a stop to it.

When Mark had asked what happened to the guy, he'd been answered with a low snore.

Need to find out how that story ended. I don't remember any calls about attempted rapes in the park. But I could've been working nights then and just never heard about it.

Maybe the woman never reported it.

Mark stepped into the breezeway. The brightness of the daylight was swallowed by deep shade. It took his eyes a moment to adjust to the sudden change in luminosity. The temperature seemed to drop ten degrees under the shelter. It felt good against the heat of his uniform and the sweat on his skin.

He approached the pale shape of the last door on the left. The bronze 4 seemed to glow above the brass knocker.

There it is.

Mark walked, rolling the balls of his feet forward, to keep his steps silent. There was no reason to be so sneaky, and he didn't know why he kept doing it.

Pinching the tiny hoop of the knocker in his fingers, he tapped it against the base three quick times. There was a peephole, so he kept his hand blocking it so she couldn't see who was on the other side.

He listened for any sounds of somebody moving around. He thought he detected faint popping sounds of feet moving across a floor.

"Who is it?" asked a woman's voice from inside.

"Deputy Varner. Webster County Sheriff's Department."

There was a short pause before the voice spoke again. "Can I help you?"

"You can by opening the door."

Another pause.

"Ma'am?"

"How about lowering your hand so I can see if you're really the police?"

Mark smirked. He knew blocking the peephole would force her to ask who was outside. Lowering his arm, he wiped his hand on his pants. It felt clammy and warm.

"See?" he asked. He tugged at the front of his shirt, angling so she

JAGGER

could see his badge. "Deputy."

"Hold on."

He heard the clicks of locks being disengaged. The door opened a crack. He saw long dark hair, a dusky bare shoulder, a lovely brown eye.

"Teresa Hawking?"

"Yes."

"Can I come in?"

She seemed to briefly hesitate before nodding. Stepping away from the door, she opened it wider for him.

Mark entered a tiny kitchen. No light was on, so when she shut the door, it looked like he was inside a cave. He caught the scent of soap and shampoo. When Teresa stepped closer, he realized it was coming from her. Her hair was slightly damp, her tawny skin gleaming under a slight moist sheen. She had on a tight tank top and short pink shorts.

"What's this about?" she asked.

"Is there somewhere we can talk?" he asked.

Sighing, Teresa walked out of the kitchen. She didn't invite Mark to follow her, but he did so anyway. A wall with a serving window was all that separated the cramped kitchen from the slightly larger living room area.

He watched her rump flex inside the tight shorts. With each step, the pink edges hiked to show the lower dark cambers of her buttocks.

Even shorter than what Amy had on last night.

Thinking about Amy made him feel guilty for ogling her friend. He didn't know why, but it seemed wrong to do so, like he was cheating on her.

We're not even friends, why should it matter?

He didn't know, but it mattered a lot.

There was a couch and a chair with a coffee table separating them. Other than a small LCD TV on a stand, there was nothing else in the room.

Teresa sat on the couch. She took a cigarette from the pack on the coffee table, lighted it, and leaned back. She threw a tanned leg over her knee. From Mark's angle, he could no longer see the pink shorts. They'd slid up so high, it was as if she were naked from the waist down.

He cleared his throat and stared at the floor.

"Sit?" she asked.

Nodding, Mark stepped around the chair and sat down on the edge. He leaned forward, resting his arms on his knees.

Teresa stuck out her bottom lip and exhaled a plume of yellowish smoke. "Now will you tell me what this is about?"

"You're friends with Amy Snider." He didn't ask her, he stated it.

"Well, yeah."

"She said you've been staying with her?"

Teresa nodded. "Broke up with my boyfriend a couple weeks ago. He keeps coming around, wanting me to take him back. She thought it would be best if I stayed there to avoid the temptation."

Mark nodded. "Is it working?"

Teresa swallowed. It made a soft clucking sound. "A little." Her leg rocked over the other, foot bopping up and down in a nervous rhythm. Though there were no lights on, the skin of her thigh reflected a pale shimmering bar. Probably from the sliding glass door across the room. "Not much."

"Old habits die hard?"

The corner of her mouth arced. "Sort of."

Mark removed the notepad from his shirt pocket, opened to the page he'd written on last night, and folded the cover down. It was too dark for him to read the words he'd scribbled down, but he was fairly familiar with the information.

"Amy said you left yesterday morning while she was out?"

Teresa nodded. "I did."

"And you didn't go back?"

"Obviously not."

Great. A snarky one.

145

JAGGER

"Why not? If you don't mind my asking…"

Teresa leaned forward and flicked the small chimney of ashes into the tray on the coffee table. She leaned even further to grab it. The front of her tank top dipped low and he saw the dark tops of her breasts. Sitting back, she placed the ash tray in her lap.

Her leg started rocking again. "I decided to come home," she said, "Any specific reason?"

Her eyebrows narrowed. Really it wasn't any of his business and didn't matter one way or the other. Hopefully she wouldn't point that out to him.

"I was tired of mooching off my best friend," she said.

Mark nodded. "Fair enough. Have you heard about what happened last night?"

Her eyes lost their edge, and for a moment he thought he saw regret on her face. Her face wrinkled when she dragged on the cigarette, killing the expression. "No. Is she okay?"

"Not really. Someone trespassed on her property and now her dog is missing."

"Jagger?"

"Yeah. Foul play is definitely suspected."

Not really, but it doesn't hurt for people to think so.

Teresa's mouth seemed to drop open. It moved as if the tank that supplied the words had gone dry.

"We don't know where he is," said Mark. He added, "Not yet."

"You said foul play? Somebody…" She gulped. "Hurt him?"

"We think so. Evidence suggests he didn't just run away. I'm putting some pieces together."

With the cigarette clamped between two fingers, she used her thumb to scratch the top of her head. Her eyebrows furrowed, putting creases in her brow that made her look older. "And why did you come here?"

Odd question. Why would you ask me that? Shouldn't you be asking

146

how Amy is doing? Or anything other than why I'm here?

"Wanted to see if you happened to go back to the house at any point yesterday."

"Why?"

Mark closed the notepad. "Just curious if you saw anything."

Teresa shook her head. "No. I didn't go over there, I mean."

"Not after you left?"

"Right. I've been here."

"All day and night?"

"Well..." She made a face that was almost a wince. "Not all day. I was out for some of the time."

Mark nodded. "Okay." He took a deep breath. "Any reason why you have been ignoring Amy's attempts of contacting you?"

Teresa looked down at her legs like a guilty child. "Um..."

"She said she's been trying to reach you."

"I know. It's just..." She raised her head. Though her face was smudged in shadow, he could see the haunted regret in her eyes. "I got back together with my boyfriend. Amy's going to be pissed about it. I mean—I just couldn't tell her, you know? Not yet, anyway."

Mark released a slow breath through his nostrils, intentionally trying to show his disappointment in her answer. "I see." Teresa watched him as if expecting him to say more. But he decided to let it go for now. "That should about do it."

"Oh? Okay."

"I'll be in touch again, I'm sure. Once I find out some more information, I'll have more questions."

"Sure. Anyway I can help, let me know."

Now that I'm leaving, she's ready to cooperate.

Standing, Mark slipped the pad back into his pocket. "For one, call your friend. She's worried about you."

Teresa quickly stood up and came to him. "I will." She looked eager to escort him out of her home.

They headed for the kitchen.

He knew he couldn't judge her for it, but she was acting nervous and strange. That wasn't anything to fret over, though. Most people acted the same way when speaking with a cop.

But he decided to say something else, to judge her reaction.

"Oh, one more thing," he said, stopping.

She paused, turning to face him. "Yeah?"

"Know anybody that owns a white van?"

The color seemed to drain from her face, making her even paler in the murky light. "A white van?"

"Yeah. Neighbors reported seeing one in the area yesterday. No windows in the back? Kind of like a maintenance van? Know anybody who drives one?"

Teresa looked as if she'd become lost in her thoughts. Her eyes stared just off to the side of Mark, as if she was watching something happen behind him. He glanced over his shoulder to make sure there wasn't anything.

Just a blank wall with cracks in the paint.

"No," she said in a scratchy voice. She cleared her throat. "Not that I can recall."

Liar.

Mark nodded. "Okay. It was worth a shot."

Back in the car, Mark sat behind the wheel, enjoying the feel of the cool air blowing from the vents. The kids were no longer on the playground equipment. Maybe the heat was too much even for them.

"She was lying," he said to the empty car. "Why?"

Mark had no idea. Teresa knew something about Jagger, he was sure of it. He'd almost mentioned the cigar but decided to hold back. For now. He'd use it later. Right now, he would let Teresa squirm for a bit.

He grabbed the mouthpiece from the CB and raised it to his mouth. "Dispatch."

"Is that you Unit five?"

"Sure is."

"What do I owe the pleasure of this little call?" asked Carla's distorted voice.

"Afraid it's official business."

"Aw, pooh. A girl can dream, right?" She laughed.

Mark smiled. He liked her laugh. "I sent something over to Pierce to be checked for DNA. Has he left a message for me?"

"As a matter of fact..." She paused. He heard the whispery sounds of rustling paper. "Yes. He wants you to call him around four. Said he should have some information for you by then."

"Four?"

"That's correct."

"Sounds good. Thank you very much."

"Got any lunch plans?"

Actually, I was going to drop in on Amy.

"Afraid so," he said.

"Oh, pooh, again. It's not my day at all."

"Talk to you later."

"Take care of yourself out there."

He returned the microphone back to the base. He looked through the windshield toward Teresa's apartment.

How do you fit into this?

Hopefully Pierce might be able to shed some light on that mystery.

CHAPTER EIGHTEEN

Clayton raised the cigarette to his mouth with a trembling hand. He had trouble getting his lips around the filter from how badly it shook. There was another sizzling zap of the cattle prod, followed by a throaty wail from Jagger.

Jesus H. Sounds like Freddy's killing him.

Jagger's cries overpowered the range of barking from the pens in the back. It was as if the other mutts knew one of their own was being tortured.

Stan had said the dog would stop feeling pain, and Clayton hoped it was soon. Right now Freddy was trying to make him mean, but to Clayton it seemed to not be working.

"Fucking shit!" Freddy shouted from inside the barn. He'd sounded like a shrieking woman.

Clayton stood outside, leaning against the barn's wall. His legs felt weak and stringy. If he had to walk at this moment, he knew he wouldn't be able to. Never before had he felt this way during a dog's *programming*. Maybe it was because Jagger just seemed to maintain so much innocence in him, a genuine display of love and trust.

Asshole had even licked Stan's hand, as if telling him he forgave him before being stuck with the needles.

Six times. Stan had injected the large dog six times, and Jagger had handled it just fine. The last two had seemed to actually hurt him, though the others acted as if they'd had no effect.

"Make sure he gets plenty of water," said Stan. "The water will speed up the process."

Well, Jagger has had nothing but water.

Sometime today they would start the raw meat feeding. Getting the taste of blood in his mouth. Raw meat made the dogs crazy, especially if it was *all* they ate. Freddy guaranteed by the time he was finished with Jagger, his new name would be *The Terminator*.

Clayton heard the dull strikes of Freddy's fists pounding Jagger. The dog yelped and cried, which seemed to make Freddy hit him harder.

He wished he had some music to listen to, something to drown out those anguished whines.

"You like that, fucking cock-sucker!?!" Freddy shouted. "How about this?"

Zzzzzz.

The cattle prod's zap seemed to linger much longer than needed. Jagger shrieked and groaned, as if begging Freddy to stop.

Asshole.

Who was Clayton to judge Freddy? He was the reason the dog had been brought here. Feeling sorry for the stupid thing or despising Freddy for his blatant mistreatment of animals would do nothing to cleanse his soul. If there was a hell, he was surely going there, along with Freddy.

Clayton felt vibrations in his leg. At first he thought his muscles were starting to give out and he would finally drop from having to listen to Jagger's anguish for so long.

Then he realized it was only his phone.

Tugging it out of his pocket, he read the screen. Teresa had sent him a text message. He'd left this morning while she was still sleeping. After going home to change his clothes, he'd come to the barn to find Freddy had already began working on Jagger. He'd claimed he'd been up all night, pounding hell into the poor dog, and Clayton didn't doubt it was true.

He thumbed the button on the phone so he could read the message.

Cop came by. Somebody saw the white van. Asked questions. I think he knows somethin'.

Clayton suddenly felt cold in the stifling heat. The sweat trickling down his body felt like ice water.

He wanted to ask Teresa more about her visitor, but replied with: *Ok. Talk later.*

Before he'd even lowered his arm, she had already responded.

Ok. I love you.

Seeing she'd written that did nothing to make Clayton feel better. He felt worse. Guilty. As if he'd somehow ruined Teresa, and she was too stupid to realize it.

I have. She's fucked too, if we get caught.

"Ow!"

Freddy's cry of pain snapped Clayton out of his self-blaming mood. Turning around, he looked into the darkened entrance of the barn.

"You damn bastard! Bite *me*, will you?"

A moment later a leathery snap resonated from the shadows. Jagger's yelps sounded worse than before.

Clayton guessed Jagger had finally had enough and let Freddy know it by biting him. Now Freddy was teaching him a lesson with the whip.

If Jagger lashed out at Freddy, the programming was working. Before long, Jagger would be the monster Clayton needed him to be.

Chapter Nineteen

Amy hoped her disappointment wasn't noticeable when she opened the door. She'd finally gotten dressed and was about to take a walk through the neighborhood to look for Jagger when somebody knocked on the door. Expecting it to be Mark Varner, she'd hurried to the door and opened it.

Ellie Riley stood on the other side, a plate sheathed in aluminum foil propped on the flat of her hand. She had on a sundress, blue with white flora printed across. Her graying hair was pulled back on her head. The sunlight seemed to magnify her eyes, making them sparkle like glass.

"Good morning," said Ellie, from the other side of the storm door.

Smiling, Amy unlocked the door, and pushed it open. Ellie took it. "This is a surprise," said Amy. She stepped back to give her neighbor room to enter.

"Hopefully I'm not intruding."

"Not at all, come in."

Ellie stepped past Amy, into the hall. "Brought you some breakfast. Have you eaten?"

Amy caught the salty scent of bacon and felt her mouth fill with slobber. She shook her head. "Not yet."

"Didn't think so." She gave Amy the plate. "It's been wrapped since I cooked it, should still be warm."

Amy felt heat seeping through the bottom of the paper plate. Her stomach trembled from the food. She hadn't felt like eating all morning since the throbbing head and the soreness in her eyes had ruined her appetite.

But this plate in her hand had changed her mind.

"Come sit down," said Amy. She started down the hall. Looking back, she saw Ellie following her. "I really appreciate this, Ellie."

"It's not a problem. Not exactly breakfast in bed, but it's the best I could do." She smiled.

"It's perfect. Thank you."

They stepped into the living room. Amy walked straight to the couch and sat down. She put the plate on the coffee table. From habit, she checked for Jagger to make sure he wasn't going to come and try to snatch the food away from her.

He's not here, moron.

It hit her again. The realization that he was gone seemed to drain the delight she was beginning to find.

Ellie must have noticed. "Not doing well this morning?"

Amy shook her head. "I keep forgetting he's not here."

Frowning, Ellie nodded. "I know the feeling."

Forcing a smile on her face, Amy looked up. "Now what have you brought me?"

"Open her up and find out. I didn't bring a fork, so I'll grab one of yours."

"Okay. First drawer when you go into the kitchen."

Nodding, Ellie walked into the kitchen. She stepped behind the counter, looking. "Ah." A drawer opened. Silverware clattered. The drawer shut. Then Ellie returned, holding out a fork. "Here you go."

"Thanks," said Amy, taking it. She unwrapped the foil as if it were a present. It made soft squeaking sounds that made her teeth tingle when she folded it away from the plate. "Oh, wow."

Two fried eggs with a thin layer of white covering the yellow bulges, three pieces of bacon, two pieces of sausage, a scooping of hash browns and a biscuit.

All it was missing was a bowl of grits, but Amy wasn't going to complain. This was the best looking breakfast she'd had in a while.

"This looks delicious," she said.

"It is. I'm a cocky bitch when it comes to my cooking."

Amy laughed. Her cheeks warmed. Something about hearing a woman Ellie's age use language like that made her blush. "Do you cook like this every morning?"

"Not exactly. Big Jim wondered what the occasion was. I told him I was making enough for you. Should've seen his face light up. He thought you might be joining us."

Amy saw Jim in the woods, watching her as she pretended to sleep on the blanket. The heat of the sun had slicked her body with sweat. She had untied the straps of her top and folded the patches down. All that had kept them from falling off her breasts had been her hard nipples.

She pushed the memory away. Nothing would ruin this meal.

Ellie sat down on the love seat against the wall. She sighed as if it felt good to be off her feet. She crossed her leg over a knee. The creamy shade of her skin glowed. Though she had no tan, Amy couldn't ignore the nice shape of Ellie's legs.

She stabbed the fork into the flimsy hump of the egg. Yolk oozed out. Taking a bite, she moaned at the delicious taste.

"Good, huh?" asked Ellie.

"Amazing."

Ellie laughed. "Well, thank you." She rubbed her knee. "I hope you don't mind, but I walked around asking some of the neighbors if they've seen your dog."

"Oh, Ellie. I wish you wouldn't do that. Some of our neighbors aren't exactly...decent."

"Don't I know it? No worries, I didn't go to the other side of the park. Just this side."

"Nobody's seen him?"

Ellie shook her head. "Afraid not. I take it he hasn't come home, either?"

Amy clamped her teeth on a bacon strip and snatched off a chewy portion. "No."

Frowning, Ellie nodded. "That sucks."

"Yeah." Amy swallowed. "I was about to walk around and call for him. Maybe even walk around the woods for a little while. Who knows, he might be out there. Might've gotten hurt."

"You don't think so?"

Amy shook her head. "No."

Ellie absently stroked her shin, her sandal hung from her toes, leaving her heel bare. "What are you going to do?"

Amy shrugged. "I have no clue."

"Well hurry up and eat. We'll go out there and look around."

"I couldn't ask you to do that."

"You didn't. I volunteered."

Amy smiled with a mouthful of hash browns, nodded. She didn't want to drag Ellie into it, but she also wasn't eager to go out there alone. She'd probably just keep putting it off if it was left up to her.

"Sure," said Amy. "That'd be fine."

After Amy finished eating, Ellie took the plate and dropped it in the trash. She set the fork in the sink. Returning to the living room, she brushed her hands together. "Ready to go?"

Amy, standing by the back door, slid her feet into her sandals. "As ready as I'm going to be."

Probably going to regret going out in the heat with so much greasy food in my belly.

Breakfast felt heavy in her stomach. Maybe the walk would help. They could hike the horseshoe road and back. With Ellie, she wasn't too worried about walking to the other side. Nobody had ever tried anything with her before, but she wasn't going to risk it. It helped being the one who owned the land, though she doubted it mattered too much to some of the residents.

Plus, Carlos would probably be outside with his buddies and all their roaming eyes. Maybe they won't be so obvious with their gawking if Ellie was with her.

Amy grabbed her keys from the board on the wall, and slid them into her shorts. She opened the door, bumping the storm door open with her hip.

Janice's envelope was still there. Amy had forgotten all about it.

"Got mail?" asked Ellie from behind her.

"Whoops."

Bending over, she grabbed the envelope. It felt a little thick. Some amount of lot rent was definitely inside. Not wanting to count the money in front of Ellie, she stuffed it into her other pocket.

At the end of Amy's driveway, they went to the right, heading toward the main strip of Eagle's Nest.

"Hot as hell already, isn't it?" Ellie asked.

"Very."

Felt like a muggy foot was squashing down on her back. Sweat wiggled down her sides, tickling her. Her hair on her neck made it worse. She wished she'd put it up like Ellie's before leaving.

Too late now.

"You sure Big Jim isn't going to mind you being with me?"

"Bah," said Ellie, waving her hand. "Don't mind him. If he had his choice, we'd spend all our time with those damn chickens."

Amy laughed, though she knew she probably shouldn't. Peeping actions aside, she found Big Jim to be a pretty depressing guy. She could tell he constantly annoyed Ellie with just his presence, and she felt sympathy for him in that regard. After spotting him lurking just beyond her property last month, she kind of was afraid of him now. Hopefully she'd get over it, since he'd never done anything to cause her discomfort until then.

They walked in silence for a while, listening to the birds chirping. In the distance, a lawn mower droned on. It was a comforting sound that blended nicely with the birds.

"Well," said Amy, "guess I better start." Cupping her hands around her mouth to amplify her shout, she called for Jagger. The name echoed, growing fainter until it dissipated.

JAGGER

Approaching Ellie's driveway up ahead, Amy saw a pinwheel sitting crooked beside the mailbox. Weeds reached up through the spokes, waving in a breeze that Amy's sweaty skin couldn't feel.

They left Ellie's house behind, passed by Janice's and Amy called for Jagger again. He didn't come. Other than the birds, the woods were quiet.

Ellie walked along the other side of the road, staring into the woods beside her, calling for Jagger in a way that made Amy think was how she talked to Jim's chickens. Whistling and hooting, she'd add a *"Come on, now!"* every so often.

The road straightened out as the isolation of the woods began to thin. They paused in front of an abandoned trailer that was falling apart. The windows had been busted and the screen door barely hung on by one hinge. The weed-choked lawn swayed lazily in the subtle breeze.

Amy stared ahead. A scattering of rundown trailers was further beyond the empty trailer, lined closely together. The grass running alongside the road shifted from green to a tobacco brown. A group of people stood in one of the front yards, huddled around an orange Impala.

Carlos and his buddies.

She spotted Carlos right away. Even from this distance she saw he was shirtless, his dark skin shining as if it had been oiled. He leaned against the front of the car, his hands moving while he talked to his friends.

"Want to head back?" asked Ellie. Sweat dotted her brow. In the brightness of the sunlight, Amy could see the wrinkles in the corners of her eyes and mouth.

Amy sighed. "I guess so. Didn't really do a whole lot of looking, did we?"

Ellie opened her mouth to respond, but the sound of tires crackling over gravel stopped her. She turned to look, and Amy followed her stare.

A police car was approaching from the direction they were heading. Carlos and his cousins stopped talking long enough to make obscene gestures with their hands.

Is that Mark?

The sun glinted off the windshield, making it impossible to see through. The grumble of the engine seemed to soften as it neared.

The car slowed to a stop. The window buzzed down and Mark leaned out, a smile on his face. Amy felt her heart speed up.

"Good morning, ladies," he said.

The shouts of Carlos and his buddies carried over. Amy heard Carlos warning Mark to leave her alone, that she wasn't doing anything wrong.

Amy waved at them. "It's okay," she shouted. "He's a friend."

"A friend?" Carlos shouted back. He laughed. "Ain't no cop anybody's friend, baby!"

"Hop in," said Mark. "Sounds like the natives are getting restless."

"Good idea."

Amy opened the backdoor and climbed in. She scooted over so Ellie could join her. Holding her dress between her legs, Ellie slid in beside Amy. Once she was settled, Ellie pulled the door behind her.

The A/C felt great. Amy sighed as cool air washed over her.

Mark started driving. Amy could see his eyes in the rearview mirror, glancing from the road to the backseat. They were a unique shade of green, hard around the edges yet soft and friendly.

"Looking for Jagger?" he asked.

"A little," said Ellie. "We got about as far as you saw us. Decided not to go any farther."

"Good idea. Some of those guys see two pretty ladies walking around, might get them worked up."

Ellie's pale skin turned crimson. Seeing her blush made Amy smile. Then she felt a fresh wave of heat in her own skin and realized she was blushing as well.

"You can drop me off at my driveway," said Ellie. "It's up here on the left."

"That one," he said, pointing at the crooked pinwheel.

"That would be it. You don't have to pull in, just let me out by the mailbox. Need to check my mail anyway."

"You sure?"

"Yeah, it's fine."

He stopped the car at the mouth of her driveway. "I'll have to let you out."

He flung the seatbelt behind him, opened his door, and got out. As he stepped over to Ellie's window, she glanced at Amy and wiggled her eyebrows. Amy laughed.

"Good luck," she said.

"I'll keep looking..."

"No. With *him*." She angled her head toward Mark as he opened her door. "I'm pulling for you." Winking, she scooted to the side, holding her dress in place. She got out.

Ellie's hoping for a hook-up.

She heard Ellie tell Mark 'bye' before he closed the door. She watched him pass by the windows on his way to his seat. He climbed back in and sat down.

Mark let out a long whistle before shutting the door. "It's damn miserable outside."

"I know. I think Ellie and I would have suffered a heat stroke before too long."

"Well, it's a good thing I came by. Don't want you collapsing in the middle of the road. Might get cooked."

"Road-fried human," said Amy.

Mark laughed softly from the front seat.

Outside, Ellie pulled a large stack of mail from her box. Amy wondered if all of it was from today. She rarely got anything other than bills in her own mailbox, unless she'd ordered something online. Sometimes she was surprised by a magazine she'd never subscribed to, or a coupon booklet.

Ellie waved before heading to her trailer. Big Jim was standing on the front steps, wearing a pair of coveralls and a trucker's cap. He looked concerned, probably wondering why his wife was dropped off by a sheriff's deputy.

"Her husband?" asked Mark.

"Yeah."

"Nice guy?"

"He's harmless, but I don't know if he's nice."

"Oh?"

She debated telling him about the peeping incident, but decided not to. Once Ellie had reached Jim, Mark started driving.

"So," he said.

"So?"

"Got any lunch plans?"

Her stomach cramped at the mention of food. The late breakfast she'd had telling her it wasn't settling well.

"How about I make you a sandwich?" she said.

"I was thinking of Lily's Drive and Park. Best burgers in the county, if you ask me. You know, they get their meat from local farmers."

"Maybe some other time."

Mark's shoulder's slouched some. "Sorry. I shouldn't have..."

Amy realized he'd taken her answer the wrong way. "No. Not you. You did nothing wrong."

"Feels like I did."

Amy laughed. "Of course not. Ellie brought me breakfast a little while ago, and I think the heat and the grease aren't mixing well."

"Ah. Okay. Belly ache?"

She felt a series of pops in her stomach. "A little."

"Tell you what. I'll drop you off and maybe we can take a rain check?"

"No. I'd really like to make you a sandwich. Plus I've got some cherry doctor pepper in the fridge. Nice and cold."

JAGGER

"I'd feel like a jerk if you made me something to eat. Like I'm imposing or something…"

"You'd be a jerk if you say no."

"How could I say no to that?"

"You can't. I won't let you."

Mark laughed. It was good to hear.

The woods that surrounded her property filled the window.

Almost home.

She couldn't believe how far they'd walked in the heat.

Her stomach gurgled again, followed by a tugging cramp. She changed how she was breathing, performing an exercise that reminded her of a pregnant woman giving birth.

Before she did anything, she would have to visit the toilet. A combination of the food, the heat, and her nerves. The beer from the night before probably didn't help.

Mark turned onto her driveway. She looked for Jagger in the woods as they rode by. She didn't see him anywhere.

The trees spread out as they took the curve. She saw the carport, her Jeep underneath. Though she knew Jagger wasn't there, she looked in the backyard on habit, expecting to see him jogging back and forth.

And felt heartbreak all over again.

Chapter Twenty

Janice clicked the plastic tray in place over Nathan's lap. She set the cookie monster plate with chopped up hot dog on the tray. Then she handed him his apple juice. It was in a cup with a firmly attached lid and handles on the sides.

She'd gotten the chair from a consignment shop. There were some stains on the yellow tray she hadn't been able to get off, and a corner had melted into hardened ridges. It didn't look great, but it had been cheap enough for her to afford. Plus, Nathan didn't mind. He ate from it every day without protest. Soon he wouldn't be able to fit in it anymore.

Janice walked over to the TV and cut it on. She heard Nathan laugh with excitement.

"SpongeBob!" He cheered from behind her.

"I know, I know."

SpongeBob didn't come on at this time of the day, but she kept a DVD in the player at all times. She used the remote to change the video input. The DVD player was on the bottom shelf of the TV stand. Using her toe, she pushed the power button.

A couple minutes later, she had *SpongeBob* playing. Nathan watched with a smile on his face, stuffing tiny hot dog chunks into his mouth.

She walked into the kitchen. Nothing separated it from the living room except for a change in the flooring where it went from carpet to tile.

Opening the fridge, she heard cans rattle in the door. Two rows of Bud Light. Her tongue tingled. She wanted to drink one so bad. Last night had been hell. She'd only had two and had hardly slept.

She'd woken up two hours before Nathan, had paced the living room, chain-smoking. Any other day, she wouldn't have been awake to hear Ellie's knocking at the door. She'd told her about Amy's dog and had asked if she'd seen him. Janice hadn't, of course, but had promised to let somebody know if she did.

After Ellie was gone, Janice had paced even more, thinking some things over. She'd decided to take Amy Snider a payment for the lot rent. With her mind a little clear, she'd began to worry Amy would grow tired of her negligence with the money. After what had happened at Amy's last night, she might be in a mood and looking for someone to take it out on.

She'd left Nathan sleeping, walked to Amy's, and had left her a payment on her past due amount. Just one month's worth.

But it better smooth things over. I'll have to be even tighter than normal now.

Nathan laughed from the living room. How he still found those same scenes he'd seen countless times funny, she didn't know. Just the sound of the cartoon made Janice's head hurt.

A beer would help that.

Her tongue felt like it was drying out. She imagined how the beer would feel streaming over it, rehydrating it, quenching her thirst.

I can't do this. What was I thinking?

She was going to fail. Making the decision yesterday to ease up on the drinking had seemed like a good idea then. Now that a lot of time had passed, she saw how impossible it was going to be.

Don't do it.

She'd hoped going without the beer would somehow mellow her detestation for her life. And the detestation she'd been developing toward her son.

Janice's hand shot past the beer and grabbed a can of Pepsi instead. She popped the top. She guzzled half the can with an arm braced on the fridge door, head titled back.

She belched.

"Ewww, Mommy!"

Then Nathan belched.

Janice laughed, which triggered laughter from Nathan. She stepped away from the fridge, swaying out a hip so she could shut the door. She stepped up to the where the floor met the carpet and watched her son eat. He looked so happy. Janice wondered if she'd ever been as happy in all her life as Nathan was at this moment.

I seriously doubt it.

Maybe when she was married, she'd been happy. And how had she shown her appreciation? By fucking somebody else and getting caught. Not just caught, but knocked up.

And Nathan was all she had now.

And I'm all he has.

This realization caused tears in her eyes. The only person in Nathan's life wished he wasn't in hers.

I want him here.

Did she really?

"Eat your food, Nathan."

Nathan looked back at her, the smile never leaving his face. "Okay, Mommy." He grabbed a mushy bit of hot dog and stuffed it in his mouth, still smiling.

And Janice saw herself slapping his face. It seemed so real, she gasped, thinking she'd actually done it. But Nathan was already looking away from her, watching TV and chewing, his lips sliding around as he carefully munched.

Her hand gripped her throat in a painful squeeze. She pried her fingers away, leaving burning marks on her skin.

She hurried past him, walking down the short hall to her bedroom. Inside, she closed the door. And locked it.

Sitting on the edge of the bed, she started to sob. She should be in there, nearby to Nathan in case he choked. Instead, she was locked away and alone, so she could feel sorry for herself some more.

She wanted a drink so bad. There was no way she'd be able to resist all day. She'd promised herself to only drink a couple after Nathan had gone to bed. That way, she could spend time with him without any headaches, any blurred vision or dizziness.

And she wanted him to get to know his mother without the influence of beer.

She was going to fail. Maybe not today, but by tomorrow, she would have caved.

Wiping tears from her eyes, she leaned back her head and peered up. There were dark blemishes across the ceiling from several roof leaks. She hadn't had the money to get them patched, so when it did rain again, she would have to break out the pots to catch water.

What a sad sack of shit I am.

Sometimes she liked to pretend she could turn it all around. Go back to school, get a certification or some kind of degree and start fresh for herself. And for Nathan.

But she had nobody to babysit Nathan so she could go to class. Whenever she did work, she left him at the free daycare sponsored by the Southeast Baptist Church, but they closed at five every day. Her parents blamed her for the divorce, and wouldn't acknowledge Nathan as their grandson since he'd come from her adulterous ways. Being ardent southern Baptists, they looked at their own daughter as a bride of Satan, and Nathan was the demon spawn.

Not that it mattered. She couldn't even afford the tuition or any book costs. Her credit was shot, so there would be no loans.

And this realization always killed her fantasies of getting the hell out of this trailer park.

Then there was Nathan—the mascot of all her failures. She didn't used to regard him in such a way. It was only over the past year or more. She hadn't even given him a birthday party two months ago when he'd turned four. Hadn't celebrated it in any way. She'd been too hung over to make a cake, and too depressed to care.

She'd loved him as a baby. Loved him when he turned one, two, and even a bit when he turned three. She wanted to love him again.

Though he had nothing but devoted love for Janice, Nathan would grow up to hate her like everyone else. It would be her fault, just like it was with the others in her life.

And then she would have nobody.

Janice wondered if that would be best. Maybe she could spare Nathan the misery of growing up with such a terrible mother.

The sleeping pills in the medicine cabinet seemed to call out for her.

Come get us! they cried from behind the mirrored cabinet.

"Mommy!"

Nathan's voice made her flinch as if she'd been slapped. She used her thumb to wipe away the tears.

"What?"

"Come watch!"

Janice took a deep breath, and tried to convince herself she could do this. Change started with your mind. And if she could get her mind to believe things could be different, everything else would follow.

What a crock of shit.

CHAPTER TWENTY-ONE

Clayton grunted as he hefted the dog's dead carcass. He swung back his arms and stepped forward, tossing the dog onto the fire. Ashes showered upward in blinking dots of heat. He fanned the smoke away from his face, and stepped back. The heat was unbearable. His clothes were soaked with sweat, molded to his body like an awkward second skin.

The flames quickly enveloped the pit bull.

His eyes landed on the crater where the dog's stomach had once been before Jagger's massive jaws had ripped it out. The ragged edges around the large wound were crispy with dried blood. He could see white bands of the lower rib bones and what few organs that remained inside.

Two minutes. Two fucking minutes!

Clayton couldn't believe how quickly Jagger had killed the pit.

Freddy had said Jagger would probably take a beating before he finally fought back. But he'd been so incredibly wrong. The pit hadn't even approached Jagger yet when the huge mastiff had charged and snatched the dog up in his teeth. Hanging out of his mouth like a squirrel, the pit had yelped and squealed in immense pain, its legs flailing and kicking as Jagger's jaws clamped together around its stomach.

Then Jagger had vigorously shaken his head.

Clayton could still hear the cracks of the pit's bones snapping. The juicy tearing sound that had followed. He still saw the pit flying through the air.

It had been dead when it'd landed.

Then Jagger had sat on his haunches, chewing the meat in his mouth. Blood had matted the fur around his snout.

The nauseating stench of burning hair filled the air. Clayton stepped further away from the fire. He'd piled twigs together and had used lighter fluid to ignite them. It hadn't taken long for the fire to cling to the dehydrated wood.

The flames had already eaten much of the dog's skin and had charred the muscles and bones into firm black rods. He didn't want to be anywhere near the burning dog, but the drought had left the area dry, so he needed to be close in case the fire tried to spread into the grass.

He saw movement in the corner of his eye. He turned. Freddy's tubby form hobbled towards him, peeling the paper away from an ice cream sandwich. Grimacing, Freddy waved his hand. "That *stinks*. Never get used to that smell, do you?"

"Why would I want to? It's awful."

Freddy stepped beside Clayton, and gazed down at the burning body. He frowned. "What a damn waste. That's two pits we've lost."

"Yeah."

"But man, I tell you what, I think you've got a damn monster on your hands. He already exceeds all my expectations."

"Where is he now?"

"In the stall. I gave him a chicken to eat. He's already almost done."

A live one, no doubt. That was a reward Freddy gave the winners. He let them relish the thrill of the kill and the satisfaction of munching on its meat.

"Water him?"

Freddy nodded. "He's got a bucket now. I don't want to spoil him, though. So once it's empty, it'll stay that way until I decide otherwise."

"Stan said we have to keep giving him water…"

"Fuck Stan, the crazy asshole."

Frowning, Clayton looked at the fire. The flames were starting to die. Without any kind of heavy breeze, there was nothing to keep them stirred. The dog-shaped charcoal briquette lay on top as the weak flames continued to crackle.

"Come on," said Freddy. He started walking. "Time for another lesson."

"But the fire..."

"It'll be fine. It's almost out, anyway."

"You just want to leave the dog like that?"

"For now. Come on."

The feathers choked him. Hacking, he cleared them from his throat, using his tongue to get them out of his mouth. Some remained bonded to his tongue, but it was easier to swallow the meat now.

Though it felt good going down his throat, and seemed to sedate his budding rage, it did nothing to satisfy his hunger. He still felt antsy, still trembled all over.

But he was no longer frightened.

He no longer feared the men who'd hurt him with the sharp things. The sharp things had made him think of the long car ride to the smelly place with the other dogs, being put on a table and the woman who pretended to be nice while she stuck stinging things into his back. In that dark place, the scent of dead dogs all around, he'd been terrified. And when he'd been brought here, he'd noticed a lot of those same smells. He'd shaken so much it had caused him to urinate.

All of it was gone, replaced by a seething rage that seemed to flourish, seemed to spread a suffocating blackness in his mind. The only thing that remained clear was his craving to hurt.

And blood. The sweet taste of blood.

A bone crunched in his teeth. He felt little nicks of splinters inside his mouth from the crushed bone as he chewed. It didn't hurt. His pains from the beatings were all but gone, just a phantom soreness he hardly noticed. Nothing seemed to hurt him now, except the hunger. The hunger made his stomach twist and fold, feeling relentlessly empty, though he could feel the meat dropping into it, the blood quenching his thirst, it seemed to never fill him up.

His feelings confused him, which caused more anger. He'd never felt like this, never wanted to harm anything. He thought of Amy, her underneath him, playing with his ears and scratching his chest. For a moment, the memory soothed the rage that boiled through his massive body.

But it didn't last.

She'd left him behind. He could see her getting in the car, waving, driving away. Then the others had come. He hadn't trusted them. But he'd seen Teresa, and had felt more at ease with the strangers' presence.

Then Teresa betrayed him.

Just like Amy.

He'd never pined for vengeance before, but now he did. He wanted to hurt, maim. He wanted to kill.

Footsteps in the barn called his attention. Raising his head, his ears perked up to listen. He recognized the smells drifting into the dark stall where he lay on the floor. The men were back.

A corner of Jagger's lip curled, but he kept the growl low in his chest.

They would not hurt him again.

Standing outside the stall door, Clayton peered in through the feed window. Jagger was in the far corner, concealed in shadow. He could see the dog's massive shape, dark against a heavier blackness behind him as he rose into a sitting position. The dim white of his pointed teeth seemed to stab the darkness, the foam of his drool like a frothy bleak cloud.

The coppery scent of blood radiated from the small window, making Clayton's eyes water. There was also a hint of raw meat that reminded him of tearing the cellophane away from a pack of chicken legs.

The dog stopped panting. The teeth vanished as the maw closed.

It had noticed Clayton watching. Though he couldn't see Jagger's dark eyes, Clayton could *feel* them studying him.

A rattling growl emanated from the darkness.

Clayton's skin went tight. The deep rattle coming from inside the old horse stall was unlike anything he'd ever heard before.

The door pounded, throwing Clayton back. Screaming, he landed hard on his rump, the dry dirt floor joggling his spine. He looked at the stall door. It shook in its frame, rattling as if something evil was trying to break its way out of the stall. Though bowing and jerking, the door was held closed by a twisting bolt lock as deep angry barks and growls resounded from the other side.

"Jesus Christ..."

Sounded like a monster was in there.

Freddy's little-girl laughter blended with the growls. The pudgy man stood at the launch of the stable area. The half melted ice cream sandwich was clutched in his chubby fingers. Chocolate clumped on his fingernails, smearing brown trails up to his knuckles. More chocolate clung to the corners of his mouth.

"Careful," said Freddy. He stuffed the remainder of the ice cream into his mouth. "Bastard'll take your head off."

Groaning, Clayton got to his knees. It reminded him too much of the other night when Freddy made him do some *convincing*, so he stood up, though it hurt his back to do so. "Sounds pissed off."

"I'm sure he is. He doesn't like us very much right now, but he'll learn to respect us." Slurping the ice cream from his fingers, he pointed with his pinky over Clayton's shoulder.

Clayton turned, unsure what Freddy wanted him to see. Then he spotted it hanging from a hook on the wall.

The horse whip.

Clayton looked back to Freddy, who was giggling with a mouthful of finger.

"Again?" Clayton asked.

JAGGER

Freddy nodded. "Mmhmm." The finger came out of his mouth with a wet pop. "Don't shit your britches. Makes them tough. This dog needs it more. He's big, but he's also a house mutt. His victory could be a fluke, never know. We have to make him a killer. I don't trust your buddy's drugs, either. Probably just injected him with cola or something."

Clayton hadn't told Freddy about the first dog, or how its heart had grown so big it had burst through its chest. He also hadn't shared the long list of side effects Stan told him about: the rage, the inability to feel pain.

The insanity.

Could a dog really go insane?

Listening to the din of frenzied sounds coming from inside the stall, he supposed it was a distinct possibility. Jagger was already on his way to being a killing machine before Freddy had started working on him.

The door quaked in its frame, scaring Clayton. Even Freddy seemed a little shaken up by the ferociousness on the other side of the door.

"Grab me the whip, will you?"

Clayton stared at Freddy.

"Don't tell me you feel bad for this bastard," said Freddy.

"Well..."

"If you want this fucker to be mean, then you have to make him *mean*. He'll get eaten alive in the pit, just like Bruiser. You babied that fucking dog too much, and you're in a heap of shit because of it."

Clayton nodded. "Yeah, okay."

Feeling numb, he walked over to where the whip dangled. It looked like something used to tame lions. He curled his fingers around the handle. It felt dry and leathery in his hand as he took it down. The thin strap was spotted with old blood. How many dogs had Freddy beaten with this thing?

He held it out to Freddy, who crossed arms. "Nope," he said.

"What are you talking...?"

176

"You're going to do it."

"What?"

"It's your damn dog. You get him riled up."

"I..."

"It's your turn."

The whip suddenly felt too heavy to hold. His arm dropped down by his side.

Laughing, Freddy said, "Time to get your hands dirty." Reaching into his pocket, his hand dug around. When it came out, it clutched his cell phone.

Gonna get video of this, too.

Fucking asshole.

In all his time working with the dogs, Clayton had never been the one to rile them up. It was always Freddy, and the overweight retard usually didn't mind.

He's doing this to fuck with me.

And he seemed to be enjoying himself. Laughing, Freddy walked over to the trembling door. Jagger was still pounding against it. His claws scraped the inside, grinding across the wood.

He reached out with his empty hand, fingers delicately gripping the lock. "Ready?"

"You know something, Freddy?"

"What's that?"

"You're an asshole."

Laughing, Freddy kicked the door. An expression of pure madness knocked the smile away. "Get back, fucker!"

The banging and growls immediately abated. Soft whimpers came from inside the stall. Freddy glanced back at Clayton with a confident smirk.

"Get ready. If he starts to run out, just whack one good time in the face. He'll change his tune real fast."

Clayton felt sick as he watched Freddy pull the lock out of the eye clasp. His hand moved down to the handle and pulled it back.

The light from the barn pushed the darkness inside the stall back.

Clayton sucked in a jittery breath when he saw Jagger. Feathers were glued to the sticky clumps of fur. The blood matting his mouth, neck, and chest looked like dark ink. But it was Jagger's eyes that made Clayton's testicles retract into his body as if trying to hide. The once hearty brown orbs had turned a mustard shade of yellow and now oozed clumpy fluid that had dried on his snout like urine-colored mud.

What was left of the chicken was by Jagger's paws—a little bit of bone and feathers inside the blood-soaked puddle his paws stood in.

Jagger snarled.

"Now!" yelled Freddy, starting to step out of the way.

Clayton threw his arm up and jerked it back down. The whip snapped outward.

And ripped a line across Freddy's back, tearing his shirt, leaving a red welt on the skin underneath. The cell phone flew from his hand, vanishing in the thick darkness inside the stall.

"Shit!" cried Clayton. The whip slipped from his shaking hand.

Freddy screamed as his hand reached over his shoulder, patting around as if trying to find the wound. His feet tangled together, and flew out to the side. Spinning around, Freddy faced Clayton, his eyes stretching open with fear and shock.

He started to fall.

His back pounded the ground inside the stall. His chubby legs flew up, rolling him back.

Hitting Freddy with the whip had been an accident. But the idea it spawned was not. Clayton dashed forward, grabbed the door, and slammed it shut.

"*What are you doing!?!*" shrieked Freddy. "*Clayton!?!*"

Clayton rammed the bolt into the clasp and twisted it down, locking it.

Freddy's face appeared in the window, tears filling his eyes.

"Clayton!" He tried to open the door, rattling the lock in the clasp. Seeing it was locked, his mouth started moving, spitting out sounds before he was able to form words. "Let me out! No! What'd you do? Please!"

A chubby arm extended through the feed window, slapping at the door, trying to find the lock. The fat of his arm squished and bulged inside the tight space, expanding around his elbow. The doughy skin kept him from reaching far enough out. He pulled his arm back inside, and put his face to the open space.

"Clayton! Come on, man. Let me out!"

"Shouldn't have made me do that, Freddy..."

"Do what? It was your idea to get the dog..."

"Not that..."

Freddy's eyes looked away, as if searching through a catalog in his mind of instances where he'd wronged Clayton. He must have found it, because regret washed over him. "I was just messing around! Come on, man! Don't be mad about that. It was a joke!"

Jagger's growls overpowered Freddy's pleads. Freddy whipped around, putting the back of his nearly bald head to the window.

Clayton took a step back.

"Stay back, dog!" Freddy shook his head. "Jagger! Stay back! Sit!"

An angry growl resonated from inside. Freddy's back pounded against the door, pushing it against the lock. The bolt started to bend.

Moist tearing sounds combined with the tearing of fabric, and Freddy's screams rose in pitch, shrill and childlike. Through the small open space, Clayton could see Freddy swinging his fists in a downward thrust. If he was actually hitting the dog, it had no effect.

Slowly, Freddy began to slide down. His cries lowered in volume, becoming gurgled and phlegmy.

His head dropped out of the frame.

And then all Clayton could hear were the juicy crunches of Jagger's chewing.

A blob of blood oozed out from the crack of space at the bottom of the door.

Chapter Twenty-Two

Mark was called to the scene of a gas station robbery and had been held up with questioning and reports until after six. He was supposed to swing by the station to see Pierce at four, but was just now getting there.

He parked his cruiser in his designated spot, shut off the engine, and climbed out. The building blocked the sun, which left the parking lot draped in shade. On his way to the rear entrance, he twirled his keys on a finger.

Though it was definitely cooler back here, the sticky heat still made it hard to breathe. Like trying to inhale through a plastic bag. By the time he reached the back door, his hair was damp. His armpits were sweaty and made squeaky sounds as his arms moved.

Mark pulled the door, stepped inside. Cool air swarmed him, making his skin prickle. It felt great, yet made him flinch when his damp shirt brushed his back.

He took the hallway to the break area. He entered. A firm rump was sticking out of the opened fridge, swaying slightly as small tanned arms dug around inside. A brown skirt was hiked up high on the sleek legs. Hands pulled a lunch bag toward her.

Mark recognized the curvy shapes right away.

"Hi, Carla."

Her pretty face appeared over her shoulder as she looked back at him. "Well, hello there." Her eyebrows curled upward with her rising eye. She made a face as if she'd been caught doing something naughty. "Guess you're getting an eye full, huh?"

"Nothing that's hard to look at."

Laughing, Carla grabbed a water bottle. She stepped back, stood up, and shut the fridge. She leaned against it, jutting out her breasts. Her shirt was made out of a material that made it look wet and shiny under the light. She started to smile, but it fell a little flat. "You look like you've been swimming."

Mark laughed. "Feel like a roasted hog."

"You need this more than me." She tossed him her water bottle.

"Thanks," he said, catching it. "You sure you don't want to finish it?"

"I'm sure. That much sweat, you're probably pretty parched."

"Understatement of the year."

Dimples appeared in her cheeks when she smiled. Carla was short, but her body was lean and curvy and packed in the right places. She was a little pudgy in her stomach, but it was hardly noticeable unless she was sitting down. The African American officers always commented on her ass, which Mark had to agree was plump and perfect. There was a tiny dark dot of a mole above her lip which he found incredibly sexy.

Seeing her now made it even harder to resist her. So far, he'd done so without making her think something was wrong with her, though she joked often that she thought he was gay.

He unscrewed the cap, raised the bottle to his lips, and gulped down the rest of the water. It was cold and refreshing as it washed over his tongue and down his throat.

Finished, he lowered the bottle and sighed. "That hit the spot."

Carla smiled, watching him. "I bet so. I liked watching your throat work."

Mark felt himself blush, which brought a laugh out of Carla.

"So," he said. "Done for the day?"

"Yep. A little late, but not too bad."

"I was surprised to see your car still out there. Any problems?"

She shook her head, hair bouncing. "Not really. Just that robbery. Was it bad?"

Nobody was killed, which is always a plus.

"Not really bad. The lady was in pretty rough shape, mentally."

"The employee?"

Mark nodded. "Took her a long time to stop crying."

"Well, I guess that's what having a gun shoved in your face will do." Carla winced. "Sorry, I shouldn't have said that."

Mark knew she was referencing his own gunshot incident. "No harm."

"I say the stupidest things sometimes."

"Hey, it's fine. Really. Don't worry about it."

"How about you come over tonight? You get off in what—half an hour?"

Mark checked the time on his watch. Not quite half an hour, more like forty minutes. "Close enough," he said.

"I can cook you some supper?" Carla lifted her eyes, sucked in her bottom lip. "What do you say?"

It was hard to decline her offer. Really hard. But for some reason, he kept thinking of Amy. Like he was letting her down in some way. Lunch had been fun, though she'd spent a block of the time in the toilet. She'd claimed it was the food not settling well, but he knew it was really nerves. She was a wreck inside, though holding up a good front. Being someone surrounded by people like that on an almost daily basis, he could see through her charade.

"Rain check?" he asked.

Carla's disappointment was easy to pinpoint, but she quickly put on a smile for him. "Sure. The offer always stands. You know that. I don't offer to cook for everybody, just so you know."

Her voice sounded different now, lower, not quite as chipper. "Thanks," he said.

Mark walked to the trash can, stepped down on the footswitch, and watched the lid fly up. It was pretty full inside, but not so much that the bag needed to be changed. It was station policy that whoever opened the can when it was full had to change the bag. He dropped the bottle inside and took his foot away. The lid slowly shut.

JAGGER

"Well, I'm going to head home," said Carla. "If you change your mind, call me. I'll whip up something for you real quick."

"Thank you, Carla. I'll let you know if I do."

Her lips tightened. She nodded. "Good." She used her elbows to push herself away from the fridge. She started walking. Her shoes made soft popping sounds against the bottoms of her feet. She had on sandals, with a strap running up between her big and second toes. They sparkled against her dusky skin. "Oh, I almost forgot."

Mark stepped forward. "Yeah?"

"Pierce left an envelope for you. I put it on your desk."

"Is he here?"

"No, he took off right at five. Guess he had to hit the golf course. You know how he is."

Mark laughed. "Yeah. Did he say anything about it?"

"Nope. Just wanted you to have it, so I put it on your desk."

"Thanks," he headed for the doorway. Turning back, he saw Carla hadn't moved from in front of the fridge. She just stood a couple inches away from it, her lunch bag dangling beside her leg.

She wants me to say I changed my mind.

Instead, Mark sighed. "Have a good evening."

"You, too."

Mark hurried out of the breakroom before she could say anything else. Each time she handed him an open invite to come to her house, he turned it down. Why? He should just get it over with. It would be fun. He wanted her, she wanted him. So what was the hold up?

Me.

He didn't want any flings right now. Didn't really want a girlfriend, either.

But what he *really* didn't want was to continue being alone. That really sucked. He needed somebody to occupy his time away from the station and he was sure Carla would gladly take that responsibility.

She might want more.

And that was where the real problem derived. He could tell she actually had feelings for him that she hid behind her constant flirting. If he gave in to her just once, she would want him to every time. It would lead to her wanting something else from him.

Again he thought of Amy, and didn't know why.

He nodded at other officers as he maneuvered through the small maze of cubicles. He hated this layout. Back when he'd first started, the desks had been out in the open and everybody could see each other. With these thin walls standing around him, he felt like he was in a cheaply-constructed cage. It was meant to add privacy, but all it really did was amplify their voices, making it easy to eavesdrop on conversations.

He saw a couple of the officers from the robbery moving around, papers flapping in their hands. They didn't seem to notice him as he headed to his desk. Stepping around one of the walls, he turned into the cramped space. His desk was against the flimsy felt wall. Papers were scattered across the top. To anyone else it would be a mess, to Mark it was organized chaos. He knew exactly where everything was.

The manila envelope was on top, his name written on the front with a black marker. Sitting down, he spun the chair around to face the desk. He took the envelope and leaned back, hanging his ankle on his knee.

Shaking the envelope, he could tell it wasn't very thick. Felt like maybe one or two pieces of paper were inside. He flipped it over. Pierce didn't seal the top, just used the brass bracket to hold the lip down. He opened it, stuck two fingers in and stretched them. Just as he'd thought, only a couple sheets inside. Upturning the brown packet, he shook the papers into his hand. Two of them. A note had been taped to the front page.

Found a match pretty quickly. Hope it helps—Pierce.

The top page was Pierce's report, which Mark put on his desk. He hated reading them. Too technical for his tastes. Seemed as if guys like Pierce used too many words to say something simple.

JAGGER

The second and final page was a mug shot. Mark didn't need to read the name to know the face. He'd had a couple run-ins with the chubby man personally.

Freddy Cormack.

Frowning, Mark leaned back the chair and propped his feet on his desk. It felt good stretching out his legs, tingling as comfort settled in.

Freddy's father was Dean—Big D—Cormack, used to own Cormack's towing. When he'd died, Freddy sold it, but had kept the farm and all the land.

Now why had he been smoking a cigar at Amy's place?

That was a good question. And Mark was afraid he already knew the answer. More than once Freddy had been implicated in animal mistreatment. The hushed rumblings of a dog fighting ring that this town secretly thrived on spread around the station like a bad cold. He'd heard about it more than once, but had never had any evidence to back up the claims. No one had. Though it was right in there faces, the evidence seemed to not exist.

And now Jagger's missing, and Freddy had been at Amy's. He wondered if he should ask Amy if she was friends with him.

No. If she doesn't know him, it will only get her thinking. She might decide to look him up herself.

Trying Freddy first would be the best choice. He'd swing by the farm on the way home. Right now he had to finish his paperwork and turn it in before he could do anything.

CHAPTER TWENTY-THREE

Teresa ended the call. She set the phone in the compartment under the car's radio. Though she hadn't been fired from her job, she didn't feel any more relieved than before she made the call. She'd lied to her boss and told him there were issues with her family, so he gave her a few more days to sort things out.

Should've just let him fire me.

The only way she would ever leave Honkers was if they made her. A sad truth, but it was one she'd accepted a long time ago. She was the only employee with seniority since she'd been there the longest. Other girls came and went in a cycle that seemed endless.

Another year they might give me a pen to show their appreciation.

Smirking, she leaned forward, taking a cigarette from the pack. She'd just gotten it lit when the light turned green. She put her foot on the gas and started going through the intersection.

A cattle truck soared in front of her, its horn blaring. Screaming, Teresa stamped the brakes, stopping just an inch or two from the truck. Cows gazed at her through the tiny windows as if bored. The odor of manure drifted through the vents with the cool air.

"Asshole! Don't you know red means *stop!?!*"

The driver couldn't hear her, but she didn't care. Shouting at him helped her feel better. Did nothing for the painful knocks of her heart that seemed to jut in her throat, or the jitters in her hands as she gripped the wheel. She checked both directions this time, saw it was clear, and drove on.

That'd be the way to go. Getting killed on my way to the barn.

A fitting end, Teresa decided. Would serve her right for what she'd done to Amy. At least she'd finally stopped texting her. When Teresa had gotten last request to come over, Teresa told her she couldn't and hoped to see her tomorrow. It seemed to have worked.

But she couldn't keep avoiding her. Eventually she'd have to go over there.

Just not tonight.

How would she act in front of Amy? Could she pretend she knew nothing about Jagger?

I better be able to.

Just play dumb and sympathetic. She'd done it before, she could do it again.

Civilization seemed to vanish as she drove. The familiar farmland appeared on either side of the road. Dusk had come, laying a purple hue across the land. The sky was vibrant with orange and red, as if the sun had burst and spilled colorful fluids over the clouds.

Usually the sunset was a vision she enjoyed, however, this evening it filled her with dread. She hoped to be over these emotions by now, but with that cop visiting her this morning, she'd been a wreck all day.

Hopefully seeing Clayton would sooth her uneasiness some. He didn't know she was coming and hopefully he wouldn't be mad. He'd told her this morning he would come over around five. He was two hours late, so she was going to see him.

Teresa slowed the car down, gazing out her window to find the driveway. She'd drive right past it if she wasn't careful.

There it is.

She spotted the faded path on the left and eased her car onto it. With the radio off, the crackling sounds of her tires rolling over gravel filled the cab. The trees around her blocked out what little bit daylight that remained. It looked like night as she drove, so she turned on the headlights.

Coming out of the trees, the headlights swept a bright path over Clayton's truck and Freddy's white van. The barn stood beyond the cars, dark except for the dim bar of light between the closed doors.

He's inside.

Driving up beside Clayton's truck, she put the car in park. She sat there, car idling, staring at the barn. The dark boards, rickety structure and rotted sections gave it a haunted look. Like the kind of place kids are warned to stay away from because of boogeymen.

I should stay away from here, too.

Teresa turned the air down. The buffeting hiss coming from the vents softened. Vaguely, she could hear crickets and frogs cheeping from the woods. Other than the usual nighttime soundtrack, all was quiet.

Teresa shut off the car. She unclasped the safety harness. When the metal tip knocked against the paneling, she jumped. Putting a hand flat on her breasts, she laughed at herself.

So jumpy.

Opening the door, she climbed out. The air was damp with humidity, licking her skin with a bland moistness. She thought about taking her purse with her, but decided to leave it behind.

Something clattered from inside the barn. Clayton yelled, "Shit!", and Jagger barked.

That wasn't a bark.

Sounded more like a roar. She'd heard Jagger bark enough to recognize it, though its tone was strange and deeper.

Angrier.

Though it was thick and stifling outside, Teresa suddenly felt cold. Hugging herself, she started toward the barn. Her feet crunched over the gravel, made whispering sounds in the grass as she approached the front doors.

The barking turned to guttural growls. More hammering sounds followed, as if somebody was pounding the walls with steel mallets. Standing outside the doors, Teresa took deep breaths to calm down.

It didn't work.

She reached for the handle with a palsied hand. The metal felt slick and cool as her fingers curled around it. Slowly, she slowly pulled the door. Hinges groaned. Light spilled out through the gap.

The noises from inside became louder. She could feel them on her, puffing her hair. An odor like spoiled meat came with it, mixed with another stench that reminded her of old metal.

Teresa entered the barn, walking slowly, her feet dragging the floor.

The tumult of violent pounding and vicious snarls ricocheted off the walls, making her flinch and jump. She covered her ears with her hands. "Clayton!"

"Teresa?" He shouted back. "What are you doing here?"

She couldn't remember why she'd come here. Trying to recall her motives was like reaching into a dark pond and hoping to grab a fish. "What's happening?" she shouted.

"Get back here and help me!" cried Clayton.

Teresa ran on legs that felt weak and rubbery, heading to the back. She could see a row of horse stables to the left. Clayton stood in front of one, his shoulder against it. At first glance, it looked as if he was convulsing as he leaned onto the door. When she got closer, she saw he was actually bouncing from the vibrations of something on the other side slamming against it. Something that wanted to break out. The door bowed outward from the frame before Clayton jammed it back shut.

The growls were even more intense this close, as if some kind of demon was locked up behind Clayton.

"Is that...?" she said.

"Yes," he said, knowing what she couldn't say.

"Why does he sound like that?"

"Don't worry about that now!" He pointed behind her. "See the tools over there?" His body heaved forward. He reared back, pounding his back against the door. "See them?"

Teresa turned. There was a workbench with tools scattered across the top. More hung from a pegboard above it. "Yes!"

"Grab me a hammer and some nails!"

"What?" She turned around, looking at him. Her face hurt from the wide grimace of her confusion. *"Why?"*

"Just do it!"

Clayton's face was red with strain. Veins jutted on his neck in thick chords. His hair was stringy and wet, plastered to the sides of his face. She could see the dark stains on his shirt, gluing it to his chest. At his feet were shallow gullies in the dirt from his shoes digging in to keep him propped up.

The door continued to quake behind Clayton as Jagger's roaring growls made Teresa's lungs tremble.

"Hurry!"

Clayton's shout kicked her into motion. She ran to the workbench, putting her hands flat on top. She scanned the top two times before noticing the hammer.

"Ah!" she squealed, snatching it up.

The nails!

She looked for the nails, expecting them to be gathered together near where the hammer had been. She saw none.

"Teresa!"

"I'm looking!"

"Hurry up!"

"I said I'm looking, damn it!"

Clayton yelled, but said nothing else.

She couldn't find them. No stray nails, no box with them inside. Nothing.

Sweeping her hand across the table's warped surface, her fingers knocked against an old coffee can. It turned over with a jingling rattle. Nails rolled out.

"Got them!"

Teresa used her hand to gather the spilled nails back into the can, then picked it up. She turned around, holding the hammer up in one hand and the can in the other.

JAGGER

Clayton saw them in her hands and smiled.

Then the door broke away from the hinges with a crackling snap.

It pounded against Clayton's back, knocking him forward. He crashed to the floor, the door landing on his back and smashing him down.

Screaming, Teresa dropped the coffee can. It hit the floor by her feet and tipped over. The nails sounded like breaking glass when they poured out.

Jagger clambered out from the darkness. His paws made deep thumps on the wood as he stepped up onto the door.

"Oh my god," whispered Teresa, shaking her head. "Dear Jesus, no..."

The dog was somehow bigger, swollen, his legs thicker. The once healthy pelt that had looked glossy under the sunlight was matted and clumped together with blood and dirt. His face was smeared in a crimson paste, feathers stuck to it like fluffy hairs.

Growling, the saggy flaps writhed around his sharp teeth.

"Jagger?" she said.

His mouth closed, an ear perked up. He tilted his head as if her voice confused him.

"Jagger, buddy, it's me. It's Aunt Teresa."

A sweet whine emanated from his throat. The patch of hair that had been sticking up on his back sank. Lowering his head, his rump raised, tail extended as a stretch worked its way through his muscles. He looked as if he was about to roll over and offer his stomach to Teresa for scratching.

She lowered her stare to below the door. Though Clayton didn't move, she could tell he was awake. His arms reached out both sides of the door, motionless. She supposed he was trying to remain still so he wouldn't do anything to set Jagger off again.

With another soft whine, Jagger slowly walked forward. He stepped off the door, onto the dirt floor. As he neared Teresa, Clayton quietly wiggled his way out from underneath the door.

Putting the hammer behind her back, Teresa sunk to a crouch. "Come here." She could feel the coolness of the hammer's metal through her shirt. The solid flat of its head was reassuring. "Come on, boy."

Jagger licked his lips, whined again. Head sagging, he kept coming, like a dog about to be reprimanded. The large dog was in front of her now, blocking her view of Clayton. He sat down on his rear, putting his forepaws flush in front of him. His head hung low as if he was ashamed for his behavior.

"There's my big boy," she said in a soft voice.

Teresa noticed movement behind Jagger. Peering over his giant head, she saw Clayton had gotten out from beneath the door. He was on his knees, working his arm back and forth as if trying to get feeling back into it.

Jagger whimpered, his head lowering to the hand resting on her leg. Tensing up, she prepared herself for a bite. Instead, she felt a tickling wetness.

He was licking her.

"That's a good boy," she said.

Clayton held his arms out, as if asking her what he should do. Shaking her head, she cautiously lifted her other hand from behind her back.

Clayton nodded when he saw the hammer.

"Jagger?" Her voice remained soft, gentle. Trusting.

He kept licking, his plushy tongue dabbing her thigh.

She poised the hammer above his skull, reared it back. Jagger stopped licking. With his head down, his eyes raised up to look at her. They moved past her head, to her pulled-back arm. The hammer was mirrored in the dark yellow of his eyes.

A deep growl rattled in his chest.

"Sorry," she said.

She brought the hammer down.

Jagger's jaws opened and caught her arm between them. They

JAGGER

snapped shut like a trap, sharp teeth tilling into her skin. Pain exploded through her arm. Teresa screamed when he gripped harder, his teeth crunching her bone.

The hammer dropped from her hand.

Jagger jerked his head to the side, yanking her forward. She landed on her stomach, arm reaching up before her. She started moving, being dragged toward the stall.

Screaming and crying, Teresa patted the floor, trying to grip onto something but only leaving narrow lines in the dirt with her fingernails.

"Help!"

Where's Clayton? Help me, Clayton! Why aren't you helping?

She slid over the door. Her breasts hit the wooden ridge, stopping her movement. Jagger jerked harder. Her breasts bounced over the edge, pulling the front of her dress down. The tops of her breasts scraped the wood. Her bra shielded her nipples, but she could tell it was beginning to slip down.

"Clayton!" she cried. "Help me!"

Jagger's claws spaded the dirt floor, locking in place long enough for him to wrench her further. With each jerk of his head, more pain blasted her. How her shoulder crunched whenever it moved, she figured it was dislocated.

"Jagger! *Stop!*" She looked up, flung her hair out of her face. "*Stop!*"

Her arm looked nearly flat inside his mouth. Her hand hanging from the other side like a lettuce leaf, fingers limp.

"I said *stop!*"

She pushed against the floor, arching her back as if attempting a push-up.

And locked her eyes on Freddy's mangled corpse inside the stall. She screamed even harder.

Freddy had been gutted, his stomach torn open and hollowed out. She could see the lumps of his spinal column through the deep wound, intestines strewn out like grease-colored confetti.

Jagger killed Freddy!

Ate him! Jagger *ate* Freddy!

And he's taking me in there! I'm next!

"Noooo!"

Teresa tried to pull her arm away. She pushed against the floor, felt her palm burrowing into the dirt. She strained, shoved.

And kept sliding.

Sliding toward the stall.

A flicker of movement caught her eye.

"Clayton!"

He appeared behind Jagger, raising the hammer with both hands. He brought it down on the dog's head. It made a sound like something hard hitting raw beef. Blood shot out. Teresa felt it sprinkle her face.

The hold on her arm was released. She dropped to the floor, rolled away, and pulled her ruined arm close. She felt her shoulder crunch and crackle with each movement. Her forearm dipped down, like a hose without water. Puncture wounds from Jagger's teeth leaked blood down her arm. Her skin was painted in crimson.

"Oh...shit..." Clayton's voice.

Looking up to see, but her hair blocked her eyes. She flung her head to clear her view.

Clayton, standing over Jagger, gripped the hammer with both hands. It shook in his grasp. The flat end had a small clump of bright pink skin and dark fur affixed to it.

Jagger raised his head as fresh streams of blood sluiced down between his eyes.

How is he still awake? That hit should have killed him!

But it didn't. Jagger's thin lips trembled around the rumbling growl coming from his throat.

Clayton's arm shot up, hammer prepped to strike again. He swung downward.

Jagger jumped away, twirling a circle and snapping his jaws. His teeth clapped like rocks as they searched for something to bite.

Screaming, Clayton backpedaled, feet kicking up dirt as he tried to avoid Jagger. His left foot kicked against his right, throwing it out from under him.

He started to fall.

Those meaty jaws snapped shut between Clayton's legs, catching him. Suspending him in air with his back slightly bowed as if doing a stretch.

As if she'd been the one bitten, Teresa felt pain in her stomach. "No!" she cried, reaching out with the arm that wasn't hurt.

Jagger raised his head, lifting Clayton with him. A leg hung next to each of Jagger's ears, his arms reaching down, hands pushing against the dog's head. His face twisted in agony as his lips formed an oval that produced moans and wails.

Teresa scrambled to her knees, holding her hurt arm to her side. She searched the ground for the hammer.

And couldn't find it.

Looking back at Jagger, she screamed as he bit down, making Clayton's legs extend outward to perform a split. Clayton's screams turned to high-pitched screeches, like a tape being eaten inside the player.

"Clayton!" she uselessly cried.

He looked at her, tears in his eyes, his face pink. Drool hung from his lips as he tried to speak. It was hard to tell for sure, but she thought she heard him say: *"Run!"*

And she did.

Jumping to her feet, she dashed away from the stalls and into the barn's front area. The door was still open, just as she'd left it.

Her injured arm dangled beside her, slapping against her side. The pain of its bouncing slowed her down, so she reached over with her good hand and held it still. It seemed to help a bit, but not enough to matter.

Teresa heard heavy padding in the dirt behind her, the deep huffs of Jagger's enraged breaths. He was coming after her like a furry locomotive, and he was gaining fast.

She wanted to peek over her shoulder and see just how close he was, but didn't dare. Her exit was just a few steps away. Leaning forward, she kicked her legs harder to increase her speed. She shot out of the barn, skidded to a halt, and spun around.

Jagger was just a few short steps away. Screaming, she grabbed the door and slammed it shut. The latches clicked. She wished she had something to slip through the handles to make sure it stayed closed. She didn't, so the latches would have to do. They would at least give her some time, and any time would do.

Turning, she prepared to run. She put weight on her front foot, started to push off.

Jagger's head crashed through the door, breaking the boards. Teresa flung herself sideways, avoiding a sailing plank that stirred her hair as it went by. In her spinning vision, she glimpsed Jagger halfway out the door, his forepaws scratching at the dirt to pull him out all the way. His hips seemed to keep him wedged there.

Teresa shook her head, unable to comprehend this dog was Jagger. Nothing about him seemed the same, even his appearance was different. Altered, slightly sick and mutated. The split in his head caused from the hammer had no effect on him and looked like a jagged bleeding grin between the curves of his floppy ears.

Jagger snapped and roared, as if he could make his jaws stretch to find Teresa's tender flesh.

He's lost his mind...evil...

Still shaking her head, Teresa walked backward, not taking her eyes away from the dog. He saw she was leaving and his attempts to get free became more desperate as he hurled himself forward. His paws slapped the ground, claws raking lines through the dirt. They latched onto something and Jagger pulled forward.

"No-no-no..."

The wood groaned as it bulged out like a wooden sphincter trying to shit out a furry turd. Jagger pulled harder. Splintering sounds came from the door, expanding in a bubble of wood around his shoulders. Any second now it would pop!

Teresa put her back to Jagger and started to run.

The door exploded behind her, triggering a scream from her lungs. She ran harder. Her arm flapped beside her loosely and out of control. The other arm pumped, elbow out for balance.

She saw her car and wished she was already in it.

Jagger, behind her again, pummeled the ground with his huge feet. His breaths sounded like a winded giant as he neared.

"Stay away, Jagger! Stay back!"

He barked in response. Teresa felt its depth in her chest, and it caused her to scream again.

"I'm sorry, buddy! Please, stay back!"

It was pointless to try reasoning with a dog, but she hoped maybe Jagger would hear her voice, the fear and regret, and decide to leave her alone.

He growled with such rage behind her that her bladder nearly released. Her voice *was* helping—helping his decision to kill her. It seemed that each time she spoke, it made him want to get a hold of her even more.

Crying, Teresa neared the car.

She recognized its familiar shape through her tear-blurred eyes.

Almost there!

If she tried to get in right away, Jagger would be on her in an instant. She should run around the back, circle around the other side as a way to throw him off. It would confuse him and she might get back around to the driver's side before him.

Running past her door, she made her way to the back. Jagger followed her just as she'd expected. She circled around the other side and darted up along the passenger doors. The galloping pursuit became fainter as she left him behind.

It's working!

Teresa ran around the front and was passing the first headlight when Jagger appeared from the other side to intersect her.

"Shit!"

Digging the balls of her feet into the ground, she spun around and went back the other way.

How did he know?

Head thrown back, Teresa rounded the front corner, holding her arm in place. She could hear Jagger behind her. Could feel his slobber spattering the backs of her legs. Abandoning her plan, she reached for the passenger door handle and lifted.

It was locked.

"*Yaa!*"

She pushed away from the door, just missing Jagger's lunging jaws. She heard them scrape the car's shell as his mouth shut.

Reaching the rear of her car, she stole a fleeting peek over her shoulder. Glimpsed Jagger turning away from the car and starting after her again. There was more distance between them now, but it wouldn't last. She faced forward once again, pumping with all she had to pick up her speed.

Reaching the driver's side door, she jerked back the handle and nearly fell when it shot open. Not taking the time to regain her bearings, she dived into the car. The top of her head grazed the door frame as she landed on the seat. She turned to pull the door shut.

And Jagger leaped in after her.

His mass crushed down on her, throwing her against the compartment. The emergency brake jabbed her side. His massive size eclipsed her vision, filling her line of sight with fur that felt sticky and warm as it wriggled over her arms and thighs. She kicked at him, barely catching him with her heels.

"Jagger! Stop!"

His breath huffed in her ears.

She felt it on her neck, warm and dripping saliva right before his teeth punctured her throat.

Teresa's screams turned to gargled cries.

And she knew there was nobody left to hear them.

CHAPTER TWENTY-FOUR

Amy opened the door. Dim light filled the frame, making her a lovely pale shape. Her hair was mussed and hung around her face in strands.

She'd been sleeping.

And I woke her up, knocking.

When she saw Mark, her groggy expression turned grim.

"What's happened?" she asked.

Mark took a deep breath. "Can I come in?"

Sitting on the couch, Mark watched Amy in the kitchen. She had on a long T-shirt and when she bent inside the fridge to get the beers, it hiked up her waist. He glimpsed a pale tip of a buttock. The light spilling out from the fridge turned the shirt's white fabric translucent. He could see the dark shapes of her breasts, swaying slightly as her arms reached in.

Mark looked away, not wanting her to catch him staring.

A few moments later she entered the living room carrying a carton of Bud Light bottles by the cardboard handle. They clinked softly when she set them on the coffee table. She sat down beside him. Only a small gap of space was between them. Mark was reminded of last night, how they'd sat on this same couch with much more distance between them.

Things have changed. We trust each other more now.

What she had on should be evidence of that. She hadn't even taken a moment to put on some real clothes. He supposed he could have suggested her to get dressed first, but the idea had never occurred to him.

I could say something now.

Amy leaned forward, her dusky knee bumping his leg. He decided to let her wear whatever she was comfortable in.

JAGGER

She took two bottles from the carton and gave him one. There was a synchronized hissing pop when the caps were twisted off. The gulping sounds of beer being guzzled interrupted the silence.

When she lowered the bottle, half the beer was gone. "Are you going to tell me now?" she asked in a breathy voice.

"Well..."

He didn't know where to begin. There was so much she needed to know.

"It's not good, is it?" she asked.

Mark saw the barn awash in the glow of their work lights. Saw photographers taking pictures of the busted door. Flashes from their cameras popped across the dark sky. Another was crouched at the prints, tearing open a bag of plaster to make a cast. Others were huddled around more prints, measuring their size with tape.

"No." He took a deep breath. "I have to tell you that...Teresa's dead."

Amy stared at him. "What?"

Nodding, Mark sipped his beer. It was no longer refreshing and now tasted bitter. He nearly shivered as it went down. "Jagger killed her."

Her hand started trembling. Beer spilled from the mouth of the bottle. Mark quickly took it from her and put it on the table. He threw his arm around her and pulled her to him. She didn't resist. She fell against him, her face pushing against his chest.

"Are you sure?" she asked.

An image of the car's interior flashed in his mind: the blood dripping from the ceiling, coating the windshield in gloppy red, innards strewn all over.

He saw Pierce and a couple of the officers, wearing gloves, loading the pieces of Teresa's body into black bags.

He felt his stomach quiver, threatening to eject what little was inside. "Yes."

Amy shook against him, sniffling. "Jagger did it?" Her voice was thick and bubbly.

"Pretty damn sure he did, yeah."

"Why do you think so?"

He stroked her back. Her skin was warm through the thin shirt. "The cigar in your backyard had Freddy Cormack's DNA all over it."

Amy sat up in a hurry. "Freddy Cormack?"

Mark nodded. "Know him?"

"Well...yeah, I mean, when we were kids, through school and stuff."

"Does he come over here?"

"No!" She grimaced. "No way in hell."

Mark nodded. "He's dead, too."

"My God..." Teresa looked pale. She shook her head. "Did... Jagger?"

"We think so. Won't know for sure until the dog saliva taken from the scene is matched with what your vet has on file. But judging the severity of the damage..."

"God," she muttered, falling back against the couch.

"There's more," Mark said.

Amy closed her eyes, as if preparing herself.

"We found a third body, Clayton Fortner."

Amy opened her eyes, turned to Mark. The shock must have lost its edge since her reaction wasn't as severe. "Teresa's boyfriend?"

"He's the one?"

She nodded. "Yeah."

"Here's my theory and there's already plenty of evidence that supports it. I believe those three came here while you were away at the gym and took Jagger."

Amy's lip curled, baring teeth. "Why? That makes no sense at all."

"Yes, it does," he said. "We found the bodies inside a barn on the outskirts of town. Way out in the sticks. We believe the barn was being used as an arena for dog fights."

JAGGER

Amy looked as if she was pain. "Jesus..."

"There have been reports of such activity going on, but we've never been able to get anyone involved. Hell, we couldn't even find somebody willing to *talk* about it. With these deaths, an entire ring will probably be exposed. I've already heard rumors of cops being on the payroll to keep things quiet."

"Holy shit, are you serious?"

"Afraid so."

Amy reached up and grabbed her beer. Her breasts moved freely behind the T-shirt. Sitting back, she raised the bottle to her lips and guzzled three heavy swallows. She lowered the bottle letting out a heavy breath that puffed out her cheeks. "And Teresa was involved with this?"

"We don't know to what extent, but I'm willing to guess that she wasn't very heavily involved. Probably mostly her boyfriend."

"And Freddy."

"Yeah."

Mark studied Amy. With her head low, she had the beer resting where the shirt draped her lap. It pulled the fabric taut around her thighs and pushed it down her groin. If he looked harder, he could detect a pale band of skin between her legs.

He chose not to look.

"So," she said, eyebrows narrowing. "What does this mean for Jagger?"

"Sorry?"

She looked at him. "Will he be put...down?"

Mark was angry at himself for not already telling her about Jagger. How could he have forgotten? A glimpse of Amy's legs showed him why the fact had slipped his mind.

"We don't know where Jagger is."

Amy's mouth dropped. "You don't?"

Mark shook his head. "He's out there *somewhere*. People are combing the Cormack property for him right now. There're a lot of acres to cover, and in the dark..." He shrugged. "Won't really get to explore until the morning."

"I want to help."

He shook his head. "Not a good idea. Besides, the sheriff wouldn't allow it."

"You already asked?" She somewhat smiled.

"I thought it would help if Jagger heard *you* calling for him." Mark shrugged. "The sheriff thinks it'll just put you in unnecessary harm. He's probably right."

"Do *you* have to go hunt?"

"Not right away. I'm supposed to keep looking into the dog fights. They have a team handling the search, but I'm supposed to keep my eyes open and look around some while digging up info about the dog ring. Nobody even knows I came here."

She smiled. "You wanted to be the one to tell me?"

"I guess so, yeah."

He definitely didn't want one of the other guys coming over in the morning and unloading all this information on her. He doubted she would have handled it as well coming from anybody else. He recognized she was putting on one of her tough fronts for him. Inside, she was probably ruined.

"What if they don't find him at Freddy's? Then what?"

"They've already put a call into animal control. I'm sure Jeremiah is chomping at the bit to get started."

He immediately regretted mentioning it the moment he stopped talking.

"Who's Jeremiah?"

Mark sighed, swigged some beer. "An asshole that takes his job way too seriously. He was in the army for a couple years and treats each animal like a mission."

"Great," she said, ruffling her hair. She looked at Mark as if deeply troubled. Her earthy eyes glistened with tears and her lips were curled.

JAGGER

"Be honest with me."

Mark's throat felt dry as he nodded.

"Was it bad?"

He'd hoped for any question other than this one. Sighing, he felt his posture slacken. He realized he'd been putting on a front of his own and Amy had just knocked it down with one question. "Yeah," he said. "Very."

Her lip quivered and she sucked it into her mouth. Turning away, she put her hand up to her face. "Poor Teresa..." She started to sob.

Mark wanted to hold her again, but the Bud Light was still pressed in her lap. He was afraid to reach for the bottle. It was too close to her groin, and he didn't want to risk her thinking he was making a pass at her.

But he also didn't like sitting here while she cried so hard. Her front had diminished and pure emotion was pouring out of her, making her shake.

Groaning, Amy grabbed the beer bottle and threw it. The glass shattered against the wall. Mark jumped back against the couch. He turned to Amy, his heart pounding from the sudden heated gesture.

She leaned forward, elbows on her knees and face buried into her palms.

He reached over, putting his hand on her back. He rubbed circles between her shoulder blades.

She acted as if he wasn't there.

And sobbed.

Should I leave?

He didn't know if he should wait around until she calmed down or if she should be alone to process all he'd told her.

"Want me to go?" he asked.

She shook her head, face sloshing against her hands. She looked back at him. Her pink cheeks were slick with tears. A few beads clung to her upper lip. Wiping her mouth with her arm, she continued to stare at

206

him. "I want you to kiss me."

A cold hand grabbed his stomach. "Amy..."

She leaned back, turning on the couch and bringing a leg onto the cushions. Her knee pushed the T-shirt open and he could see the smooth skin of her pubic mound. "Kiss me," she said, again, starting to crawl toward him.

He knew he shouldn't. Just like last night, he couldn't allow her vulnerability to persuade him to take advantage of it. "Listen, we shouldn't..."

She put an arm behind him and another on the couch beside his leg. She brought her other leg onto the cushions and sat up straight, folding her legs under her. Reaching down, she grabbed the bottom of her shirt. She pulled it up. Her breasts lifted as she tugged her head out of the shirt and lowered when she tossed it away.

Her breasts were firm and sat high on her chest. They weren't overly large, but definitely weren't small, either. Her nipples were dark points in the front.

She started crawling toward him again. She put her arms on either side of him. "I know we shouldn't. But right now, I don't give a shit. Just kiss me. Now."

Mark stopped fighting and kissed her.

CHAPTER TWENTY-FIVE

Jagger awoke with a yelp. The nightmares of being beaten were already fading from his mind, the accompanying shouts dwindling away in ghostly resonances. Looking around, he couldn't remember where he was or how he'd gotten there. Pointing his nose in the air, he sniffed. A pleasant breeze stirred the trees, making the leaves rattle softly. Scents wafted into his nose and, as he became more alert, his memory returned, bringing with it the tastes he'd found so pleasurable and satisfactory.

He'd traveled all night and most of the morning—sprinted for a while, walked even longer, and had eventually curled up under an Evergreen near a stream.

He'd slept.

Now he needed to urinate. And his muscles ached. His stomach felt as if it was being stomped from how hungry he was. He remembered the blood's taste, remembered glugging it like water on a hot day. The meat, warm and tender, springy with flavor as he'd chewed. There had been an immense satisfaction that had come with the kill, a soothing rush that had made the buzzing in his head stop. That had made the hunger pains causing his stomach to feel as if it was trying to eat itself go away.

Jagger rolled onto his stomach. Looking around, he kept his ears open to the sounds around him. He heard birds singing far away. Wings flapped from somewhere nearby. Twigs snapped and leafage rustled as things scurried about. The sounds of flowing water nearby reminded him how thirsty he was.

Those didn't interest him. Somehow he knew they could do nothing for the craving that made him sick with need.

Crawling out from under the shade of the Evergreen's bushy branches, he squinted at the forest's brightness. Pine needles dangled

JAGGER

from his filthy fur.

Looking from side to side, he saw trees that seemed to carry on endlessly. He sniffed the breeze and didn't detect any suspicious scents.

Last night, he had been sniffing Teresa's tires when the first car had arrived. He'd heard it coming and was already fleeing into the woods when the car had shown up.

From the bordering woods, he'd watched the man walk around. The temptation to attack him had been so strong, it had made Jagger shake. He'd known better than to try. The man had had something in his hand that Jagger knew could hurt him, so he'd kept his distance.

The man had also had fragrances clinging to him that Jagger sensed above all others, an aroma Jagger had once enjoyed, had once loved...had once trusted.

Home.

Amy.

Jagger had also smelled Amy in Teresa's car, traces of his old home had been all over the tires. He'd collected a range of scents from the rubber treads and had them stored away. Without any conscience thought, Jagger had decided to trace those smells back to home.

Nose to the ground, Jagger searched for a place to urinate. He didn't want to claim any of this territory as his, so he was careful to avoid areas he sensed other markings. He finally found a spot near another tree that looked dead and bare among the luscious timber. He cocked his leg and relaxed his muscles. A heavy stream of urine poured out, pelting the ground. It felt great and seemed to take some of the edge away from his thoughts. When he finished, he turned a circle and squatted. Once his bowels were empty, he felt better and lighter.

But the hunger remained, mingling with the anger inside that he couldn't calm, brewing into an inner storm that seemed to be growing stronger.

A vision of Amy lying next to him, stroking his fur, appeared in his head. He used to love sleeping next to her. The feel of her hand

210

petting the length of his back had once brought him peace. Now, the image caused rage to twist his insides. His colorless vision appeared to flicker with blinding flashes, tearing through his skull in spiky jabs.

Such thoughts confused him. And the confusion brought about even more anger. He blamed Amy for his pain, for his abuse. She'd betrayed him, had broken their bond, had allowed him to be taken, to be hurt. She'd caused the turmoil in his brain, the constant pains in his body that made him want to lash out.

In the vision, Amy's hand reached under his chin and lifted his head. She moved in to kiss his nose.

And Jagger opened his mouth and snapped his curved teeth down on her face.

The clap of his jaws connecting echoed around him, bouncing off the trees. So embroiled with his fantasy, he'd absently acted out the glorious bite. He huffed through his nose, licked his lips, and started walking.

He made his way to the stream and began to drink. He lapped up water for several minutes before turning away. Water ran down his jowls as his nose worked. Filtering through the odors around him, he processed those scents he'd store away. He wanted to find one that matched. He walked a long time before the scents spliced together perfectly like a piece of tape.

Jagger knew he was going in the right direction. It might take him some time, but eventually he would be home.

Chapter Twenty-Six

Mark stood behind a tree, unzipped his pants, and pulled out his penis. He started to urinate. Though he'd already peed a couple times today, his pee still came out in sputters from all the sex he'd had last night.

Four times.

It had taken that long for Amy to finally climax. He'd started to think it wasn't going to happen. They'd done it on the couch, lying on their sides and facing each other. The floor in the living room, with her bent over the coffee table and Mark slamming into her from behind. Moving to the hallway, he'd hoisted her against the wall and pounded into her until reaching his third release. And after a short break to catch his breath, he'd taken her into her bedroom and allowed her to get on top. It hadn't taken long before she'd begun shuddering on top of him, her head leaned back and crying at the ceiling.

With her release finally spent, Amy had come back to reality—quiet, distant. She'd all but told him to leave, saying she'd wanted to get some sleep and in the morning had to get some things done.

Her way of letting me know not to come around this morning.

And he hadn't. It was going on eleven and he hadn't even called her.

She hasn't called me, either.

Tapping the head of his penis, he winced at the tender ache he felt there. He zipped his pants and started back to his cruiser. He'd left it parked on the shoulder of the road. Being nowhere near a bathroom, a quick stop in the woods worked just fine. Wouldn't be the first time he'd had to make a quick pit stop on the side of the road.

Back in his car, he checked his cell phone for any missed calls or text messages. There were none. Amy would probably get in touch with him before too long. The shame of what she'd done last night would eventually wear off. She'd call. Might even apologize.

Hell with that. I'll apologize to her.

Shouldn't have let it happen.

How could he have refused?

I did *refuse. Kept telling her we shouldn't do it.*

He couldn't pretend he'd tried very hard.

I could've been anybody. Wouldn't have mattered to her.

Maybe, maybe not.

Checking the road for cars, he saw nobody coming from either direction. He drove off. Mark sipped some iced coffee through the thin straw poking out from the cup. It was melting and made slurping sounds as it traveled through the straw.

Driving along Goodson Lake Road, he took turns gazing out the passenger and driver side windows. This morning, the sheriff had told him to patrol for the dog until told otherwise. He'd probably get called off and put onto the dog fight investigation at some point, but right now, Mark was on Jagger duty since responded to the call. Though Pierce hadn't confirmed anything, they were working this as if Jagger was the killer dog.

Mark preferred it like this, really. Let the guys making the big bucks handle the rest. Besides, deep down, he wanted to be the one to find Jagger. He felt he owed it to Amy, especially after last night.

Yawning, Mark drank more coffee. He got three hours of sleep last night and was feeling it in every part of his body. He felt achy, sore as if he were coming down with something. It was supposed to be another scorcher of a day and the heat would only make him feel worse.

My own fault.

And Amy's.

He saw the sign warning him of a sharp curve ahead, so he slowed his speed. At the point of the curve, he spotted a large white truck parked on the turnoff before a large field that separated the wide expanses of woods. Blades of sunlight stabbed golden arcs through the clouds, making the thick grass twinkle like golden specks.

It was hard to read the words on the truck's door, but once he saw the cages in the back, he knew those words spelled out Animal Control.

Jeremiah.

Mark sighed. He eased the car onto the gravel border of the road, parking at an angle behind Jeremiah's truck. He leaned over so he could see out the window. He didn't spot Jeremiah right away. A light mist hovered around the area, glowing under the sunlight. It was actually a very lovely sight, but knowing Jeremiah was over there killed any admiration he might have for the scenery.

Get this over with.

He climbed out of the car, gently shutting the door. His feet made whispering sounds as he walked through the tall grass alongside the road. Patting his pocket, he felt the lumps of his keys through his pants. He didn't remember putting them there.

Mark stepped up to the rear of the truck and peered into the cages in the back. None of them looked large enough to hold Jagger.

Obviously Jeremiah didn't get my description of Jagger's size.

At the rear of the truck, Mark looked around. He saw no one. Birds chirped in the distance. Insects buzzed and chittered, the volumes growing and shrinking in alternating patterns. He saw some hay bales scattered out through the field like giant straw bunkers.

But he didn't see Jeremiah.

Mark walked beside the truck, heading to the front. On top of the hood, a man's elbow came into view. It jutted out, the tanned skin coming to a point. He followed the arm to where it was folded under a ball cap.

There he is.

Mark walked around to the front passenger wheel and stopped. Jeremiah was stretched out on the hood of his truck, a foot propped on the bumper and the other braced on his knee. He looked like someone enjoying a relaxing day on the beach, lying back as if relishing the feel of the sun. Though he had on dark sunglasses, Mark guessed his eyes were closed behind the shaded lenses. His face had a light brushing of stubble on the cheeks. His mouth hung partway open.

Mark detected the soft rattles of a snore.

Getting a few winks?

Mark wished he could too. But since he was on duty, he couldn't. And neither could their expert animal control officer.

He kicked Jeremiah's leg away from the bumper. The young man slid down the hood with a *"Whaaa!?!"* Arms flailing, he reached out, trying to grab onto something. He slipped off the front, quickly bringing his legs down and landing on his feet. He spun around, and leaned over the hood. His hands slapped the metal as if holding himself up.

Panting, he looked around. His face was pale with shock and confusion. After a moment, he turned to Mark and smirked.

"Funny, Varner."

"Good morning. Have a nice nap?"

"I wasn't sleeping," said Jeremiah. Taking off his cap, he scratched the closely cropped hair on top. He'd been out of the army for a couple years now, but had kept the hairstyle. "I was letting my eyes rest for a few minutes."

"Ah. So the snoring helps with that?"

Jeremiah took off his sunglasses and rubbed his tired eyes. "What do you want, Varner?"

"Saw the truck and thought I'd check in with you. You weren't at the briefing this morning."

"Didn't see why I needed to be. Figured that was about the dogfight stuff. Not my foray. I'm all about the animals, Varner. I leave the rest to you guys."

"Well, you should have at least been there to hear about the kind of dog we're looking for."

"I know. A Mastiff, right? I've seen them before."

"Not like this one, I'm sure."

"Maybe not. But one Mastiff is like any other."

Mark restrained a groan. "Not like this *one*."

Jeremiah puckered out his bottom lip, raising his eyebrows. He nodded. "All right. Color me intrigued. What's so special about this dog? I've got the report, his description, the whole works. What can you tell me that I don't already know?"

"This dog killed two grown adult men and a one adult woman without slowing down. We found some of its skin and fur matted to the end of a hammer. Pierce believes one of the victims attempted defending themselves."

"A good assumption."

"Do you know how hard they would have had to hit the dog to get a clump of its skin on it?"

"Pretty hard, I'd imagine."

"And it didn't affect this dog enough to even slow it down. After being bashed with a hammer, it *still* killed these people."

Jeremiah's face was already a little pale from fatigue, but Mark watched as it turned an even lighter shade. "I'm prepared for all kinds, Varner. This isn't my first day on the job."

"What cage do you expect to haul him back in if you *do* catch him?"

"The big one."

Mark remembered the one on the end. Though it was big, it was not enough to contain Jagger. "This dog weighs nearly two-hundred damn pounds, Jeremiah. Vet records confirm it. How do you plan on cramming something that big inside that thing? Going to fold him up like a piece of paper before putting it in an envelope?"

"It'll be fine. I've hauled coyotes and even a panther in that damn cage. Ain't no dog going to make me change my procedure, Varner. All these animals are the same, you know that. I know we don't like each other very much, but the one thing about you I always admired was your abhorrence to these bastards. You hate them nearly as much as I do. But don't you dare think you can come here and tell me how to do my fucking job. I'd put my foot in your ass before I'd allow that to happen."

"Wow," said Mark. "Threatening to kick my ass?"

"I'm not threatening anything. I'm just saying—*fuck off.*"

Mark felt heat rising from the collar of his shirt. Sweat had broken out along his hairline.

Jeremiah turned away from him, walking toward the field. "I parked here because I know he'll come this way. I read the report. It stated footprints put him going west, into the woods. Since no one has reported the dog's termination or capture, I figure he's still on the move. He'll stick to the woods because he'll feel safer there, concealed, away from the open areas. He'll have to cross this field to get to these woods." He pointed to the woods on his left.

Jeremiah turned back to the dense woods on the right. "Hell, he might even be out there now, watching us, sizing us up. Seeing if we're any kind of threat to him."

Mark looked toward the thick bushy trees that stood close together with darkness filling the gaps between them. Jagger could easily be hiding out there, shrouded by the cover the woods provided.

"And you'll be here to nab him," said Mark.

Jeremiah looked back at Mark from over his shoulder. "That's right." He smiled.

"With your tiny-ass cage."

Jeremiah's smile sagged. "Don't you have somewhere to be?"

Mark figured he could probably get along fine with Jeremiah if his personality wasn't always ruining it. He came from Boston, though he'd lived in North Carolina long enough to lose some of the sharpness from his accent. He was one of those types that thought he was surrounded by idiots, and Mark was inclined to agree with him for the most part. However, Jeremiah conducted himself on the job as if he were levels above his fellow officers in skill and knowledge, as if he were light years ahead of them.

And Mark could never fully like—or respect—somebody like

that.

"I just want you to understand," said Mark. "I've seen pictures of this dog. And he's a beast. I doubt even you, in all your infinite wisdom and experience, has seen anything like him."

Mark pulled the crumpled sheet of paper out of his back pocket. Carla had handed him a stack of them before he'd left the station this morning. Flattening it out, he saw Jagger's happy face on the front. The information was printed below it.

"The vet's office emailed this picture to us this morning. He's so big they took pictures of him to hang on a bulletin board in the waiting area."

He handed the paper to Jeremiah, who studied the image for a few moments. There was a brief flicker of concern that passed on Jeremiah's face.

Looking up at Mark, Jeremiah smiled. "I welcome the challenge. Ain't no damn dog going to beat me."

CHAPTER TWENTY-SEVEN

On her back, the sheet pulled over her breasts, Amy stared at the ceiling. Daylight filtered through the curtains, filling the room with a calming brightness. She felt a combination of guilt and relief from last night's activities. That enjoyable soreness inside was back after such a long absence. And it was a feeling she was glad to have, though she hated how she'd gotten it.

And she really hated how she'd acted toward Mark when they'd finished.

What's wrong with me?

Sighing, Amy had no answer for that one. She sat up. The sheet fell away from her, and she kicked it off her legs. Last night had been a great distraction from the news Mark had delivered to her. After she'd coldly forced Mark to leave, she had a restless night of sleep, tormented by nightmares. Her body felt great, less bogged down after her powerful release, but everywhere else she felt incredibly drained.

Bad dreams of Jagger attacking Teresa had replayed in a constant cycle.

In the nightmare, Teresa had begged Amy for help.

"He's going to kill me!" she'd screamed.

Amy had shaken her head. "That's not like Jagger."

Then he'd arrived and suddenly they were in the woods, and Amy had stood behind a tree, her hands gripping the rugged bark while Jagger tore Teresa limb from limb. She'd tried commanding him to stop, but her orders had been ignored. And during the process, she'd kept thinking: *This isn't like him. He's a good dog. A good dog.*

"He's a good dog," she muttered.

But three people were dead because of him. One of them was

someone he considered a friend.

He was just defending himself.

Amy knew that was only a smidgen of truth. Mark's explanations of the attacks proved there was too much evidence of brutality for it to have simply been a defense kill.

He'd eliminated them, picked them off one by one.

And now he was on the run.

Still, she couldn't fathom that her Jagger had done those things. This was the same big goofball she'd watch roll around on his back in the yard, kicking his legs in the air and spinning circles as he scratched all the itchy spots. This was her cookie eating companion. Though he wasn't picky with his choices, lemon-flavored sandwich cookies were his favorite. Whenever Amy brought them home from the store, he knew what she had just by the particular crinkling the packaging made inside the shopping bag.

She'd never seen Jagger act hostile toward anybody. Other than the guy in the park, his only other enemy was the UPS man. And Amy had to admit she was glad Jagger showed the man his teeth whenever he came to drop off a package. He was a good looking guy, but very creepy and awkward. She got the feeling whenever he looked at her that he was trying to picture what she looked like underneath her clothes.

With Jagger gone, who will protect her from him?

The UPS guy? Really?

Who would protect her from the people living around her?

What would she do if an intruder broke in? Or if Jim came back to spy on her lying out in the sun?

When she'd finally decided to move into her father's house, she had known she would need to get a dog. A big one, too. And Jagger was perfect for her. Nobody messed with her whenever she walked around collecting lot rent with Jagger on the leash.

If Jehovah's Witnesses came knocking on the door, usually all it took to run them off was the deep thunder of Jagger's barking.

KRISTOPHER RUFTY

I want him back!

Tears misting her eyes, Amy crawled out of bed. She wasn't going to cry right now. She'd done enough crying the past two days and enough was enough.

For now.

Standing beside the mattress, she stretched her arms high. She pushed up on the tips of her toes. The movement pulled at her muscles. She felt a tingling lug work down her back and into her calves. Then she bent over, touched her toes, and felt another wave wriggle back through her body. When she stood up straight, her muscles felt loose and relaxed. The tightness from her fitful sleep was gone.

She needed to do something. She had no idea what, but she couldn't sit around here all day again.

I have to get out there.

Amy wanted to find Jagger herself. The cops would just kill him on sight. To them, he was a dog who'd turned wild and needed to be put down. Even if he had gone mean, she wouldn't be convinced he was the monster Mark had told her about until she saw him for herself.

She got her clothes together and left her bedroom.

Inside the bathroom, with the hiss of the shower tapping the tub as the water heated, she stared at herself in the mirror while it slowly fogged up. Her mind was a fury of thoughts and worries. She dreaded finding him maybe a little more than not. She was scared to learn what kind of wild animal he'd become.

Under the shower's hot spray, she washed herself as her thoughts continued to stampede in her head. She understood how slim her chances of finding him were, but she was going to try.

What do I do if I see him?

That was another concern she had no resolution for.

CHAPTER TWENTY-EIGHT

Kenny threw the flat stone at the pond. It stabbed into the water at an angle and skipped across the surface a couple times before plunging into the murky depths. "Just like that," he said.

Brianna scrunched her face, poking out her bottom lip as she tried to hold the stone he'd found for her. She reached her arm back and even before she tossed it, Kenny knew it wasn't going to do anything.

It crashed into the water.

And sank.

"Oh, hell," said Brianna, shaking her head. Her red ponytail rocked behind her. "I suck at this."

Laughing, Kenny bent over and grabbed another stone from the collection he'd gathered earlier. "No, you don't. Your form's just wrong."

"My form?" She arched an eyebrow. "I thought you liked my form."

Kenny smirked. "This form, yeah." He reached out, cupping a breast. The fabric of her bikini top was slick under his hand. He felt the point of her nipple pushing against his palm, hard and stiff.

Closing her eyes, Brianna smiled. "I thought so."

The sunlight made her freckles seem darker than usual. Her creamy skin was speckled with them as if she'd drawn them on with marker. She was embarrassed by them, but to Kenny, the faded dots made her even lovelier.

He pulled his hand away from her breast and replaced the springy feel in his hand with the flat hardness of the stone. Curling his forefinger around the top, he angled his thumb under the bottom, turning his hand into a backwards C around the gray shard. "You hold it like this," he said.

Brianna crouched in front of him, and sorted through the rocks.

JAGGER

He liked the shapes of her legs, how they bowed out, lean and curvy. He could see the imprint of her groin through the purple sheath of her bikini bottoms.

His swimming trunks became tight as his erection grew.

Finding a rock she was happy with, Brianna stood up. "How's this one?"

"Good," he said. "Now hold it like this."

He watched her awkwardly struggle to get her fingers just right. She needed to use her other hand to push her thumb down into the correct position. Finished, she held her hand out. "How's this?"

"Looks okay to me," he said. "Now turn sideways."

He turned his body so he was facing her. Mirroring his stance, she put her back to him. He glimpsed the muscles in her back pulling taut as she raised her arm, the milky skin tightening and freckles lurching. Her rump jutted out, pushing against the shiny seat of her briefs in a smooth arch.

"And when you throw," he said, "stop your arm and flick with your wrist. Know what I mean?"

"Sort of," she said, looking at him from over her shoulder. A few strands of fiery red dangled around her eyes. "Show me, again."

He threw his stone, watching it twirl as it lowered to the water. It smacked the surface and bounced four times before sinking. That was his best one yet today.

Brianna laughed and cheered. "Way to go!"

"Now you do it."

"Okay," she said, turning away from him.

He watched her body move as she got the stance just right. She pulled her arm back, hips turning slightly. He glimpsed a pale strip of breast behind the bikini. Then she pivoted on her heels, flinging her arm out, and releasing the rock. It twirled away from her.

The rock went out further than his had before hitting the water. It pranced across a couple times, then was snatched under by the cloudy water.

Bouncing, Brianna clapped her hands and cheered. She spun around, hopping in place. Her breasts shook and jiggled with her celebration. "I did it!"

"Yes, you did!"

"Did you see that? It skipped right across!"

"I saw it. A champion quality display."

She came to him, pressing her warm body against his and hugged him. "You really are a great coach, you know?"

"Well, you're my star player."

Moaning, Brianna writhed against him. He felt the slickness of her bikini rubbing his bare chest. She looked up at him with her gray eyes, the outer corners narrowing to points to give her a constant expression as if she were doing something naughty. "Got a prize for your all-star player?"

Smiling, Kenny leaned down and kissed her. Her lips were smooth and moist, a thin upper strand and plump bottom made it easy for his mouth to insert into hers. He felt sweat dotting the skin above her upper lip, smearing over his as they kissed.

During moments like these, it was easy to forget how wrong their relationship truly was. He was twenty-six and the coach of Brianna's softball team. She'd just turned sixteen back in April and had gotten her license on the last day of school. It made meeting her easier, but the risk of getting caught would never completely go away.

Sometimes he thought his sister suspected he was closer to Brianna than he should be, but she'd never accused him of anything. She was the reason he'd taken on coaching the team in the first place, so this was, in a way, her fault as much as it was his.

Nice try, Kenny. Can't blame her for your stupidity.

He'd known he had a connection with Brianna from their first conversation. He'd called all the players to introduce himself and talk about his plans for the season. She'd laughed at all his jokes and had talked openly with him. Her voice had hooked him right away. It had a husky tone to it, like a sweet whisper, as if she were talking to him in secret. And when she laughed, it flowed out of her loud and smooth. Their phone chat had lasted longer than all the others.

But it wasn't until the night after the team's third practice that things became interesting. He was sitting in his car, parked in line at a drive through when she'd texted him.

Doing anything?

He wasn't then, but had been ever since.

But I'm happy. Damn it, I'm really happy.

And so was she, at least he thought so.

Brianna pulled away with a smack. "Ready to go swimming?"

Kenny turned his head to look at the water. Where the rocks had skipped, he saw dirty clouds swirling just beneath the surface. He felt himself wince. "In there?"

"Sure! Why not?"

"There're probably leaches in there."

Laughing, Brianna pressed her breasts tighter against his chest. "You're so silly. There aren't any leaches out here."

"I hate to disagree with the lady who's rubbing her hot body against me, but this is the perfect place for them to be. One dip in there and we'll have them clinging to us."

Brianna rolled her eyes. "Whatever!"

"And this is Dinky's Pond, right?"

"So?"

"Isn't that where they found that dead body last year?"

Brianna frowned, thinking. "I think you're right." She stuck out her bottom lip to form a fake pout. "Aw, boo. Now I'm sad."

"Let me make it up to you," he said, rubbing his finger down her sweat-slick neck. It slid down the hollow of her throat, dipping into a shallow puddle of perspiration. He ran it lower, over the ridges of her chest, turning it to glide over a slope of her breast. His finger slipped

228

behind the bikini patch.

Brianna sucked in a gasp. "Kenny?"

Smiling, he looked up at her. "Lay down on..." His words petered out when he saw the horrified look on her face. "What's wrong?"

"There...look." Her wide eyes didn't blink. Her lips curled around her teeth, nearly a grimace as she thrust her chin up.

"What are you talking about?"

"*Look!*"

Kenny turned his head to look behind him, not knowing what to expect. The smile still hung on his face, though it felt strange, like a plastic appliance. His first thought was he was going to see her father standing somewhere behind him with a shotgun.

He saw no one, and kept his awkward-feeling smile.

It dropped away when he saw the impossibly huge dog. Its dark fur was disheveled on its bulky body, caked with filth and some kind of paste that was not unlike strawberry jam. Its hackles were raised from its snout all the way to its tail like a dingy Mohawk. The dark lips trembled around teeth that curled out like hooks. Water streamed down its chin, dripping onto its puffed out chest.

The dog must've been drinking from the pond when we showed up. How did we not see it?

Because they were too involved with each other, holding hands, prancing around each other and sneaking kisses. Not realizing that something so ridiculously monstrous was just feet away from them.

And now we're screwed.

An assembly of chaotic thoughts scaled his mind, most of them hoping neither he nor Brianna were bitten. How would they explain what they'd been doing to an ER doctor? Her parents would find out they were together and then he'd have to convince them he wasn't being uncouth with their daughter.

The dog put a beefy paw forward.

"Oh...shit..." Kenny muttered.

JAGGER

Brianna pressed against him. "What do we do?"

"Don't run..."

"Oh, Kenny..." Her breaths were hot and quick on his sweaty skin.

"Start walking backwards," he said. "Slowly."

"O...okay..."

He heard a squeaky moan resonate from Brianna as she took a small step in reverse. The dog didn't move. It watched, growling.

It was Kenny's turn to take a step of his own.

And the dog did as well.

Brianna started to cry.

Putting his hand on the small of her back, he felt her skin quivering. "Calm down," he told her. "Just keep going. He'll see we don't mean him any harm and he'll go away."

Though, Brianna didn't reply, she gave a quick nod. She sucked her lips inward, biting down.

They moved back a little more. The dog followed, keeping a slow, stalking pace. His erect tail stuck out behind him like a furry saber. Kenny had never seen such a big dog in all his life. It easily reached his hips in height, and the dark color of its pelt gave it an overall semblance to a small bear.

It wore no collar, but its claws looked manicured.

Somebody owns this bastard.

Man's best friend to Leatherface.

"He's still coming," said Brianna in a shouting whisper. Her husky voice was choked and sharp.

"Yeah," said Kenny. He wished he was more educated on how to handle situations like this. But how could he have known to prepare for such an event? "Here's what we're going to do."

He felt Brianna turn slightly, her head twisting toward him. When he looked at her, he saw her eyes were spilling tears down her face. She looked so vulnerable, scared. And alone. He quickly leaned in, kissing her softly. Her lips were moist and salty from her tears.

"We're going to turn around," he said. He felt her tensing up, trying to pull away from him. "Stop it."

"I don't want to..."

"Listen to me." Brianna stopped fighting, her body going slack. Her head dropped down. "We're going to turn around and keep walking. Okay? If we show him we're no longer interested, he'll stop trying to defend himself. He wants the damn pond so bad, he can have it."

"Will it work?" she asked without looking up.

He thought, *I have no idea* but he said, "I think so."

Looking over his shoulder, he glimpsed the dog. It hadn't budged. It watched them, probably waiting to see what their next move would be.

Kenny faced Brianna. "Ready?"

"No..."

"Let's do this."

Kenny turned first, putting his back to the dog. It felt much worse this way, knowing it was there but not being able to see it. He could feel its angry eyes all over him.

"Your turn," Kenny said.

Brianna screamed.

Kenny was turning around when he felt something like a horse kick on his back. The impact threw him forward, sent him crashing to the ground. His chin scraped the damp earth.

Dazed, he looked up. His vision was jittery, tilting in all directions. He could make out Brianna stepping away from him, her hands up to her mouth as she sobbed.

"Bri...?"

The weight pounded him again, pressing him into the mud. Hot breath wafted across the nape of his neck, making the hairs stand up. He felt warm droplets of the dog's slobber trickle across him, getting in his hair.

Kenny reached out for Brianna. "Help!"

231

JAGGER

She acted as if she were about to come forward, then hesitated. Before Kenny felt the dog's mouth on the back of his neck, Brianna ran away.

Leaving Kenny behind.

He cussed her in his mind.

Then the dog bit down, igniting a brief flurry of pain before Kenny went numb from the neck down.

His last thought before he died was something about being paralyzed.

Jeremiah was opening the cooler he kept in his truck when he heard something that might have been a scream. He listened, but heard nothing more than the buzzing of June Bugs.

He stuck his hand in the cold water, grabbed an ice cube and pulled it out. He rubbed it across the back of his neck, cringing from the brutal frigid kiss. The ice quickly melted, trickling down his shirt in a chilly path. He flicked the excess water from his fingers, then reached inside the cooler's cold pool again. This time his hand found a can.

Stepping back, Jeremiah let the lid close with a soft thump. He used his knee to shut the passenger door. The Pepsi was slick and wet in his hold, dripping across the ground as he walked back to the front of the truck. Using his index finger, he popped the tab, then raised it to his mouth and guzzled. The soda was cold and sweet, wonderful on his throat as it swished down.

Damn, it's getting hot.

His clothes felt hot and uncomfortable on his body, itchy on his skin. The hat kept the sun off his face, but did nothing to shield him from the heat. He was starting to think hanging out here hadn't been such a good idea.

It's better than being cooped up in the truck.

There was no A/C in there, so no matter how hot it was out here, it was nothing compared to how stuffy and unbearable it would be *inside* the truck.

He'd hang out here a little longer, praying for the sun to move behind the trees so he could have some shade. He had a sandwich in the cooler that his stomach growled to have, but the heat had ruined his appetite.

Damn. Varner was right. I'm going to have a damn heat stroke out here. What the hell am I doing?

Waiting for the dog to come through, simple as that. He was certain that it would. Dogs stuck to a formula in their behaviors, moving on an autopilot they probably didn't even realize they had. If it had fled west, it would continue west until finding a spot to claim as home.

He'd hoped it would have gotten here a little sooner. The idea of spending all day out here was not something he was anxious to do.

Jeremiah guzzled more Pepsi. His stomach was starting to hurt a little from how fast he was drinking. He didn't care. The soda was refreshing. He might even have another.

Someone screamed from the woods.

Jeremiah jumped. The can slipped from his fingers and smacked the ground. He could hear the fizzy gulps of soda pouring out. He stepped toward the field, pausing when his feet crunched dehydrated weeds. Staring across the tall stagnant grass, his eyes moved along the trees. He saw no one, but he was certain he'd heard a scream. There was no mistaking it. Sounded like a woman.

Not a woman, a girl. Young.

Jeremiah turned away from the field and ran to the back of his truck. He saw the rubber guard of the catch pole poking out from between the cages. Reaching over the tailgate, he pulled it out, letting the end drop to the ground. He held it like a staff as he returned to the front of his truck.

He patted his left hip and felt the hump of the tranquilizer gun.

JAGGER

A dart loaded for a hundred pounds was inside, plus he had two more in the clips with the same mixture. With such a big dog, the first shot would only slow it down, hopefully long enough for him to reload and shoot it again. A third shot would kill the dog, but it was there if needed.

And if for some reason the sleeping sauce wasn't enough, he had his 9 mm Browning on his other hip.

More screams resonated from the woods. Closer now.

He started running.

Brianna dashed through the woods. Low-hanging limbs whipped her exposed skin, leaving pink stripes across her milky flesh where the bikini didn't cover. All she had on her feet were flip-flops, and though they made running more difficult, she didn't want to lose them. Not on this uneven terrain where roots seemed to be jutting up from the ground everywhere she turned. She wished she would have at least thought to grab her shirt. It wouldn't have protected her from much, but maybe her skin wouldn't be hot in a flurry of stings.

You bitch. Kenny's dead and you want your damn shirt!?!

Tears filled her eyes, turning her vision blurry. Poor Kenny, poor stupid Kenny. He'd brought them out here so they could be alone without worrying somebody might see them together.

And now he was dead.

His head was nearly bitten off!

In one bite, the dog had left a large conduit in Kenny's neck so deep that the top of his spine could be seen through the gross tendons and meat. And something that looked like a clear hose. It hung out of his throat, off to the side, curling out from the gore.

Hopefully it didn't hurt much. Hopefully it was quick and he didn't suffer.

What do you care?

She cared plenty. Kenny had been great to her, better than anybody ever had been, including her parents. She loved their time together. Maybe she even loved *him*.

And he's dead. Because he wanted to be with me, he's dead!

What was she going to tell people when they found out? What was her dad going to say when he learned she had been fooling around with someone almost ten years older than her?

He's going to hate me. He'll say something about being right about me.

Mom would probably go into her bedroom and pray for days, and fast from food.

But Brianna would have to find her car first before any of that could happen. She'd met Kenny in the gravel parking lot beside the ball field and they'd hiked out to the woods from there. She had no idea which direction she was heading now, but she doubted it was the one she needed to be going in. She was all turned around and confused, running anywhere that would take her away from the dog.

Where's it at? Is it still following me?

Slowing down so she wouldn't crash into a tree, Brianna stole a quick glance over her shoulder.

The dog wasn't far behind, keeping his pace steady as he leaped over a fallen branch.

Brianna screamed. She turned around and pushed herself harder. Her arms worked at her sides, fists thrusting into the air. She felt her breasts bouncing in front of her, the straps of her bikini hauling them back.

She cut to the left, and rushed toward a throng of large Evergreens. They stood tall in even rows that went on for a great distance. How perfectly they were arranged and consistently spaced, Brianna supposed somebody had planted them. Maybe she was getting close to a house, or a farm.

Please!

Brianna entered a corridor between the Evergreens. Darkness

dropped over her, messing with her vision. From the bright light of the woods, she felt as if she had suddenly put on sunglasses. She saw flashes whenever she blinked. Tiny splotches burst ahead of her. A sweet odor that reminded her of Christmas hung in the air. It felt so much cooler in this piney chasm than it had in the woods.

She kept running. Her legs hurt, feet throbbed each time they slapped down on the ground. A funny tingling feeling spread through her thighs. The flip-flops slid on the carpet of tiny needles and loose dirt.

Brianna was over halfway through the Evergreen fortress when she saw a blinding sheet of daylight up ahead. It looked as if a portal had opened at the end of the sweet-smelling stretch. At first she wasn't sure what she was seeing, but as she neared it, she realized it was the end of the line. The woods were ending on what she believed was a field.

This gave her exhausted body a surge of encouragement. She kicked her legs harder, stretched them wider to increase her gait. Hopefully the field was close to a road and not just a random clearing. If she got out there and saw she was still in the middle of nowhere, she might just give up.

No! I won't!

She didn't chance looking behind her. The heavy pants and grunts of the dog were back there, so she didn't need the visual confirmation to know it was still after her. It seemed no matter how hard she pushed herself, she couldn't get ahead. The dog was playing with her, allowing her to stay in front of him. If it wanted, it could end this chase and have her.

And kill me just like Kenny!

Why didn't it? Was this a big game?

Brianna was so lost in her thoughts, she didn't notice she'd exited the woods until the sun was blinding her. It reminded her of her dreams, how they always seemed to be washed out, burning her eyes with brightness. The glare caused tears to stream down her face. The soft ground that had been padded with needles and fuzzy bristles quickly turned hard and bumpy.

She stumbled to one side, almost falling, losing one of her flip-flops in her near tumble. Thick grass brushed her legs, making them itch.

"This way!"

A voice?

Staggering, Brianna looked right and could see a smeared moving shape. It looked like a blurry movie as the dark form seemed to stretch and wave from side to side.

"Help me!" she cried.

"I'm coming!"

Brianna shuffled through the high grass, her feet dropping into hovels, throwing her off balance. She stumbled, fell onto her knee, but quickly pushed herself back up and ran. Now she had lost her other flip-flop, and her bare feet slapped down on spiky earth.

Vision clearing, she began to make out she was in a field. The weeds were very high, tickling her hips. She spotted a few bales of hay that looked like giant pieces of wheat cereal along the edges. She looked forward and loosed a wild cackle of relief when she saw the man.

He was dressed in the tan markings of a police uniform. In his waving hand was a gun of some kind.

"Come to me," he shouted, hurdling through the tall grass as if he were running in snow.

Then she remembered the dog. It had been right behind her. Spinning around, she peered at the border of Evergreens. The corridors between the trunks were filled with impenetrable darkness. She saw no dog, only specks of shimmering sunlight cutting through the shadows.

"Is it coming?" she heard the man shout. "The dog? Is it after you?"

Brianna turned around. How'd he know about the dog? "Yes!"

The man halted, holding the gun away from him and angled up. His eyes scanned the area. "Where?"

"I don't know! It was right behind me!"

She was close enough to him now that she could see his nod. He ushered her forward with his other hand. "Come on. I'll get you in my truck. You'll be safe there."

Safe.

A word that had never held much meaning to her before had become the most gloriously spoken form of the English language. She felt a smile tug the corners of her parched mouth so high they burned.

Brianna was about to start heading his way when the cop's eyes widened in frenzied shock.

"Shit!" he yelled.

Then he was yanked down. He vanished into the abyss of brown weeds.

Brianna screamed, clawing at her own face as if she could somehow scrape away what she'd seen.

The weeds trembled. She heard short angry growls, juicy ripping. The cop unleashed a tormented wail that bordered on a howl. Blood sprayed up in a thick mist, thinning as it splashed the weeds.

More screams were like a slap on her rump that threw her back in this nightmare.

She ran.

For the second time today, she left somebody behind to die so she could live.

Guilt would probably come eventually, but right now all she could focus on was her own survival.

She spotted the cop's truck. It wasn't very far away, but at the rate she was moving, it could have been two miles. The ground titled and dipped every few steps, making her stumble. Her bare feet snagged holes. Sharp things jabbed her. Something sent a stinging pang up her leg that she assumed was a wasp.

Almost there!

The truck grew in size as she neared. She glanced behind her, expecting to see the dog still busy with the cop.

He was just a short distance behind her, tearing through the weeds. They parted around his bulky front, his big feet scraping up dirt as they yanked him forward. Crimson froth coated his jaw like a foamy beard. His evil eyes were the color of piss.

Screaming, Brianna nearly lost her balance. Her foot slipped out to the side, but she was quick to counter the weight. She turned in a circle. When she straightened, she was off her path. The truck was over to the right now. She would have to cut across at an angle to get to it.

Bearing right, she dashed in front of the dog, feeling the hot wind of its snapping teeth. One foot in the field, the other on cut grass, she rocked each way as she made for the truck. Her arms flapped, keeping her upright as if she were walking a tight rope.

Spinning around, she glimpsed the dog exiting the field. She angled toward the truck. The dog's feet pounded the ground, sounding like rocks raining from the sky.

Brianna wouldn't have time to open the door, so she bypassed it. Headed for the rear tire. She threw her wasp-stung foot forward, briefly noticing how much it had swollen. Her toes hooked the edge of the tire, fingers curled over the lip of the truck bed. She heaved herself up and forward. A cold moistness streaked the back of her calve, marking a path down to her heel. She recognized it as being the dog's wet nose, narrowly missing the meaty chunk of her lower leg. Her foot rose above the powerful clamp of its jaws.

She dived into the back of the truck. The top of her head bumped metal. Her legs carried her over, flipping her, the heels of her feet banging against jagged objects. Things clattered, scooted around as if to make room for her. She landed on her back, her legs spread and bent, feet hooked above her.

Something slammed against the truck, rocking it as if a car had crashed into the side.

Sitting up, Brianna noticed her feet were hooked over the edges of cages. Different sizes and widths, a taller cage had lifted her right leg higher than left, making her thighs burn with tightness. She pulled her feet down, dragged her legs to her, and hugged her knees to her chest.

The dog growled and barked below, banging against the truck, his claws squealing across the metal. It made a sound like knife blades slashing steel.

Burying her face between the tight valley between her thighs, Brianna cried.

Chapter Twenty-Nine

Mark sat beside Brianna in the back of the ambulance, staring at the blank page of his notepad. He'd hoped to get some useful information before the paramedics escorted her to the hospital and she was pumped full of drugs.

Not happening.

The girl was too succumbed by shock to offer him any information. He couldn't blame her. After what she'd gone through, she was lucky to not have died from fright.

A paramedic stuck her head in. She was a thick woman, not fat by any means, but buff and stocky, with short dark hair.

"We've got to get going," she told him, annoyance in her voice.

Mark looked at Brianna, lying back on the stretcher. A sheet was pulled up to her throat. She had a natural fair complexion, but the day's events had left her skin in a sickly, almost green hue around the dark red of sunburn.

He tightened his lips, exhaled through his nose, and nodded. "All right," he answered the stocky woman.

Mark, keeping to a slight crouch, stood up from the bench. He gave Brianna one last glance, then dropped down from the bus.

"She give you anything valuable?" asked the medic.

Mark shook his head. "She's too far gone."

The big woman grunted as she climbed into the back of the ambulance. "Come by the hospital tomorrow afternoon, she might be able to talk then."

Tomorrow afternoon will be way too late. Jagger will be long gone by then.

Mark forced a smile. "Thanks."

JAGGER

He stepped back to avoid the door swinging past as the medic's partner closed it. He was much smaller and thinner than his female counterpart, and barely acknowledged Mark when he passed in front of him to get the other door.

"Varner!"

Mark turned around, recognizing Pierce's voice above the others who were shouting at each other and conversing all over the field.

The dark skinned man ran toward him, waving his hand above his head as if Mark might not know he was the one calling for him.

"Yeah, Pierce?"

Mark headed to meet the running man as the ambulance's siren began to wail. He heard it leaving the scene within seconds.

Pierce stopped at the front of Jeremiah's truck. Putting a hand on the hood, the other found his waist. He bent over slightly, panting. He was a thin man, but had a sagging gut that showed how little he exercised. His face was glossy under a sweaty sheen.

"What's wrong?" Mark asked the winded man.

"Deputies found another body."

A cold pang hit Mark's insides. "Where?"

"In the woods. A young man, probably early twenties."

Though, he didn't need to ask, he did so anyway. "A dog kill?"

Pierce nodded. "Yeah."

"Damn."

"We're about to cordon off the entire area and examine the scene."

Nodding, Mark put the pad into his shirt pocket. "All right. I'll be there in a couple minutes."

"I have to grab some things from my van, I'll walk with you."

"Fine."

Pierce jogged to the white van parked on the other side of Jeremiah's truck.

Mark stepped into the field. The sun had moved to the opposite side of the sky, veiling the field in much-needed shade. The woods would probably feel even cooler. It was late in the afternoon, though the temperature hadn't changed from its hottest peak.

All this from a dog that was once scared by a damn cat.

Nothing seemed to scare the dog now.

He looked at Jeremiah's truck and felt a pinch of remorse. The asshole had been right about the dog coming through here, but Mark was right that the animal control specialist had underestimated the severity of the dog's rage and strength. Jeremiah hadn't truly known what he was up against.

And now he's dead. Counting the man in the woods, that makes five.

Five people killed by one dog—a very large dog that had been a domesticated pet just a few days ago. Mark didn't understand how so much could have changed in such a short span of time, but he supposed that was irrelevant for now. The damage had happened, and Mark needed to stop it from continuing. He could worry about the causes later.

If only I would have come by sooner.

Mark had decided to swing over here and check on Jeremiah. After finding nothing all day, he'd wanted to see if the *animal expert* was having any luck.

And he'd stumbled upon a nightmare.

He saw the top of Pierce's black hair through the truck's windows. His bangs were bouncing above his eyebrows. He came around to the front of the truck, gripping a leather medical bag in his hand.

"Ready?" he asked.

Mark was not, but nodded. "Sure."

Pierce took a deep breath, held it a moment, and let it out, puffing his cheeks. "Let's get this over with."

Switching the bag to his other hand, Pierce started to turn, but paused. He looked over Mark's shoulder, eyes squinting as if doing so could make him see better. "Who's that?"

"Huh?"

Pierce raised his chin to point behind Mark. "There."

JAGGER

Mark turned to see what he was talking about. "Oh, shit," he muttered.

"Know her?" asked Pierce.

"Damn. What's she doing here?"

"Who is she?"

"Amy Snider. Damn dog's owner."

"Oh, shit."

"Yeah."

Amy looked rough as she stood on the shoulder of the road. She wore a baggy pair of gray lounge pants and a red tank top that clung to her front. The curves of her breasts and dots of her nipples were easily decipherable through the wispy garment. Her hair was pulled behind her head with golden sprigs hanging down the side of her face. Even from where he stood, he could tell she'd been recently crying. Her face was swollen and puffy, a little red as if she might have been drinking.

She spotted Mark and waved.

Turning to Pierce, he said, "Why don't you run along and I'll catch up in a few minutes? Going to see what she wants."

"Uh..." Pierce blinked several times as if waking from a trance. "Yeah, sure." He turned away and started walking, looking over his shoulder every few steps.

Mark watched him walk for a bit before turning back to Amy. She had stepped off the shoulder and was now at the taillight of Jeremiah's truck. Sighing, Mark headed to her.

Before he'd reached her, Amy said, "Did you find him?"

"What are you doing here?" He stopped in front of her. "You shouldn't be here. This is a crime scene."

"Crime scene? Oh, God..."

"How did you hear about this?"

"Wha...?" She looked at him. Her eyes were pink and watery. "I didn't hear about it. I was driving by. I've been out looking for Jagger all day...I'd given up and was on my way home when I saw..." By the end of her sentence, her voice had gone bubbly.

Mark thought he smelled beer on her breath.

"Okay," said Mark. He put his hands on her shoulders. "You need to go home. I'll be by in a little while, okay? I'll tell you all about it…"

"What happened?"

"Not now. You should get home…"

"*Tell* me." Though she didn't shout, the tone of her voice suggested she would soon if Mark didn't tell her something.

And he knew she'd been drinking. The smell seemed to radiate off her skin.

Sighing, he rubbed her shoulders gently. He shouldn't be showing her this kind of affection in front of so many people from the department, but he hoped touching her might calm her some. "Two people are dead. One survived. We're trying to sort out the details."

"Was it…Jagger?" Her lip trembled and she bit down on it. A tear budded in the corner of her eye, quivering as it prepared to drip.

Closing his eyes, Mark took a deep breath. When he opened them, he nodded.

Amy's shoulders bounced in his hands. Tears filled her eyes and trickled down her cheeks. "Oh…God…" Lowering her head, she acted as if she was about to lean against him, but suddenly jerked from his hold. She slapped his chest with both hands. "Don't fucking *touch* me!"

Mark jumped back, nearly gasping. He looked over his shoulder and noticed officers had assembled by the van. A couple held rolls of yellow tape in their hands. They'd paused on their way back to the field.

And were now watching the show with interest.

Heat ran up the back of Mark's neck. Turning to address Amy, he saw her swing at him a moment too late to avoid the punch.

It knocked his head to the side. He felt his jaw already swelling and trying to lock up as a dull throbbing sensation worked up to his ear.

"*Bastard!*" she shouted. "You took advantage of me! You were *fucking* me while Jagger was out here hurting people!" She swung her hands, slapping his chest over and over.

Mark tried to catch her wrists, but she was moving so fast. He couldn't grab her quick enough. Reaching for her arm, she twirled away, dodging him. Then she started running into the field.

"Jagger!" she cried. *"JAAAGERRRRR!"*

With her arms stiff at her sides, she ran slightly bent forward, continuously screaming for her dog. Mark couldn't believe what he was seeing and could only watch her in a sort of dumb silence. His jaw hurt, gums swelling inside his mouth. He was embarrassed and his feelings had been hurt by what Amy had said.

You were fucking me!

She'd made it sound just as he'd feared.

He'd taken advantage of a distressed woman.

And she's losing her shit.

Mark didn't chase after her.

She'd only run a few feet past Jeremiah's truck before Deputy Squirewell had dropped his roll of tape. Being a large guy who'd played college football, it took no effort for him to wrap his arms around her waist from behind and lift her off the ground.

Swinging her fists and kicking her legs, Amy continued to scream. She clawed at Squirewell's large hands clutched around her belly. Punched them. At one point, she tried to bite them. Her breasts shook loosely behind the thin shirt. Any moment they might fall out if she didn't calm down. It'd really give the other deputies an eyeful.

Mark could only shake his throbbing head as he watched Amy.

She's having a breakdown.

He saw Squirewell's head peek above Amy's shoulder. His eyes were just as wide as Mark's probably were. Though he didn't speak, he knew Squirewell wanted to know what to do with her.

"Just let her go," said Mark.

"She assaulted a deputy," said Squirewell.

"Two of them," offered somebody. Sounded like Deputy Bartlett.

"Jagger!" Amy screamed. Making a sound that was part hyperventilating and part maniacal laughter, Amy looked around with eyes that might pop from her skull. "Where are you!?! *Jaggerrrrrrr!*"

"I'm not going to book her for hitting me," said Mark. "I deserved it."

Amy slammed her elbow into Squirewell's ribs. He let out an *Oomph* and dropped her. She landed on her knees, started to get up, but Squirewell quickly pushed her back down. He wasn't forceful, or even abusive, but he was very *firm*.

Amy was on her stomach, kicking and pounding the ground like a kid pitching a wild tantrum. Squirewell, on one knee with another leg stretched across her back, pulled her arms behind her back.

He dug out his cuffs. "You might not book her for it," said Squirewell. "But I sure as hell am. Unlike you, I didn't *deserve* to get hit by this crazy bitch. Plus, she smells like she took a bath in beer!"

Amy tried to roll over, but Squirewell's burly leg wouldn't allow it. "Get off me, you *fuck!*"

Mark said nothing. There was nothing he could do at this point. He started walking toward the field.

Seeing he was leaving, Amy lifted her head. "Where are *you* going!?! What's this guy doing to me!?! *Ow!* Stop it, you fucking *fuckhead!*"

"You're going to jail," said Mark without looking back. "And I'm going to survey the damage your goddamn dog has caused."

He left Amy shrieking behind him.

Walking through the field, he felt eyes behind him and in front of him. He chose not to acknowledge any of them and keep his head straight as he made his way to the woods.

His jaw was really starting to throb, but he kept his hand gripping his belt so he wouldn't rub it. He didn't want the other deputies seeing how badly her punch had hurt. It would probably bruise and he'd get teased about it later.

Once he was behind the trees, he leaned against one and allowed himself to breathe. He felt jittery and humiliated.

Half the damn department witnessed that!

He was going to be in trouble. Word would get back to the sheriff that he'd had relations with Jagger's owner. He'd hear about her insane display on a crime scene. Sometime tomorrow Mark would be called into the sheriff's office…

Damn.

Mark might even get suspended, or demoted. He did not want to go back to working nights, no matter how much he sometimes missed it.

But, he supposed, if he got fired, going back to school would become a reality instead of a mild fantasy he toyed with on occasion.

He'd have no other choice.

"Mark!"

Pierce.

Pierce's voice had come from deeper in the woods.

"Yeah!" Mark fired back.

"Thought that was you. What was all that screaming about?"

Mark felt a burst of cold in his chest.

Whether he was reprimanded or not, he would never be able to live this down. He'd lost so much respect in a matter of minutes and soon would be the biggest joke in the department.

Finding Jagger was now a top priority, even more than it already had been. There would be hell to pay if the dog killed anyone else, so he needed to successfully bring the dog in to regain any kind of credit Amy had ruined for him.

Amy.

He felt bad for her. But he knew it wouldn't last once he suffered the repercussions from how riotously she'd behaved.

CHAPTER THIRTY

Amy was the last one left in the holding cells when the guard came to tell her she was going home.

Ellie got my message!

She'd left it on Ellie's answering machine this morning with her one phone call. She'd begged her to come bail her out and promised to explain later and promised she'd pay her back. But the day had carried on, and she was beginning to think Ellie wasn't coming.

Today wasn't as bad as last night.

She'd had to share a cage with a Latino woman who had shoulder-length black hair on one side of her head, and the other side was shaved bald. Words in Spanish had been tattooed to the exposed skin.

Amy had feared the Latino woman would be a talker or force her to *do things.*

But the woman had been silent the whole night and Amy had found herself wishing the woman would say something. *Anything.* The quiet had somehow seemed worse than if she'd been blubbering uncontrollably. Amy couldn't read her thoughts, so she never knew what was going on behind those cold dark eyes.

Thankfully the Latino mute was hauled out earlier this morning.

As Amy was being escorted down the hall by an officer who was probably somebody's grandpa, she wondered what time it was. She'd eaten three meals in the cage, waiting on Ellie to come. It had to at least be late evening, some time.

It doesn't matter now. I'm going home.

It took a few more minutes to get processed and her purse back, but she was finally allowed to leave.

Ellie was sitting on a bench in the side hall, reading from a Dean

JAGGER

Koontz paperback when Amy was let out. She looked up and smiled when she saw Amy approaching.

She closed the book. "There you are," Ellie said.

Amy sighed. She felt exhausted, as if the walk up to this point had sapped what energy she'd had left.

Frowning, Ellie put the book in her large purse and stood up. "Everything okay?"

Amy shook her head. "Not really. Nothing like a night in jail to make you realize how badly you screwed up to get put in there."

Ellie put an arm around her shoulder. "I bet so. Let's get out of here."

In Ellie's car, Amy stared out the window. It was dark outside, but the restaurants had lighted the street up in a gallery of neon beams. She saw the doughnut shop and her stomach grumbled. It was crowded for a weeknight, teenagers mostly, occupying the tables set up outside. She heard the clicking of a lighter and turned to find Ellie putting the flame to the tip of a cigarette.

"Don't mind do you?" asked Ellie.

Amy shook her head. "It's your car. Your rules."

"Don't worry," said Ellie, cracking her window. "I'll give you a ride to pick up yours from the impound lot in the morning."

She'd hoped to get it tonight, but the lot had closed at six.

Amy smiled. "Thanks. You've done enough already. And don't worry; I'll pay you back tomorrow too."

Ellie waved her hand. "Don't worry about. How about you just give us a few months free on the lot rent and call it even?"

"How about a year's worth?"

Ellie's eyes rose above her cigarette. "Even better."

Amy was apt to give her free lot rent for life for coming to her rescue tonight.

"I have to be honest," said Ellie. "I was more than a little surprised when Jim and I got home this evening and heard your message."

Amy squirmed in the seat. She felt the same as she used to whenever her mother had learned of something Amy had done wrong.

"I wasn't happy to make that phone call," said Amy.

"Care to tell me what happened?"

Amy didn't want to talk about it. She knew it would seem even worse hearing her voice speaking about it.

"Can we talk about it later?" asked Amy. "I just don't want to get into it right now. I'm so tired."

"It's fine," said Ellie. "Did your deputy lover come visit you in the cage?

Mark.

Remembering how she'd punched him, the things she'd said to him, made her feel tight and sick inside.

"Oh, God..." she muttered.

In the corner of her eye, she saw Ellie give her a glance. Though she said nothing more about Mark, Amy figured Ellie wanted to.

After a few long moments of silence, Amy finally spoke. "Did Big Jim mind you paying my bail?"

Ellie dragged off her cigarette. "No. I think he was just upset I was going to be leaving tonight."

"Aw," said Amy. "That's sweet."

"Not really. Tonight's our night to...you know..."

Ew. But they're so much older...

Amy hid her disgust and said, "Ah. I see."

"And I was glad to delay it!" Ellie laughed.

Amy laughed as well. It was mean to poke so much fun at Jim, but it felt good to laugh. Then she saw Jim leering at her from behind the trees and the laughter choked off.

I wonder if he thinks about me when they're...

"So, he can wait a little while," said Ellie.

Amy was thankful she'd spoken and stopped her mind from finishing that thought.

JAGGER

Ellie did most of the talking on their way back to Eagle's Nest. Amy responded here and there, but for the most part was very quiet. She figured Ellie wanted to know more about what had led to her spending a hair over twenty-four hours in jail. But the sweet woman didn't ask anything else about it.

Ellie also never mentioned Jagger.

Amy wondered if he'd been found yet.

I would've heard.

Maybe not. She'd been in jail, so there was no way to know for sure.

Mark would have told me.

He was the kind of person who'd keep her informed even after what she'd done to him.

I can't believe I said those things to him!

She'd *punched* him. Screamed like a lunatic.

Thinking back to it made her sweat. She felt heat rising from the clothes she'd had on for almost two days.

Though she wanted to apologize to Mark for how she'd acted, she was too mortified to contact him. If he came to see her, or if she bumped into him anywhere, she would tell him, then.

I can't call him.

Maybe tomorrow she'd send him an apologizing text.

Ellie drove them through Eagle's Nest. The trailers were long pale blocks in the night. Some were lighted by the glow of floodlights, others stood in darkness. Some had on lights inside glowing through the windows, some porch lights were on as if they were expecting company and others looked abandoned.

She glanced past Ellie and saw Jim had left a light on for his wife. She pictured him lying in bed, waiting on Ellie to come home and felt a ping of nausea.

Janice's trailer was dark, but she noticed a dim flickering inside from a TV.

They arrived at Amy's house. No lights were on at all. The only light came from a floodlight at the top of a power pole on the other side of the yard. Under the empty carport was a thick blackness.

Amy's Jeep was gone. Teresa's car was gone.

Teresa's car would never be parked under there again.

She felt her throat tightening.

I wonder when her parents are going to make the funeral arrangements.

She hadn't heard from Teresa's mom yet. She imagined she would soon. After all, it was Amy's dog that had killed her.

Hopefully she knows it wasn't my fault. Teresa was the one that took Jagger.

If Mrs. Hawking tried to blame Amy, she would remind her of that.

"Want me to walk you in?" asked Ellie, putting the car in park.

Amy swallowed the forming lump in her throat. "No thanks," she said. "Jim's waiting on you."

Ellie laughed. "I know. I'm probably in for a long night."

"Do you mind picking me up around nine?"

"To get your Jeep?"

Amy nodded. "Yeah. I want to get there as early as possible. It feels so weird, it not being here."

"I know. Kind of like you're trapped."

Trapped.

That was exactly how Amy felt.

"Got your keys?"

Amy checked inside her purse. She saw them sitting on top of her wallet. "Yeah."

"Well, come here."

Ellie reached over and hugged Amy. It felt good. There was nothing in the hug except for complete nurturing affection. No hidden meanings. Just a motherly embrace that Amy needed and was glad to have.

JAGGER

When the hug was over, Amy felt herself wanting another.

"Try and have a good night," said Ellie.

"I'll try my best."

"See you in the morning. I'll bring breakfast."

"Sounds good."

Light burst inside the car when Amy opened the door. She climbed out. As she headed for the back door, Ellie started backing the car up. By the time Amy reached the deck, Ellie was gone.

And Amy entered a dark house that seemed to smother her with its emptiness.

He was sleeping when the sounds of a car stirred him awake. Raising his head, he stared at the trailer. Headlights raked across the yard, burning his eyes as they swept by. He looked away.

A car door banged shut.

The crunching of footsteps called his attention back to the trailer. He saw the woman vanish on the other side. Different sounds came from inside, probably the man moving about.

A door opened.

"I'm home, Jimmy-tot!"

Then another door bumped shut. The sound of muffled voices drifted out from the trailer, but he'd already stopped paying attention to them as he laid his head back down. The urge to attack was there, but it was sedated and faint.

He'd walked all night and day, keeping away from the roads, avoiding people though his impulses had told him to attack. He'd ignored the rage, the cravings. His lust for blood had nearly forced him out of the seclusion the woods had offered multiple times.

But he'd kept moving.

And moving.

He'd walked in a continuous, slow and steady pace, heading in one direction.

Eventually the strange scents surrounding him had become familiar again, and he'd followed them like a map leading him here.

Now, his sated belly made him tired. And all he wanted to do was sleep.

His eyes fluttered shut and stayed that way.

The chickens had been enough food. He'd probably sleep all night.

CHAPTER THIRTY-ONE

Jim snuck out of bed, leaving Ellie sleeping. The sheets reached her ribcage, leaving her large breasts open to the dim morning light in the room. Her breasts looked smaller, more normal when she was on her back. They seemed to fit her body better, a natural plumpness to her lean frame.

They'd had another one of their awkward rutting sessions last night. That was about the only way Jim knew how to describe them. He was just thankful they could still do it at all, even if they had to lie on their sides with her facing the wall. Both of them were too old and Jim was too out of shape for their sex life to be anything other than strenuous, but the reversed position got the job done, and usually left him feeling slightly lighter in the morning.

This morning was no different as he left the bedroom and headed to the bathroom with a small bop in his step.

He emptied his bladder, enjoying the quietness of the trailer. Ellie would sleep late this morning, giving him time to himself that he would relish.

Finished, he flushed toilet, and grabbed his robe from the hook on the back of the door. He put it on, tying it shut as he walked into the living room.

Usually by this time he could hear his rooster cawing outside, announcing it was time for the hens to wake up. It was also his signal to Jim that they were ready to eat. Other than the light cheeping of birds, he heard nothing.

Strange.

Frowning slightly, he walked to the back door. His loafers were on the floor mat where he'd left them. He always left them there so he'd always know where they were when he needed him. He slipped his calloused feet into them, unlocked the knob and pushed the door open wide.

The day was hazy and thick. It caused his skin to feel sticky when he stepped outside. His robe rubbed his penis, making him flinch. The tip was tender from his night, and the friction of the robe left him with a deep itch he couldn't scratch. He adjusted himself, pulled the fabric belt tighter.

The gray clouds blotting out the sun suggested it might rain and Jim hoped the bottom would fall out. His yard was nearly brown from the lack of moisture. He'd read in the paper yesterday that the town was under a water restriction, so he wasn't allowed to spray the grass with his own damn water hose. Shouldn't matter, since he had a well, but the law was the law.

The steps wobbled as he climbed down them. The ground sounded like dry hair when his feet stepped into the grass. He looked around the yard, trying to spot his chickens. He didn't see any. Usually they came running when they heard the door open.

Not this morning and Jim felt a small knot of worry in his stomach. He hadn't put them in the coop last night. He rarely did. They weren't a flock that liked to wonder *too much*, so he never needed to. If he took Ellie into town and knew they would be gone for the day, or if they were going to be away over night, he locked them up.

Where are they at?

Jim clucked his tongue, making a ticking sound with his mouth. When that didn't work, he curled his bottom lip inward and whistled. It pierced the peacefulness of the morning like a high-pitched blade, reverberating through the trees beyond his backyard.

Nothing.

Jim felt his frown deepen, sinking into his already creased face. Leaning over, he grabbed the basket from beside the steps. It had been his daughter's Easter basket when she was little, but now he used it for gathering the chicken's eggs. It worked just fine.

He stood up straight, scanning the yard for any kind of movement.

His eyes landed on the tiny coop at the verge of the woods. The ramp was speckled with white from the chicken's constant shitting, and led to a small orifice of shadows.

Something moved in there. Subtle, but Jim noticed its slow swipe across the tunnels of light peering in through the fenced windows in the back.

Jim had thought seeing some kind of evidence his chickens were okay would have settled his nerves some. The slight movement seemed to rustle up the tingling sensations inside his gut even more. He knew why it bothered him, though he didn't want to admit it.

The shape was too big to be his chickens.

"Shit..." Jim whispered. His voice sounded dry and strange in the quietness that felt heavy on his shoulders. The birds that had been chirping minutes ago had gone silent. Everything seemed to be watching him with uneasy anticipation.

No thanks.

Dropping the basket, Jim headed for the shed. It was a tin building on a plot of dirt that he kept locked with a padlock. He never actually clasped it, so he didn't need to go back inside for the keys.

On his way, he glanced behind him every couple steps. The chicken coop was suddenly different to him, somehow more dark and ominous now, as if housing wickedness inside.

All because of a shadow.

He didn't care what was making him so shaky. Something wasn't right with his chickens, and he was going to find out what it was.

Jim yanked the padlock's curved shackle from the door's clasp. His robe was old and the fabric thinning with age, so instead of putting the lock in his pocket, he dropped it on the ground. He slid the door back on its rollers. The groan it made was loud and shrill. Jim looked back, expecting to see something wild charging out of the chicken coop.

Nope.

Nothing moved over there. Maybe the shadow he saw earlier had been a trick his eyes had caused.

It wasn't.

He wasn't completely senile yet. He knew what he saw and it wasn't anything his mind had conjured up for him.

Turning away from the chicken coop, he entered the shed. It was stuffy and dank inside, a trap that seemed to collect the heat of every summer day within its walls. No matter how he tried, he'd never been able to air it out. He kept the small rolling window in the back open all summer and all it did was allow bees to enter and build their nests. He could see a hornet's nest hanging in the corner, the little white bulbs of their eggs stuffed into the combs.

What he wanted was right inside, leaning in the corner with the other yard tools.

He grabbed the pitchfork. A prong scraped the shed's wall with a sharp *shnick* that reminded Jim of sword fights in the movies.

He left the shed, enjoying the cooler air outside. Sweating heavily now, the robe glued to his body. His pale legs glowed as if coated with wax.

Holding the pitchfork in front of him with both hands, he started walking toward the coop. He had a rifle inside, but if Ellie saw him getting it she would have something to say about it. And if it turned out nothing was wrong with his chickens, she'd tease him for how much he'd been worried about them. The gun was better than the pitchfork, though he wasn't going to risk his wife's ridicule for it.

His loafers crunched across the stiff grass, making a sound like walking on dry cereal. The bald patches of dirt were dry and hard, lined with twisted cracks. His steps were nearly silent as he walked over them.

Had a coyote gotten into the coop? About five years ago, a coyote had been seen around the area, but last he'd heard animal control had shot it.

But *another* one could have come by.

And I left the chickens out like an idiot.

He could just imagine Ellie's reaction to that one, and hoped with all his might that he was being overly paranoid. However, his gut told him he was not.

Jim was a couple steps away from the ramp when his foot slipped in something moist. He used the knobby end of the pitchfork's post to stop him from falling. Looking down, he lifted his foot to look at the bottom of his shoe. Red smeared across in a clumpy line. Dry grass was adhered to the crimson streak.

Jim looked past his foot to the ground below it. He saw feathers poking out from a gooey mound.

"Oh, no..."

His throat tightened. The markings on the feathers looked like Jackie's. Yes, he'd named all his chickens, though he'd never told Ellie that. Something had devoured her, ground her up, and all that was left of her was a dark pulpy mound.

With tears welling in his eyes, he turned away. His gaze landed on another pile just to the side of Jackie's remains. This one was brown and lumpy, narrowing at the top like an anthill. Chunky grits were buried in the compacted logs with more feathers and grass.

To Jim, it looked like a substantial pile of dog shit.

He turned to the chicken coop. The tears stopped. He felt his quivering lip stiffen into a tight line.

A coyote for sure.

Ain't no mangy mutt going to kill my chickens and get away with it.

He stepped onto the ramp. His hands trembled with the need to impale the mutt with the pitchfork. He yearned for it so much, his old shriveled penis started to wake up.

After he stabbed this damn coyote to death, he might go inside and take Ellie again. Just climb on top of her and stick it in. The mood he was in right now, she would know better than to resist.

He reached the doorway. The top of it came to the bottom of his ribs, so he had to lean over to look inside.

From the brightness outside, the inside of the coop was like trying to see with his eyes closed. There was a bright shimmer in his vision and he blinked several times to dim it. When his eyes finally adjusted to the murky room, he saw the hutches in the back. They were open as he'd expected, but spread out along the floor, he saw the leftovers of chicken feet, more feathers, and a lot of blood.

Jim felt his blood pressure rise. Fuming, his breath huffed through his nose.

Then he looked down. There was a large lump on the floor that was slightly dimmer than the surrounding darkness. It moved.

Before Jim could get the pitchfork ready, he saw a quick flash of white. In the instant it sprang forward, Jim noted how it looked like teeth.

He didn't have a moment to scream before the large mouth closed over his face.

The long trip and gorged belly had exhausted Jagger. He hadn't even noticed the man was coming until he was walking up the ramp. His nose had caught the man's approach much sooner than his ears.

The man was weak, and his meat tasted foul and stringy to Jagger. But the kill was just as appeasing as the others had been. His prey had hardly struggled, and Jagger was glad since he still hardly had the energy to attack. Once the blood had slid down his throat, he was strong again. Alert.

And ready to kill again.

Jagger left the meat on the man since its taste didn't interest him, and walked out of the chicken coop.

On the ground, he raised his nose in the air.

The scents flooded in. He could smell the old blood of his chicken feast, the animals hiding from him in the woods, and something else that seemed to cut through the rest. Fresh. Sweet.

The smell pulled his attention to the trailer, to the back door that hung open, slightly swaying in a mild breeze. Jagger angled his nose in that direction and sniffed again.

The smell was more prominent, overbearing. Something inside was calling him closer. It would settle the rage inside him, would soften the pain pounding behind his eyes. The reprieve wouldn't last, he knew this. The calm seemed to be coming less frequently, which made him antsy and very angry. And he had to find something to quickly fulfill the painful cravings that came over him.

He couldn't make the urges stop. He'd felt the changing inside for days now, and it seemed to be altering him into something lethal. At first, Jagger had tried to fight those painful cravings, but with each kill he found himself relishing the victory a little more. Now it was all he thought about. He was consumed by the bloodshed, addicted to the hunt and felt a great release whenever he killed.

Jagger extended his forepaws and dipped his back to the ground, stretching his tired muscles. Standing up, he shook away the tingling sensations. His body felt loose, more relaxed, his back no longer ached.

Then he started for the trailer, heading to the door that seemed to be open just for him.

CHAPTER THIRTY-TWO

Mark held the door open for a woman with a cat carrier. She wore a long coat, even in the muggy heat, and had on pants the color of plastic Easter grass. Looking at him, she smiled as she exited the vet's office.

"Thank you so much," she said.

"No problem."

He heard the cat inside the carrier meow through the air holes. It sounded weary, depressed. As if going home with this woman was somehow worse than the vet visit it had just underwent.

Mark hated cats. He'd grown up in a house full of them because of his mother. She had six that she treated as if they were members of the family. It had driven his father, his sister, and even Mark crazy. And he still despised them. They always scratched him, or bite him whenever he wasn't giving them the attention they thought they deserved.

Little freeloading bastards.

Mark entered the office. Cool air rushed over him. It felt wonderful, though an odor like a petting zoo hung in the air.

Approaching the counter, he smiled at the woman behind it. She was hanging up the phone when he laid his arms across the top, leaning against the front. When he glanced down, he saw the newspaper. An article about the exposed dog ring had made the front page.

It's all the buzz these days.

At least it was keeping the focus away from Jagger. There was hardly a mention about the massacre at the farm on the news last night, and Mark was thankful for that.

He turned his eyes from the paper to the woman behind the counter. She was really cute, with short hair styled like a pixie. She had on heavy eyeliner that curled into points around her eyes.

JAGGER

Polly was printed on the name badge pinned to her left breast. Mark wondered if the name was some kind of joke.

"Good morning," she said.

"Hi," Mark said back. He removed his notepad, and flipped to the page he wanted. He found the name he'd underlined. "Is Dr. Alasba in?"

"Yes, she is. Is this an appointment or..." She glanced at his badge. "Other matters?"

"Other matters."

Polly nibbled at her lip, looking worried.

"It's okay," said Mark. "She's not in any trouble."

Smiling, Polly let out a deep breath. "That's a relief. You just never know these days." She tapped a finger on the newspaper. "With all this mess going on..." She shook her head. "You just never know."

"No, you don't." Mark cleared his throat. "Is she busy?"

"She just finished up with Ms. Goldman, so she's in-between appointments, at the moment."

"Would she have time to talk to me during that moment?"

Smiling, Polly said, "I'm sure she would. Hang on." Polly lifted the phone to her ear, punched in a short set of numbers and waited. "Hi, Dr. Alasba?" She smiled. "Yes. There's an officer here to talk to you."

"Deputy," he whispered.

"Oh, sorry. A deputy."

Mark cheeks warmed. He didn't know why he always felt the need to correct somebody when they got it wrong.

A deputy for now, anyway.

As he'd feared, word had gotten back to the sheriff about Amy's outburst the other day. He was supposed to be at a meeting in the sheriff's office at three, and he didn't expect things to go smoothly. So the way Mark saw it, he had a few hours left to get as much done on this Jagger ordeal.

Polly nodded, though Dr. Alasba couldn't have seen it from the other end of the conversation. "Will do. Thanks." She hung up the phone, looked at Mark. "She said to head on back." Leaning forward, Polly pointed over Mark's left shoulder. "See that door?"

Mark turned. He saw a door in the corner. It had no sign, or even a handle, just a bar window with frosted mesh glass. "Yeah."

"Head over there and someone will come let you in. They'll show you to her office."

"Great. Thank you."

"No problem."

Mark turned away from the desk and started toward the door. Before he reached it, he heard a click from the other side that sounded a lot like a shotgun being jacked. A moment later, the door swung open. A man, who looked close to fifty, dressed in brightly colored scrubs, stepped out. He held the door open with his back.

He smiled at Mark. "Hello."

Mark nodded. "Hi."

"Come on back to the dungeon."

The man didn't escort Mark. He only pointed to a narrow hall and told him to follow it to the right. Dr. Alasba's office was the first one on the right after it veered. Mark thanked him and started walking.

It smelled even worse back here than in the lobby. A combination of medicated shampoo, feces, and stink blended into a repulsive odor that was heavy to walk through. The lighting in the hallway was dim and a little spooky. It reminded Mark of the long walks to the morgue he'd have to take whenever going to see Pierce. He'd never get used to the cold feeling it gave him. Checking his arms, he saw they were stippled with gooseflesh. He rubbed his skin, feeling its bumpy texture.

The hall ended at a T, branching into two directions. Mark followed his instructions and went right. Dr. Alasba's office was immediately next. He saw the plaque outside the door with her name on it. The door was open.

Poking his head in, Mark lightly rapped his knuckles on the door frame. All he saw inside was a desk with two monitors, blocking his view of whoever sat on the other side.

A head appeared above the monitors. Dr. Alasba was not of Indian descent as he had assumed. She was a white woman with long curls of auburn hair, a pretty face clear of make-up, and very young.

"Dr. Alasba?"

"I am. So you're the fuzz?" she asked.

Mark smiled. "That would be me."

"Well come on in, Deputy Fuzz."

Nodding, Mark stepped into her office. In front of her desk were three chairs. He stood behind them.

"Have a seat," she said.

"Thanks."

Mark chose the one in the middle. As he sat down, Dr. Alasba separated the monitors, opening a space between them to look out.

"So you caught me, huh?" she asked.

"Caught you?"

"Isn't that why you're here?"

Mark felt a small pinch of alarm. "Um…" It went away when she started to smile.

She turned the monitor around. A game of solitaire was on the screen. "Caught me not working. And being *paid* for it." She gulped.

Laughing, Mark held up his hand. "No, no. If that was a crime, I'd be guilty of it myself."

"Well, that's a relief. So what does bring you by? More questions about the dog fights? I've already talked to the detectives about that."

Mark shook his head. "No, this is different, though it's connected."

Dr. Alasba nodded. "Am I safe to assume it involves Amy Snider's dog?"

"Very safe."

She nodded again. She raised a coffee mug to her lips, softly blew inside, and sipped. Her tongue licked off the small line of coffee from her upper lip. "When I got the report about Jagger, I couldn't believe it. Have you found him?"

Mark sighed. "Afraid not."

"Really?" Her mouth hung open. She spoke as if he'd somehow let a terrorist slip through his fingers. "It's been three days since..."

"Since he killed somebody?"

Dr. Alasba winced. Nodded.

Mark scratched his head. "Two days, actually. We're keeping the others quiet for now."

"There were more?"

"Yes. I'm sure you know Jeremiah..."

She gasped. "I do. Oh my God..."

He gave her a very brief report of the events. By the time he'd finished, her pretty eyes were grim.

"Dear God," she said. "What a nightmare."

Mark thought, *You have no idea,* but said nothing.

"How's Amy?" she asked.

Mark saw Amy trying to bite Deputy Squirewell and quickly shoved the image away. "Not good, as you can imagine. I haven't spoken to her in a couple days."

"I bet she's falling apart," said Dr. Alasba. "That dog is everything to her. You know, some people adore their pets as if they were children..."

Mark thought of his mother and those damn cats.

Dr. Alasba shook her head. "But Amy..." Her nose wrinkled, as if thinking hard. "She almost seemed to adore Jagger as if he were her... companion."

He considered telling her about Amy's conduct the other day, but decided against it. "Isn't that what all dogs are?" he asked.

"Not that *kind* of companion."

Mark felt his face harden. His stomach bubbled. "You mean..."

Dr. Alasba quickly held up a hand, patting the air. "No. God, no." She laughed. "Gross. I'm not suggesting Amy was into bestiality. Yuck."

Mark smiled. "Sounded that way."

"Sorry. Spend so much of my time talking to animals I forget how to talk to humans."

"Must make for an awkward social life."

"Please. This is my social life right here." She waved a finger to Mark and back to herself. "Our conversation."

"That's just sad."

Laughing, Dr. Alasba raised her mug. She shrugged. "My life." She took a sip, set the mug back down. "What I mean is she treats the dog as a mate. Like a person that cares about her as much as she does for him. She threw him birthday parties, cooked meals for him. She's even referred to him as her significant other more than once. She's a very lonely person, and coming from someone with a drab life as myself, that's saying a lot."

Mark could feel his mouth lowering into a frown.

That would explain her acting guilty the other night.

No wonder she ran him out of the house. She was somehow devastated because she'd *cheated* on Jagger.

Very strange.

"In some odd way," said Dr. Alasba, "she might be suffering from separation anxiety herself."

"Great." Mark sighed. "Should I suggest she talk to somebody about it?"

"Wouldn't hurt."

Mark nodded. He would have to come up with some way to approach her about it. Tell somebody they needed help, they automatically refused any offer. He'd better tread lightly in the matter.

Besides, she wouldn't be delighted to see Mark anytime soon.

"So I'm sure you didn't come here to talk about Amy." Dr. Alasba tilted back her mug and guzzled what was left of it. "Oh, where are my manners? Can I get you some coffee?"

"No, thanks. It's too hot outside for it."

"Yeah, but it's *freezing* in here. It's perfect coffee drinking temperature."

"I'm good."

"Suit yourself." She flung herself away from the desk, rolling across the floor in her chair to a small table against the wall. Mark glimpsed a bare leg through the slit in her long skirt where the white lab coat didn't quite cover. The skin was pale, but looked very smooth and fit.

On top of the table was a coffee maker, a couple mugs, a bag of filters and a column of paper plates. A microwave was on the other side of the plates. She took the coffee pot from the burner and began preparing her cup.

"I came to see if you could offer me any insight," he said.

"On?" she asked, without looking up from her mug.

"Jagger. I can't believe I'm saying this, but I was wondering if maybe you have any kind of information about his...personality. His traits. Maybe even give me an idea of what he might do next."

"Well, the fact that you haven't captured him yet is a little unnerving, to be honest."

"Please, don't point out how inadequately I'm doing my job. I do that enough on my own."

"No offense."

"None taken."

"Feral dogs usually keep to isolation, only venturing into the open for food. They rarely attack, unless they are provoked."

"Jagger's not feral, not really."

"He is now," she said. She spooned in three scoops of sugar and mixed the concoction together. "Really, once a dog tastes human blood, they will eventually become feral. Never fails. Might take a long time before they crave it again, but they always do."

She twirled around in the chair and rolled back to her desk, this time moving slower and more careful. Probably so she wouldn't spill anything on her white lab coat.

"Also," she began, settling behind her desk, "feral dogs usually keep to the same patterns, traveling the same path, usually in packs. If they aren't in one, they'll find. But I doubt Jagger will seek out a pack. He's a loner now." She put her finger down on the desk and drew a circle. "A cycle. And these dogs keep at it until something forces them to move on. But that's talking as if Jagger hadn't been neutered, which he has been. So explaining his behavior is just like throwing darts at a board, hoping one of them sticks."

"Jagger seems to be constantly moving," he said. "His attack at the barn, then the next day, many miles away, he killed two more. All we've found of him are a few hairs and of course…what DNA he's left on the bodies. Plus, a lot of…droppings."

Dr. Alasba gave an understanding nod. "Maybe he's so erratic, his behavior is too hard to predict, even for himself." She sipped some coffee, looking slightly below Mark's arm as if seeing something. "He might even have a destination already in mind."

A prickling sensation sprinkled up Mark's spine. "He does?"

"I'm not *saying* that," she said. She set the mug on her desk, leaned forward, and crossed her arms flat. "But I don't see him just wandering around and killing randomly. There has to be some kind of motivation to his rage."

Mark rubbed his eyes. He felt the early inclinations of a headache brewing. If he didn't take something for it soon, it'd become a real problem.

"And Jagger," she said. "He's probably so angry at her…"

"Amy?" Dr. Alasba nodded. "Why? He's the one hurting people."

"Whatever he's done is a direct result to his hostile feelings towards her."

"Think she's what's motivating his rage?"

"It's very possible. And probably accurate."

"Would he try to make his way back to her?"

"I don't think so. I think if he was to see her somewhere on the street, he might try to approach her with cruel intentions. But once the bond is broken, rarely does a dog return to the person he no longer trusts."

"Even if he wanted revenge?"

Dr. Alasba laughed. "This isn't a bad B-movie, Deputy. Dogs don't hold grudges and seek out all those who've wronged them like in *Death Wish*."

Mark held up a hand, as if surrendering. "Humor me. Let's erase facts, knowledge, practical training, and even common sense from the board for a minute. Let's shut off our doubts and open up our imaginations and gut instincts. All right?"

"Sure." She smiled as if expecting the punchline to a great joke.

"Would it be *possible*, even a smidge possible, he would travel across the county to get back to Amy, so he could…I don't know…make her pay?"

"Go that big of a distance, just to attack her?"

Mark nodded. "Yes."

"That would be *very* farfetched, not to mention seriously impossible. I believe he would die from exhaustion before ever reaching her."

"Again, let's wipe all the bullshit away, and just open up the possibilities, even if they're slim."

"A hair's width slim?"

"Yes. Even if it's that close to impossible…could it maybe be a *hair* possible?"

Holding up her hand, she pinched her thumb and forefinger together. The space between them was hardly noticeable. "Even this much of a possibility is an exaggeration."

"It's all I need," he said, standing.

"What are you going to do? Put up roadblocks for a dog?"

"Please. Nobody's going to believe me if I tried."

"What *are* you going to do?" The humor had left her, replaced by genuine concern.

Ignoring her question, Mark said, "This conversation stays between us. Got me?"

"Yes, but…"

"Have a good day."

"Want me to come with you?" she asked as he was leaving the office.

"No, but thanks."

Mark hurried up the hall, not quite jogging but very close. He went through the door and into the lobby. Waved at Polly at the front desk on his way to the exit.

"Everything get worked out?" she asked.

"It did. Thanks."

"No problem!"

Mark walked out of the vet's building, and stood under the brick awning. The fresh air was wonderful, though thick with heat. He detected a faint odor of urine from the bushes around him. He checked the time on his watch. It was getting close to nine. He still had a few more hours before his meeting.

He'd checked this morning and Amy's bail had been posted last night, so Mark headed for his cruiser, not knowing what he was going to do, but realizing that he needed to see Amy.

CHAPTER THIRTY-THREE

Ellie had dreamed of sex. She rarely remembered her dreams, but this one had been a doozy. She was her present age, and the man shoving into her had been Tom Doleson. She'd known Tom when she was a teenager, and though they'd never dated or hardly even spoken to each other in the past, the version of him in her dream was from that time period.

Young and fit, his muscles had flexed as he'd gripped her thighs while thrusting forward. His penetration had been dominating and a little painful, stretching her to make room. Her cries of delight were what had woken her from the wet dream. When she'd opened eyes, she'd seen her familiar ceiling, stained from many roof leaks throughout the years.

Now, the dream was beginning to fade, thinning as her senses reassembled, as her mind came into focus.

Jim!

Ellie looked beside her and was relieved to find the spot empty. Probably outside messing with those damn chickens. For once, she was glad. He would want to know what she'd been dreaming about. She could lie and tell Jim it was about him, but even he wasn't dumb enough to believe that.

Tom Doleson.

Smiling, Ellie reached out her arm, pawing at the nightstand beside the bed. Her fingers tapped her cigarettes. Grabbing the pack, she brought it over and set it on her bare stomach. She flinched slightly at the coldness of the cellophane wrapping. She removed a cigarette and was still smiling when she put it between her lips. Though she was thirsty, and the cigarette would be harsh on her dry throat, she couldn't start her day without having one. It helped settle her nerves and prepare her for a morning with Jim.

Ellie lighted the cigarette, letting the lighter drop from her hand. It pegged her breast when it landed, stinging slightly and sending a soft jitter through her.

I'm really in a mood now.

It wasn't often that she woke up feeling frisky. She could remember the last time being Fourth of July three years ago. She'd rolled over and mounted Jim while he'd slept. Though he was nearly comatose, he'd reacted to her advances and she'd rode him until finishing. It hadn't taken her long that morning. He'd never gotten his, but hadn't seemed to care.

Dreamed about Eric Foster that night.

He was the son of Ben Foster and had just turned sixteen that week. She'd stopped by Foster's Market to get some groceries and to give the boy a birthday card. He'd been running register that Saturday, and Ellie would still swear he'd been flirting with her. He'd all but told her to come meet him when he got off work.

Their conversation had stayed with her all day, and though she'd never asked him to elaborate on the hidden meanings to what he'd been saying, she'd fantasized about it often. Ellie wasn't a cheater in a physical sense. Never had been and she wanted to think never would be. But in her daydreams, she fooled around on Jim quite often.

I'm a mess.

Raising the cigarette to her mouth, she wondered what her daughter and grandchild would have to say about that.

Something growled from the doorway.

Ellie's hand froze in place, her body tensed.

The hell was that?

A fusty odor like a dozen skunks and rotten meat drifted into the room. The stench was awful, singeing her eyes.

"Good God, Jim. What the hell did you get into?"

She looked up and gasped.

Jagger stood in the doorway, the front of his body in the room and the rest in the hallway. He was filthy and coated in mud and blood, his fur dingy and matted into gnarly tangles. On top of his head, Ellie could make out a wound that had split his hair in an oval shape. The green puss and pale scabs revealed a massive infection. His face looked as if he'd shoved his head into a bucket of red paint that had dried into streaks across his dark hair. Light pink foam hung in thick strips from his droopy jowls.

What happened to him? Why does he look like this?

Ellie's skin turned cold and her stomach cramped. It was his eyes that scared her the most. The yellow orbs looked hard and unreal, like yellow metal that oozed spoiled milk.

For a moment, she thought he was rabid, but she couldn't think of any form of rabies to make a dog's eyes look like *that*.

"Juh..." She gulped. "Jagger?"

The dog's lips lifted, baring a patch of sharp teeth.

"You know me, boy."

Another growl. He stepped forward.

Though Ellie's body didn't move, she flinched on the inside. "Just stay back, okay? Don't come in here." Jagger studied her, as if daring her to do something. "Go on. Shoo!"

Jagger barked. The angry outburst echoed off the thin walls around her. Ellie jerked in the bed. Her heart painfully sledged inside her chest.

"Jagger. Go on, *get*. Go home. Want to go see Amy?"

The dog tilted his head, obviously recognizing the name.

"Huh? Want to see Amy?"

His tail lifted as if it were about to wag. Then it stiffened to a point, the hair standing firm to show his warning.

God, he looks like he wants to kill me.

"Stay back," she said.

Everyone had heard about what Jagger had done, the killings at the barn. And until seeing him now, she'd had a hard time believing it.

JAGGER

Sure, he was a big dog that intimidated a lot of people. But never Ellie. He liked her and she liked him. She used to tease Amy about how gentle the dog was, saying he couldn't be a guard dog if he was too busy wanting to be friends with everybody he came in contact with.

But Ellie understood Jagger was not here looking for friends.

Something hot and powdery sprinkled between her breasts, nearly causing Ellie to shout. She looked down at her chest and saw the dark flakes of cigarette ashes on her skin. The gray flakes had become too long and dropped off the cigarette. Slowly, she stabbed the cherry tip into the ash tray.

With caution, Ellie moved the ash tray from her stomach to beside her on the mattress. She slowly scooted back, pinning the sheet to the front of her body with her hand. "Jagger, sit."

He remained standing, motionless, but his eyes turned to follow her.

Putting her back against the headboard, she cautiously pulled the sheet up and around her shoulders. "I said go on!" She ushered him away, flicking her wrist.

Jagger tensed, pushing back on his forepaws. She heard his claws scraping the carpet as he prepared himself to pounce.

Ellie slowly extended her arm from under the sheet. Jagger paused, studying her motions. She lowered her arm, opened her hand. Her fingers squeezed the rim of the ash tray. She didn't know what it was made out of, but it was hard and bumpy and would hurt if used as weapon. Ellie hoped it would be affective on a nearly two hundred pound crazed dog.

"Just stay right there, Jagger, okay?" She reeled back her arm. "Be a good boy."

Jagger's eyes lifted, watching her arm.

"I'm sorry, boy," she said. She tilted her hand, feeling ash and cigarette butts sprinkle down her arm. "I'm sorry."

Ellie threw the ash tray with all she had. It soared across the room, spinning like a disc. She could tell right away that her aim was good. The twirling gray blur was heading straight for Jagger's face.

Ellie was starting to get out of the bed but stopped when Jagger caught the ash tray in his mouth. It was such a natural reaction, with very little effort, that Ellie could have tossed him a piece of bologna.

He lowered his head and dropped the ash tray on the floor. Looking up, his tongue licked his stained lips.

"Oh...shit on me..."

Jagger lunged.

Screaming, Ellie flung herself sideways, pulling the sheet with her. It wrapped her body as she fell to the floor. When she landed on her stomach, Jagger dropped onto the mattress. She felt the bed shake beside her, the metal frame bumping her arm as she scurried to get away.

Above her, Jagger reached down, roaring. His jaws snapped at her. The sheet was snagged by his teeth and pulled. Growling, the massive dog viciously shook his head with the sheet clamped in his mouth.

Ellie bounced in the wispy cocoon, kicked at the sheet. Her legs were mummified in its tight coil. She could feel her body being dragged back to the bed. Hands slapped the carpet, fingernails trying to dig in. She felt one become lodged and snap off. The burning sensation hurt, but she ignored it as she fought to free herself.

Jagger loosened his grip for a moment, probably to change his position for better leverage. It was all the chance Ellie needed to jerk her legs away. The sheet came with them as she flipped back. She got on all fours, and looked up. Jagger was situated the same as her, but looking down at her. Waiting to see what her move was going to be.

Her move was to *run!*

She scrambled to her feet and was heading for the door within mere blinks. She felt more than heard Jagger leap from the bed. The floor shook under her with his landing, rocking her to the side. As much as she wanted to pull the door behind her on her way out, she knew she couldn't take the time to do so. It would slow her down just long enough for him to nab her.

JAGGER

In the hallway, Ellie could hear the claps of Jagger's jaws as he bit at her ankles, could *feel* his saliva spattering her heels. Screaming, she slapped along the walls on either side to keep her moving. Without their support, she'd surely fall.

"Jim! Help me!"

Where is he?

In the bedroom, during her stare down with Jagger, she hadn't thought about Jim. But now she realized how wrong his absence really was. The dog was *inside* the house. How could that have happened? Entering the living room, she realized Jim was most likely already dead. Jagger had gotten him first and moved into the house to get her.

She saw her proof when she spotted the open back door. That was where she would go. Out the back, screaming for help. Sure, this was a lousy neighborhood, but there were some decent people left who'd hear her cries. They'd come help.

Ellie veered to the left, heading for the kitchen. Her feet left the carpet and slapped the cool tile of the kitchen floor.

And slipped out from under her.

She saw her feet fly up beside her before the weight of her shoulders angled her down. She pounded the floor, taking most of the impact on her left shoulder and neck. Her legs swung around next to her, burning as they squeaked across the tile. The air exploded from her lungs.

Wheezing, she rolled onto her stomach and got her knees under her. Standing up seemed impossible, so she crawled, making her way to the open door. The hazy glow from outside was like a threshold to freedom. If she could get out there, she'd be safe.

Her hands found the frame, dropped down onto the wooden step and gripped the lip of the top plank. She saw the broken finger nail of her ring her finger, the dark blood seeping out thick and slow. A smile pushed at the corners of her mouth, arching her screams into hysterical laughter.

She'd made it!

Then she was jerked to a halt, her neck yanking back with a fierce pop. She felt a tremendous burst of pain in her foot when Jagger's mouth engulfed it. His teeth pierced her calf muscle, sinking in deep. Her foot felt as if it was being sucked down a moist tunnel.

Rocking onto her side, she looked down her naked body to see Jagger had swallowed her halfway up her calf. Her foot was down his gullet and still traveling.

Ellie screamed as she was pulled back into the kitchen.

CHAPTER THIRTY-FOUR

The meat had been better than the man's, but still not very nourishing to Jagger. He'd liked the meat in her legs the most. There the meat had been lean and tight, easy for him to chew, and juicy when he'd bitten into it. Everywhere else hadn't tasted as good, and he'd sampled it all.

Raising his head, Jagger looked around the kitchen. It was dark and empty and didn't interest him. He lay on the floor beside the body, forepaws extended in front of him while he licked the blood from his mouth. He felt some in his nose, but couldn't get his tongue to reach it. The lapping triggered a sneeze that shot spatters of blood across the floor.

He shook his head, flapping his ears.

And detected a distinctive sound not far off.

Youth.

His bloodthirsty mind conjured up images of torn meat, ripped flesh, and blood. So much blood.

A growl crawled up the back of his throat.

The sound came again, this time louder—a strident squeal of happiness, a kind of laughter that had once brought him great joy. Now it made him ache. Hardened his muscles with rage. Infected him with a yearning to kill.

He wanted to kill everything, and couldn't stop the cravings. Needed the blood, the meat. It was all that mattered now, all that could calm him, though the bouts of peace were brief.

Jagger could smell the source of the sounds now. The scent was maddening, bringing him to his feet, his nose aimed forward. The familiar smells sent images into his brain that he divided and sifted as recognition took hold.

JAGGER

He saw the boy in his mind.

Running around the yard with the high grass, laughing. Jagger remembered how sad the boy seemed to be on the inside. Nobody but Jagger could really sense it, and whenever he was near the boy, he hunkered down and allowed him to stroke his back. It caused the boy to emit that sweet laughter that rattled the back of his throat.

He would also offer his belly to the boy, rolling over with his legs spread so he could be scratched. Amy was the only other human he'd permitted this honor to. And the boy would become happy because of Jagger's affection, truly happy, the sadness washed away.

More laughter came now.

Jagger's growl loudened, vibrating his chest with its deep pulsations.

He walked out of the trailer, leaving a trail of large prints in the dead woman's blood.

The boy's scent would guide Jagger to him.

Amy hung up the phone. Though the news she'd received was mostly good, she didn't feel any better than before the phone call to Jacob, her lawyer.

"No worries, Amy," Jacob had said. "The only thing they have on you is disorderly conduct."

"That's it?"

"You sound surprised."

And she had been. The way she'd acted, she thought they would have hit her with a lot more.

"Well, they said you reeked of beer," added Jacob. "But there were no empty containers in your car and you passed the sobriety test, correct?"

"Yeah."

"So no worries there. All I see happening is a hefty fine. Nothing else."

"And what about…Jagger?"

There was a long pause. Then he said, "Well…that I can't say for sure yet. Nothing's been said about you being held accountable for his actions. I don't see any trouble with the authorities since the deputy's report backs your claim that Jagger was taken from your residence. But… relatives of the victims might want a payout. Especially when they realize how much you're worth."

Amy's anger had made her skin feel as if it were popping. "How could they, Jacob? I wasn't *here* when Jagger was taken. I've even spent a *fortune* on obedience lessons for him, his shots are up-to-date, and he's never done anything bad. I mean—he hasn't before…this…" Amy had taken a deep breath. "He's a good dog, anybody will tell you that."

"Calm down. I'm not saying anyone's going to come after you. I'm just saying be prepared…just in case."

"But I didn't do anything wrong!"

"They'll find something with legs to stand on. I mean—Jagger was outside, not on a leash."

"But he was behind a fence."

"Not one that was constructed for a dog. Not a *pen*. I can hear them now using that as their defense." Jacob then altered his voice to make himself dumb. "'But she just let him run around in her backyard, making it easy for anybody with ill motives to come by and snatch him up'."

The phone trembling in Amy's hands, sweat had broken out across her forehead.

"Like I said," Jacob had told her, "no worries. We'll be ready if they do come after you with their greedy hands open for cash."

They'd talked a few more minutes. He'd told her there shouldn't be any problems getting her Jeep back. She would have to pay the tow fee and the impound fee, which would run her somewhere near a thousand dollars after all had been calculated.

JAGGER

Amy didn't care how much she had to pay. She wanted to get her Jeep.

Now she sat on the couch, her feet on the coffee table and her legs spread wide. She stared at the empty beer bottles lined on the table between her open knees and felt ashamed.

Pathetic.

She counted nine that she had drunk all by herself last night after Ellie dropped her off. This was becoming a habit, and she was worried about herself.

Not a good idea, going to get my car with a hangover like this.

Her head felt sore, as if her brain had been squeezed and pulled and pounded.

Why was she doing this? Punishing herself?

Over a damn dog.

That was all Jagger really was, just a dog.

But why does it hurt so bad?

Her body ached with sadness. The hangover probably boosted it, but mostly it was the depression and feelings of abandonment that had caused this pain. She had no memory of going to bed last night, but she'd awakened in it, wearing the red tank top she'd had on during her search for Jagger. The rest of her clothes were on the floor beside the bed, slightly damp and reeking of jail, stale beer and sweat.

What a pity-party I had, huh?

Amy shook her head, triggering a pounding ache behind her forehead. Wincing, she put her hand up to her temples. Her hair was damp from the shower, but at least it no longer felt sticky, like when she'd be eating pancakes and accidentally dip her hair into the syrup.

She quietly burped and tasted the sour residue of vomit.

Oh God...

The burning vapors in her throat made her eyes water. And it reminded of her of the mess she'd awakened in.

Puked myself last night.

She'd rolled over this morning and thrown her arm into a wide, chunky puddle.

"Oh, gross..." she'd muttered. Then she'd jumped out of the bed, holding her dripping arm away from her.

Amy had quickly undressed the bed, carrying the giant ball of sheets and covers to the laundry room. The lid of the washer was already up, so she'd stuffed the sheets in, added the detergent and then started the machine.

Then she'd rushed into the bathroom and taken a quick shower.

With her hair still wet and soaking through the back of her shirt, she got off the couch. Inside the kitchen, she grabbed a trash bag and returned to the living room and began cleaning up.

She took care of the bottles first. Once she had them all in a bag she tied it, and set the clinking white sack on the back deck. Then she returned with another bag to get the rest of the mess.

She found cereal-bar wrappers on the floor, lots of tissues that had hardened from her tears and snot, and a pizza box with two slices left. It took her a moment to remember she'd gotten pizza last night. She'd ordered it from Krispy Krust sometime after Ellie had left and had forgotten to tip the delivery guy.

I'm such a bitch.

She used to get pizza and share it with Jagger. She'd sit on the couch with the box in her lap. Jagger, sitting on the floor beside her legs propped on the coffee table, would patiently wait for his servings.

"Want a slice?" she'd ask.

Jagger would respond with an enthusiastic slurp.

Holding the slice by the crusty edge, she'd dangle it above his mouth. Like a baby bird, his mouth would open impressively wide enough that she could set the slice inside. Then it would gently close, so he wouldn't catch her fingers, and chew.

Those were our *nights.*

Every night was their night, she realized. They'd spent them all together for almost four years and Amy had loved it. Sure, the dog worked her nerves sometimes, but she would rather have all the annoyances than not have him at all.

I'll never have him, again.

The idea pounded her, stole her energy. She dropped onto the couch, not trusting her legs to hold her up.

He would have to be put down, for sure.

Amy felt something wet and warm trickling down her cheek and realized she was crying. She used a knuckle to wipe her eyes.

No point in crying, won't change a thing.

Jagger was gone forever, no matter what. Might as well get used to it.

Her body shuddered as a sobbing fit threatened to come on. She fought it away and stood up, hugging the pizza box to her side with one arm. The trash bag bumped her leg as she headed for the back door again, stepping over the now clear coffee table.

She'd left the main door open, but the screen door was closed. Bumping it with a hip, she held it wide and dropped the bag and pizza box next to the other trash. She needed to carry it all to the trash can. Tonight was pick-up night, and she needed to make she had everything ready to go.

Wonder what they'll think when they hear glass rattling in so many of the bags.

Probably think she's an alcoholic. Like Janice.

And most of the others that live in this neighborhood.

Can't beat them, join them.

Amy hated herself. She hated how weak she'd allowed herself to become. And she knew it was mostly because of how desperately dependent on Jagger she was. She didn't used to be like this and wondered how it had happened.

Probably started with Nick. She'd trusted him. Trusted Teresa, too. And they'd fooled around behind Amy's back. If her longtime boyfriend and best friend of so many years could betray her, she'd begun to think everybody would. Given the opportunity, anybody would stab her in the back.

But not Jagger.

She'd always known where his loyalty was. With her. And hers was with him.

He's probably so mad at me.

She hoped Jagger somehow understood that this wasn't her fault.

I'll never know. They'll have put him to sleep before I get the chance to tell him how sorry I am.

Fighting back more tears, Amy went inside the house. She checked the time on the wall clock and saw it was past nine. Ellie had promised to bring breakfast this morning. Hadn't she? Amy thought she remembered that. They were going to eat breakfast, then go get Amy's Jeep out of impound.

Ellie was late.

After a long night with Jim, she's probably running behind.

The idea that Ellie was having sex with Jim last night threatened to make her throw up again. She resisted the disturbing images of their lurid night from manifesting.

Maybe she should walk over to Ellie's. If Amy showed up, it might get Ellie moving quicker. She wanted to get her Jeep. Being without it felt weird, on top of everything else.

Trapped.

Ellie had said that last night.

Amy headed for her bedroom. If Ellie hadn't shown up by the time she finished getting ready, then she would walk over there.

Chapter Thirty-Five

Janice stared at the dirty dishes filling the sink. They needed to be washed, but she decided to wait. Nathan would have to eat lunch later, so there was no point in washing them only to dirty more soon after.

She turned around and was shocked again by the condition of the living room. Still couldn't believe it. So clean. She'd dusted, washed the walls, and vacuumed. To keep herself busy and her mind occupied so it couldn't convince her to drink, she'd started cleaning. She'd cleaned *all* day yesterday.

Nathan's room had been first. She'd organized his toys, hung up posters that had fallen, moved his mattress to the other side of the room so he could see out the window. Then she'd washed all his sheets and pillowcases and the pillow itself.

That had taken a long time. Then she'd moved on to her bedroom and had made it look as good and clean as possible.

By the time she'd started on the living room, it had been nearly time for supper. She'd stopped for the day, and had finished this morning.

So the dishes could wait a little while. She'd cleaned plenty already.

Janice looked down at herself. She debated changing out of her denim cutoffs and white T-shirt. It hung down her legs, covering the frilly threads that tickled her thighs.

Forget it.

She was comfortable in what she had on.

Nathan was outside, playing some kind of war game. She could hear him making the explosions with his mouth and telling imaginary soldiers to get down. His laughter broke through the faux demands, killing any kind of illusion that he was in a real battle.

Janice stepped up to the window in the living room. She could see

JAGGER

Nathan spinning around, hopping from foot to foot. The grass reached his bare knees.

"Watch out for snakes!" she said.

Nathan jerked rigid. "What?"

"Snakes!"

Nathan's nose wrinkled, baring his teeth. "Ewwwww."

"Just be careful."

"Okay, Mommy!"

Then he was hopping around again, as if there was nothing to worry about. Most likely there wasn't, and this was the first time Janice could recall fretting about anything in a long time. So much alcohol over the past year had not only numbed her to her own pain, but to Nathan's as well. It had kept her blind to the real problems.

Amazing what a few days without a drink had done for her. She trembled constantly, had sharp stomach pains out of nowhere, and a thirst that wouldn't go away, but her mind was clear, absolutely clear. She saw hope beyond the black rotting wall that was once her heart.

If only I can stay this way.

She hoped she could be like a real mother once again—a mother that cared about her son. For so long Nathan had been a dependent to claim on her taxes for a decent check that would be gone within days after catching her up on delinquent bills. But lurking in the recesses of her hope was fear, a quickly spreading death that would surely consume her once again. It missed her and would reclaim her at the first opportunity.

Janice didn't know how to be a mother. When Nathan was a baby, it had been so easy. It had felt hard at the time, but when she looked back on it, she could see the pattern to it all. If she stuck to the pattern, all was fine. Once he'd started moving on his own, constructing sentences and developing a personality, the design had been destroyed. She'd never been one who could quickly adapt to any situation, even motherhood.

I suck.

Janice pushed the thought away, knowing it would only lead her to more self-damaging remarks about herself. And that would open the door to the slithering darkness of defeat and fear.

Welcome back to the family, Janice. Have a drink.

God, she wanted a drink. So bad.

Taking deep breaths, she closed her eyes, and focused on nothing. She felt sweat sliding down her forehead, slipping down the side of her face. More dribbled down from under her arms, tickling her sides. As the speed of her breaths began to reduce, the sounds of Nathan humming filtered through the rush of her doubts.

Opening her eyes, she took one last deep breath. She felt better. Not great, but not as close to falling over the edge.

Janice looked out the window again.

Nathan was sitting on the ground, legs crossed, and waving a stick around the tops of the weeds that choked her yard. She needed to mow it. Not only were snakes a concern, but ticks were probably everywhere. Maybe this evening, when it wasn't so hot, she would drag the push-mower out and cut the damn grass.

Janice gave one more look at Nathan and started to turn away.

And her eyes locked on the dog.

She stiffened as her back felt like it was being gouged with a frozen dagger.

A gasp tickled her throat.

The dog was so *big*. Huge. His thick hair looked like dingy carpet, soaked in a dark, syrupy substance that dripped from him in thick glops. He stood under her fig tree, nearly hidden by its shade. Fins of light cut through the leaves, writhing bright splotches across his nasty fur. Mouth open, an elongated tongue dangled, dull in color which made Janice think of sickness.

And he was staring at Nathan, whose back was to the dog, oblivious of his presence. Her son continued to hum and swipe the stick across the grass, making it sway like hair.

It's...Jagger.

JAGGER

She'd heard about his disappearance, everyone in the trailer park had. The news had reported something about some people being killed by a dog a few days ago. She hadn't really paid much attention to it. But seeing Jagger now, she had no doubt he'd been the dog to do it.

And now he was here. Outside. With Nathan.

"Oh my God…" she whispered.

Her first impulse was to rush outside and pluck Nathan off the ground and run back in. *Bad idea.* She wouldn't make it down the steps by the time Jagger had pounced her son.

Her son.

My *son.*

A fluttering sensation traveled through her. She felt slightly dizzy as it worked from her head and down into her chest. Her heart seemed heavier as it beat, thudding slowly.

An image of the Grinch flashed in her mind, his heart growing bigger.

Her mother instincts seemed to click on as if a switch had been flipped. It had been so long since she'd felt anything like this that it nearly overwhelmed her with sorrow.

I'm sorry, Nathan. For everything.

She'd been a shitty mother. Nathan deserved better than her, better than this shithole they'd been banished to and forgotten about. No more. She was not about to let him be in danger because of Jagger.

I don't give a shit how big the bastard is.

Quietly, she snuck back to the kitchen. Her cast iron pan was still on the burner, the filmy remnants of scrambled eggs clinging to the insides. It had been her mother's, and she'd given it to Janice as an early wedding present. Her fingers curled around the crispy handle. She lifted it from the burner and silently hurried back to the window.

She peeked outside.

Nathan was still there, lost in his fantasies. He hadn't moved.

And neither had Jagger. He continued to gaze at her son,

motionless as if he'd been lodged there.

Going out the front door would only call attention to her, so she hurried back through the kitchen to the back door. She slipped the chain out of the catch, and quietly opened the door. Another set of timeworn wooden steps were back here that wobbled as she stepped down them.

The backyard was more overgrown than the front. It had been almost two months since she'd last mowed it. The grass was nearly waist high, and she'd forgotten to put on shoes.

Janice waded through the weeds. Her legs itched. Her feet were jabbed and poked by various things. Reaching the corner of the trailer, she poked her head around the side.

And couldn't see anything from this angle.

Shit.

Janice started walking again. Her footfalls sounded like loud whispers as she moved through the high grass.

Please don't step on any snakes. Or a bee.

She expected any moment to feel a stinging pinch on the bottom of her foot.

Nothing happened.

She reached the other corner without any trouble.

Peeking around the edge, Janice saw Nathan. No longer was he facing away from Jagger. Now he was turned around, his tiny back to Janice.

On his knees, he patted his thighs with both hands.

Trying to get Jagger to come to him!

"Nathan," said Janice in a harsh whisper.

Her son didn't hear her. He slapped his thighs, bounced a little as he tried to get Jagger to come forward. "Come here, Jagger," he said, clucking his tongue. His voice sounded even higher than normal. "Come on."

"Nathan," she repeated, louder this time, but very shaky.

This time Nathan heard her, twisting his body to look back at her. His face lightened up and a silly grin stretched across his mouth. "Mommy! Look!" He pointed at Jagger. "Jagger's here!"

"I see him, Nathan," said Janice. "Come on over here to me."

"But…"

"Now, Nathan. We have to get inside, okay?"

His smile fell away. "Mommy, I wanted to pet Jagger."

No!

"Nathan," she said, her voice more stern than she'd meant for it to be. "You *can't* pet him."

Nathan's expression showed he didn't understand. And how could he? There had never been a problem before. Whenever Amy would march around the neighborhood for the lot rent, she always had Jagger with her. And the dog had never showed any hints of aggressiveness toward Nathan in the past. Or if he had, Janice had been too numb to notice.

"He's filthy," Janice said. "Look at his fur."

Nathan glanced back at Jagger, who still hadn't moved. A gentle breeze ruffled some loose strand of fur that weren't matted down.

This seemed to work for Nathan. When he looked back, his nose was wrinkled into a childish grimace. "Ewww. Okay."

He started walking toward Janice.

Jagger started following.

"Nathan, stop!"

Nathan jerked to a halt. He looked up at Janice with his teeth bared and his eyes wide. "What'd I do, Mommy?"

Janice's heart nearly broke at the question. It was more proof of how much she had failed him as a mother. Because her voice had risen, he'd instantly assumed he'd done something wrong.

"Nothing, Nathan. You did just fine, I promise. But stay there, okay? Let me come to you."

"Okay."

Keeping the iron pan behind her back, she started walking. The grass parted as she made her way closer to Nathan.

From the other side of Nathan, Jagger was also making his way closer.

And Nathan looked from his mother back to the dog, over and over. Worry began to appear on his innocent face as if he was starting to suspect the danger of what was going on.

"Mommy...?"

"Almost there, Nathan."

He raised a finger to his mouth and rubbed his lips.

Jagger was much closer to Nathan than she was. If Jagger broke into a sprint, he would beat her to Nathan by a few seconds. And it would take nothing for Jagger to...

Don't think it. Don't allow that thought to register.

Kill him.

No! Not Nathan.

Janice felt a buzzing inside her head, could hear the rushing sound of blood in her ears. Though she was sweating, her skin felt cold and icky, as if she'd been drenched in ice water. Something bad was about to happen. Her entire body sensed it.

A few days ago, Janice probably would have been dozing on the couch. She wouldn't have heard a thing and would have come outside to get Nathan for lunch. He'd have been gone or...dead.

But I'm here now. I'm here now. I'll show them all how much I care. Mom will know that I can be a good mother. She'll know...

And more important than her mother knowing—*Janice* would know.

Jagger stopped just a few long steps away from Nathan. Janice still had a short ways to go before reaching her son.

"Mommy, he's growling!"

"Calm down, Nathan."

High-pitched wheezing came from her son as his shoulders bopped up and down. She could see his chest expanding and dropping behind his blue shirt. He was terrified, on the verge of panic. Any moment now, he might try to run...

"Just stay there, Nathan," she said. "*Don't* run."

"I'm scared..."

"I know. Mommy's almost there."

Shouldn't have let him outside. Not without me out here to watch him. This is my fault. My *fault!*

But if Amy would have kept the dog locked up like she was supposed to...

Nathan started to lift his leg, as if he was about to take a step back.

Janice's arm felt weighed down and very slow as she started to raise it. "No, Nathan!"

Everything seemed to slow down: Nathan's leg bent and moved back, his foot dropping to the ground. The grass crunched when his foot pressed it down.

Then like a gun blast, everything kicked back into normal speed.

Before Janice could move, Jagger had already leaped with a single bark, signaling his attack.

Nathan managed to gabble out a gasp before Jagger's beefy paws slapped his chest.

Janice watched Nathan go down into the tall grass, with Jagger dropping down on top.

"*No!*"

Nathan's screams tore through the tranquility of the day, stopping the breeze, killing the sounds of birds and distant audible noise.

Janice ran, raising the cast iron pan. "Get away from him!"

Jagger lifted his head, cocking it slightly. A tattered piece of Nathan's shirt dangled from his lips.

She slammed the pan against the dog's face, feeling the impact tremor up her arms like a baseball bat hitting stone. The vibrations made her hands lock up. Unable to keep a hold of her pan, she watched it fly away with Jagger's twisting body.

The pan vanished into the grass an instant before Jagger crashed to the ground on his back. The grass folded under him. He rolled onto his side, back facing her, and didn't move.

Janice dropped to her knees.

Nathan was bloody. He lay on his back, arms covering his face. Crimson streaks covered his bare arms. His shirt was ripped down the middle. She saw a few scratches on his chest and belly, but nothing major.

And he was crying.

He's alive!

"Nathan, I'm here!"

Janice pulled his arms away from his face and gasped when she saw the swollen bun around his eye. The eye itself didn't look damaged, just banged up really bad. He should be fine.

"Mean…" cried Nathan.

"What?"

"Jagger's mean now, Mommy!"

Now Nathan wailed. Janice felt tears in her own eyes as she reached for him. Her hands curled over his shoulders and started to lift him.

Nathan's shrieks made her turn sideways.

And in a flash, she saw Jagger diving for her. His yawning mouth was wide, and teeth dripping.

CHAPTER THIRTY-SIX

Amy patted the pocket of her shorts to make sure she had her keys. She felt the lumpy bulge and heard them jangle. Then she pulled the locked door shut.

She'd waited another fifteen minutes for Ellie to show up. Giving up, she'd decided to walk over there. Hopefully she wouldn't be interrupting anything.

She said she would be here at nine. She's nearly forty minutes late. She would do the same if it was me.

Amy picked up the pizza box, stuck it under her arm, and gathered up the few trash bags. It was a tad awkward, but she managed to carry everything down the steps and into the yard.

She walked over to the trash can beside the house. Pulling the lid toward her, she hefted the bags and dropped them in. The newest additions filled it to the top, so she had to pound the pizza box flat to get it all to fit. Then she flipped the lid over and closed it.

She was on her way to the gate when suddenly the air became a tumult of shrill screams. They sounded a ways off, hollow and thin as the resonances reached her.

Sounds like a kid!

Without thinking, Amy dashed out from inside the fence. She ran up her driveway, kicking up rocks behind her. She felt their tiny stings whenever they bounced off her calves.

A woman screaming carried above the other, crying out. Something deeper was added to the high-pitched wails.

Barking!?!

Within a few short seconds, it all stopped.

Pausing on the gravel road of Eagle's Nest, Amy listened. A

terrifying stillness returned. The direction of the screams was hard to pinpoint. But on this side of the park's horseshoe road, she only knew of one child.

Nathan.

And the screaming woman must have been Janice.

What's going on?

It clicked.

The bark. The screams.

What Mark had told her about the attacks, about Teresa's death, the crime scene she was at the day of her meltdown. She saw it all in a quick series of flashing images.

"Oh, shit!"

Slapping her shorts, she expected to feel the skinny hump of her cell phone in one of the pockets. All she felt were her keys. Her cell phone was somewhere at home. Probably in her purse. And she couldn't call Mark without it.

When the woman's screams returned, Amy realized she wouldn't have time to go back for it.

She started running toward Janice's.

Her legs seemed to not want to cooperate. They felt as if they were weighted down by lead, lagging when she needed them to pump.

The screams continued, becoming louder as she followed the bend in the gravel road. Up ahead to her right was Ellie and Jim's trailer. She could see the old pinwheel, the weeds growing between the spokes, at the mouth of their driveway.

And just as she'd suspected, the screams were coming from her left.

From Janice's.

Amy ran harder, the trees zipping beside her in a blur of green. As she neared Janice's lot, the screams diminished. Now all she could hear were the blubbery cries of a child.

The woods ended on a yard that looked more like a field used for grazing. Amy scanned the bank of weeds from one end to the other.

At first, she couldn't find anything that would suggest trouble.

Then her eyes landed on Nathan.

He stood alone in grass that reached his thighs, crying, his arm reaching out. His short fingers were splayed wide, wiggling slightly. His face was red and pinched, his cheeks puffed out as he bawled for his mommy. Even from here, she could see he was bleeding. His shirt looked torn, hanging open like a vest.

Amy made a long stride over the ditch, nearly stumbling when her feet slapped down. "Nathan!" she shouted.

The boy didn't hear her above his own wails.

Amy was closing in on him when her feet stumped something hard. She felt it spin around. A stiff narrow piece knocked her in the shin. It threw her foot back and her upper body forward, causing her to splash flat on the ground at Nathan's feet.

The wind was banged out of her. She wanted to lie there a moment, allow herself a minute or two to catch her breath. But she couldn't. She needed to get up.

Nathan stood just inches from her, shrieking in a wild frenzy, calling for his mommy. One eye was inflamed and puffy, leaving only a wink of white between the two blobby lips. His cries rose and squeaked when he took a breath.

Crawling to her knees, Amy hooked an arm around Nathan's back and jerked him to her. He acted as if he didn't notice, still screaming. She put a hand on the back of his head and pulled him close. She felt his warm tears smearing across her chest, dashes trickling down between her breasts. The boy's body felt hot and feverish as it trembled against her.

She tried shushing him, but the boy couldn't be silenced.

Pressing him tightly to her, she hobbled around on her knees. The ground was hard and rough, scraping her skin. She saw what had tripped her lying in the grass a few feet away.

A thick frying pan.

JAGGER

Adhered to one of the sides was a chunk of pink flesh. Hair that matched Jagger's fixed to the end of it.

Janice must have bashed Jagger.

But where are they now?

Nathan squirmed in her arms, trying to turn around. He must be looking for Janice. Amy couldn't even begin to imagine what this little boy had witnessed.

"*Mommmeeeeee!*"

"We'll find her, Nathan, we'll find…"

Amy's words died in her throat when she followed the path of Nathan's stare.

A cold, spikey hand gripped her insides.

Jagger waded through the weeds, carrying Janice in his mouth by her spine. She hung from his snout, arms dangling, hands brushing the grass. Her legs drooped from the other side of Jagger's mouth, knees dragging the ground alongside her hands. The skin of her back had been torn away, along with her shirt. The spaces around her spine hollowed out, the jagged column clamped between Jagger's teeth.

Just like he would carry his play rope, she realized.

Jagger saw Amy and stopped. Lowering his head, he set Janice on the ground, as if presenting what he'd done to Amy.

"Jagger…what's happened to you?"

His fur looked stiff and mucky, congealed with blood to form clumpy spikes. She could see where Janice had clobbered him with the pan—a wide gash that started on his snout and spread up to the top of his head, sagging around the skull. The gray of bone was exposed and coated in red. It was like a mask that had been unzipped partway and left hanging around the face.

How he had survived the hit, Amy couldn't understand.

And his eyes were all wrong now. No longer a soft brown, they'd turned a septic yellow, oozing from the corners in clods that looked like egg salad.

304

Jagger lowered his head, looking up at her with his eyes. She got a clear view of the wounds on his head. Blood had dried to a crust on some, but the fresher areas seemed to spill it down between his eyes.

His jowls juddered with a growl that sounded unlike anything she'd ever heard come from her dog before. She felt it in her toes more than heard it.

"Jagger, easy..."

His growl turned to a snarl, teeth dripping with thick dark foam. She saw little threads of flesh stuck in his gum line.

Nathan cried harder, so she pushed his face against her shoulder, muffling his sounds. His tears rubbed wetness across her skin.

"It's me, baby boy," she told Jagger. "It's *me*." The sound of her voice seemed to agitate him even more, seemed to make his growls more vicious. "Don't you want to go home?"

This seemed to confuse him. Though his mouth remained an angry snarl, his eyes shifted. She heard a whine somewhere behind the rumbling growl. It was as if a part of him wanted that very thing, but the rest of him wanted nothing but slaughter.

And that part of Jagger was winning the inner turmoil she could see working inside her dog. His eyes lowered back to their scowl, the growls overpowering the tortured whine.

"Jagger...let's go home. Okay?"

He barked. Spatters of foamy heat hit her legs. There was nothing excited in his bark, just anger that told her he would not be going home.

Tears welled in her eyes, throat tightening. How could Jagger do this? How could he have done any of the things Mark said he had? She realized she was more hurt by this than she had been when she'd learned about Teresa and Nick. More hurt than any of the times her father had made her feel worthless, insufficient, and isolated.

She also realized that Jagger was all she'd ever needed in this life and now he had turned on her, just like everyone else had in the past.

Amy had never felt more alone, more betrayed. She knew it was

JAGGER

selfish, feeling this way when so many others had been hurt or killed, but she couldn't help it. Jagger was *hers*, and he'd hurt her more than anyone, broken her heart, decimated her soul.

"How could you do this to me?" she cried, squeezing Nathan against her. "Huh? What did I ever do to *you!?!*"

Jagger's forepaws slapped the ground with his hateful bark.

Nathan screamed against her, shaking. She felt the back of his shorts turning wet, felt warm streams going down his leg as he peed himself.

"You do this after all I've done for you? You're just like the rest of them! You're a fucking scumbag!"

Jagger hopped forward, his hair pushing up on his back. His tail was stiff.

"I treated you like a king…You…goddamn…*bastard!*"

Jagger lunged, snapping at Amy's legs. The sound of his jaws clacking together shattered the red that had been blinding her vision. Blinking, her eyes returned to normal. She felt warm liquid on her arm, could smell urine. Grasping that she had scared Nathan as badly as Jagger had made her feel lousy.

"I'm sorry," she muttered as she turned around.

Nathan's screams turned rocky when she started running.

Jagger's teeth tore at Amy's heels, ripping lines through her calves. It lit up her legs in a flurry of stings, but she kept moving.

She headed for the front door of Janice's trailer.

Nathan was heavy and hard to hold, but she hugged him close with both arms, not allowing him to fall. His screams tore through her ear, triggering the pounding of her hangover against her brain. Any other time she could have easily maneuvered with the boy in tow. But her night had left her sluggish and achy.

Jagger bit down on her foot, his teeth slipping behind her shoe and plucking it off. She kept going, leaving Jagger a few hops in the rear as he spat out the shoe. Now her pace was uneven and more difficult.

But she reached the steps, skipping the first and jumping to the second one.

Jagger's mouth clamped on the bottom plank, tearing out a wide chunk of wood.

Amy grabbed the handle of the screen door, jerked it wide.

She dived.

Releasing Nathan, she glimpsed him tumble away from her when they landed inside. Behind her, his screams were frenzied as she spun around on her knees. She crawled forward to the doorway.

Jagger lurched forward.

Amy grabbed the edge of the front door and threw it toward the frame. Jagger's head sounded like a giant's fist against the door when it banged shut.

CHAPTER THIRTY-SEVEN

Nathan sobbed uncontrollably behind her. Amy, her back to the door, leaned her head flat against it with her eyes closed.

Why does he look like that? What made him so violent?

She rubbed the backs of her calves and felt sticky wetness. Raising her hand, she saw her fingertips were dotted in blood. It wasn't heavy, only a couple thin runnels of crimson, so she should be okay.

Lifting her head from the door, she looked at Nathan. Crying, he sat on his bottom, shirt hanging open over a row of scratches. His eye looked very swollen above his opened mouth and trembling lips.

"It's okay, Nathan..."

The boy shook his head. Even at his young age, he knew that nothing would ever be okay again. And Amy began to cry, knowing the same.

She crawled to him. She checked his wounds more closely. Some of them had already stopped bleeding. The ones that still bled were barely a trickle. His eye looked the worst. Probably poked by one of Jagger's claws. Hopefully there wasn't any permanent damage.

"Stay right here, I'll be back."

Nathan only cried, not responding to her statement.

Standing, Amy looked around the living room. It was cleaner than the last time she'd been here. A lot cleaner. She thought she detected the scent of Pine-sol in the air.

Something banged against the front door, making Amy jump. The sudden pounding caused Nathan to shriek. Another sound like tearing metal derived from outside.

He's clawing the door.

It was a thin tin design that wouldn't hold Jagger out for long. She needed to devise a plan. Quickly.

Maybe Janice has a gun.

She thought about asking Nathan.

He won't know.

Then she realized she had just contemplated shooting Jagger and felt grief wash over her.

He's not Jagger, not anymore. Doesn't even look like him anymore, not really.

Amy could search for a gun, but it might take forever.

She checked on Nathan. He hadn't moved from his spot on the floor and still bawled. His face was soaked in tears and slightly pink from the bleeding.

More scraping sounds came from the door. Something pounded. The ferocity in the noises showed how desperate Jagger was to get inside.

Amy spun around and scanned the kitchen. She saw the counter, the stove, the sink. She looked to the other side. Another counter, a breadbox on top, a basket filled with what looked like coupons.

And a knife rack.

Bingo.

She hurried into the kitchen in a shuffling jog. It was annoying moving around with only one shoe, but she wasn't planning on shedding the other one to even out her movements. Leaning over the counter, she looked at the handles jutting from the wooden block. She saw the biggest one and grabbed it. She pulled out a large butcher knife, the kind she'd seen used in many horror movies. The blade was slightly tarnished, but looked very sharp.

With the knife by her side, she turned around. She was about to head back into the living room when she glimpsed a phone mounted to the wall.

A phone!

"Thank God," she muttered.

Amy ran to the wall, snatching the phone from its base. She

raised it to her ear as she reached for the keypad with the hand clutching the knife.

No dial tone.

"What?" She tapped the switch on the base several times. No dial tone came on. "No!"

Amy looked at the phone, angry at it for not working. Janice didn't have much money, so she probably couldn't afford to keep the line connected.

Amy screamed again. She slammed the phone down.

Before defeat could take its hold on her, the idea to find a cell phone struck her.

Surely Janice had one somewhere, even if for emergency purposes.

She found one on a wobbly end table in the living room. It was plugged into the wall, charging. She yanked it from the chord and was raising it to dial when she noticed the screen.

Balance: $0.00 Please add money now.

"Damn *it*!"

Nathan screamed.

The door pounded, metal twisted. Jagger's frantic growls drifted inside.

Amy dropped the useless cell phone. It hit the carpet with a soft *bump*. She was trapped in this substandard trailer with Nathan. If Jagger kept tearing at the door, he'd get inside before much longer. There would be no way to escape him, no way to defend herself or to protect the boy.

Amy looked at the knife and nearly laughed at how inadequate it seemed. What could a blade like this do to a dog Jagger's size?

She remembered going to the breeder—an older man, with kind eyes and glasses that rested on the bridge of his nose.

"He'll be a *big* boy," he'd warned her. "Are you sure you want a dog that big?"

"I do."

"That's good," he'd said. "Although they get *really* big, these kinds

JAGGER

of Mastiffs are the sweetest dogs in the world. They like to cuddle, so when he's trying to get in your bed, don't be surprised."

His attempt at a final warning had made her decision for her. She'd *wanted* a dog like that.

Now the dog was trying to kill her.

Amy didn't notice Jagger had stopped trying to get inside until Nathan's bawling settled down. Sniffling, he whined and chewed on his finger.

"Stay there, Nathan," she said, though it wasn't needed.

Amy crossed the room to the front windows. She looked out. From where she stood, she couldn't see the steps, but she knew Jagger was out there somewhere.

She searched the yard for any signs of movement. She saw only the tall grass, slightly swaying. From this spot, she couldn't even locate where Jagger had left Janice.

Soft crackling sounds pulled her eyes to the road.

Mark's police cruiser appeared.

"No!"

Before she could shout for him, he'd already driven by.

CHAPTER THIRTY-EIGHT

Mark stared into the rearview mirror.

I could have sworn...

He checked both side mirrors as well, to be sure. Nothing was back there.

He thought something had flitted across the road behind him. Something *big.*

Nothing's there now.

Must be his nerves.

Shaking his head, Mark slowed the car down as he neared Amy's driveway. He steered onto the narrow pathway and drove into the corridor between the trees. Shade fell on the car, blotting out the glaring light of the sun. He stretched his eyes, blinked. Even with his sunglasses on, he'd been heavily squinting. The constant tightness in his eyes was making his head hurt.

As he came out of the trees, he spotted Amy's small brick house.

The carport was vacant.

He felt a pang of dread as he parked the car.

She's probably home.

As far as he knew, her Jeep hadn't been retrieved from the impound lot yet.

Maybe she's cooled down some.

He knew she wouldn't want to see him, not after the other night. But he needed to check on her. After his visit with Dr. Alasba, he was even more worried about her mental stability. The more he thought about what the vet had told him, the more things about her had begun to make sense.

Mark left the car running, enjoying the cold air blowing from the vents.

I'm dawdling.

He looked at the house through the windshield, then the backyard. Other than the trees and jiggling leaves from the small breeze, he saw no movement.

Heard no sounds other than the motor and the fan of his car.

He shut off the engine. The cool air died. Stuffiness was already suffocating the comfort level inside the car. He removed the keys, opened the door.

And was hit by something big that slammed him back inside the car.

Dropping into the seat, Mark was crushed under the heavy burden pounding down on top of him. A barking mouth, spitting foam, rose above his flailing arms.

Jagger!

Stupid, so stupid! He should have checked before opening the door.

Jagger's weight pinned Mark down. One of his legs was free and he kicked it wildly, trying to peg the dog with the heel of his shoe. He struck the door, the frame, Jagger's tail, but his foot couldn't connect how he needed it to.

The dog's snout snapped at him, teeth clacking together. Drool spattered Mark's face with hot dots.

He managed to get his hands under Jagger's chest and throat. Holding the dog back, Mark writhed underneath, trying to lean his face away from the chomping mouth.

Jagger's strength was incredible. It took all Mark had to keep him back. And he knew it wouldn't last. Soon, Jagger would overpower him. In this position, Mark had little hope of winning this struggle.

A paw slapped down on Mark's chest, raking him with claws. The buttons of his shirt plopped off as the paw swiped downward and left rows of fire on his torso.

Mark called out in pain.

Gritting his teeth, he growled, "Get off!" and tried to shove the massive dog away. Pressing down harder, Jagger wedged Mark farther down into the car.

Jagger bit and growled, jaws snapping in Mark's ear. A clump of skin and hair was plucked from his scalp. He felt the warm trickles of blood running down his forehead.

He couldn't think of way out of this.

But he knew for certain he couldn't keep this fight going.

Mark wiggled in the seat, towing his other leg under Jagger. Planting his foot in the cushion, he dug his knee into the dog's stomach. With his knee lodged under the dog, Mark kept his right arm under Jagger's throat and pawed at his belt with the left.

Jagger jostled downward in an almost stomp, pushing Mark's arm down and nearly clamping his jaws on Mark's gullet. Mark gave a thrust back, with all his strength, shoving Jagger back up.

He slapped at his belt, fingers tapping the smooth polished leather around his waist. Getting his gun would be impossible from this position. He'd have to somehow roll onto his side just to get his arm around to reach it. Trying to switch arms was too great a risk. He might not get an arm up in time to stop Jagger's bite.

But he *could* reach the small canister clipped to the side.

He tugged until it popped free.

Jagger bounced, putting all his weight on Mark's arm and knocking it back. He heard a snap, felt the bone break with a sharp jolt of pain, and cried out as his arm dropped by his head in a limp fold.

Jagger's teeth clamped down on the space between Mark's shoulder and neck. Screaming, Mark felt Jagger's teeth dig in deep, finding his collar bone and crunching it. Pain exploded in Mark's chest. His body stiffened as his screams ripped his throat raw. Jagger's head jerked violently, as if he were trying to extricate Mark's collarbone through his shirt.

Raising the pepper spray with his free hand, it trembled as if Mark were lifting a brick between his thumb and forefinger. He thumbed the nozzle. Thick foam sprayed from the tip, spattering Jagger's face. Yelping, the dog jerked back, bonking his head on the ceiling hard enough to shake the car.

Mark held the button down. The dog's whines turned to howls as his eyes were washed in frothy white. Jagger scrambled on top of Mark, pushing against him and digging his claws into his stomach to find purchase. His back legs locked into place, forepaws scraping Mark's chest as he tried to get away from the spray. The dog rolled sideways, and dropped backwards out of the car.

Mark wasn't quick enough to catch himself and followed Jagger out. Landing on his stomach beside the car, he pounded the hard ground. His arm was crushed underneath him. Legs bent behind him, his feet hung inside the floorboard.

Mark tried to rock to the side and was met with a jolt of immense pain from his shoulder. Moving to the other side, he struggled to get onto his back, but his legs stayed stretched into the car. It hurt his hips to lie this way, but the relief in his shoulder was greater than the pain.

His firing arm dangled from the injured shoulder, unable to operate. He wasn't as good with his left, but he could still get the job done pretty affectively. Reaching across his stomach with his left hand, he grabbed his handgun. It took some effort, but he got the gun out. Holding it up by his head, the barrel pointing at the sky, he looked around. From the ground, it was hard to see much. He checked under the car, beside him, tilted his hips lower to see under the door.

Jagger wasn't around.

Gotta get up. I'm just asking for it down here.

Easier said than done. It hurt him all over to move, though the bulk of his injuries seemed to be in his arm and shoulder.

Bastard broke my arm.

He checked his shoulder. Saw the torn fabric of his uniform, and the blood. So much blood. His shoulder was ruined. A small part of his mind wondered if he'd ever be able to use it again. Would it heal right?

Mark scooted back, pushing against the inside of the car. His back scraped the gravel of Amy's driveway.

If I don't get off this damn ground, I'll never live to know.

Where was Amy?

There was no sign of her. If she were home, surely she'd heard his screams, or Jagger's.

Either Jagger got her, or…

No. She's probably not home.

She might have found a ride to the impound lot. Ellie, probably. They might be on their way back.

Or maybe Jagger already got her. She's lying dead around here somewhere.

No. He wasn't going to think that way. She was okay.

Mark pulled his legs out of the car, and pushed them between the door and the rocker panel. As if performing a sit-up, Mark strained with his stomach muscles and pulled himself up to his knees. He hugged his left arm around them, pointing the gun into the car.

He stayed that way, huffing and holding himself, his face flat against his knees. Sweat streamed down his face, soaking in his eyes. He was banged up, but not entirely defeated.

I'm not dead.

His eyes gazed into his cruiser as he tried to get his bearings. It took a moment before he realized he was staring at the radio. He saw the mouthpiece, the coiled chord dangling below it.

And remembered he could call for backup.

Shit! I'm such a damn idiot!

During the chaos, he'd completely forgotten about it.

He dug his shoes into the gravel, squirming back to make a base. Then he put his weight on his legs and thrust upward with his hips. Surprised by how quickly he rose to his feet, he started to tumble back, but threw his arm over the door to catch himself. He could see his 9mm through the glass, his hand clutching it so strongly his fingers had turned white.

With the door acting as his support, he scanned the yard from one side to the other. Then he turned, looking at the woods to his left. Though the wind wasn't blowing, he saw limbs slightly shaking. They came to a stop as he watched them.

Through there.

Jagger wouldn't get far with his eyes messed up. Mark could call in backup and assemble hunt teams. They'd find him this time, for sure.

He wondered if the dog was running blind or…

The quick padding of footfalls on gravel came behind him, crunching through the dirt and rock.

Mark spun around.

He glimpsed a large rushing blur with grubby fur.

Saw it launch.

He didn't have time to move, didn't have time to raise his gun.

As if he was being rundown by a motorcycle, he felt the hurling mass of Jagger plow into him. The impact threw him against the door. Instead of stopping him, the door flew back, bending in a way it shouldn't. The hinges groaned and quickly snapped, just as Mark's arm had.

Mark crashed to the ground with Jagger on top of him.

CHAPTER THIRTY-NINE

Amy stood at the window, slapping the glass. She continued calling for Mark as if he might somehow hear her and come back. What felt like several hours had gone by, but most likely, it had only been a few minutes.

If only he'd hear her calling.

After all, she'd heard Janice's screaming...

Nathan's bawling had ceased to a sniffling blubber behind her. She could feel his frightened eyes on her back, watching her. He was judging her, seeing how she would handle their situation so he would know how he was supposed to react. Right now, he was probably confused, wondering why Amy continued to shout at a window and slapping it as if it had told her bad news.

It did. Told me Nathan and I are going to die in here.

Amy rested her head against the window. The glass was cool against her sweat-slick forehead. Her arm dropped to her side. She tried to think.

Please God...show me a way out of here. I know I don't ask you for much, but please...

Amy waited on a response, as if she'd expected the clouds to open a large hand to reach down and carry her to safety.

All she got was Nathan's pitiful moans.

Mark will see I'm not home. My Jeep's there, but I'm not and he might think something's up.

Wait...

Her Jeep was *not* there. It was locked up. Just as she'd been until last night. When she didn't come to the door, Mark would assume she wasn't home and he'd leave.

JAGGER

Maybe he would stop by Ellie's to ask if she'd seen Amy...

Ellie!

Amy jerked her head away from the window, bent slightly forward and looked out. She could see barrier of bushes and trees at the front of Ellie's yard, her mailbox. Why hadn't Ellie come to see what all the noise was about? Surely she'd heard it. There was no way she could have mistaken the frenzy of screams and crying for anything other than what they were. So, why hadn't Ellie, or *Jim*, come to help?

Maybe they aren't home.

No. They had to be home. Ellie was supposed to give her a ride this morning.

Maybe they were sleeping.

Amy had to try something to get their attention.

She looked down at the window and saw it was only partway open. She gripped the edge of the window and yanked it up. It flew high, smacking the inside of the sill. The open space was still too low, only reaching her breasts. She sunk to a crouch and propped her arms on the window pane.

"Ellie!"

Her voice was loud in the room, startling Nathan enough to start him crying again.

Amy leaned against the screen, pushing her mouth against it and called for her friend a second time. Then she added, "It's Amy! I'm across the street. With Nathan! We need help!"

She waited a bit, hoping to see Ellie appear at the end of her driveway.

She didn't come. Neither did Jim.

And Amy suddenly felt sick inside. They *had* to be home.

What if Jagger...?

She wouldn't allow herself to think it, though she'd already convinced herself it was true.

Jagger had gotten them. Then he'd come over here to get Janice and Nathan.

Why?

Picking them off…getting them out of the way…

But why!?!

"To have me to himself…" she whispered.

And now Jagger was gone. And Mark was most likely at her house.

"Oh…God…Mark…"

Mark was in danger, she knew it. Jagger had gone after him.

Amy gazed outside for several more minutes.

She heard no gunshots to indicate Mark had killed Jagger.

She pictured Mark firing several rounds into Jagger and was surprised she felt no grief at all.

He's not my dog…

It helped that he looked nothing like his old self. Made it easy to push aside the good memories she had of him.

A shadow emerged on the gravel road beyond the front yard. Small at first, it seemed to stretch and fill out, widening across. A bar of light danced in the middle of growing shape. She realized what it was a moment before she spotted the frontend of a car coming into view.

Her first thought was Mark had come back. Maybe he'd heard her shouting for Ellie.

But the direction was wrong.

This car was taking the same route Mark had come from.

Unless he circled around, drove around the horseshoe.

That idea died when she saw the color of the car was orange and much longer than a police cruiser. She recognized the Chevy Impala, its polished, metallic orange smolder. The fancy rims that reflected light onto the ground around it as if it had suddenly materialized from a portal.

The only difference this time was there was no Spanish music blasting from its speakers. And the windows were down. She saw a dark-skinned face peering out from the open frame, long hair pulled into a tight ponytail.

Jose!

Carlos must be driving. Why was he going so slowly?

Yes, the car was creeping along, but it would be gone in a matter of moments.

Amy threw herself against the screen. She heard mesh tearing as she worked to get her mouth facing out.

"Help us! Carlos! Heeeeeelp!"

Jose's head turned back into the car, his ponytail bopping as if saying something.

The car jerked to a halt.

Though Nathan was shrieking again, Amy started to laugh. Jose had heard her.

"Jose! It's me, Amy! *Help!*"

The passenger door flew open and Jose jumped out. He was naked down to the shorts that hung past his knees. Though he was incredibly short, his body was lined with tight, skinny muscles.

"Jose! Here, at Janice's!"

Jose, gazing across the yard, didn't move. He stood at the edge of the ditch. Carlos emerged from the driver side. He walked around the back of the car to join his friend. Carlos had a chain wrapped around his fist, a length dangling by his leg.

Jose reached behind his back and brandished a long-bladed knife.

Good job, guys!

Carlos gave a terse nod, and at once he and Jose started into the yard.

Amy shuffled away from the window, snatching Nathan from the floor on her way to the front door. She flung the door wide and kicked open the screen door with her shoeless foot.

She was down the steps and in the grass before the guys had made it halfway through the yard.

Amy hobbled in uneven strides toward the pair of men.

Seeing her, their slow skulk turned into a run.

They met her.

"Amy? What the hell's going on, huh?" Though of Spanish heritage, Carlos barely had an accent. His English was flowing and nearly southern in tone. Jose, on the other hand, couldn't speak a word of English.

Jose saw Nathan and his eyes widened. He turned to Carlos and spoke in a rapid fire of Spanish. Nodding, Carlos held up his hand.

"Are you all right?" asked Carlos.

"Not really," she said. "Jagger's gone…mad."

"Your dog?"

"Yes," she said, and felt her throat thickening.

"Damn." Carlos wrinkled his nose into a grimace. "I heard about that shit at Freddy's on the news. Never liked the guy, but still…" He made a sour face. When he looked at Nathan, it dropped away. "Is the boy all right?"

"He's hurt a little bit, but he'll be fine."

"His mom?"

Amy shook her head.

Carlos sighed, closed his eyes a moment. She thought she heard him mutter something in Spanish. Sounded like a prayer. When he opened his eyes again, his look turned serious. "We heard the screams. At first we weren't sure what was going on, but when they kept coming we decided to check it out."

Amy was so grateful that they had. Usually, she felt intimidated and even a little frightened of Carlos and his friends. Right now, she was very glad to see them.

"Thank you…"

Carlos shrugged. "We're all neighbors, right? We've got to look out for each other."

Amy felt herself smiling at his noble proclamation.

"Where's the dog now?" asked Carlos. He looked around the yard as if Jagger might be hiding nearby.

JAGGER

"I don't know," she said. "He took off, shortly after I saw…"

Mark.

"Oh, God…"

"What's wrong?" Carlos asked.

"Mark, I saw him go by. I bet Jagger went after him."

Carlos nodded, though he couldn't have known who Mark was. "All right. Think he went to your house?"

"He must have."

Carlos turned to Jose, said something in Spanish. Jose nodded. Carlos kept talking, using his hands to emphasize a point he was trying to make.

Jose responded in the same agitated manner.

Carlos turned to Amy. "Here's what we're going to do. You and the boy are going to go with Jose back to my place. You can use my phone to call the police and an ambulance. I'll go to your house and check on your friend."

Amy couldn't believe how wrongly she'd judged these guys. She'd convinced herself they were gang members. And maybe they were, but in this moment, it didn't matter.

They were heroes.

But she also couldn't let Carlos go by himself.

"No," she said. "I'll go with you."

"I'd rather you…"

"He's my damn dog, Carlos. I'm going."

Holding out his hands, the chain jangled slightly in front of him. "If you want."

He relayed the information to Jose in Spanish. Jose nodded, put the knife away and stepped forward. He opened his arms for Nathan.

Amy had to pry Nathan away from her, but once he was in Jose's arms, the boy hugged the short Spanish man just as hard. She noticed a slight smile of affection wash over Jose's hard features.

With Nathan clutched close and wrapped around his torso, Jose turned away and started across the yard. It was hard for him to run with the boy clinging to his front, but his legs worked quickly, though stiff. He reached the car in moments and fought Nathan loose to get him inside. She heard the click of the seatbelt engaging, then Jose stepped back and shut the door. He gave a quick look around before hurrying to the driver side. There, he hopped in. A moment later she heard the transmission click and watched the car zip away in reverse. A thin cloud of dust hung in the air, swirling where the car had just been.

Carlos took a deep breath, turned to Amy. "Ready?"

"Not really." She looked at the chain wrapped around Carlos's closed fist and realized she'd left the knife inside, by the window. She wasn't going back inside for it.

"Let's get moving," said Carlos.

They started through the tall grass. Amy searched the ground as they walked.

"What are you looking for?" Carlos asked.

"My other shoe…"

She spotted it on the ground and slipped her foot in. Her stance was balanced once again. She was about to walk back over to Carlos but caught a dim twinkle in the grass from something close to the ankles of Janice's mangled body.

"Stay there," she said. "Janice is…over here."

Carlos didn't respond.

Amy walked a short distance and squatted, keeping her body angled away from Janice so she wouldn't have to see her again.

Her fingers curled around the handle of the cast iron pan. Gripping the heavy object, she felt a tad better. She started jogging, the wound on her calf jabbing her as she made her way back to Carlos.

He looked at her weapon, puckered out his bottom lip and nodded.

Now she was ready.

CHAPTER FORTY

Amy saw Mark's cruiser and gasped. She stopped walking. Carlos paused beside her. She lowered the pan by her leg.

My God Almighty…

The door was open, pushed toward the front of the car and flat against the front tire. She saw torn shreds of metal poking through the gap between the door and car like sharp jagged leaves. There was a large blob of a dark stain on the ground beside the car. It looked like a puddle that was quickly drying in the heat.

"What happened here?" she heard Carlos ask. It sounded as if he'd spoken more to himself than to her.

"Mark?" Amy called, her voice reverberating around them.

Though her voice had come out flat and very afraid, Carlos shushed. She listened. All she heard were her heaving breaths and Carlos's slow heavy huffs through his nose.

A breeze gently shook leaves on the trees near them.

"A…Amy?"

"Mark!"

She took a step forward and her arm was gripped. She was snapped back. Carlos stepped beside her.

"Wait," he said in an angry whisper. He held up his chain-wrapped fist.

"Carlos, it's…"

"Hush."

Amy listened. Her mouth hung open a moment before slowly closing. She saw the intensity in Carlos's expression as he leered at the cop car.

"It came from over there," he whispered. He gave his chin a quick thrust toward the car.

Amy turned her head. She looked past the damaged door, to the left overhang of the bumper. She could see the tire, angled slightly inward.

And then a hand came down on the loose dirt.

The fingers, arched and trembling, dug in. The sleeve around the arm that flexed and pulled was tattered and torn. Blood slicked the skin in crimson through the threadbare rags.

"Mark?" she said, her voice low.

A deputy clambered out from the other side of the car, pulling himself with his left arm. She only knew it was a member of the law by the color of his uniform and the belt around his waist.

The face on the bobbing head was a monstrous ruin. An eye dangled from the pulpy mask like a plucked radish. The other eye was a narrow white slit through the red and brown mush.

Amy's muscles turned soggy. She started to drop, but Carlos still had a grip on her arm and held her up.

"My God," she said, "No, Mark, no!" She tried to pull away from Carlos. Couldn't. His grip was firm and strong, but not painful.

"Don't," he said.

"But it's Mark, he…"

Mark rolled over, dropping to his back. From the chest down was a mess. His stomach had been torn open, intestines reaching out of the flaps of bloody skin like tentacles. They hung in brown coils on his thighs, hanging over the edges and dragging the ground. His right shoulder looked flat and rumpled compared to the left. And it was easy to see his arm had been broken, how it laid in odd angles to the side of him.

"Amy…" said Mark. His voice was jittery and filled with phlegm.

Amy tried to go to him, and again Carlos wouldn't allow it.

"Stop," he said.

"I have to *help* him!"

"It's a trick."

"A what?"

"A trick." Carlos looked around, his eyebrows lowered into a patchwork of concern. "He's drawing you out."

"My *dog?*"

Carlos slowly nodded. "He wants you to go to the cop, so he can attack…"

Amy turned to Mark. He lay several feet away, on his back, body trembling. A soft quacking sound came from the back of his throat.

So close to death and Jagger hadn't finished him off. Why?

Because he's using him as bait. For me.

No way in hell could that be real.

But it was. Now she could clearly see the workings of a trap.

But she couldn't let Mark just lay there, in so much pain. He was…dying.

As if sensing her thoughts, Carlos added, "He won't make it, anyway."

Tears filled Amy's eyes. She felt a cold space open up inside.

"Let's get out of here," said Carlos.

"We can't just leave him there!"

Carlos jerked her closer by her wrist. "We're going. There's nothing we can do for him."

Through her wet lenses, she looked back to Mark. Though blurry, she could tell he was still alive and in a lot of pain. More pain than she could imagine.

"G…go…" she heard Mark say.

"Mark…"

"Goooo!" His voice sounded strained and filled with agony.

She felt Carlos pulling her back, toward the driveway.

"No," she said.

"I said we're leaving."

"We can't go back that way. There'll be nowhere to go if he comes after us!"

Carlos seemed to consider this. He looked around.

JAGGER

"It's too risky to go for your house," he said. He gnawed at his bottom lip. "The car. We'll *drive* out of here."

The car was awfully close to Mark. And the door was broken. She didn't feel much safer being in there with such a wide open space for Jagger to come through.

But it was their best option. Better than going for the house. And a lot more secure than walking in the open.

"Okay," she said.

Carlos pulled her as he ran for the car. She tried to avoid looking at Mark lying at angle in the front, but it was impossible not to see him.

He no longer trembled. It was hard to tell if he was even breathing.

Amy hated how she'd acted the last time she'd seen him. She'd been so awful, and it would be their final encounter. She wished she'd never hit him, or slapped him.

"Mark," she heard herself whisper.

Then she turned frontward, facing the car. Her arm stretched in front of her, hand clasped in Carlos's sweaty hold. Carlos turned toward the maw of the car's damaged ingress.

All units! All units!

Carlos and Amy gasped. The stocky man stepped in front of her as if to shield her from harm.

Report to Eagle's Nest Mobile Home Park, right away!

Amy sighed with relief. Jose had come through. Help was coming.

The feral dog has attacked again. Report to Amy Snider's residence at 111 Eagle's Nest Circle!

"The cavalry's on their way," said Carlos. He turned toward her, smiling. "God bless, Jose."

I have been trying to reach Deputy Varner and have been unsuccessful. Proceed with caution!

"This'll be the first time I'm *glad* to see the cops," he said.

Repeat! Calling all units to respond to a call from Eagle's Nest Mobile Home Park!

330

Amy felt herself laugh at Carlos's statement.

Laughing, he turned toward the police car.

And Jagger sprang from inside, as if he were a giant, furry missile being launched.

Carlos had no time to react. He barely uttered a scream before Jagger slammed into him. She felt Carlos's hold on her arm tear away as he dropped with Jagger on top of him. The chain clanged when his hand bashed Amy's knee on its way down.

She felt a wild blast of pain in her leg as it shot out to the side, twisting her around. Her back pounded the ground a short distance from Carlos.

She could hear his screams, the juicy tears of Jagger devouring him.

Amy propped herself up on her elbows. Through the V of her legs, she saw Jagger had straddled Carlos with all four legs. His snout was buried in Carlos's stomach, tearing and ripping stringy stretches of flesh away.

No! Not him, too!

He'd come to her aid, had saved Nathan.

He tried to help.

She wouldn't let Jagger do this, not to Carlos. She'd been too late to help Mark, but she wouldn't let Jagger do this.

Amy tried to stand, but quickly dropped back down when her hurt knee folded. The hard ground scraped her skin as she wiggled to her side.

The pan was there.

She grabbed it, and fell back onto her back.

Carlos had stopped screaming.

"Jagger!" screamed Amy.

The dog ignored her as he tore out thick chunks of Carlos's innards. Sinewy strips hung from the corners of his mouth like bloody jerky.

JAGGER

"Jagger!"

The dog stopped his riotous chewing. Snout deep into Carlos's stomach, Jagger's eyes shifted to Amy. The left eye was nearly white, thick and gloppy like vanilla pudding. The other was swollen and the yellow bulb was encircled by a crusty, red halo. Damage had been done to his eyes since she'd seen him last.

Good job, Mark...

He didn't go without some kind of fight.

But he's dead. Carlos is dead. Janice is dead. Teresa is dead. Jagger killed them all...

The one she'd considered her world had destroyed what world she'd truly had.

And she was going to kill him. If she died doing so, that was fine.

"It's *me* you want!" she shrieked.

Jagger lifted his head, slowly chewing what was in his mouth. Blood spilled from his jowls. He stepped over Carlos, dodging the dead body with his paws.

He stood on the other side of Carlos, facing Amy. Only a short span of space separated him from her feet. If he went after legs, her plan wouldn't work.

Plan? I have a plan?

The heavy firmness of the pan reminded her she did.

A terrible plan. But it was...something.

Slowly, she turned the cast iron pan in her hands. The handle jutted out, the angled tip pointing high.

"Come on, you bastard!"

Jagger snarled, snapping his jaws. Bloody spit shot forward.

"It's just us now! Isn't that what you wanted!?! Huh? We're all alone!"

Far in the distance, Amy heard the whine of sirens. She figured they were heading this way.

Jagger lifted his head, turning his ear to the sky. He listened. He took a step back. It looked as if he was preparing to run away from Amy, not toward her.

"Jagger!"

The dog stopped. He looked back to her.

She slapped her bare thigh, hard, causing her swelling knee to throb. The smack echoed.

Jagger flinched.

"Get over here, now!"

His lip curled, baring teeth. The gaping slit running up his head seemed to tremble.

Now it's working.

"I said, *now!*"

She slapped her leg again. It stung around the ruddy handprint on her thigh. Her skin felt as if it was tightening.

Jagger's snarl spread across his mouth, the growl rising in his throat.

Another slap on her leg triggered a quick, angry bark. Foamy strings hung from his upper teeth and stuck to his lower set.

"You want me? Here I am!"

She slapped her leg again. Jagger hopped in place, hunkering down. His upper body lowered as his tail rose higher.

They used to play like this. She'd smack her thighs to get him worked up, then they would run around the yard. Amy would laugh and Jagger would let out quick happy barks.

There was no playing this time. This was foreplay to a fight.

"Come on, you bastard! Come and get me!"

Jagger shot forward. Ignoring her legs, he ran between their spread. A heavy paw slammed down on her groin, her stomach, her chest.

She couldn't breathe with his abundance of weight on top of her. His head dipped, mouth opening.

And she rammed the handle of the cast iron pot into the yawning chasm of his mouth. It met some resistance and probably wouldn't have

JAGGER

kept burrowing if Jagger wasn't already bringing himself down. His own momentum made it easy for the handle to crunch through his skull.

A sharp whine tore from Jagger as he hurtled down onto Amy. She kept her grip on the ring of the pan, pushing it further into his mouth. The thin stiff edges of iron dug ruts into her palms, lubing the pan with her blood, making it slippery.

Gritting her teeth and growling, she gave one final shove with all her strength.

The handle burst through the back of Jagger's skull, glazed in blood under the skin that lay like a pitched roof over its tip.

Jagger went limp on top of her, burying her underneath his furry mass. His jowls were distended around the pan, forming a wide disk of iron that forced his mouth wide.

She quickly jerked her head sideways, dodging his face as it came down. The pan clamored softly when it hit the ground.

He didn't move.

The full force of his weight pushed her down into the dehydrated soil.

Underneath Jagger like this reminded her of her last morning spent with him. She'd hugged him, wrapped her legs around him as if he were a boyfriend who'd woken her with kisses. Just as she'd done every morning leading up to the final one.

She hugged him now, though she couldn't lift her legs. One was trapped under him, and the other had a hurt knee that felt hardened like a rock.

Amy squeezed his neck, holding her hulk of dog tightly. Though the light hurt her teary eyes, she gazed up at the flat blue sky. It was cloudless and vast, a gorgeous color that reminded her of swimming pools.

And she cried.

The tears made her face wet and itchy, as did the foul hair rubbing her cheeks. Jagger smelled terrible, a combination of infection and rot. She didn't care. This was her final moment with him. And she wanted it to matter.

"I'm so sorry…" She cried harder.

The sirens grew steadily louder until they chiseled through her brain like a spike. She heard the crunching of tires coming up her driveway.

The sirens were all over her now, vibrating her clothes, pounding her brain. She winced against the shrilly howl.

A car grinded to a halt. The siren died. She heard a door open and rapid footfalls on gravel as they hurried to her.

"My God, what is this?"

A man's deep voice.

"Jesus Christ!" A female, most likely his partner.

"Shit, Deputy Varner's down!"

She heard footsteps running away, the car squeaked slightly.

"We have an officer down at the Snider residence! Deputy Varner is down. Send an ambulance immediately!"

A shadow fell over Amy, shielding her from the brightness of the sky. She couldn't see a face, but from the strands of hair curling out above the shoulders and the slightly bowed waist, she could tell it was a female.

"Amy Snider?" The voice was hesitant, and a little frightened.

"Yuh-yeah…"

"Are you all right?"

Amy didn't know why, but she laughed. Nothing was funny about this situation. Knowing this did nothing to stop the wild guffaw that shook her underneath Jagger's immense bulk. Couldn't this cop see that nothing was all right?

As quick as Amy's laughter had come about, it was replaced by sobs that she doubted would ever quit.

KRISTOPHER RUFTY

Kristopher Rufty is the author of The Lurkers, Pillowface, A Dark Autumn, and Prank Night. He has also written and directed the independent horror films Psycho Holocaust, Rags, and Wicked Wood.

But what he's best at is being married to his high school sweetheart and the father of two crazy children who he loves dearly. Together, they reside in North Carolina with their hulk-like dog, Thor, and numerous cats.

For more about Kristopher Rufty, please visit his Website www.lastkristontheleft.blogspot.com

He can be found on Facebook and Twitter as well.

43746338R00188

Made in the USA
Lexington, KY
11 August 2015